THE
EMERALD
ANACONDA

THE
EMERALD
ANACONDA

TIM TINGLE

authorHOUSE®

AuthorHouse™
1663 Liberty Drive
Bloomington, IN 47403
www.authorhouse.com
Phone: 1 (800) 839-8640

Published by AuthorHouse 12/17/2015

ISBN: 978-1-5049-6859-1 (sc)
ISBN: 978-1-5049-6860-7 (e)

Acknowlegments

Thanks to Helen Dunnavent for her reading and editing skills on this story. Thanks to my wife Nanette for her many hours of painstaking scrutiny over the details. Thanks to Matthew Denaburg for allowing me to use a photo of his snake, *Ozzy,* on the cover.

1

Travis considered himself very lucky to still be alive, and have his freedom, after the botched mission he had carried out in Egypt the previous November. Though it could hardly be called *his* error, because he was working off flawed intelligence provided to him by the CIA, and those guys were not supposed to make mistakes of that magnitude. He had been sent to covertly capture or kill a man that was believed to be Osama Bin Laden, the leader of Al Qaeda, who was thought to be hiding in a small town in Egypt. However, the man he killed, was actually a very convincing double for Bin Laden, and was also a well respected Muslim cleric named Mohamed Nasser Hassan. The Muslim Brotherhood did not take kindly to someone coming into their midst in the middle of the night, and decapitating their beloved spiritual leader. It literally set off a chain reaction of events that threatened to destabilize the entire Middle-East.

The United States officially denied any knowledge of the hit. In *their* version of the incident, all they knew was that an unidentified Egyptian man showed up at the U.S. Embassy in Cairo with a decapitated human head in a sack, and claimed that it was the head of Osama Bin Laden, and said he was there to collect the $25 million dollar reward money. Apparently the man thought the similarity to Bin Laden was close enough to claim the reward. But he didn't know they would verify the identity by using DNA. The man never returned for the reward.

At least that was the official U.S. explanation, of how they came into possession of the head. That was their story, and they were sticking to it. It was a perfectly plausible explanation, and it was accepted by the Egyptian government. And eventually, at least on the surface, the up-roar died down over the killing. But in private circles, on both sides, the actual truth was known, and from the radical Muslims a vow of vengeance was sworn to, by some very cut-throat individuals.

The 'Agency' (no, not the CIA) endorsed the above explanation about the killing, because it couldn't let Travis take the heat for it, because they obviously had bigger plans for him down the road. Their 'war on terrorism' was going to be a long and treacherous road, and those in high places knew the value of holding in reserve a valuable pawn like Travis Lee. When the game turned ugly, they needed a player who knew how to trump ugly with *uglier*, because he had done it before.

So Travis was able to walk away from the whole mess. For the time being at least, he was free to go back to his farm in Laurel Grove, Alabama, and to his wife, Janice. (They had five grown kids together.) He was free to go back to his old job at Fly By Night Investigations, where he worked sporadically as a crash scene investigator. He was also free to go back to his writing career. He was a best selling author, with several novels in print, and a contract to churn out a new novel every 12 months for his publisher, Jester Books, of London England.

His latest adventure in Egypt would make an incredible story, that would surely allow him to hit the best seller's list again, but alas, he would not be able to touch that story in any form, because it was classified as 'top secret'. *Damn!* Travis thought, *Most of the really good stories I know, and could write about, are 'Top Secret'!* And the secret 'Agency' he sometimes worked for, kept close tabs on what he wrote, out of fear that he would leak something that was classified. Travis did them the courtesy of sending them a manuscript copy of his newest novel, three weeks before he sent it to Jester Books, just in case they found a part that was 'questionable' and wanted it tweaked a bit.

Travis had been in Special Forces during the Vietnam War, where he became notorious for taking the impossible missions, and somehow surviving them. He was highly decorated, including five Purple Hearts, for wounds received. After his third tour in Vietnam, he returned home, and retired from active service, finishing out his 20 year pension in the Reserves. (Actually, his time in the Reserve was served out by being on call for a very secretive outfit known only as the 'Agency'. A half dozen times he was activated by the Agency to do covert activities in Central and South America. Most of his missions were behind enemy lines in Nicaragua, during the Sandinistas rule. He was also a sniper in both the Granada and Panama operations.) His time in the Reserve overlapped with a twenty year career in the coal mines, from which he retired in '99, and went to work for FBN Investigations. He liked FBN, because he was able to travel the world, and see things he never thought he would see.

So Travis stayed pretty busy, between traveling for FBN Investigations, meeting his writing quota, and keeping up his farm, (and since the 9-11 attacks, being back 'on call' for the Agency.) But he *liked* to stay busy. He believed that a person who did not stay busy, just sort of wasted away. He reasoned that there was plenty of time for that when he reached 80, if he lived that long.

Yes, if he lived that long.

Travis had not had a call with FBN for two weeks, when he got an unexpected call from his childhood friend, Steve Meredith, who had been working for Exxon for the past three years in Ecuador. When he saw Steve's name on the caller ID, he was eager to see what his old friend had been up to.

"Hello, Steve!"

"Hello yourself! How's the world been treating you, Travis?"

"Well, we don't want to get into all that."

"That bad, huh?"

"If you only knew!" Travis assumed that his call was concerning their 'Full Moon Society' meeting that was coming up in about a month, and he mentioned that to Steve.

"Oh, that's right! I almost forgot about that! Of course, I've missed every meeting for the past three years, because of this job with Exxon. But no, that's not why I called. I talked to Homer, so I know you are making tons of moolah with this new job of yours, so I thought you might want in on the ground floor of a really good deal."

Almost afraid to ask, Travis did anyway. "What kind of deal?"

"A real estate deal in Ecuador."

"I don't know if buying land in Ecuador, or *any foreign country,* is such a good idea, Steve."

"At least hear me out."

"Okay, let's hear it."

"Well, you know I've been working for Exxon down in Ecuador for the past three years, helping them locate new oil fields and so forth. I found out that Exxon has been buying up large tracts of land, along with the mineral rights, down there for the past 30 years. They probably own more land than the Ecuadorian government does! They bought it dirt cheap, hoping to find oil beneath it. And in many cases, they *did* find oil, thanks to me. But they own thousands of acres that do not have oil fields, and so, to finance further drilling, they are selling off some of their 'worthless' land. But having been there, and seen the land, I can assure you that some of that land is far from worthless!

"In Ecuador, just like most Latin American countries, there is a lot of under-handed deals. If you are not a member of that country's elite class, you don't know about a lot of the really sweet deals. But because I have been so valuable to Exxon, one of their executives let me in on a 'hush-hush' land sale that will take place in just a few days. The land will go to the highest bidder, but most of the bidders have agreed to bid very low, so that one of them will get a great deal. Then on the next great deal, they will all agree to low bid on that one, to benefit another of their cronies. It's rigged to make the rich richer, and keep the poor people down."

"So how does that help you, if you don't know what the highest bid is going to be?"

"That's just it. I *do* know what the highest bid will be! All I have to do, is rake together enough money to back up my bid."

"Okay, so tell me about the land you are bidding on." Travis said.

"It is a 900 acre tract of prime property, covered with virgin rainforest hardwood trees, with almost a half mile of riverfront on the Napo River!"

"Prime property, huh? Tell me what makes it valuable."

"I mentioned the virgin forest. That means 900 acres of huge, valuable mahogany and teak trees! Some of them are just massive! Trees like that are worth a mega-fortune! And also, think about that half mile of river-front property! There used to be road access to the property, because Exxon had to get in there to drill test wells. But when the oil drilling came up bust, the well sites were abandoned, and you know what happens to things like that in the rain forest. Within a year, the roads grew over with jungle again. Now there is no evidence that Exxon was ever there."

"So is that a good thing? No road access?"

"Well, the river is the access. Down there, the rivers *are* the highways."

"And because there is no road access, I am going to assume that there are also no utilities? No electricity or running water?"

"Yes, you would be correct in assuming that."

"So we could buy the land, and log the trees off it, and make an insane fortune from the rare woods?"

"Well, no, not really. You see, Ecuador, like most South American countries, they have laws against cutting too many of the old growth trees. The tree-huggers have gotten to them, and convinced them to protect the old growth rain forests, because they are more valuable as living trees, because of pharmaceutical research, and tourism. The red tape and permits required to cut a mahogany tree, for example, make it not worth the trouble. It is a nightmare to try to cut a tree legally. They will literally tax you more than the value of the tree itself. And illegally cut trees will get you a stay in prison longer than if you murdered someone!"

"Okay, so, the fact that the property is covered with virgin rainforest, isn't really a plus either, huh?"

"Not unless you just like trees."

"Well, I've got to say, Steve, you're not exactly blowing my skirt up at this point, if your aim is to convince me to go in with you on buying this property."

"I know. That's probably why I was booted off the debate team in high school. But listen to this: I have inspected the property, and closely examined the geology of the area, and guess what I found?"

"A lost Inca city of gold?"

"Well, actually,…almost!"

"What do you mean, almost?"

"Not a city, and not gold, but something almost as valuable!"

"So you're going to keep me in suspense? What is it?"

"Emeralds!"

"Real emeralds?"

"Of course, real emeralds! I'm a geologist, remember? I found that there is a very rich deposit of emeralds on this property!"

"And Exxon doesn't know that they exist?"

"Not a clue! They are going to sell it off as worthless land! When they gave me orders to examine the land for the prospect of oil, they said nothing about reporting anything I found besides oil! Oil company executives have a one-track mind. If there is no oil, they don't want to hear it!"

"I don't know, Steve. I'm pretty sure they would take an interest, if you had told them that there were emeralds there!"

"Well, in the prospectus, it is customary to list all the minerals that were found on the property, and so I was bound by custom to include all that. And yes, I did mention that there were trace elements of the minerals beryl, chromium, and vanadium on the property. In case you didn't know, those are the three minerals that usually make up emeralds! Hey, it's not my fault if the Exxon executives don't know that those three minerals add up to make emeralds! If they sell me the land, and later find out that there are emeralds on the land, they will have no legal grounds to sue me, because I did disclose that information! If they go back and read my prospectus, they will see where I plainly told them ahead of time that there were deposits of beryl, chromium and vanadium minerals there!"

Travis shook his head. "So, later, after you've bought the land, and started mining emeralds, they can't say you didn't tell them about it?"

"Something like that. Only I wasn't exactly planning to let them know about the emeralds at all. Because remember? I said that they are only selling the surface land. Exxon will still retain the mineral rights, so technically, I can't mine emeralds, or anything else on or under that land, because the mineral rights will still belong to them."

Travis chuckled. "So, what you are really saying is that you want me to go in with you in buying 900 acres of land that is rich with emeralds, and is covered with rare, exotic trees. But we can't cut the trees, and we can't mine the emeralds, and we can't even access the land except by boat? You're saying that you want me to put up a ton of money to buy this land?"

"That's right."

"I'm sorry, Steve, but it sounds like a 'white elephant' to me. It would be neat to own, but what could we do to ever get our investment back?"

"Well, Homer and I have been discussing this, and we think we might have a solution."

"Oh, so Homer is in on this too?"

"Yes, I went to him with the proposition first, then to Doc. You are the third one I've approached about it."

"So what do they think about it?"

"Homer is all for it, but Doc said he wants to wait and see if you go for the idea."

"Well, what I've heard so far doesn't sound very good. But you said that Homer has an idea?"

"Yes, but we shouldn't discuss it over the phone. Homer suggested that we get together for lunch, and talk it over. And he will explain his plan."

"I'm always open to lunch. But I've got one more question. How much of an investment are we talking about here?"

"That's a valid question. It depends on how many partners we have on board. I'll go ahead and tell you that my bid was $600 per acre."

"Ouch! That sounds like a lot for land in a third world country, and for land with no access to anything!"

"I know, but I had inside info that the low bid was going to be $550 per acre, and I wanted to be sure and win. That's a total of about $486,000, so the more partners we have, the more ways we can split it. Three ways will be $162,000 each. Could you handle that?"

"Probably so, if I can see a way of making it pay off."

"$162,000 is going to be every dime I can scrape up." Steve said, wistfully. "But if you and Doc come on board, it will drop our individual investment cost to only $121,000."

"That would be pocket change for Homer."

"Yeah, that's what he said. I hate it when he gloats about how rich he is! But I'm glad he has deep pockets, because it might take his deep pockets to get this plan off the ground. He offered to pay 50% of the total, but I didn't want any one of us to have controlling interest. We need to keep it an equal partnership."

"Yes, that would probably be for the best. Win or lose, we do it equally. Well, I'm going to have to hear Homer's plan before I jump in with both feet. When and where do we meet for lunch?"

"Homer suggested Red Lobster, in Arlington, at about one this afternoon."

"So soon?"

"Hey the bid will be awarded in three days. We need to get our cash together ASAP, to be able to pay it on the spot, otherwise, it will go to the next bidder."

"I'll need to talk to Janice about this first. Because the money I use will have to come out of our retirement accounts, and we'll have to discuss that."

"Sure. I understand."

"But I'll be at Red Lobster at one. I want to hear Homer's plan."

"I think you will be impressed!"

⇥ 2 ⇤

Travis knew it was going to be a hard sell to get Janice's approval for such a deal. In fact, he wasn't so sure about it himself. It would help if he knew what kind of plan Homer had in mind, so he could share it with her. He knew Homer was a pretty bright businessman, and even though he was rich, he still didn't invest money unwisely. If Homer thought it was a good investment, he would trust Homer's judgment. The fact that Doc didn't want in, unless *he* was in, probably meant that Doc didn't have enough money to invest, unless there were more investors, and thus, smaller amounts required from each.

He thought about not even telling Janice, just investing the money, and hoping it paid off, but he was old enough to know that it was folly to do such a thing. If it back-fired, his name would be mud. Better to just tell her about it, and let her decide if it was a good investment or not. If it bombed, she couldn't blame it all on him.

"You want to buy 900 acres of tropical rain forest?" Janice asked. "Travis, I thought the rain forest made you paranoid? Remember when you took Jenny to Peru a few years ago? She said you were seeing VC behind every tree!"

"Not *every* tree! And I knew there were no VC in Peru!"

"But you told me that it made you feel uncomfortable, because it reminded you of Vietnam."

"Well, maybe I've gotten over that by now. I've been to a lot of rain forests since then, and I think I'm over it."

"Okay, I believe you. But 900 acres of rain forest? What in the world do you plan to do with it?"

"Steve said that Homer has a plan, and he wants to meet for lunch today to discuss it."

"So maybe you should wait to see what his plan is, before we decide to pour that much money into it.

"Yeah, that was what I was thinking."

"After you hear his plan, then tell me about it, and we will decide if we want to risk our money on it. Where are you meeting for lunch?"

"Red Lobster."

"Ooh! Maybe you should take me with you! I like Red Lobster!"

"Well, this is more of a business meeting. A guy thing. Tell you what, I'll take you there tonight for dinner. How about that?"

"Okay, but over dinner, you have to fill me in on everything you talked about."

———◆◆◆———

As it turned out, Travis didn't have to worry about taking Janice to dinner at Red Lobster, because when he got there that afternoon, the parking lot was vacant, and the sign said: 'Closed for Renovations'. He took out his cell phone and called Steve."

"Closed for renovations?" Steve asked. "Oh well, I guess we'll have to meet somewhere else. What else is close by?"

"Well, right next door is a Milo's burger joint on one side, and on the other side is what looks like a bar, called The Pearl Harbor Tavern."

"Is the tavern open?"

"Yeah, it appears to be."

"Well, that works for me. All we need is a place to discuss business. Go ahead and get us a private table in the back. I'll call Homer and tell him about the change of plans. I'm 10 minutes away."

Travis pulled into the tavern parking lot, not a crowded place itself, and noted the elaborately painted sign on the front of the building. It was the scene of a tropical island paradise, with palm trees, and parrots, and monkeys, and an oriental looking 'rising sun' on the horizon, with rays of red sunshine emanating from it, eerily similar to the old Jap battle flag.

'The Pearl Harbor Tavern', the sign read, and under that, in smaller lettering, it also said, 'Come in and get bombed!'

Hmm, Travis thought. *I bet he doesn't get many WWII veterans as customers.* But that was nothing compared to what he saw when he got inside. The entire bar was decorated with all kinds of Japanese WWII memorabilia. Kind of like a Japanese version of the Hard Rock Café. But it made more sense when a young Japanese man approached, and introduced himself as the tavern owner.

"Welcome to the Pearl Harbor! Would you like a table or booth?"

"A booth against the back wall." Travis replied. "Two friends will be joining me in a few minutes."

"Great! Right this way, sir." As they walked he told Travis that they served great sushi, as well as steamed and fried sea foods. As he sat down, Travis asked about the tavern's name, and the invitation to 'come in and get bombed'. Did it ever make anyone mad?

The owner laughed. "Yes, I got a lot of curious responses, and angry remarks from older customers. When I chose the name for this place. I wanted something that would turn heads, and stir a little controversy, and it did. But hey, it's been over 50 years since WWII, and the name is a sort of, tongue-in-cheek way of making light of a very serious past event. But believe it or not, some of my most loyal patrons are old war veterans. And it helps that I give a veterans discount."

"In that case, I'm glad I came in." Travis said. "Here come my friends now."

Homer and Steve saw him and came on back.

"Gentlemen, I am Mr. Moto, the owner! Welcome to Pearl Harbor! What would you like to drink?"

"Actually," Steve said, "We are here to discuss a business deal first, then we will order later. So if we can meet undisturbed for awhile..."

"Of course! But new customers get a free round of drinks on me! So what will it be?"

"Free booze!" Homer exclaimed. "I'm an Indian! I never pass up free booze! What about it, guys?"

"Bring us Sake, Mr. Moto." Steve said.

"A good choice!" He left to get the drinks, as they were seated.

"So how have you been, Travis? You stay so busy that you never call me anymore." Homer said.

"I know. This new job with FBN Investigations is keeping me on the move. And I have a demanding contract with Jester Books, to churn out a new book every 12 months, so I stay busy!"

"You're writing career must be really taking off. You should quit that Private Eye shit, and write full time!"

"Are you kidding? That Private Eye shit, as you call it, is where I get a lot of my good ideas to write about!"

"Well, perhaps we can all three just retire and watch our money roll in off this investment in Ecuador!" Steve said, trying to get to the reason for their meeting.

"Yes, I am anxious to hear the details of this plan, and so is Janice."

"So she's reluctant to let you jump on in?" Homer asked.

"Well, yeah, but so am I, until I get more information."

"That's why we are here," Homer said. "I think you will like our plan."

Mr. Moto returned with a half bottle of sake, and three glasses. He poured them a round, then left the bottle on the table.

"Looks like a bit more than a round, Mr. Moto." Steve said.

"A round,…a bottle,…it's my treat! Enjoy, gentlemen! Just wave to the waitress when you are ready to order."

After he was gone, Travis said, "I think he is trying to make us his regular customers."

"It works for me!" Homer said, as he knocked back his shot of sake, and poured another. "What is sake anyway? Is it rice wine, or rice liquor?"

Steve took a drink and coughed as he set his glass down. "Oh yeah! It's liquor all right! Pretty stout stuff!" Everyone sampled it, and agreed that it was good.

"Okay, lets get down to business." Steve said. "Homer and I have already kicked around a few ideas, and I think we have found a way to make it work."

"Just for clarification," Travis said, "Let me first recount what I already know, based on what you told me over the phone."

"Okay." Steve said.

"We are buying 900 acres of rain forest land in Ecuador, on the banks of what river?"

"The Napo River. It's one of the biggest tributaries of the Amazon River."

"We will be paying $600 per acre, for the land, which does not include the mineral rights."

"That is true." Steve said.

"The land has no utilities, and no access road whatsoever, and is only accessible by the river."

"True." Steve said.

"The land is covered with valuable hardwood trees, that, if harvested, could be worth millions. But because of government red tape, the trees cannot be harvested. Correct?"

"You are correct." Steve said.

"The land also contains emeralds, but because we won't own the mineral rights, we cannot mine them. Is that correct?"

"Again you are correct, sir!" Steve admitted.

"So the question I have is this: Why should I sink $162,000 of my life's savings into this property, if there is no way to recover our investment? I mean, it might be pretty land, and $600 per acre is cheap by our standards, but how is it going to pay off in our lifetime? I'm seeing it as a giant sucking money pit."

Steve looked at Homer. "You start it off, Homer."

Homer took another shot of sake, and replied, "I can sum it up in two words, Travis: Eco-lodge!"

"Technically, that is one hyphenated word, Homer." Travis corrected him.

"Well excuse the hell out of me for not being as literate as you! After I have a shit-pot of novels published, I will probably know better!"

"Travis, do you know what an eco-lodge is?" Steve asked.

"I should. I've stayed at enough of them in Peru and Central America. It's an ecologically friendly lodge out in the jungle where visitors can go to see and experience nature up close and personal."

"Give the man a cigar!" Homer said. "That is the key to how we will make money off this deal."

"By building an eco-lodge on the land?" Travis asked. "At $50 per person, per night, it will take forever to pay off the cost of the land! Plus you would have the expense of *building* the eco-lodge, and staffing it with competent people. I just don't see us doing this, and not getting deeper and deeper in the hole."

"Perhaps because you are not seeing the whole picture." Homer said. "Allow me to back up and explain this deal from an investment point of view. I have already consulted my tax lawyers, and took the liberty of having them crunch a few numbers, and the facts might surprise you, as they did me. Step one: We buy the property, and make sure it is legally transferred into our names. Step two: We split the property in half. We keep the 450 acres that have the river-front access. The back

450 acres, that has no access at all, we donate, yes, I said *donate*, to the International Nature Conservancy, as a *huge* tax write-off. Underscore the word huge! What that means is, even if we never do another damn thing with that property, it provides all three of us with a tax shelter for the rest of our lives! The International Nature Conservancy is a world famous non-profit organization that is recognized by the United States Government as a legitimate charity. What that means to us, is that starting this year, no matter how much money our businesses in the States make, we will owe *no taxes* to the Feds, because the projected value of our 450 acre donation of teak and mahogany trees is worth literally tens of millions of dollars! We don't have to cut and sell the trees, as long as we can get tax credit for leaving them as is! So for a paltry investment of $162,000, I can recover that amount in less than two years of tax savings from my businesses here at home."

"So it's a great investment for you, because of the huge tax savings, because you own a giant business, but what about me and Steve? Are we going to get our investment back with eco-lodge profits?" Travis asked.

"No." Homer said. "Both of you will benefit from the tax break too, though not as much as I will. But we are all going to maximize our profits by mining emeralds from the 450 acres we are keeping."

"But Exxon owns the mineral rights." Travis reminded him.

"That is true," Homer said, "And that is why we can not *openly* mine emeralds, but that brings us to the *real* reason for building the eco-lodge! It will be a front,…a cover for mining the emeralds!"

"Wait. Hold it right there!" Travis said. "I used to be a miner, and I know better than anyone, that you can't operate a mine without making a big mess! There's no way we could covertly mine emeralds without someone figuring out what we are doing!"

"That is Steve's specialty. Tell him, Mr. Geologist." Homer said.

Steve reached in his briefcase and took out a large print-out from Google Earth. The photo showed a large river snaking its way through a rain forest. "This is a satellite view of the land we are looking at. I drew off lines here to approximate the boundaries of the land we are buying. This horizontal line is where we propose to divide the land. That half will go to the Nature Conservancy. The land bordering on the river, we will keep. The place I found the emeralds was here, on the beach, in this crescent shaped inlet. Notice the strip of high ground bordering on the river. This is a protrusion of rock that was pushed to the surface millions of years ago, by pressure exerted from tectonic plates shoving one plate under the other. This protrusion of rock is what I am speculating contains the emerald-bearing rock. But strangely, not on the surface. I did test holes all along this protrusion, but found emeralds nowhere along it. Away from the protrusion, still no emeralds. But in and around this crescent shaped inlet, it was a different story! This area was *littered* with emeralds! What caused this formation, and where did the emeralds come from? Best I can tell, this semi-circular formation is actually an *impact crater*. I speculate that it was caused by a *meteor* impact around 10,000 years ago. I know this, because I rented scuba gear, and went down and examined the gravel beds in the bottom of this bay. There I found pieces of iron meteorite, indicating that this was indeed a meteor strike. This too, just adds to the uniqueness of this site! How often do you find a meteor crater on the earth, that you can *identify* as a meteor crater? Very seldom! But what really excited me was this." He took a hand ball size green rock out of his briefcase, and set it on the table in front of Travis.

"This is a 109 carat emerald I found among the gravel in the bottom of that crater! Go ahead. Pick it up and look at it. Do you see anything interesting about it?"

Travis turned it over in his hand, admiring the beauty of the dark green crystal. He asked a stupid question. "Are you sure this isn't just glass?"

"I had it appraised by Victor Carranza in Bogota last week. He offered me $100,000 for it on the spot! I thought I'd better hold on to it for awhile, and get a second appraisal. I think it is worth much more."

"Who is Victor Carranza?" Travis asked.

"He is the biggest emerald producer in the world. Most of his mines are in Colombia. He has been called 'The Emerald Czar'. He also buys raw emeralds. If we are able to start mining, we will sell our emeralds to Victor, because he will give us the best deal. When I told him that this emerald came from Ecuador, he would not believe me, because he said he has never known of this kind of quality emeralds to come from Ecuador. Now, do you see anything special about that emerald, Travis?"

"It's not like I see emeralds every day. What am I supposed to be looking for?"

"Turn it into the light. See that?"

"Yes, I do. What is it?"

"It is a six-pointed star pattern within the emerald itself. Kind of like the star inside a sapphire. It is caused by rays of carbon impurities that formed inside the emerald. It is a very rare occurrence, and is known as a *trapiche emerald*. It makes this emerald worth double its usual value. Before I found this one, the only known trapiche emeralds had come from one of Victor's mines in Muzo, Colombia. Now here is the shocker: Half of the emeralds I have already recovered from my test holes on this property are trapiche emeralds! We simply *must* buy this property, if for no other reason, than to get at these emeralds!"

Travis was trying to get this clear in his mind. "So the emeralds were formed by this meteor impact?"

"No! Absolutely not!" Steve said, getting agitated. "You don't know anything about crystal formation, do you?"

"Well, I thought I did, but apparently not. So where *did* the emeralds come from?"

"The emeralds formed deep underground, and were brought up near the surface by the shifting tectonic plates. But the random meteor strike exposed them to the surface! The meteor did not cause their formation, but it did blast them out of the ground, when it smacked into the side of that protrusion. That is my speculation, but it is consistent with where I found the emeralds. That tells me that there could be emeralds beneath the surface all along that raised protrusion. That's why we need to acquire this land!"

"I agree." Travis said. "But that still doesn't answer my question of how are we going to run a mine without someone recognizing it as a mine."

"The answer is this: The emeralds are only found on the surface, around this crater, and in the river gravel itself, where the protrusion has eroded into the river. Therefore, the place we will construct our Eco-lodge, will be on this protrusion. That way, we will not be mining, per say, but will be doing necessary excavation work for the construction of the eco-lodge! We will have to dig holes for septic tanks, and field lines, and even a couple of swimming pools. We can come up with no end of reasons to continue digging and improving the eco-lodge. And as for the meteor crater itself, we can use that as a protective harbor for tourist boats to come in and dock to the eco-lodge. And even there, we can find reason to dig. We can say that we need to dredge out the gravel in this harbor, to allow bigger boats to enter. I know a dredging company from Coca that we can hire to dredge out the bottom of the crater for us. Of course we will carefully screen all the gravel they dredge out. That was where this big emerald came from. We can actually mine that whole site without anyone suspecting a thing! And in the process of constructing the eco-lodge, we can determine whether or not there really are emeralds beneath that protrusion. If so, we can covertly sink a shaft from the back side, to mine the emeralds. An old style mine, in which all the digging is done by hand. All tailings from the mine will be hauled out in containers that will be loaded onto a supply boat, and under the cover of darkness, hauled out into the river to be dumped. As big and as strong as the Napo River's current is, no one will ever notice the small amounts of rock we dump into it."

"It sounds like it will be a very labor intensive operation." Travis said. "Where are we going to find enough workers that we can trust, to run this place? And the key word is *trust!* Because if word of the mine gets out, there will be a flood of unauthorized miners digging all over the area, trying to strike it rich. Not to mention that we could be sued by Exxon for stealing their minerals."

"Leave that to me." Steve said. "I have been working down there for almost three years now. I own a house in Coca. And I have met dozens of good, hard-working people that we can trust to run this place. As long as we can pay them well, and provide them a place for their families live on the property, they will be fiercely loyal to us. We can staff the eco-lodge, the mine, and even have our own security personnel to watch over the place. Ecuador is very friendly to Americans, especially when they are benefiting from the deal. Considering the isolated area we will be in, it would benefit us to sort of start our own local community, with a good school, a resident doctor, and a company store, to provide for their every need. Our personnel would have no reason to leave, or even want to leave, as long as we take care of them."

"It sounds like you have put a lot of thought into this." Travis said.

"I have. What I have shared so far is just scratching the surface. I have put a lot of thought and planning into every aspect of this. And if we go through with it, I will live on site, just to make sure that everything goes smoothly. I need to be there through every phase of construction, so I can solve problems that might come up."

"The deal is sounding better all the time." Travis said. "So all that is required from me, is my share of the money?"

"Basically. Of course, you guys can come down and help me all you want. I know that you stay busy with lives of your own, but any help you can give the first year will be appreciated. Getting the eco-lodge built, and starting the mining operations will require a lot of planning. In order for this plan to work, we will have to really take on guests at the lodge, but even with guests coming and going, we will have to keep the mining operation a closely guarded secret."

"I assume that the lodge construction will require a lot of building materials to be brought in by boat?"

"Yes, everything that comes in, will have to come by boat. But most of the building materials can be had on site. I can hire a local lumberyard to bring a portable saw mill out to the site, and saw up all the lumber we will need to build the central lodge, and all the individual accommodations."

"Wait, I thought we couldn't cut the trees?" Homer asked.

"We can't for commercial sale. But if I submit a plan to the Ecuadorian Interior Department, explaining that we will be building a structure that will promote international tourism, then that is different. I will have to show projections of how our eco-lodge will bring money-oozing tourists into Ecuador. If I can persuade them, then I can secure a permit to cut just enough trees to provide our building supplies. They make deals like that all the time. And be sure, they *will* have inspectors on site to make sure we don't cut more than we need. But of course, a little money to 'grease palms' always helps."

"Bribery?" Travis asked.

"No, just an 'incentive' to sometimes look the other way on little things. There will be no OSHA to oversee the construction, so we will be our own quality control. The construction of the buildings will be simple, yet sturdy. Most of the poor, tropical countries are starting to realize that the real value of the rain forest is not in logging the trees, but in preserving them. They are learning that tourists will pay good money to come to these unspoiled places, to see the wild proliferation of plants, animals, and insect life. They want to see natural beauty. That is what makes our plan so perfect, because it fits right in with the latest trends, and the government will help us all they can. Outwardly, we are constructing an eco-lodge that will enhance their country's natural beauty. And the very fact that we give half our land to the Nature Conservancy should convince even the skeptics that we are on the level."

"While the whole time, we will be mining emeralds right under their noses!" Homer said. "It's a beautiful plan!"

"Okay, so we begin mining the emeralds." Travis said. "We are going to sell them to that buyer in Colombia?"

"Yes, Victor Carranza. He will buy all the emeralds we can produce. We will sell them to him anonymously. I have already applied for a seller ID number. All transactions will go smoothly. With each sale, he will wire the money back into Ecuador, into private accounts that we will set up. I suggest that we set up an account for each of us in Quito, as well as a general account, to be used for expenses incurred by the operation of the eco-lodge, at least until it becomes self sustaining."

"So Homer and I will have to open up a banking account in Ecuador."

"Yes, and you might as well apply for dual citizenship as well. All it requires is for you to maintain a banking account with a minimum balance of $25,000. And You should have that with our first deposit. And of course, anything you put into that account will be tax free, because of our donation to the Nature Conservancy."

"So Homer, are you convinced that this is a good move?" Travis asked.

"Of course! I wouldn't risk my money, if I didn't think it would work!"

"So you need a decision from me right away?"

"The sooner, the better." Steve said. "If you come on board, Doc said he would also. That will bring down our investment to $121,000 each. I can sell this big emerald and pay for most of my part. Which is a good thing, because I am strapped for cash right now."

"And I suppose our payments need to be in cash?"

"A money order will work." Steve said.

"Well, call Doc, and tell him that I'm 'in'. Once he gets in, the amount will be $121,000?"

"That's right."

"Then let's do it!" Travis said.

With that statement, he could not have envisioned the can of worms he was opening.

≈ 3 ≈

Travis figured that he had *better* take Janice somewhere nice to eat dinner, to break the news to her that their retirement account was going to show a $121,000 withdrawal. And since Red Lobster was closed for renovations, he consulted the yellow pages for another expensive restaurant. Preferably near the hospital, in case she took the news badly, and tried to kill him. The Olive Garden looked like a good choice.

When she asked how his business meeting with Steve and Homer went, he said he would lay it all out for her at The Olive Garden.

"What happened to Red lobster?"

"They were closed for renovations. We had to meet in a tavern next door, called Pearl Harbor."

"A nice place?"

"Just a bar. Oh, I got you a souvenir from there."

"An ink pen?"

"Read what it says."

"I got bombed at 'Pearl Harbor'? That's cute."

"I thought you would like it."

"Did you get 'bombed' at Pearl Harbor?"

"Homer did, on the Sake. We almost had to carry him out."

"Okay, I guess The Olive Garden will do."

They talked about the kids, and the possibility of grandkids, as they drove to Arlington. As they sat down in The Olive Garden, and ordered tea, Janice said, "Okay, I know you want to invest in this land deal, so let's have the details."

"How do you know that? I might not be interested at all."

"Travis, I can read you like a book! The fact that you haven't said a word about the deal, means you like it, and want to do it. If you didn't like it, you would have said so before now. So go ahead and tell me about it."

He told her all the facts, which didn't exactly add up to a good deal, until he got to the 'secretly mining emeralds' part.

"So this eco-lodge will just be an elaborate front for an illegal mining operation?"

"No, the eco-lodge will be real. It will make money, after the initial investment. But in the process of building it, we will 'have our eyes open' for loose emeralds that just might be uncovered by our construction digging."

"Yeah, right!"

"What? You don't believe me?"

"I know better than to think that Steve is going to build an eco-lodge on top a fortune in emeralds!"

"He figures that we will find a fortune in stones just during the construction."

"That doesn't even make sense! Just go ahead and tell me the truth, that the emerald mine will be an on-going thing, and it will be concealed by the eco-lodge!"

"You guessed it. But it's not illegal, in the sense that we are not going to be hurting anyone, by running the mine. It's only illegal, because Exxon owns the mineral rights. And they don't even know the emeralds are there. As far as we are concerned, it's finders-keepers!"

"I'm not impressed. This is about on par with that bogus story you spun for 'Whisperings Magazine', about your first book!"

"But that worked out, didn't it? The same way this will work out."

"Tell me how you are going to run a mine without everybody knowing about it!"

"Anybody who knows about it will be working for us, and making a good living. Part of the good wages we will be paying, will be a reward for keeping the mines existence a secret. Every miner will be responsible for making sure his family stays quiet. Nothing sinks ships quicker than loose lips. Steve knows the people down there, and he thinks we can pull this off."

"But $121,000 is a lot of money!"

"Figure it up. At my present income, the tax savings alone will save us that amount in 5 or 6 years. And that is if I never make a dime off the eco-lodge or the emeralds! So from that perspective, that's a good investment of cash money."

"But you have to give up your citizenship?"

"No, I said we could have *dual* citizenship. We will still be U.S. citizens, but we will also be citizens of Ecuador. A lot of people who have investments overseas have dual citizenship."

"So we could live there if we wanted to?"

"Absolutely! In fact, we could use that as our winter home, to escape the cold winters here at home. Wouldn't that be nice?"

"It sure would! Okay, so how soon does Steve need the money?"

"As soon as possible."

"Then go ahead. I'm willing to take a chance on it."

Janice didn't know it, but Travis had already withdrawn the money, and bought the money order. But he was glad to let her think that he had gone ahead on her approval.

4

Steve's bid of $600 per acre was the winning bid. (But what Steve *didn't know*, was that the next highest bidder was only $55 per acre. He had been scammed by one of his Exxon 'buddies' into bidding almost a half million dollars, when they could have won the bid with less than $54,000. The Exxon executives laughed as they divided up their profits off that, what they considered to be 'worthless land'. But they wouldn't be laughing if they had known about the emeralds.)

Immediately after Steve confirmed ownership of the land, he went to Quito to get the ball rolling. He presented his plans to the Ecuador Department of Interior, and got their blessings to build the lodge. He also got the necessary permits to cut and mill enough lumber to build the lodge. He also got the digging permits to install septic tanks for 16 units, and also for one swimming pool. This would be a good start.

Next, he flew to Coca, a large bustling 'wild west' boom town on the banks of the Napo River, just 12 miles down stream from their property. He immediately contacted local friends, and hired a company with a portable sawmill to get to the site, and start up the mill.

He met with a few of his most trusted local workers, over a pitcher of beer, who advised him on prospective employees for the new lodge. Men who could be trusted, who would bring their entire families, and live on site.

He met a local surveyor, who went to the site and made sure of the boundaries, and helped Steve plan the lay-out of the eco-lodge. Workers cleared the underbrush, then marked the trees, so that the sawyers would know which trees to cut, and which to leave, to enhance the beauty of the place.

During the clearing process, the workers found a 43 foot long Anaconda snake, and were about to kill it when Steve stopped them.

He explained that the reason tourists would come to a place like this, was to see all the creatures, and exhorted them to spare anything else of natural interest that they came across.

Many of the families set up temporary shelters on the property, so they could be near the work. Later they would build nicer, more comfortable habitations, as the lodge took shape.

Sawyers used cross-cut saws and axes to fell giant mahogany trees, de-limb them, and man-handle the logs into their portable sawmill. The lodge would be constructed from massive slabs of mahogany, notched and skillfully fitted together, by local workers who were used to working with such materials. The slabs of fresh milled mahogany were stacked in ventilated layers, so they could air-dry and cure for a few weeks, before the construction began. During this time of preparation work, Steve was busy trying to keep up with a dozen different crews on jobs scattered all across the site. He also kept an eye to the ground, in case emeralds turned up in unexpected places. And he had found quite a few.

When the foundation of the main lodge and kitchen was being excavated, he stayed there constantly, to make sure no one found anything of value. But he quickly saw that he was not going to keep the emeralds a secret, because in digging the foundation, they hit what looked like the mother lode. He quickly closed the site, and called his foremen together. In a closed meeting, he admitted that there were emeralds on site, and that he could make it well worth their while to keep it a secret. He explained to them in no uncertain terms, how keeping this a secret could benefit them all in the long-term, much more than they would gain from *not* keeping the secret. He laid out the terms of their agreement. He could guarantee them long term employment, which meant long-term security for their families, good educations for their children, and better health care than they could get anywhere in Ecuador, if they could help maintain this 'secret'. Steve knew what their reaction would be, because he knew he had loyal employees from the start. Such an agreement to the average Ecuadorian was like winning the lottery. There was unanimous agreement among them that they would loyally protect this secret. They, in turn, would make sure that every man in their crews would keep this, or they would not have a job.

Steve quickly counted the number of locals who were going to be privy to this secret, and counted 23 workers. Of course, if these workers were sequestered into living here on the property, they would have to be allowed to also bring their immediate families, who would also have to be taken into confidence on this matter. That was taking a big chance, but he knew that going in. These same workers, who were presently helping develop the property, would have to be the same workers and their families who would later staff the eco-lodge, and become the miners who would operate their secret mine. If there were no defections of personnel, then the secret could be kept. It would all depend on keeping the workers happy and content enough to stay here. His foremen, once they understood the terms of their agreement, assured Steve that there would be no defections.

At the end of the day, Steve breathed a great sigh of relief. With this matter settled, he knew he had cleared the major hurdle to carrying out their plans for the property. He knew he had to move quickly to keep his end of the bargain, so he called Homer, to begin the process of looking for a good doctor willing to move to the Ecuadorian jungle to staff their future health clinic. And to find a hearty-souled teacher willing to come here and educate the workers' children. He would immediately designate property upon which the workers could, in their spare time, construct their private homes. He would also survey locations for the health clinic and school. It was probably more important to get the latter two buildings constructed even before the main lodge itself. The health clinic would be a necessity for the eco-lodge as well, to treat ailments that might arise among the lodge's guests, so it made sense to build it within close proximity of the lodges. A general store would also be a necessity, and it would require a full time store keeper, to order stock, and make sure the store had everything that his workers needed.

With everything falling neatly together, it looked like the deal was going to come together exactly as they planned. This bewildered even Steve, who had started such ventures as this before, only to have someone, or something shatter the plans at the last minute. The last time, it was his wife (now ex-wife) who dropped the bombshell that shattered all his plans. But this time it looked like smooth sailing, from his perspective.

But that was when the unexpected bombshell hit. And it came out of the blue, in the form of a phone call from Travis.

"Travis! I didn't expect to hear from you so soon!"

"There has been big change in plans, Steve! How is the Lodge construction coming along?"

"Great! Everything is proceeding as planned. So what is this big change in plans?"

"Is the lodge far enough along that I can move down there with my family?"

"Uh, you mean to live here on site?"

"Yes, do you have basic necessities in place?"

"Well, no…not yet. We've got a dozen projects going at one time, and everything is progressing, but it's going to be awhile before we'll have descent living quarters available. Why? What's going on?"

"I need to move my family somewhere immediately, for their safety. I'm talking about Janice, Calvin, and maybe even Rebecca. Our present address is no longer safe."

"Why is that?"

"I just killed two Al Qaeda assassins right here in my living room! They were sent here to kill me in my home, in retaliation for a job I did recently in Egypt."

"Are you kidding me?"

"As I speak, their blood is soaking into my carpet, Steve! Janice has been terrorized out of her mind. I haven't even called the police yet. I made sure they were dead, and that there were no more outside, and then I called you, to find a safe place to hide my family. I know that this is just their first attempt to kill me. When they find out they didn't succeed, they will try again. I need a secure place to send my family, while I try to resolve this issue."

"And you want to send them down here?"

"Yes, as soon as possible. Can you think of a more remote place?"

"Er,…like I said, nothing is really set up yet. Those of us who are living here now, are basically living in tents. Things will improve in a few months, but right now, it's really primitive."

"Didn't you say you own a house in Coca?"

"Yes, and that is about 12 miles away from here, down the Napo River."

"So it's not being used right now?"

"Uh, well, it sort of is. You see, I have an Ecuadorian girlfriend, and she kind of keeps up my house in Coca when I'm away. But it's a big house, by Ecuadorian standards. I'm sure that we can make temporary arrangements to accommodate your family, since this is an emergency."

"That's great, Steve! I really owe you one! I'll have everyone on the first flight out of Birmingham this evening. I haven't even checked on connecting flights, but I can probably have them in Ecuador by tomorrow morning."

"Okay, here is what you do. Book your flights to Quito, the capital city, with a connecting flight to Coca. The Coca flight will be a short 200 mile flight up and over the Andes Mountains. Coca is on the Napo River, deep in the upper Amazon Basin. If you call me back with flight information, I will be there to meet you at the Coca airport tomorrow morning."

"I might not be with them." Travis said. "I have business to attend here."

"Okay, then I'll be there to meet *them*."

"Great! I'll do that. Thanks Steve!"

Steve hung up and rubbed his forehead. Knowing Travis, and how he loved his family, he suspected that this 'business' he had to take care of, might involve something that he was better off not knowing about.

But he had a lot to do. He had to make sure that all the crews here were understanding their immediate tasks, before he left for Coca. In Coca, he would inform his girlfriend that they would have house guests for a few days. That would require reshuffling a few things to make room, and cleaning up the place, and then, going to the grocery store to stock up on food. As though his life wasn't busy enough already, it was about to step up a notch. But that was what friends were for.

5

Back in Alabama, the day had started off ordinary enough. Calvin and Rebecca had just left for school, and Janice was on the phone talking to one of their grown kids. Travis finished off the left-over bacon, then went outside to feed the chickens, and gather eggs. Since his chickens were free-ranging, it was a challenge to gather eggs, because most hens were prone to lay eggs wherever they happened to be when the urge struck them. He was ever finding new nests in the most unlikely places. It was like hunting Easter Eggs.

That was when he got his first hint that someone was watching the house. He caught a glimpse of someone moving in the trees on the west side. Then he caught the glint of sunshine off the lens of a pair of binoculars, or perhaps a rifle scope. He owned several acres of wooded land on both sides of his home site, so there was no legitimate reason for anyone to be out there watching him, unless they were trespassing, and up to no good. Of course, he didn't let on that he had seen anything. He continued to gather eggs, then went back to the house. He set the egg basket on the counter, and told Janice to go to the bedroom.

"Why?" she asked.

"Because someone is prowling around outside. Now let's go to the bedroom." He accompanied her to the back room, and immediately got his Desert Eagle pistol out of the gun safe, and shoved in a full clip.

"That's an awfully big gun to scare off a prowler!" she said, noting the size of the .50 caliber bullets.

"You just stay here and keep your head down." he said. She complied, because he had been on edge, ever since he had gotten back from Egypt last November. She knew something had happened there, but he never told her exactly what. She figured this was just his latest installment of paranoia over whatever it was that was worrying him.

That was when the dog started to bark, indicating that there *was* someone out there this time.

"Travis, don't you shoot one of our neighbors, thinking it's a bad guy!"

"Don't worry about that! Now stay down. If you hear shooting, don't come out unless I call for you. Okay?"

"Sure. Should I call the police?"

"No. Not right now."

"What is it that you're not telling me, Travis?"

"I'll explain later. Stay down, and be quiet until I find out who this is."

The dog continued to bark in a manner that told him that someone was on the front porch. He peeked out the curtains to see a brown UPS truck in the yard, about the time he heard a knock on the door.

"Mr. Lee, this is UPS! I have a package for you!"

He didn't believe it, because he knew the only two UPS delivery men who serviced this neighborhood, and that voice didn't match either of them. He also knew what the hit-man tactics were, so he did not go to the front door, but instead went to position himself where he could see the back door entering the kitchen.

The dog continued to bark at the man on the front porch, at the same time Travis saw a human shadow fall across the back door.

The door knob turned, and a strange man armed with a large caliber hand gun appeared in the doorway. There was no hesitation. Travis fired two quick rounds into the man's chest, then whirled around in time to see the front door burst open. The stranger in the UPS uniform entered the room with an AK-47, yelling, "Allah Akaba! This is for Sheik Muhammad Hassan!" He opened fire, spraying a row of bullets across the living room wall, where Travis had been standing, but Travis had dove onto the floor, taking aim at the man, as he ran into the room. One shot from the Desert Eagle stopped the man. The second shot lifted him off his feet and deposited him like a rag doll on top his wife's coffee table.

He waited to see if there was a third gunman. Apparently not. The dog was peering into the living room from the front door, to see what happened, but decided he'd best go patrol the yard. If his master was *that* pissed off at the UPS man, there was no telling what he would do to *him*.

Travis got up to make sure the gunman on the back porch was dead, which he was. A .50 caliber. hollow point magnum made a hell of an exit wound. The man looked to be ethnically an Egyptian, which made sense, because it was the Muslim Brotherhood who most likely would be sending someone after him. He rolled him over to get his wallet, to identify him, and was not surprised to see no ID at all. He surveyed the yard, then went to examine the dead guy at the front door. Same story,…no ID, except the ID of the real UPS man, who was obviously not this guy. They had probably killed him, in order to get his van.

His mind was racing, considering every possibility. Was the gunman at the back door, the same man he had seen creeping in the woods? If not, then there was the potential of a *third* man still out there. He didn't think so, because everything he had studied about Muslim hit-men, indicated that they operated in pairs. But still, he had to be sure. He got a scent off he dead man, then crept out to the woods, to examine the area where he had seen the intruder. It was the same scent, which meant he had gotten them all.

Travis returned to the house and started to call the local police, but then thought about who that would be. Laurel Grove's ageing police Chief Stone, and his incompetent *Barney Fyffe proto-type*, Deputy Dangler. He would just as soon call the neighborhood gossip committee. He wanted to keep this whole thing as low-key as possible. It would be better to call General Morgan, and let The Agency handle this clean-up. *Like it never even happened.*

But first, he wanted to make arrangements for his family's safety. His first thought of a place to hide them, was the place he had been thinking a lot about lately, so he called Steve, in Ecuador, and made arrangements to send them there immediately. Then he called General Morgan.

"Good morning Travis! Good to hear from you!"

"Listen General, I just had an incident here at my home."

"It sounds serious."

"I just neutralized two Muslim Brotherhood hit-men, who showed up here to kill me!"

"Are you okay?"

"Yeah, I got them first. I thought you might want to handle the 'clean up' operation. Know what I mean?"

"Yes, I will immediately dispatch a unit there to clean things up. Have you called anyone besides me?"

"No, I thought you would want to be the first to know."

"Good! You did the right thing. I'm at Fort Benning. I can get a chopper and be there within an hour. The 'clean up' crew will be there before I will. Show them what they need to see."

"How did this happen, General? How did they track me to where I live?"

"I think I know. I'll explain it when I get there. Stay alert, in case they try again."

"Oh, I'm alert alright!"

He thought about Janice, who was still hiding in the bedroom, and went to get her. He didn't want her to see this mess before it was cleaned up. She would need help in packing for her trip to Ecuador.

"Janice? Everything is okay. You can come out now."

She appeared from the closet, pale as a ghost.

"What just happened, Travis? Are you okay?"

"I'm fine. But you don't need to go into the living room right now. Things are kind of messy!"

"Who were you shooting at?"

"I don't know. I never saw them before."

"Are they gone now?"

"Yeah, they're gone. Listen to me, I just called General Morgan, and he's sending a crew out to clean up this mess, so don't let it bother you."

"General Morgan? So this was something to do with your 'top secret' dealings? Is that what you are telling me?"

"Yeah, but I don't know how they knew me, or where to find me."

"Does it matter? Someone comes here and shoots up my house, an you're worried about that? Let me go look at the damage!"

"No, what you need to be doing is packing a suitcase, because we don't need to be here right now. I called Steve, and he said that we're welcome to come to Ecuador for awhile, so that's what we need to do. Calvin and Rebecca need to go too. Who are you calling?"

"I'm calling Rebecca, to get her home from school. She can go by and pick up Calvin."

"No, don't call them yet. Wait until this mess has been cleaned up first. But you can go ahead and pack your things."

"Have you not called the police?"

"Morgan will take care of that."

"I want to see what happened, Travis! Out of my way! This is my house, and I want to see what happened!"

"Fair warning, you're not going to like it."

Her mouth fell open when she saw the dead man on her coffee table, and the splatter on the wall and furniture from his exit wounds.

"Travis, I thought you said he was gone!"

"He *is* gone, Dear! He's in that happy Muslim Heaven where he gets his 72 virgin! Unless he doesn't get them, because he failed in his mission to kill me. In that case, he probably goes to the Muslim Hell, where he is fed pork, and spends eternity getting the shit beat out of him by 72 red-necks with baseball bats!"

"You killed the UPS man!"

"No, he was just pretending to be a UPS man. See that AK-47? UPS men don't carry those."

"Travis, there is a *dead man* in my living room,...*again*!"

"Well, I knew you weren't going to like it!"

"Look at all those bullet holes in the wall!"

"Fair warning, you probably won't like what's on the back porch either."

She brushed past him, to go into the kitchen, where she saw the dead man on the back porch.

"You killed *two* men?"

"Well, yeah. But remember, they were trying to kill me! Hey, at least this guy isn't bleeding on your carpet! Blood is easier to remove from concrete, especially since we paid extra to have the sealer put on it. Remember that the next time you want to give me a hard time about paying extra to have the sealer added!"

"Travis, I don't care about the concrete! Do you not seem to understand that you had a *shoot-out* in our *home*? I mean, I'm still upset that a *dead man* was found in our living room last year! And now you bring your 'job' home with you! You have a shoot-out right here where we live, and you expect me to just laugh it off? Do you not realize that I can't take much more of this? My nerves are shot! How can I *ever* feel safe here in my own home again?"

"That's exactly why I say you need to take a long vacation to Ecuador! Get away from this place, and all your worries, in a place where you can feel safe! And in the meantime, I intend to solve this problem! I intend to make you feel safe in your home again, by finding out who is responsible for this!"

"Oh Travis! You can't fix everything! I don't care what you do, I'll never feel safe here again!" She burst into tears.

He knew that she was right. On one hand, it angered him, that this had happened here, because this had been his home all his life. They could move, but he certainly didn't want to. On the other hand, with all the kids grown, now they could move, and it wouldn't be as disruptive. No, he wasn't even going to consider moving! This was his home, and he would do whatever he had to do, to make it safe again. But he needed time to do that. With her and the kids safely in Ecuador, he would explore the options. He wasn't leaving his life-long home without a fight.

He was about to suggest that they go start packing for Ecuador, when the dog began barking again, meaning that someone had just driven up. Morgan's 'cleaning crew' couldn't be getting here so soon. He looked out the window and was startled.

"Janice, your parents just drove up!"

Drying her tears, she said, "What! They almost never come to visit! And never without calling first!"

"Well, here they are! And we've got a dead body at the front and back doors! How are we going to explain that?"

"I don't know!"

"You've got to go out and meet them at their van, and stall them from coming in! In the meantime, I'll try to do something with the guy on the back porch. Try to give me at least five minutes! And dry those tears up before you go outside!"

"It will take them awhile to get out of the van, because she can't walk very well any more."

"Well stall them as long as you can, and when they do come in, bring them in the back door!"

"I'll try!" She stepped gingerly over the body on the back porch, and went around the house to greet her parents. Travis, meanwhile, had to find something quick to do with the dead guy. Where could he put him? There was nothing handy. Dig a hole? No, it would take too long. Suddenly, he got an idea.

Janice tried to put on a happy face, as she rounded the end of the house to face her parents, but they were sure to see that her eyes were red from crying.

"Paw-Paw, this is an unexpected pleasure! I haven't heard from y'all in awhile."

Her Paw-Paw took his cigar out of the corner of his mouth, and said, "That might be because we just got back from our month-long trip to Alaska! How's my baby girl?" He opened his arms to greet her with a big bear hug.

"That's right! I forgot you were gone to Alaska! When did you get back?"

"Last evening. We went by Marla's house first, but she wasn't home, so we came on down to see how you and Travis is doing!"

"We are just fine, Paw-Paw!"

Maw-Maw spoke up. "Janice, have you been cryin'?"

"No, Maw-Maw, I've just got an allergy to something, the doctor says."

"Probably to that *husband* of yours!"

"Hush, Maw-Maw!" Herston said. "I ain't brought you here to be stirrin' up trouble!"

"Yes sir." she said.

"Where is Travis?" Herston asked.

"I think he's around back. I don't know if he saw you drive up or not."

"Looks like the UPS man is here," Herston said, nodding toward the brown van.

"Oh,…no…he…his delivery van broke down. He caught a ride back to town. A tow truck is on the way to get that one." she lied. "So tell me about Alaska! How was it?"

"Well," Herston began, "You know we drove all the way, most of it on that dad-burn Alaskan Highway. I tell you what, that's got to be the dustiest road I have ever seen! We had the winders rolled up, and the dust *still* got all over everything inside!"

"Wasn't the road paved?" Janice asked.

"Yeah, most of it, but the sections that was jest gravel, *those* were the dustiest spots! And man, there wasn't nothing but eighteen wheelers passing us, and when one passed, we'd just have to pull over and let the dust clear out so we could see again!"

"But I guess it was a lot better once you got up there?" Janice asked.

"Oh yeah, yeah! Beautiful country! Everywhere we went, was jest as pretty as a post card! Your Maw-Maw got plenty of pictures, but they ain't developed yet."

"Yeah, it was so pretty up there!" Maw-maw said. "You should have seen all the pretty hummingbirds! They were everywhere!"

"You crazy old woman," Herston scowled, "I done told you a hundred times, them *wasn't* hummingbirds! They was *skeeters*! Janice, them skeeters was big enough to tote you off!"

"Nah! They was hummingbirds!" Maw-maw insisted. "Mosquitoes don't get that big!"

"They was skeeters! I know, because they put whelps all over my arms! I squashed one inside a magazine, and I can show it to you!"

"You're full of mud!" she replied. "I need my walking stick out of the van." As she went back to the van to get it, Herston whispered to Janice,

"I'm startin' to worry about your Maw-maw. Her mind is startin' to go, even worse than it was before. She can't remember much, and what she does remember, she remembers it all wrong. I have to watch her pretty close these days. Sometimes she says some hateful things, but don't take it personal, because she ain't really herself. Every passing day, she's getting to be less and less the Maw-maw we used to know."

"Really? I hate to hear that." Janice said, though she wasn't so sure she meant it. Her Maw-maw had been so mean to her when she was a girl, that she figured that any kind of change in *that* mind had to be an improvement. While she was thinking this, her Paw-paw was making his way to the front porch, saying,

"Well, I got to use your bathroom in the worst kind of way. How about you helpin' your Maw-maw waddle on to the house."

"Uh,…Paw-paw, you can't go to the front door,…it's locked."

"Locked? Since when did you start locking your doors?"

"Since we found that dead man in the house over a year ago."

"Yeah, I reckon that would cause me to start lockin' my doors too!"

"Go around by the back door. It's not locked." Janice said in a loud voice, hoping that she had given Travis enough time to move that body. When Herston went around the corner of the house, he saw Travis with the garden hose, washing off the concrete.

"Hey, Herston! I didn't hear you drive up! Is Maw-maw with you?"

"Yeah, she's coming, but she's a little slow. I've got to use your bathroom. Is this door open?"

"Yeah, but let me go in and move some junk before you go in."

"I ain't afraid of no messy house. You've seen where *I* live!"

Travis went in ahead of him, and closed the door to the living room, and used a kitchen towel to discretely wipe up a few spots of blood before his father-in-law saw them. He put on a pot of coffee in the kitchen, because he knew his father-in-law would want a cup. By this time, Janice was guiding her mother through the back door into the kitchen, and sat her down at the kitchen table. She was worn out from the short walk. Travis looked at his watch, knowing that the 'cleaning crew' was going to be there soon.

"So, Maw-maw, tell us about other things you saw in Alaska."

"Oh, there was a whole bunch of stuff that we saw. We saw bears, and mountain goats, and moose! Them moose was as big as your house!"

"That's pretty big, as big as our house!" Travis said.

"So I reckon you're callin' me a liar then?"

"No, I'm just saying that they probably just *looked* as big as our house."

"No, they was *as big as your house!*" she insisted.

Herston returned from the bathroom in time to hear this. "What kind of tale are you telling, old woman?"

"I was telling them about the moose we saw that was as big as their house, and he's callin' me a liar!"

"No I didn't! I just said that was hard to believe." Travis said.

"See? He's callin' me a liar! You ought to whip his ass Herston! He's callin' both of us liars!"

"Now wait a minute, old woman, I think you be talkin' about that moose *statue* we saw somewhere up yonder. Remember? You got pictures of it. It was in the town square, in one of them small towns up there."

"It wasn't no statue! It was a *real* moose!" she insisted.

"We did see lots of real moose, but that one that was as big as a house was a fake moose, made out of concrete, I think."

"You're full of mud! It was real! I know it was real!"

"Well, it doesn't really matter," Travis said. "Mosquitoes as big as hummingbirds, and moose as big as a house. Tell us about some other things you saw."

Maw-maw looked at him with a straight face, and said, "You talk too much! I'm going to cut your head off!"

"Okay," Travis laughed.

"You can't pay no attention to her!" Herston said. "The old woman is getting battier every day! We was wanting to do some salmon fishing while we was there, but the salmon run was late, and we missed out on them. But we did buy some smoked salmon from the Injuns that live there. Talk about some good eaten 'that is some good eatin'."

While he was talking, Maw-maw got to her feet, and shuffled over to the kitchen sink, and began opening drawers, looking for something. When she got to the knife drawer, she pulled out a big butcher knife, and was looking at it.

"Now, just what the hell do you think you're going to do with that?" Herston asked her.

"I don't know. I forgot." she said.

Travis got up and slipped up behind her, and carefully took the knife out of her hand, before she remembered.

"Well, I can see right now, I need to get you home and give you your medication!" Herston said.

"But we just got here." she said.

"We been here long enough! Sorry, Janice, but I need to get her home."

"I understand." Janice said. She was shocked that her mother's mental condition had worsened to the point she had just witnessed, and she felt sorry for her Paw-paw, for having to put up with her.

"Well, if we're leaving, I need to go to the bathroom before we leave."

"Okay, but make it quick." he said. "Do you need me to help you get to the bathroom?"

"No, I reckon I can still go to the bathroom by myself!" She ambled down the hall, and they heard her close the bathroom door. Janice took the opportunity to speak candidly to her father.

"Paw-paw, she needs to go to a nursing home, as bad as she is getting. Before long, she won't even recognize you any more. And she could be dangerous too! You saw her going to get a knife, to cut Travis' head off!"

"I know, Janice. I've seen old folks that wasn't as bad as her in the nursing homes, so I know that they would take her. But I love her, and as long as she's still able to recognize her family, I think I need to keep her at home. But I sho ain't taking her on no more road trips! I was thinking that the change of scenery would do her good, but I think it just made her worse! That trip to Alaska just about killed me!"

"That's what I mean, Paw-paw. I don't want you trying to take care of her, and her sending you to an early grave!"

"I know what you are saying, Janice. But I do still love her, and as long as she still knows who I am, I want to keep her at home."

"Well, at least promise me that if she does start to not recognize anyone, you will put her in a nursing home."

"I can't promise that right now, Hon. It's a call I'll have to make when the time comes."

"What does Marla think about it?"

"Marla? Humph! She wanted her committed two years ago! I don't put no stock in what Marla says."

They heard Maw-maw coming back from the bathroom, but it sounded like a different door closing than the bathroom door. There was a second door going from the hall to the living room, but Janice and Travis both thought there was no reason she would try to come back that way. They were both shocked when she opened the door from the living room to the kitchen. That meant she had walked right past the dead man in the living room. Janice got up and quickly closed the door behind her, and they both held their breath, waiting on her to blurt out the fact that there was a dead man sprawled out on their coffee table. But to their surprise, she said nothing about it. They knew she *had* to have seen it.

"Are you ready to go now, old woman?" Herston asked.

"I reckon so." she replied, and she began shuffling her way to the back door, with Herston right behind her. They walked them out to their van, and helped Maw-maw get in. As she was getting in, she said, in a calm voice,

"Herston, did you know that they have a dead man in their living room?"

"Say what?" He replied.

"I said, did you know that Travis and Janice have a dead man in their living room? And he is bleeding *all over* the floor in there!"

Herston looked at them, and Travis, who was out of sight from Maw-maw, was making a circular motion with his finger around the side of his head, as though to say *'she's crazy, remember?'*

Herston looked back at Maw-maw and grinned, "Of course they've got a dead man in their living room, old woman! Don't everybody?" He turned to the Lees, "I'll be talking to you, in a day or two." He shifted to reverse, and backed up, then headed out the driveway. Janice finally breathed a sigh of relief. "I can't believe we got away with that!"

"Who is going to believe your mother, the way her mind is?"

"What did you do with the guy who was on the back porch?"

"I lifted the lid on the septic tank, and rolled him in."

"No!"

"Yeah, it was all I had time to do, with your Dad coming around the house. I just barely got the blood washed off the concrete before he got there. Good thing it didn't have time to dry."

As soon as Janice's parents got gone, an un-marked black commercial van pulled up in the driveway. The driver rolled down the window and asked,

"Travis Lee?"

"You are the 'cleaning crew', aren't you?"

"That's right."

"Okay, there's a dead guy in the living room, and the other one I had to roll into the septic tank around back."

"Okay, we'll take care of it. It will be just like it never happened. You and your wife should find somewhere to go while we work."

"We'll go into Laurel Grove."

"Good deal."

"Travis, you mean we are going to leave and let these men work in our home,…unsupervised?"

"It's Okay, Janice. They are professionals. Grab the phone book, and we'll go to town. We have a lot of phone calls to make."

While they were in the truck, heading to town, they discussed what they were going to have to do. She, Calvin, and Rebecca were going to Ecuador, to stay out of sight for awhile. This presented a few problems, which Janice pointed out.

"This is Calvin's senior year of high school. He'll get an incomplete for the spring semester, and will have to repeat it, if he drops out now and goes to Ecuador. And the same thing with Rebecca. She's in the middle of her Spring semester, and she'll have to drop out too."

"There are comparable schools in Ecuador, where Calvin can finish his senior year, and graduate. But I'm not so sure about a University in

Coca. She would have to be in Quito to attend a comparable University. But the language would be no problem, because she is fluent in Spanish."

"Are you serious? Do you think Calvin wants to graduate high school from a school in Ecuador? He doesn't know anyone there! He doesn't play soccer! Which brings up the question: Just how long are we going to be 'hiding out' in Ecuador?"

"Until I can get this issue resolved?"

"And just how do you resolve something like this? Someone tried to kill you, and they will probably try again! Exactly who was it that tried to kill you, and why?"

"You know I can't tell you anything about that."

"Yes you can, if it involves me! And if I am having to move to Ecuador *indefinitely* because of it, then *yes*, it does involve me! The very least you owe me, is an explanation of *why*!"

"Well, in a few minutes, General Morgan is going to call me, and we'll get together to discuss the options. I will run it by him, and see if I can let you in on the reason why I was attacked, if you really want to know."

"Believe me, I really do want to know!" Janice said.

The phone rang, and Travis spoke to General Morgan, and he agreed to meet them at Rocky's Pizza, for a cup of coffee, and a talk. When he hung up, he turned to Janice.

"You're about to get your chance to ask all the questions you want in just a few minutes."

≈ 6 ≈

It was mid-morning, and Rocky's Pizza was not officially open until eleven, but the owner was an old friend, and was glad to let them in for the meeting. General Morgan arrived shortly after they did, so he arrived at their table about the time the coffee did.

"Good morning Travis, Janice! It is good to see you again!"

"I can't say the same about you, General." Janice said dryly. "Your visits are always synonymous with 'bad news'!"

"Be nice, Janice!" Travis said.

"Well," the General said, "I suppose from your perspective, Janice, that's a fair assessment, and I am sorry about that. By the way, are we in a secure place? I mean, are we free to speak here?"

"Oh yeah. This is my turf. Nothing but friends here."

"The things we discuss could be classified."

"General, are you hinting that I should not be here?" Janice asked.

"Well, classified material is not to be…"

"General, I am so tired of being told that! Let me tell you something! Travis has never told me anything about what he does, or where he goes, and that's fine! I can live with that! I know he has a job to do, and I appreciate that! But when he comes home, and *assassins* follow him home, and try to kill him in his own living room, then it's time to call it *my business*! You are not going to ask me to leave the room this time, because I *demand* to know what's going on!"

"Well, top secret means…"

"General, I don't give a rat's ass about 'top secret', or this 'classified' bullshit! I want to know what's going on!"

There was a brief silence, only broken by the sound of Travis excessively stirring ice into his coffee. Morgan turned to him.

"Travis, do you vouch for her integrity? Can we entrust her with hearing classified material?"

"What about it, Dear? Can you keep quiet about what you are about to hear? That means no blabbing to anyone, not even Marla."

"Of course I can!"

"Under the penalty of *imprisonment*, if you do not?" Morgan added.

"Would they really do that?" she asked.

"They would." Travis assured her. "So think carefully, before you answer."

"Yes! Yes, I can keep a secret! That's no problem! Now tell me what is going on!"

"Okay, Janice. I will take you at your word." Morgan said.

"So, Morgan, do you know who those guys might be?" Travis asked.

"Well, I have not see them yet, but from your description, I think we both know who sent them. The 'cleaning crew' will confirm a lot. Did they say anything before they started shooting?"

"Actually, I started the shooting. There was no sense in letting them get the first shot. Besides, they were inside my home when I opened fire. But as he was firing back, the one in the living room yelled *'Allah Akaba'*, and then something like, *'Revenge for cleric Hassan'*."

"Really? Then that pretty much nails that down. There is no doubt as to why they attacked you. It was a revenge hit, plain and simple."

"Revenge for what?" Janice asked.

General Morgan looked at Travis, then back at Janice. "Your husband was recently sent to Egypt to capture or kill a major player in international terrorism."

"You mean Osama Bin Laden?" she asked.

"Um, yes, that was the intended target. The CIA gave us intel that he was hiding in Egypt, protected by the Muslim Brotherhood, and even gave us an address. Travis went in, tried to capture him, was not able to, so he killed him, and brought out the head as proof of the hit."

Janice's jaw fell open.

"However, the man he killed was actually a *double* for Bin Laden, and was an Egyptian cleric named Mohammed Nasser Hussian. This made the Muslim Brotherhood very angry, and they vowed revenge. But we figured the revenge would be directed toward the U.S. presence in the Middle East. We did not anticipate it being a personal attack, because we had kept Travis' identity a closely guarded secret."

"But obviously, they found out it was me." Travis added.

"I think I know how they tracked you down, Travis, but this is just a theory." Morgan said. "Remember when you told me that Janice had tried to call you, but got an Arabic speaking person instead on your cell phone?"

"Yes, but you told me that you called the phone company and had my phone information wiped out."

"Yes, I did that. But it appears that they recorded your information before I had it erased. Therefore, they got all the information they needed to track you down, from that one phone call."

"Wait a minute." Janice said. "Back up and explain that to me about the phone. I don't quite understand."

Travis turned to her and explained. "Before I made my attempt that night, I deleted all information off my satellite phone, in case something went wrong, there would be no incriminating information on the phone. That was the same reason I sent my passport, and wallet home with Rose. If I was caught or killed, I didn't want that information in the wrong hands."

"So why did you even take the cell phone with you?" she asked.

"Because I needed it, in case the mission was aborted, I could be notified. And I also used the phone to call my evacuation plane, to have him adjust his pick-up time. But after I made that call, I deleted even that off the phone, so that if the phone was captured, there would be nothing on it. Going into the mission, there was nothing incriminating on the phone. After I made the hit, I retreated to the landing strip to be evacuated, and I was dismayed to find that I had apparently dropped the phone, as I struggled with my target. But I thought that was okay, because there was nothing incriminating on it."

"That is, Janice, until *you* tried to call your husband." Morgan said. "When you called him, the phone caller ID recorded who the call was from, and gave your home address. Since the phone was purchased in *your husband's* name, the enemy now had the *name*, and the *home address* of the hit man who had just killed their cleric! Now, do you have any more questions about how those hit men were able to find your home?"

Her jaw fell open again. "So what you are saying is, it's *my fault* that those men attacked us this morning?"

"Janice, remember that I have always told you, 'don't try to call me, when I am gone on a mission'? To wait on me to call you? Now do you see the reason why? If you try to call me, you could put me in grave danger. And in this case, you have put our whole family in danger."

"Well *DUH*! If I had been given a little explanation about that before now, instead of this 'top secret' B.S., then I wouldn't have tried to call you! I was calling to find out why you had sent your passport and wallet home! That didn't sound right! It distressed me that you would do such a thing without telling me why!"

"Okay, blame it on *me* then!" Travis said.

"I'm just surprised that it took them four months to track you down, Travis." Morgan said. "I would have thought they would strike quickly, just to send us the message that they are capable of such a thing."

"The main thing I worry about is, will they try again?" Travis said. "If they do, they have lost the element of surprise, because I will be watching for them next time."

"It sounds like you were watching for them *this* time." Morgan said.

"No, I just happened to see someone in the woods creeping around, while I was feeding the chickens. We ain't got no neighbors that are stupid enough to do that. Only somebody unfamiliar with the area would be doing that."

"Well, it might be a while before they try again." Morgan said, "Or, they might try again later today, depending on how extensive their sleeper cells are in this country. I think it was sheer lunacy on the part of President Bush, to *not* close off the Mexican border after 911! If the radical Muslims are smart, and we have no reason to believe that they're *not*, they will be slipping their sleepers cells into this country every day, until the border is closed off. The bottom line is, you need to take measures to protect your family, in case of another attack."

"I already have." Travis said. "I know of a really good hiding place in Ecuador. And I have already made a call related to that. I told them that my family will arrive there tomorrow morning. So I need to call the airlines and buy tickets."

"And I already told you the reason why that won't work, Travis! About them missing school?" Janice reminded him.

"Well, they can make up their school later, after this has been resolved."

"And that's another thing," she said, "How do you plan to resolve this? What are you going to do? I thought you would be going to Ecuador with us?"

"No, I have unfinished business here, or in Egypt, or wherever this takes me."

"Hold on." Morgan said. "You need to let me handle this. You can go on to Ecuador with your family, and I will see that this is taken care of. We need to capture one of these guys alive, so we can question him. If you are involved, we probably won't take any prisoners! Am I right?"

"Pretty much."

"That's what I thought."

"So how do you plan to handle it?"

"We will probably set a trap at your farm. When they walk in, we will have them. Of course, we'll need your *permission* to use your farm."

"Exactly how would that work?" Travis asked.

"We are assuming that the two hit-men you killed today were acting independent of anyone else. They made up their own terror cell. They most likely slipped into this country across the wide open border with Mexico, months or even years ago, and they have been 'sleepers' here ever since. When they got the orders to go to your address, and kill you, they did exactly as they were ordered. But since you killed them both, they most likely have not gotten word out that their attack failed. When news of that reaches whoever sent them, there will be another attempt on your life, from another sleeper cell. They will keep sending them, until they succeed in killing you."

"Or until they *think* they have killed me." Travis added. "Couldn't you put out a bogus story about how I was killed, but I fatally wounded both of my attackers. That way, they would think they succeeded, in killing me, and maybe stop trying."

"I don't know what we will do yet. But that idea does have merit." Morgan said. "We will check the fingerprints of the guys you killed, to see if they match anything we have on file. In the meantime, it might be best if you leave the country with your family, and let us try to resolve this."

"That's right," Janice said. "If I have to go to Ecuador, I want you to go with me!"

"Okay, we'll go by the high school and get Calvin out, and then go get Rebecca. We'll come back home to pack our clothes, while I call to buy tickets to Ecuador."

"After you leave your house," Morgan said, "I will decide what action to take. I might have military personnel move into your house, to assume your identity, as we set a trap for the next attempt."

"Good! That means someone will be there to feed the dog, and the chickens." Travis said.

⇥ 7 ⇥

If they thought Calvin was going to upset about missing his senior year of high school, they were mistaken. He was excited about going to Ecuador, and the sooner they left, the better. But when they caught up with Rebecca on the UCA campus, she was totally against leaving school at this point.

"But I only have two and a half months left before I graduate! And then Stan and I will be getting married this Summer! He was drafted by the Carolina Panthers, so we'll be looking for a house in North Carolina this Summer too. I need to graduate this Spring to keep everything on schedule."

"Well, it will not be safe at our house, after what happened this morning. So staying there is not an option." Travis said. "Do you have any dependable friends you can move in with on campus, to finish out the semester?"

"I can check around. If not, Stan will probably rent an apartment for me, if I ask. But it needs to be right away, doesn't it?"

"Yes, today if possible. You need to find a place to stay, then move your things out of the house. Your last name is Austin, so the bad guys after me, shouldn't even know that we are related."

"I'll cut the rest of my classes today and call Stan, to find me an apartment. I hope to be out before sundown. But Janice, are you going to be okay with moving to *Ecuador*?"

"I won't know until I see it, Rebecca." she said. "But when I married Travis, I vowed to go where he goes, and live where he lives, so whatever it's like down there, I'll learn to endure it."

Rebecca knew, better than anyone, what she was in for. Moving from the Colombian rain forest to civilization, had been a big step for her. But she was afraid that it was going to be an even bigger step for Janice to leave civilization, and adjust to the culture shock of the Ecuadorian jungle.

When they returned home, they found that the 'cleaning crew' was almost wrapped up. They were right, it was just like it never even happened. When Travis examined the living room, he saw a living room carpet that was cleaner than the day it was installed new. The man in charge of the cleaning explained,

"When we cleaned the affected area, there was such a difference between it and the unaffected area, that I made the decision to clean the carpet in the entire room. I hope you don't mind."

"No, not at all! You could have cleaned the entire house if you wanted to!" Janice said.

"Well, we didn't have time to do all that."

"Did you get the body out of the septic tank?" Travis asked.

"Yes, the outside crew did. We have both bodies on ice, waiting for examination. Do you know that both men were devout Muslims?"

"How do you know?"

"By their foreheads. The scaly, discolored spot in the middle of their forehead means that they frequently stayed face down on the floor, praying, the way Muslims do."

"That's a good observation."

General Morgan entered the living room. "So how does the house look, Travis?"

"After they finish repairing the bullet holes in the wall, it will look like it never even happened."

"Good. That's what we were aiming for. I'll have soldiers in civilian clothes here within the hour to occupy the house. Designate which room you want them living in, and I will pass it on to them."

"Probably Rebecca's room. She is packing up now."

"The men will bring folding cots with them. I will instruct them to keep their impact on your house to a minimum."

"Just tell them to maintain it in its present condition, and not to mess with our personal affects."

"Of course. That goes without saying."

"And another thing, my parents live in the house up the road. Can you instruct them to keep an eye on them as well?"

"That is affirmative."

Janice spoke up, "Travis, are you going to tell your parents what's going on? You know they'll suspect something, living so close."

"Yeah, before we leave for the airport I'll stop by and tell them what they need to know."

"Shouldn't I call my parents and let them know we will be gone? I mean in case they come by here again, like they did this morning?"

"No, we seldom hear from them. We could be gone a month, and they wouldn't know it. But here's something we can do. We can use the 'call forwarding' option, to forward our house phone to my satellite phone. That way, even if we are down in the jungle, we can still receive all our calls. If we don't tell them where we are at, they will assume that we are in our living room."

"Yes," Morgan said, "And that will perpetuate the belief that you are at home. If a hit man calls, just to see if you are home, that will tell him that you are, and he will walk into a trap. Which brings me to another subject. I need to get your permission to record all your home phone calls, in case you get a suspicious caller, we can be on it immediately."

"I don't know if I want someone hearing all my phone calls." Janice said.

"It is necessary, considering the circumstances." Travis said. "Janice, just remember that someone is listening in, when you are talking to someone. Don't say anything you don't want them to hear."

"So, you are going to give away our privacy, just like that?"

"It will just be until this is resolved, Janice. Trust me, it will be okay."

I've heard that line before! Janice thought to herself.

■━◆━◆━◆━■

Calvin was in his room packing his clothes, and facing a hard decision. What to do with that ammo box in his closet, that contained the treasure trove of gold and silver coins that he and Chris had found? The soldiers who were to occupy their house while they were gone were not supposed to mess with their personal belongings, but did he want to trust them with such a temptation? True, they would have to dug down in the bottom of his closet to find them, and that would be like excavating into a Mayan tomb, but if they did, they would find a surprise.

No, he had to hide it a little better than that. He considered having his dad put it into a safe deposit box at the bank, but that would require *telling* his parents about the treasure. So far, only Rebecca knew about it, and he had taken a chance in telling her.

Desperate to find a secure hiding place, he thought about hiding it inside the wall, in the space between the wall studs and the sheetrock. The sheetrock in the closet had never been finished. It was one of those hundreds of little projects that his dad was intending to do one day, but he would probably never get around to doing them. Which was good, because he could cut out a section of sheetrock up high, drop in the ammo box, and then replace the piece of sheetrock. Hmm. Not a bad idea, so he did it.

The ammo box was slightly too big to fall down between the studs, because it was slightly wider than the 2x4 studs. But that turned out to be a good thing. He wedged it in securely, and it stayed right there. He replaced the piece of sheetrock by using gorilla glue, instead of nails. That way, no one would hear him hammering nails, and ask what was going on. When he finished, he was impressed with how it looked. No one would even suspect that something was hidden there.

Then he turned to packing his suitcase. He had no idea what he would need, or what he could get down there, so he packed his favorite clothes, and a wide variety of personal items. This included his camping supplies, and insect repellant.

——◆——

While Janice and Rebecca helped one another with the packing, Travis was in the phone with Jim Deshler, his employer at FBN Investigations. He had explained the situation he was in, after foiling the attack on him that morning, and informed Jim that he was taking his family into hiding in Ecuador. Jim agreed that it was probably a good move, as long as he didn't leave a forwarding address that the bad guys would find.

"I hate to tell you this, Jim, but I may not be able to take on any jobs for awhile."

"Why not? Just because you'll be living in Ecuador, instead of Alabama? Flying out of Quito shouldn't be any different than flying out of Birmingham."

"Yeah, I guess you're right. And with your satellite phone, you and Helen can call me there just as easily as here, so yes, I guess I can still take on investigations while I'm there."

"Atta boy! You owe me for getting you out of that tight spot in Egypt! I spent a night in jail trying to help you!"

"Actually, you spent a night in jail for trying to bribe a police captain! Yeah, Helen told me all about it! They had nothing on you, until you tried to bribe the man!"

"Hey, it usually works! It just happened that I was questioned by the only *honest* police captain in Egypt! Just my luck!"

"So give me a couple of days to get my family settled in, and I can start back to work. Maybe no jobs will come up before then."

"Okay. Call me after you get settled, and let me know how it is. I might want to come visit you!"

"Will do!"

8

Travis booked the earliest flight out of Birmingham to Miami, and they had to literally run to catch a Delta flight from Miami to Quito. They arrived in Quito at midnight. The next flight to Coca was 8:00 AM, so they found an unoccupied place among the seats where they could camp out and get some sleep. Travis called Steve to let him know what time their flight would be arriving in Coca, and they settled in to sleep and wait.

"I'm hungry." Janice said.

"So the in-flight meal just didn't do it for you, huh?" Travis asked.

"No, I thought I was going to be sick."

"Well, I think we're out of luck, finding food here, at this hour. All the airport food vendors closed up before we got here. Want me to go find a vending machine?"

"Would you? A pack of cheese crackers and a soft drink would be nice."

"Okay, I'll go see what I can find. Want to go with me, Calvin?"

"Sure."

"Watch our bags, Janice."

As they walked, Calvin asked, "Are we really in Ecuador now?"

"Yes, we are in Quito, the capital city."

"It doesn't look much different from Birmingham."

"That's because we are in the airport. Most modern airports are pretty much the same. Wait until we get to Coca tomorrow. I bet Coca won't look anything like Birmingham."

"What kind of name is that for a city,…Coca?"

"It's a local name. Maybe it is called that because they grow coca beans there, you know, what they make chocolate out of?"

"Chocolate is made out of coca beans?"

"Sure. What did you think it was made out of?"

"I don't know. I guess I thought it was a combination of milk, and butter, and something to make it look brown."

"Well, the coca beans are what makes it brown, and flavors it. I'm sure we will see coca trees where we're going. Coca beans are actually the seeds from a big fruit that grows on a tree."

"So are the leaves from the coca tree what they make cocaine out of?"

"No, that's a different tree."

"So is Coca a big place?"

"I have never been there, but from what I hear, it's a big sprawling place. It's like a frontier city at the edge of the rain forest. I visualize it as being a rough place, probably a lot of bars, because it is the jumping off point for American oil companies that are drilling for oil all out in the jungle. When those rig workers get off days, they most likely come to Coca to drink and have a good time. Steve said that only the main streets in Coca are paved. The rest turn to muddy slop when it rains. Since there are a lot of foreign workers in Coca, there are a lot of locals, who come there to sell goods and services to them. Steve owns a house in Coca, which is where we will be staying until we can get a few livable bungalows built at our lodge."

"And where is this lodge?"

"He said it's 12 miles up the Napo River. Right out in the jungle!"

"That will be cool! So you haven't been there either?"

"No, this is my first time to be in Ecuador. There's a few vending machines. You know, I bet we have to have Ecuadorian currency for the vending machine. All I have is dollars."

"There's an ATM machine, Dad. Will that have Ecuador money?"

"It should."

"It shows that it gives out U.S. money."

"Are you sure?"

"Well, that's what it says. And look, the vending machines take U.S. money!"

"They sure do. Then I guess we're good. I have a pocket full of U.S. coins." The made several selections, then gathered them up and headed back to their gate.

"Dad, do you think Mom is going to be okay with living down here?"

"I hope so. But it's not like we will be living here from now on. Hopefully we can resolve the problem, and move back home soon. But in the meantime, consider this to be just a vacation. It's not every day you get to go do something cool like this. And if this eco-lodge works out, we will have a place where we can go in the winter, to get away from the cold weather."

"What made you want to invest money in a place way down here, Dad?"

"To answer that question, wait until we get there, and I will show you." he said with a wink.

When they got back with the snacks, they found Janice digging through her suitcase. When they sat down she broke out in tears.

"What are we doing, Travis?" she said finally. "At this point in our lives, we should be getting ready to grow old together, in the place where we have lived all our lives! Instead, we throw our world into a suitcase, and run off to hide in some out of the way place like Ecuador! I have never been here before. I don't know anyone down here. It is a different culture! A different language! I don't want to like this place! I just want to go back home!"

It was Calvin who answered her. "This is just temporary, Mom! Think of it as a vacation! We'll have a good time down here, and then when we get tired of having fun, we'll go back home!"

"Your Dad has been brainwashing you already, hasn't he?"

"No, I'm just looking forward to moving down here. I hope we can stay awhile."

"You're not fooling me! This is a conspiracy by you two to make me feel better about moving down here! Well, it's not going to work! I can be miserable and home-sick if I want!"

"Dear, you haven't even been out of the country for a day, and you are already saying you're homesick! Why don't you wait and see the place we are going before you say you don't like it?"

"Because I am a woman, and I can complain if I want to! Is crackers all they had?"

"I thought you said that was what you wanted? Crackers and a soft drink. I got a few sweets too."

"It's okay. Crackers will do! I guess I shouldn't complain, because after all, us having to come down here is partially my fault too! If I hadn't tried to call you in Egypt, all this wouldn't have happened!"

"It's okay. Things happen. That's the way life is. It certainly makes things in life more interesting, doesn't it? I mean, we could be stuck at home, bored to death, but instead, here we are!"

"That B.S. isn't going to work on me, Travis! I would love to be home, bored to death, watching TV as I sit on the couch!"

"Well, maybe you will change your mind after a few days."

"Don't hold your breath!"

———◆———

The next morning, after dozing on and off, Travis went down the concourse, and returned with breakfast burritos and coffee for the three of them. Janice had slept like a rock, but woke up more surly than ever.

"When do we start boarding?" she asked.

"In about an hour. Here, drink some coffee."

"Do I have to?"

"No, but it's here if you want it."

"How long will this flight be?"

"It's only 200 miles. Probably just a 25 minute flight."

"If that's all it is, why didn't Steve just drive here and pick us up?"

"Because that 200 miles is over the Andes Mountains, which have some of the most treacherous roads in the world! Trust me, it's better that we fly."

"Ugh! I think I'm going to be sick, thinking about that! Travis, I don't think I can do this! I'm going to have to go back home!"

"You haven't even seen the place, Dear! You are letting your imagination run away with you. Do like Calvin, and look forward to this, like it's an adventure!"

"Oh I will, but if I don't like it, can I go back home?"

"You'll find something to like about it, I promise!"

They ate in silence. As boarding time neared, only a handful of people gathered at the gate. Their fellow passengers fell into two categories: the indigenous bronze skinned people who were slight of build, and the big burly American oil well workers, who were probably on their way back to work, after visiting with their families in the States.

They thought they were boarding a 727 that was parked at their gate, but as they went down the ramp, they realized they were loading on an airport bus, which would take them out a ways from the terminal, to board a small twin engine plane.

"We're flying on that? Janice said. "It looks like it should be in a museum!"

"I'm sure it is very dependable," Travis said.

"Oh yeah, it's safe!" said one of the oil workers. "We ride it all the time! Sometimes going over the mountains it's like riding the Scream Machine at Six Flags!"

Janice didn't need to hear that, and the oil worker saw it in her eyes, and added, "Like Six Flags, but in a *good* way!" Too late, the damage was done.

The plane only held about 25 passengers, and it wasn't full. With only two rows of seats, everyone had a window seat. There was no stewardess, just the pilot and co-pilot, and the latter helped everyone to their seats.

In spite of its notorious billing, the flight over the mountains was surprisingly smooth, and the landing was perfect. The one thing that impressed the Lees, as they came in for the landing, was all that *green* jungle that covered everything. They saw no roads, no fields, no buildings, as they neared Coca. The giant snake-like Napo River loomed ominously on the east, as they turned for the landing. At the last moment they saw tell-tale signs of civilization, in the form of fields and scattered farm houses.

When the co-pilot opened the door to exit, they were blasted with tropical heat, and the unmistakable smell of a rain forest frontier town,…the smell of burning wood.

"It smells like something is burning." Janice said.

"Yeah, it's hundreds of cooking fires, from mothers cooking breakfast for their families." one of the oil workers said. "They have electricity here, but most people prefer to cook over an open flame. It's the custom."

As they exited the plane, Travis asked his son, "Does it still look like Birmingham?"

"Nothing like Birmingham!" Calvin marveled.

The terminal building looked like a Butler building that had been renovated with sheets of locally made plywood, and the carpenters who did it had no measuring tapes, because it appeared to be slapped together with function in mind, not workmanship. Nothing quite fit like it was supposed to. But it served it's purpose. It said to those arriving in Coca for the first time: *Yes, we are civilized, but don't expect much.*

There was no carousel for the luggage pick-up. The passengers just stood beside the plane until airport workers arrived to open the cargo door, and hand out the luggage. And apparently there was not much in the way of security, because while they were waiting on their luggage, a swarm of trinket vendors swarmed them, trying to make a sale. It was a little too much for Janice, but Calvin thought it was amusing.

A lean, lanky man with distinct Welch features towered over the short locals, and waded through them as he hurled greetings.

"Gringos! Welcome to Coca!" Steve Meredith yelled out over the crowd merrily. "I see you've already met the local welcoming committee!"

"Steve! How are you?" Travis asked, as he shook his hand.

"Life just gets better and better! Any more, and I couldn't stand it! Hey Janice! Great to see you again, and looking as beautiful as ever! And this is Calvin? Man, have you grown up! Where is Rebecca?"

"Oh, she decided not to come. She has a fiancé." Travis replied.

"Well, too bad. I was hoping to see her too. But hey! It's good to see you guys! I'll help you grab your bags, and we'll be on our way!"

There was no shortage of things for Travis and Steve to talk about as they loaded everything into his Land Rover.

"I am going to take you guys straight to my house here in Coca, and introduce you to my girlfriend, Felicia. She will help you get situated, and then I will take you all up the river to see the site of our new eco-lodge! And by the way, while you guys are here, we need to try to come up with a good name for our new lodge. Some name that will be catchy and fresh, and have a dual meaning in both English and Spanish."

"How do you say 'Smelly Arm-Pit' in Spanish?" Janice asked with a straight face.

"Hey! Good one!" Steve said, in his ever upbeat style. "One point for Janice! Although I was looking for a name that would have, shall I say, more *pleasant* connotations associated with it. Please, no more suggestions right now. Let's wait until you can actually *see* the place, and then an inspired name might come to us."

"Yes, that will be best." Travis added.

"Oh, by the way," Steve said, "Did you guys happen to get your Yellow Fever shots before you left home?"

Travis and Janice looked at one another. "No, we were in such a rush to leave, that we didn't even think about that." Travis said.

"Well, in that case," Steve said, "I know where our first stop will be. The health clinic, and it is out here by the airport, so it will be convenient to get it out of the way right now."

"We gotta' have shots?" Calvin asked.

"Oh yeah!" Steve said. "You don't want to be here, and not be vaccinated against yellow fever, and typhoid. Actually, the yellow fever you were supposed to start three days before coming down here, but better late than never! This won't take but a few minutes. I know the doctors here."

⤞ 9 ⤝

They stopped at a plain looking concrete block building that was painted white. Inside, it looked very up-to-date and clean. Steve told the nurse what they needed, and they were all four ushered back to the lab, where the three new-comers were given a shot in the arm, and then dispensed to each of them, bottles of Lariam pills to take for the duration of their stay in the rain forest.

"See? That didn't take long." Steve said. "Now let's head to my place."

The road from the airport into Coca was paved, and the main street in the business district was paved, as well as the road that served most of the industries around Coca, the road to the port on the Napo River. But virtually every other street and alley in Coca was either gravel or dirt, which added a quaintness to the town of Coca that was all it's own. Steve pulled up in front of a row of small white houses on the paved street that faced the river port.

"Welcome to my humble home in Ecuador! It may not be much, by U.S. standards, but by local standards, this is prime real estate! Really, it looks much better on the inside. Let's grab all your bags, and get inside."

As they were unloading the Land Rover, the front door opened, and a very beautiful woman stood in the doorway. She was a mestiza, or a local Indian, mixed with European, and she was very pleasing to the eye. Her short, low cut dress barely contained her breasts, and the skirt split up to her hip did nothing to make her less appealing.

"Hey everyone, this is Felicia!"

"Buenas Dias, mis amigos!" she said with a smile.

"She can speak English as well, but she is more comfortable with Spanish." Steve explained. "Please! Everyone inside!"

The house looked even smaller from the inside, than it did from the outside, but it was very neat and clean. Basically, there were two bedrooms, and a large living room/kitchen. Travis and Janice were given one bedroom, Felicia had the other, and Calvin was set up in the living room.

"Where is the bathroom?" Janice asked.

"Uh, that's out the back door, to the right. You can't miss it!" Steve said.

"So you have an out-door toilet?" she asked.

"Yeah, something like that." Steve replied elusively.

She started to say something, but Travis pinched her, which was their signal to one another in social situations to '*don't say it*'. But usually it was Janice pinching *him*.

"You've got a nice little place here, Steve! But hopefully we won't have to impose on you and Felicia for very long. Either the situation at home will be resolved, or if not, maybe we can move out to the lodge."

"Before I left the lodge site yesterday, I gave instructions for a crew to drop off working on the main lodge, and begin work on Bungalow Number one. That will be your new home as soon as it is completed. The crew leader says he can have it ready to move into in about four days."

"Four days seems pretty quick." Travis said.

"Well, these bungalows will be very basic. No insulation of any kind. Only cold running water. Only one electrical outlet, and it will only be on from 3 till 10 P.M. After 10 P.M. the generators will be turned off to conserve energy, and preserve the ascetic beauty of the natural camp. The bungalows will be basically just a shelter from the rain, insects and predators. So taking four days to construct one is about right, if all the crews work together."

"Sounds good. I can hardly wait to see it!" Travis said.

"Then lets head that way!" Steve said. "I need to get back there to supervise anyway."

"Will it be okay to leave our things here?" Janice asked.

"Oh certainly! Felicia will be here to watch things, but this is a very safe town. Most residents don't even have locks on their doors. Felicia, we will return this evening!"

"You wish that I prepare la comida?"

"Yes, have it ready by say, five. Comida a cinco."

"Yes, I cook a big meal for all!"

"Great! This way, folks!" He grabbed his back-pack and slung it over his shoulder, and they set out walking to the port.

"We're not driving?" Janice asked.

"No," Steve said, "One good thing about having a house this close to the river front, is that I can walk to catch a boat."

"Do we have our own boat that serves the lodge?' Travis asked.

"No need for one at this point. There are so many water taxis for rent, and so cheap, that it makes sense to just use them. There are so many of them, and all are competing for your business, that a one way passage for one person to go to the lodge is 50 cents. Round trip is a dollar. If I bought a boat and operated it myself, I couldn't get there any cheaper. And there is always four or five boats hanging out at the lodge, just on the hope that they can run somebody back to Coca for parts or supplies. Before I hired a full time cook for the lodge site, I would order hot meals delivered from Coca once a day. Anything you need done, there is someone here that is willing to do it for you very cheaply. It's a very service-oriented culture here in Coca. There are the boats. See, there are five or six boats already waving at us, wanting our business!"

The boats he was referring to were twenty feet long, and very narrow, with seating for two persons across, with no sail. The boats were all covered with colorful canvas canopies. While some appeared to be constructed from planks, and sealed with resin, others were actually dug-out single logs of massive size. All of them had a large gasoline motor on back, with a propeller on a long narrow shaft, that could be easily raised out of the water in shallow areas.

"Is that what we are riding in?" Janice asked. "Those don't look safe!"

"They are actually very safe, and these experienced drivers handle them very well." Steve said, as they stepped down to the floating pier, to board the craft. He pointed to one boatman, and waved him in. "To the Eco-lodge!" he said, and handed the driver two dollars. He maneuvered the boat up beside the pier to allow them easy access.

"These boats can carry about fourteen people, but when there are just a few, like now, we must sit toward the back of the boat, near the driver, to make it easier for him to steer. And once we are seated and under way, don't be getting up and moving around, because it will throw the boat off balance."

"What are those big canvas coverings for?" Janice asked.

"Hey, this is the rain forest, Janice! We could have a thunder storm any time, but mostly in the early evening. You haven't seen it *rain* until you see it rain *here*! A down-pour in the rainforest is a *down-pour*! The canopy is not just to keep the passengers dry, but to keep the boat from filling up with rain water and sinking!"

"Mercy!"

When everyone was seated, the driver started the engine and puttered out away from the other boats. Once he reached open water, he opened it up, and they fairly flew over the water. They had to hold on to their hats. It was a smooth ride, because there were no waves. The Napo River at this point was massive. Travis guessed that it was between a quarter, and a half mile wide, but as he soon saw, it was not really very deep, except in the main channel. The biggest part of the river was very shallow with gravel beds sometimes showing on the surface. But the driver knew the navigateable areas, and kept them skimming over deep water. He was ever vigilant for floating logs and other debris, and gave such objects wide berth. They covered the twelve miles very quickly, then he cut back on the power, as he aimed for an inlet on the far shore. At idling speed, he carefully skimmed the shallow boat across a gravel bed, raising his propeller out of the water briefly to avoid the rocks, then lowered it again in the deeper water of the inlet, which became a sizeable lagoon.

Steve yelled over the engine, as he pointed out a few features.

"See this nice round lagoon? This was formed by a meteor impact thousands of years ago! The debris thrown up by the impact, created that raised bluff around the lagoon! As you can see by the clearing there, that is the place I selected for the main lodge, The bungalows will spread around the bluff, so that most of them will have a scenic view of the river!"

"It looks like you made a good choice, Steve! It's a beautiful place!"

"We haven't got a landing built yet, but we have the wood cut for it. All construction here is labor-intensive, But I have some very capable workers. To do everything I have planned, it will take time. But it will be nice, once it is built. We should have no trouble luring tourists here. Everyone be careful getting out of the boat. Remember that there are piranhas in the water!"

"And Anacondas!" said the smiling boat driver.

"That's right, snakes too!" Steve added. Once they were all safely on the top of the bluff, Steve pointed out a few things. "There will be a covered rotunda-like gazebo here where we are standing, where we will welcome our guests. The big main lodge will be over there, where you see the foundation being dug out. It will include a large dining area, and dance floor, for parties. There will be a full kitchen and restaurant inside, as well as a bar. Over here will be the big swimming pool! There on the other side of the pool, is the start of your Bungalow #1. They already have the foundation down, and the frame up, and are working on the roof."

"So the bungalows will have thatched roofs?" Travis asked.

"Yes, and even the main Lodge will have a thatched roof, so that everything will match. The frame of the lodge, however, will be built of massive mahogany slabs. See it stacked over there?"

"Wow! That's some kind of lumber! Do you know what that stack of lumber would be worth in the United States?"

"Humph! Do you know the red tape that would be required to get that stack of lumber to the United States? It is mind-boggling!"

"You've got crews busy working everywhere!"

"Yeah, and we're getting g a lot done! The portable sawmill is still here. They're working on the other side of the bluff, if you want to go watch them."

"I might do that later. Right now, I want to see your work tent."

"Ah! I know what you want to see! The *good stuff*! My tent is over here!"

Travis turned to his son, "Calvin, you asked me why I invested money in such an out-of-the way place? Well, you are about to find out! Janice, I think you'll want to see this too."

"It better be something good! I haven't seen a whole lot here that impresses me so far! Did you bring the insect repellant? Something is biting me!"

"I have some." Calvin said, and dug in his back-pack for it.

They approached the big army surplus tent, and Steve warned them before they entered, "I have been living in here for two weeks, so you'll have to overlook the mess!" He folded back the flaps, and they saw a large table on one side of the tent that was piled up with rocks. The other side was a sleeping bag and scattered clothes, as well as empty cans. "If you didn't know better, you'd think this was the abode of a cave man!" Steve said in defense of the mess. "But ignore the mess and step over to the table."

He turned on a battery operated lantern, and illuminated the scattered rocks on the table.

"What we have got here, is most of the stuff that was found when we started digging out the foundation for the main lodge." He turned to them grinning from ear to ear. "We barely scratched the surface, and hit the mother lode!"

"Rocks?" Calvin asked.

"Not just rocks, Calvin. They're *emeralds*!" Travis said. "This site is covered with emeralds! That's why I invested in it."

"Those are so pretty!" Janice said. "And there are so many!"

"Actually, what you see here were gathered in about thirty minutes of digging, before I halted the project."

"Why?"

"Because we don't want this to look like a mine site. We want it to look like an Eco-lodge! If government inspectors come in, I don't want them to see too much. After we get the lodge up and running, then we can go back and covertly start mining the emeralds. In the meantime, I have armed guards closely watching things. At least now we know exactly where to start with the mining operation. Under the main lodge will be perfect!"

"Those guards, are you sure that you can trust them?"

"Of course. I'm paying these guys really well for their loyalty, and part of that good pay, is to keep things a secret. What you see on the table right here is just a drop in the bucket to what we will mine later. A conservative estimate is that this is worth $200,000. I'll probably load up all this and sell it to Victor Carranza, to have funds to keep the construction going. If you want, you can go with me, and meet Victor. He needs to meet the other partners, in case something happens to me."

"So you will have to take these to Colombia?"

"No, we will meet in Panama. That is where I will take the stones to sell them every time. There is like, an emerald clearing house in Panama City, and that is where he conducts all his business. There are gem experts there who do nothing but grade and cut stones. It is state of the art! You will want to see it."

"I want to make a necklace out of this one!" Janice said.

"No Dear, we have to sell these stones, to finance the construction here." Travis said.

"Besides," Steve said, "That's not really a good quality stone anyway."

"It looks pretty to me!"

"Janice, if you will allow me," Steve said, "I will be on the lookout, and will save you a *really nice* stone later on, and I will even take it to Panama, and have it cut and polished just for you! What do you say to that?"

"You would do that for me?" She asked.

"Sure! We are going to be rich here, many times over! And if it will make you like this place any better, I'll even have matching earrings made to go with it!"

She squealed with delight.

"I think you just found the way to her heart, Steve!"

"Hey, I have a *way* with the ladies! Just not ex-wives!"

"So you just find these in the ground here?" Calvin asked.

"Sure! Actually, there is a geological reason that they are here, of course. I told your Dad about it, and I will explain it to you too, some evening when we have the time. You'll be amazed! Geology is my passion!"

"So whoever you bought this land from must not have known about the emeralds?"

"No, they didn't, and I don't really want them to know about it for awhile. We bought it from Exxon at a very reasonable price."

"Are you still working for Exxon?" Travis asked.

"Nope! I worked out my three year contract with them, and their parting gift to me was the option to buy some of their 'worthless' land. But I think I will get the last laugh, if these emeralds continue to come in as easily as they have been. Come with me, and we'll look at the lodge foundation."

They left the tent and Steve was confronted by a local worker, who had a question about the bungalow construction. They conversed in Spanish for a few minutes, and the man seemed satisfied.

"He wanted to make sure of how to proceed with the roof. I am impressed with the skill and attitude of these Ecuadorian workers. These guys understand that if this place is a success, it will benefit them as well as us, so they are careful to follow my instructions to the tee. Now, lets go to the lodge."

They stood looking into the dug out foundation of the lodge, seeing nothing special.

"Looks like rich soil." Travis said.

"That's what you are *supposed* to see. Actually the soil here is mostly rock and gravel, having been thrust up from deep in the earth, but that is not what you see here, is it?"

"No, it isn't."

"That's because when I realized that we had hit the mother lode, I had my workers haul in tons of rich fill dirt, and cover the natural rock strata, just so anyone visiting here will not see it. Later, after the lodge is built, we'll dig back under it, remove the layer of dirt, and start the mining. It is important that here at the start, we make this look like a lodge construction, and not a mine site, because there will be a lot of government inspectors coming around to make sure we comply with the environmental protection laws. If we can fool them, we will be home free."

Janice thought about something Steve had said earlier, so she asked. "So that little hut they are building over there is going to be where we will be staying when it's finished?"

"Yes." Steve said. "Your home away from home!"

"Are you kidding me? That thing isn't big enough for nothing!"

"Well, for the guests who stay here, it will basically just be a place to sleep, and keep your stuff. The big lodge will be the social center of the place, with the restaurant, bar, swimming pool, and places for their group to congregate."

"Well, until all that is built, we will be in that little thing? I don't think so!"

"Would you rather stay at my house in Coca? I'll be here most of the time, so if you want to live in Coca, you are more than welcome to do so. I mean you will be there for a few days before this place is ready anyway. You'll have time to decide. Felicia would probably enjoy the company of having you there."

"I'll think about it." Janice said.

"Okay, who wants to go look at the saw-mill?" Steve asked.

"I am getting eaten alive by something!" Janice said.

"Yeah, we have a jungle version of 'no-see-ums' down here. They get really bad in the evening. I'm looking into getting a special made version of bug zapper, that is supposed to take care of them, but that will be a later addition. For now it's bug repellant."

"Well, I'm going to stay in your tent, while you are gone to the saw-mill." She said.

"Sure, no problem. Everyone else, this way."

The three guys set out walking for the sawmill. They could hear it before they saw it. It was a primitive set-up all right. The enormous, dangerous looking saw blade was not covered by any kind of protective guards or warning signs. It was powered by two diesel engines, and the closer they got to it, the louder it got. To get close enough to see what they were sawing, was to loose all sense of hearing. The mill workers were communicating with hand signals and gestures. They were cutting massive slabs off a mahogany log that had been delivered to the mill with a D-6 bulldozer. Once the big log was in place, it was rolled and positioned with hydraulic jacks. The big saw easily sliced through the log, as though it was hot butter, and then positioned it to take off another slab. The board that had just been cut off was pushed out the end on a bed of rollers, then was man-handled by four strong men, who carried it to the lumber rack and stacked it. It was an efficient operation, but was labor intensive, and very loud. When the mill operator finished the log, he shut down the saw, and turned off the diesel engines, to save fuel, and blessed quiet filled the air.

"Pablo! How is it going?" Steve yelled.

"Buenos! I wait on a log! The sawyers are slow today!"

"Well good, that gives me a chance to introduce you to one of my partners! Travis Lee, this is Pablo Estrella, the owner of the sawmill."

"Good to meet you, Senor Lee!"

"The same to you, Pablo! And this is my son, Calvin."

"A fine looking young man!" Pablo said.

"Are we still on schedule, Pablo?"

"Oh si! We are ahead of schedule by two days at least. No problema! At least not on my end!"

"Is there another problem?"

"Well, it could be a problem. You should speak with your security officer, Senor Ortega. He will explain."

"Where is he now?"

"He and another security man, they are down in the jungle with the sawyers, watching for them."

"Okay, thanks. Come on, Travis. I think I know what this is about, but I need to talk to Ortega first."

"What kind of problem?"

"A security problem. But let's find Ortega, and you'll understand."

⊰ 10 ⊱

They followed Steve down off the ridge, into the jungle, walking in a swath cleared by the bulldozer. They found Ortega standing on a massive stump, with an automatic assault rifle slung over his shoulder. He was watching two sawyers who had stopped to sharpen their saws.

"Senor Ortega!"

"Aye, Senor Meredith! How are you today?"

"Buenos! This is Travis Lee, and his son, Calvin. Travis is one of my partners."

"Aye, pleased to meet you, Senor!"

"Pablo says we might have a problem?"

"Yes, I think it can be a big problem!"

"So they are still watching us?"

"Yes, I saw two today. Watching from a distance, but I am sure they are up to no good! I am closely watching the sawyers because of that."

"Who are 'they'?" Travis asked.

"We aren't exactly sure." Steve said, "But the locals seem to think that they are Colombian drug smugglers, or maybe even poachers, or lumber thieves. See, we are only about 15 miles from the Colombian border here, and there is nothing between here and there, except jungle. The Colombians have been known to use trails through this jungle to get drugs and other illegal goods to the Napo River and load it onto boats. They do that because it is closer to go through the jungle, than haul their stuff over the mountains other way. But now we own the land here, and they are curious to know who we are. But I don't really blame them. They were here before we were. And I don't think they appreciate us blocking their access to the river."

"Perhaps we can make a deal with them?" Travis suggested.

"No," Steve said, "these guys are not to be trusted, or so I am told. And we certainly don't want to enter into any kind of deal with them. That would make us complicit to whatever illegal activities they are up to. Every time we try to approach them, they melt away into the jungle, so we don't know exactly what they are up to. But it can't be good."

Ortega further explained, "I think they are very poor people, who live just across the border. They are willing to do whatever they have to, to feed their children. To them, what is legal or illegal? They are just trying to survive. They hunt jaguar and anaconda, to sell the skins, they transport cocaine base, I have even known them to kill local politicians, if the pay is good. They are poor people who care nothing for the law, because the law has done nothing for them, but make them poorer."

"But if that's who our neighbors are," Travis said, "wouldn't it be better to talk to them, and get them to agree to skirt around our property? I mean, we don't *care* what their business is, as long as they don't involve us."

"Ah, but that is the thing, Senor! They cannot be trusted to be good neighbors! They are bad people! They murder and kidnap, and steal!"

"And just imagine," Steve said, "if they found out that we are finding emeralds here! We would be their prime target!"

"Si! They would think nothing of killing us, to get something so valuable!" Ortega said.

"That is why we must be especially careful in our mining, because not only do we have to keep it from the government, but also these thieves, who are in the jungle watching us all the time. They are probably our biggest danger."

"I don't remember you mentioning anything about them, Steve, when you were trying to drum up investors!" Travis said.

"That's because I didn't know about them until we started construction here! If I had known about it before, I would have told you."

"Well, isn't that just lovely! That's all we need is for them to rob or kidnap some of our guests! That would kill our eco-lodge business quicker than anything."

"I know. That's why we have to do something about them. Co-existence is not an option apparently."

"I used to be a sniper. I can pick them off one by one!"

"That would just start a war with them, and it probably wouldn't end well. And bad publicity we don't need."

"Well that's the only solution I can offer. We can't get the government to do anything about it? I mean, these are people who are coming into Ecuador illegally, so you would think that the government would do something."

"No, out here like this, it's almost like the Wild West! The law doesn't quite reach this far. If you don't defend yourself, you are at the mercy of lawless people. That's why I hired our own security team. Senor Ortega and his men are some of the best."

"Gracias, Senor Meredith!"

"All we can do right now, is keep an eye on them, and try not to let them know what we are doing here. Senor Ortega, keep up the good work."

"Si, senor."

As they walked back toward the lodge, Steve remembered something else. "Oh yeah, I forgot to mention that Homer and Doc are coming down here in a couple of days."

"Wow, things are going to get crowded in your house." Travis said.

"Homer said he wants to see the place, and when he found out that you were going to be here, he decided to get Doc and come on down. They are going to stay at a hotel in Coca. His main reason for coming down is to open a savings account at a bank in Quito. Remember I told you that each of us needs a bank account here to deposit our earnings? And the bank account with at least $25,000 will make you eligible for Ecuadorian citizenship. Well, actually *dual* citizenship."

"That's right, I need to do that too while I am here." Travis said.

"Homer said that he can't stay long. But when he leaves, we can all go with him back to Quito, and you can open your accounts together at the same bank. Then give your account numbers to me, and I will deposit the money in each account, every time I sell a load of emeralds."

"Sounds good to me. Are you sure we can trust you with all that money?"

"Duh! Do you think I would embezzle *your* money? I have seen what happens to fools who get on your black list! I might as well just shoot myself in the head and save you the trouble!"

"You can run, but you can't hide!" Travis grinned. He started to use Osama Bin Laden as an example, but that didn't turn out well, so he didn't mention it. He knew that Steve was careless with his own money, but when it came to other peoples money, he was honest and frugal to a fault. "I think I can trust you, Steve!"

Calvin had not said much lately. He found that he learned a lot more by keeping his mouth shut and listening. He was also watching the ground for emeralds, but not seeing any. There was a lot of unusual plants and flowers and seed pods, that were totally different from anything he had seen in Alabama. He was thinking that he was going to like his stay in Ecuador.

As they were walking up to Steve's tent, Travis' cell phone rang, and he answered it.

"Hello?"

"Travis?" He recognized the voice as being Janice's sister Marla, and he knew that she didn't call to speak to him.

"I guess you want to talk to Janice?"

"Is she there?"

"Yeah, hold on." He called Janice, and she answered from inside the tent. He covered the phone and said,

"It's Marla. Remember, she is supposed to think that we are at home."

"I remember." She took the phone. "Hello, Marla. What's up?"

"I just called to tell you that Mom and Dad are back from Alaska."

"I know. They stopped by to see us yesterday."

"Did you happen to notice that Mom is getting worse? I think she might have Alzheimer's disease, and going to Alaska just made it worse!"

"I don't think the trip had anything to do with it getting worse. She's been getting worse for over a year now."

"Well this is the first time I have seen them in over a year."

"That's probably why you didn't realize she was getting worse! You really ought to go by and see them more often."

"I know, but I stay so busy!"

"Doing what? Since you can't 'run down' Travis any more, you should have a lot of free time on your hands!"

"I stay busy with lots of things! But I didn't call to argue with you! I'm just concerned about Mom."

"I'm more concerned about Paw-paw, having to put up with her!" Janice said. "He takes heart medication, you know."

"Well, I think we ought to talk to Paw-paw about putting her in a nursing home."

"He would never consider that."

"That's why we both need to go talk to him about it. Maybe the two of us together can convince him that it has to be done. What about us going to see him this Sunday?"

"No, Marla! I said he won't do it! And I don't think she's that far gone anyway. As long as Paw-paw wants to take care of her, then let him do it!"

"If you say so, sister. When does Travis leave on his next job?"

"I don't know. His jobs pop up so unpredictable that he never knows when he will get a call."

"Well, next time he leaves town, give me a call, and we'll go shopping, and out to eat, and just chew the fat."

That didn't sound very appetizing.

"Sure, Marla. But I don't know how long that will be. Listen, I've got to go right now."

"Okay, talk to you later."

She turned the phone off and handed it back to Travis.

"So, what did she want?" Travis asked.

"Oh, nothing important."

"She didn't suspect that we weren't at home?"

"No, why would she?"

"Just checking."

"So, have you and Calvin seen everything you want to see here?"

"No, there's a lot more I want to check out while I'm here. Why? Are you ready to go?"

"I have seen all I need to see for now. The insects are still eating me up!"

"You must taste pretty good to them. I haven't got a bite yet."

"And you think that I want to *live* out here in the middle of this bug infested jungle? The only thing going on here, is things eating one another! I think I would rather be in town!"

"Do you want to head back to Coca?" Steve asked her. "I can have the boat driver take you back, if you're ready."

"I don't want to go by myself."

"It's okay, really. I know the boat driver. He's an honest, reputable man. He will take you back to the same pier we left from, and my house is within sight of the pier. Felicia should be there."

"I wouldn't feel comfortable leaving without Travis. I'll wait." she said.

"I want Steve to show me a few more things before we go. You want to walk with us, or wait in the tent?" Travis asked.

"I'll put on some more insect repellant, and walk with you. I would like to hear about this place anyway." While she was gone to the tent, Travis whispered to Steve, "Don't say anything to her about those people watching this place. It'll just scare her." Steve nodded. When she returned, they walked back toward the big lodge site.

"I told you that I applied for permits to put in septic tanks for every bungalow, didn't I?" Steve asked.

"Yeah I remember something about that."

"Actually, down here it isn't necessary to install septic tanks. But if we do, it will give us all the more excuses to dig, and thus get a better sense of where the emeralds are."

"Didn't you say something about dredging out the lagoon here too?" Travis asked.

"Yes, I already know that the bottom of this lagoon is full of emerald bearing rock. By saying that we need to dredge it out to allow for larger tourist ships to enter, we can have a legitimate excuse to mine out the lagoon. There is no telling how many millions of karats we'll get out of the lagoon."

"What is this crew doing?" Travis asked.

"It looks like they are making baskets." Janice said.

"Those are fish baskets they're making out of bamboo slats. They will put those fish baskets out in the lagoon, and catch enough fish that the cook will be able to feed our whole crew. The fish, prepared with rice from Coca, and wild jungle fruits, will provide all the workers here with meals on the job. And even after the Lodge gets up and running, we'll still use local food to feed our guests. See that covered pavilion over there? That's our temporary kitchen. But the cook is the same cook we will have to cook for the guests. He is an Ecuadorian, but he was trained at a Paris cooking school. I was lucky to find him. He specializes in preparing something out of virtually nothing. It is almost lunch time. If you like, you can try it out for yourself."

"And Janice, because he cooks over an open fire, the smoke keeps biting insects away."

"Then maybe he can use help with the cooking." she said.

"No, he doesn't need help, but you can go stand in the cooking fire smoke if you want to."

"What is that over there?" Calvin asked, pointing to an elevated platform with ropes leading from it out to the trees in the jungle.

"Oh yeah, that's a monkey feeding tower." Steve said. "One of our workers said we needed one, to draw in monkeys, for the guests watch, so I told him to go ahead and build it. We stock it every morning with bananas, and the monkeys swarm in from all over the jungle to eat them. The thinking is, get them used to finding food there every day, and you provide free entertainment for your guests while they eat breakfast."

"Does it work?" Calvin asked.

"Yes, we had a swarm of monkeys there earlier today. They are something to watch! They come in from the jungle on those ropes, because they don't feel comfortable on the ground. I have seen forty monkeys on that platform at one time, but once the bananas run out, they head back to the jungle. Because we don't have guests yet, we don't put out a lot of bananas. But by putting out a few every morning, we get them used to coming here as a part of their usual feeding routine."

"I would like to see them." Janice said.

"If you are here early in the morning, you'll get to see them."

"How early?"

"Sunrise."

"No, that's too early!"

"And we can do the same thing with the tropical birds. Once we start getting guests here, we will start putting out fruit every morning, and we'll have all kinds of tropical birds flocking here to feed, and it will be a bird-watcher's delight. Anything we can do to enhance the visit here by our guests, we will guarantee that more guests will come, because word of mouth is the best advertisement."

"And the whole time, we will be mining emeralds, just out of sight of the guests." Travis said.

"Yes, that will be the icing on the cake!" Steve said. "I plan to fence off all this area back here, and make it off-limits to our guests, because this will be our mining area. The entrance to the mine will likely be under the main lodge. The mine will branch off anywhere we have to, to follow the emeralds."

"You certainly seem to have done a lot of planning, Steve." Janice said.

"I know. I lay awake at night obsessing over how things should be done, and what to do if a certain problem comes up. I over-analyze everything! I'll have ulcers before this project is finished!"

"Well, you seem to be doing a good job so far." Travis said. "I'm impressed, and I'm sure Homer will be too, when he gets here."

They passed by the main lodge and saw three men starting to lay flat rock, like the floor of a patio. Steve offered them a few suggestions, and they got out a measuring tape, and measured three or four distances, and marked it with spray paint. Steve studied the lay-out a few moments, then told them which measurement to use. As he led them away, he explained,

"They are starting to lay out the floor for the permanent kitchen here. They will put down the stone floor first, then build up the stone hearths. The cook will use wood to prepare meals. He will be here later today, to make sure the lay-out is right. The kitchen will be an important part of the lodge. So, Janice, how do you think you are going to like living here?"

"Me? I don't think I will be living here for very long. Just until the problem is cleared up at home."

"Suppose it doesn't get cleared up, and you have to live here for years? Do you think this place will grow on you?"

"I think I could learn to like it here." Calvin said. "But I don't know about Mom."

"I will have to think about it." she said. "Right now, I'm going to stand in the smoke, to get away from the insects, and watch the cook."

———◆◆◆———

Lunch consisted of grilled fish, fresh out of the lagoon, served on a bed of rice, with fried yucca roots. Fresh sliced papaya was for dessert. They seemed to have a lunch schedule, because only one crew showed up at a time to eat, probably because there was only limited seating. Over a period of two hours everyone was fed. After lunch, everyone took a one hour 'siesta' before going back to work.

"I can't change their work habits." Steve said, "so I let them keep the siesta. But they make up for it by working later into the evening. So tell me about your writing career, Travis."

"It's puttering along. I have a contract with Jester Books in London, to put out a new manuscript every eight months, so I have had to step up my writing. But that is no problem, since I left the coal mines. I have a lot more time to write."

"So this Jester Books is doing a good job of publishing your books?"

"Oh yeah."

"I remember the nightmare you had with that Canadian publisher. What was their name?"

"Maple Leaf Publications. Yeah, I'm glad that mess is over. I've been hitting the top ten list in England, with all my books so far. The royalty checks are getting bigger and bigger. But I got some disturbing news about a week ago. I heard that my first book, 'The Relic' was seen on sale in China!"

"That should be good news."

"Yeah, if I had authorized it to be translated into Chinese! No, someone in China has made a pirated version of my book, and I didn't get a dime out of it!"

"That's not good. So how many copies have sold in China?"

"I don't know, but Jester is looking into it. The Chinese are notorious for ignoring copyright laws, and so it would be useless to try to sue someone over there for it. But at this point, it's just rumor. I will probably have to personally go to China to verify it."

"So you might have sold 100 million copies in China already!"

"That would just be my luck. Oh well, no sense in worrying about it."

Janice spoke up. "So what is there to do in Ecuador, besides slap biting insects, and avoid stepping on poisonous snakes?"

"It just depends on what your interests are." Steve replied. "If you are a visitor to an eco-lodge like this, you can bird-watch, or fish in the Napo River, or go for long nature walks. If you like animals or insects, you can find all kinds of things to hold your interest here."

"What if I don't like the jungle? What is there to do in Coca, for instance?"

"Do you like to shop?"

"Does she like to shop?" Travis injected. "Does a drug addict like cocaine?"

"Yes, I like to shop." she replied.

"Then there are a lot of interesting places to shop in Coca. Get Felicia to show you around. She grew up in Coca, so she knows where everything is."

"Okay."

"And if you and Travis get the time, you might want to go to Quito, and see the old Spanish inspired architecture and museums. There is a lot to see in Quito. And I have heard that it's really neat to visit a place outside Quito, called Middle of the Earth. It is a place on the equator, where all kinds of strange magnetic anomalies can happen. Sort of a mystical place."

"That sounds interesting."

"You can visit the city of Guayaquil, down south on the Pacific Ocean, which is a really tropical paradise. And of course, if you want to really get 'out there', you can go to the Galapagos Islands, and see all the unusual wildlife."

"That sounds good too. Can we go to the Galapagos Islands, Travis?"

"We might as we'll see it while we are down here, if we get time."

"There is a lot to see, no matter where you go," Steve said, "As long as you are adventurous, inquisitive, keep an open mind, and are willing try new things, you can have fun anywhere you go. In short, anywhere they sell beer by the pitcher, is a good place to visit."

"I told Janice about you and your first wife, Dixie, going to the Yucatan, and about you doing that 'rain dance', and then it really did rain!"

"Oh yeah! That was a classic! That was about the time Dixie began to suspect that she was married to an insane man! But hey, I've got to be me!"

"You're not the only one that has to be you!" Janice nodded toward her husband. "But that's why I love him!"

"That's strange," Steve said. "That was the very reason Dixie fell *out* of love with me! Well, that, and the fact that she had more sex when I was out of town, than when I was home!"

"Yeah," Travis said, "I called your house one time to see if you were back home yet, and some hunk named 'Bjorn' answered the phone. I could hear Dixie in the background, obviously drunk, and throwing quite a party. Bjorn thought I was calling about joining the party, and told me to stop and get a keg on the way."

"You never told me about that." Steve said.

"It was a month later before I caught up with you, and by that time her behavior was public knowledge. I couldn't see throwing gas on the fire."

"So did you pick up a keg on the way?" he asked.

"Believe me, I wanted no part of that!"

"Well, it doesn't matter now. It's all water under the bridge. Actually, it was the water that washed out the bridge, and half the town! Anyway, how did we get on this subject? I've come a long way since then."

"So what are the projections for the eco-lodge? How long before it will be open for business?" Travis asked.

"This is March. I think by Labor day we might be far enough along to have the grand opening. And I might as well tell you that when we have the grand opening, we will be booked up with Ecuadorian government officials. I had to give them a special introductory offer, in exchange for a streamlining of the red tape in getting this place started."

"So this special introductory offer is what?" Travis asked.

"They and their families get to stay for free the first year. So Don't get your hopes up for making a profit off the lodge itself for awhile. The first year, our profit will be off the emeralds only."

"No problem. That's the cost of doing business down here."

"Yeah, and we certainly want to stay in good graces with the government and military. They can be our best ally, if the politics change. I figure if we can just stay in business here for five years, and secretly mine emeralds, we will be financially set for life anyway. So free stays at the lodge to the right people, will be an easy way to do that."

"Yeah, as long as no one catches wind of what we are really doing here."

"As long as we are careful, and don't get greedy, and have good luck, I think we can pull it off." Steve said with confidence.

They spent a couple more hours walking around looking at things before Steve suggested that they get back to Coca. He wanted to also get them familiar with the town before dark, since they would be spending a lot of time there

⇥ 11 ⇤

The boat ride back to Coca was quicker than before, because they were going down-stream. The pier was a lot more crowded when they arrived, because many fishermen were returning with their day's catch, and they were rushing to get it to the market in time to sell most of it to dinner shoppers.

"Look at all those fish, Calvin! I bet you've never caught fish like those from the Cahaba River back home!"

"Some of those don't even look like fish!" he said.

They hurried to Steve's little house, where they were greeted by the most delicious aroma of something cooking in the kitchen. Felicia called out to them, "You are back so soon! It is almost four. You said five o'clock! The dinner will not be ready until five!"

"I know," Steve said. "I'm going to walk them around the neighborhood until dinner time, to get them familiar with where things are."

"Okay."

"I might stay here and help Felicia." Janice said.

"She can handle the dinner," Steve said. "You'll have plenty of opportunities to help her later, but right now, you need to walk around with us, and let me show you where things are located. Things like the market, the pharmacy, the post office, the local restaurants and bars!"

"I don't know. It's a little scary to me, Steve."

"And that is exactly why you need to get out! I will introduce you to the merchants, and the pharmacist, and some of the colorful people who live here. If you are going to be living here, you need to go out the first day and meet everyone! Believe me, everyone wants to meet you too! This is a very friendly neighborhood, and it shouldn't scare you to get out and meet people. If you do not get out and introduce yourself, they will be suspicious of you, and you don't want that. You want to let them know that you are a warm, friendly person! By tomorrow, anyone you meet on the street will greet you by name!"

"Everyone?"

"Yes, everyone! And so you need to return the courtesy, by trying to remember their names too! That will please them, if you can remember their names."

"My memory is not that good, but I'll try." Janice said.

"Once you start to meet people, you'll associate faces with names." Travis said. "You'll know everyone within a week!"

They set out, and turned the corner, and the dry goods store was right there. "This is like the Ecuadorian version of Wal-Mart." Steve said. "Good evening, Marcos!"

"Good evening, Steve! Who are your friends?"

"These are my good friends from Alabama. They will be staying at my house awhile. Travis, his wife, Janice, and their son Calvin."

"Very pleased to meet you!" Marcos said.

"Marcos sells canned goods, all kinds of dried beans, rice, corn, hardware items, cooking utensils, soap, brushes, clothes, you name it, they've got it! And right here next door, his cousin Eduardo runs a fresh produce market! Any kind of fruit, nuts and vegetables can be found here. Good evening, Eduardo."

"Buenas tardes, Senor Steve!"

Steve introduced the Lees, then they moved on. "Here is the meat and fish market! Notice the smell? Everything here is so fresh, you would have to kill it yourself to get it any fresher! Raul is the butcher, and his wife is Margarita."

"Let me guess," Travis said, "Raul is another cousin of Marcos and Eduardo?"

"Close. He is their uncle. Hello Margarita! Where is Raul?"

"In the back, with the fish."

"Margarita, let me introduce you to the wife of my good friend, Travis Lee. This is Janice. They will be living in my house here for awhile."

"Hello Janice! I think we will be good friends, no?"

"Yes, I hope so!" Janice replied. Then she saw something on the display counter and asked, "What is that?"

"It is a chicken! You never see the inside of a chicken?"

"What are those things?"

"Ah, those are egg yokes! That is what the eggs look like before the shells form over them."

"So you butchered a laying hen?"

"Yes! Very good meat, and the eggs are extra!"

"Janice raises chickens back in Alabama, but I don't think she has ever seen the inside of one." Travis explained.

"You never eat your chickens?" Margarita asked.

"Are you kidding?" Calvin laughed, "She's *named* all her chickens! They're like members of the family."

"It would be like eating my own children! I would feel like a cannibal!" Janice admitted.

Margarita laughed at such a thing. "Well, these chickens did not have names, so we can eat them."

"I am showing them around right now. We'll be seeing you later, Margarita."

"Yes, later, Steve."

"Now, right across the street here is a local watering hole, and one of my favorite hang-outs, 'Cantina Perrito Feo'!"

"The Ugly Dog Bar?" Travis asked.

"Yeah, the original owner had one hellaciously ugly dog that stayed right in front of the door. You had to literally step over him to get into the bar. He wasn't vicious, just ugly! He sniffed at everybody that came in, and if he didn't like your smell, he'd growl at you, and the owner of the bar would make you leave. He was like a security system with fleas! He could sense when someone was a bad person, and the bartender wouldn't serve him! Pardon my French, Janice, but for lack of a better word, he was a jack-ass detector!"

"What was the dog's name?" Calvin asked.

"Something that I can't repeat in public, even in Spanish!" Steve replied.

"He was probably so ugly, he was cute!" Janice said. "So where is the dog now?"

"Uh, about two years ago a drunk oil worker tried to step over him. He didn't know the dog was growling because he smelled bad, he thought the dog was going to bite him, so he pulled his pistol and shot him!"

"No!"

"Yeah, and then the bartender pulled out a shotgun, and shot the drunk, and the drunk's buddy pulled *his* gun and shot the bartender! The owner pulled *his* gun, and shot the buddy! I saw it all, because I was at the table right there by the window! Actually, I was *under* the table by the time the shooting stopped!"

"Mercy! Everybody was killed, just because the dog growled?"

"Oh, nobody was killed. Not even the dog. But all four of them shared a room down at the local hospital for awhile,…even the dog."

"They let the dog into the hospital?" Janice asked.

"Well, it's not really a hospital like you're thinking about. It's more like a veterinarian clinic, where they also treat stupid people who get cut or shot in bar fights. It happens more often than you might think. We have a local surgeon, but bless his heart, he's kind of 'self taught', because he had to drop out of medical school early, and…well he's still learning. I'm sure he will be a fine surgeon one day, after he gets a few more years experience. Until then, he buries most of his mistakes."

"Are you serious?" Janice asked. "Travis, please tell me that he's joking!"

"Welcome to Ecuador, Dear."

"Well," Steve said, "everybody knows that if they need *serious* surgery, they'll be better off to get air-lifted out to Quito. They have *real* doctors there."

"So where is the ugly dog now?" Calvin asked, getting back to the original story.

"Oh, the dog is dead now. He was crippled up by the gunshot wound, so he couldn't move very fast. He was out in the street one day licking his nuts, and couldn't get out of the way of a beer truck. The bartender still walks with a limp too, but at least he doesn't lick his nuts in the middle of the street!"

Janice tried to suppress a laugh, but couldn't quite hold it, and burst out.

"Oh, you thought that was funny?" Steve asked with a straight face. "Travis, does your wife always laugh at the afflictions of the handicapped?"

"Yeah, she's bad about that." he smiled.

"I am not! I just thought that was funny, the way you said that!"

"Well, Janice, after dinner we'll come back here and have a few drinks, and you can laugh at the bartender as he hobbles around."

"No, I said…"

"Mom, you'd better stop now." Calvin cautioned her. "You're just digging your hole deeper!"

"Anyway, there is the Post Office, in case you need to send mail to someone."

"I need to send post cards to people we know." Janice said.

"Why?" Travis asked.

"Just to let them know where we are."

"Think about it, Dear."

"Oh, that's right! We don't want anyone to know that we're here, do we?"

"That is correct. We are here in protective hiding, remember?"

"Because I called you when I wasn't supposed to!"

"Correct again!"

"So all this is my fault!"

"Remember, this is a *vacation*, Mom!" Calvin said.

"Yeah, don't think of it as hiding! Think of it as a long anticipated vacation!" Travis said. "And I told you not to think of it as 'your fault'. It's just one of those things that happens. But as with most things that 'just happen', it has consequences that we have to deal with. Don't worry about it. We'll get past this."

Steve just smiled. "I can't wait to hear the explanation of all this. It's bound to be a doozie!"

"Travis, you didn't tell Steve why we are here?" Janice said.

"Well no." Steve said. "He just said that he needed to get his family out of the country immediately, and I offered my house here. I figured I'd find out all about it after you got here."

"Tonight at the Perrito Feo, I'll tell you all about it Steve, over a pitcher of beer!" Travis assured him.

"Now you're speaking my language!" Steve replied, "And Janice can get drunk and laugh at the bartender!"

"That sounds like a plan."

"I'll take you around this block, and show you all the little specialty shops, and by the time we get back to my house, Felicia should have dinner about ready."

On the back side of the block, it was like a flea market, where anyone could spread a blanket, or set up a table, and sell anything they thought someone might want to buy. Many of the vendors seemed to be jungle people, selling all kinds of herbal remedies. Most were wearing their typical clothing, which in some cases was no more than a loin cloth. Some men had huge wooden plugs in their ear lobes, to stretch them out. Steve whispered to them that this was because their women thought it made them look attractive. The wares that they offered were a bazaar collection of insects, animal parts and plant extracts.

"Oh, there's something that I need to get!" Steve said. He picked up a 10 ounce Coke bottle full of what looked like blood. The Indian held up three fingers, and Steve shelled out three dollars for the bottle.

"What is that, Steve?" Travis asked.

"It's called 'Sangre del Drago'. It's great for healing cuts and insect bites."

"Dragon's blood?"

"Yeah, that's what it's called, but it is actually the sap out of a tree that grows here, in the jungle. It's great, because it disinfects, sterilizes, and if you let it dry, it makes a water-proof artificial scab over the wound, that allows it to heal faster. I found out about it three years ago, and I keep a bottle in my medical kit. We use a lot of it out at the lodge site, because the guys get a lot of cuts and scrapes. It's kind of weird, in that it looks just like blood, but if you are bleeding, you dab a little of this out and mix with the blood, and gently stir it around, and it makes a white cream! Let the white cream sit on the wound awhile, and it dries, and turns kind of clear, and seals the wound. I am surprised that the modern medical world hasn't exploited it yet. But they probably will, in time. In fact, I'd better get another bottle, because we use so much at the lodge."

"What are all these dried bugs, and stuff?" Janice asked.

"Everything this guy sells, has a medicinal use. He is a local Indian healer. I'm sure you noticed the porcupine quill through his nose. That means he draws his knowledge of medicinal herbs from the vast knowledge that has been accumulated over the centuries by his ancestors. This man can probably prescribe more practical remedies, to more afflictions, than a modern doctor or pharmacist even knows about!"

"So this is the *pharmacy* you were talking about earlier?" Janice asked dryly.

"Yeah, this is a great source of medicines! I would personally come here before I go to a modern pharmacy!"

"Do they even *have* a modern pharmacy here?" she asked.

"Define *modern*." Steve said.

"That's it! Get me out of here, Travis! I want to go home, where I don't have to go to a witch doctor for medicine!"

"He's not a 'witch doctor', he's an herbalist!" Steve said. "And before you run for the airport, let me tell you that yes, they *do* have a modern pharmacy here, it's just that I prefer to use these guys, because they know what they are doing!"

"So where is the *real* pharmacy?" She asked.

"It's about four blocks away, beside the hospital."

"Is that the *real* hospital, or the animal hospital, where they treat dogs and drunks with gunshot wounds?"

"They are kind of one in the same." he replied.

She held her temples and shook her head.

"Look Janice," Steve said. "I know all this is unfamiliar to you, and you are feeling a little bit of culture shock, but hey, this is just your first day here! Things will look a lot better, the longer you're here! After a week or so, you'll start to feel right at home here, and you'll never want to leave!"

Oh god, I hope not! she thought.

⇥ 12 ⇤

Felicia had really out-done herself in preparing dinner for them. It was traditional Ecuadorian food, but she had been cooking for Steve long enough to know how to gastronomically please the North American tastes. It required more salt and butter than the locals normally used. It probably made what should have been a very healthy dinner into a heart attack waiting to happen, but it sure did taste good. Buttery grilled fish filets that were crisp around the edges. Wild rice smothered with a blanket of mysterious, but incredibly good white sauce. An assortment of fresh green vegetables simmered in chicken broth, and then made into a casserole topped with local goat cheese and crumbled crackers and fresh garlic. For dissert they had fresh sliced pineapple. As they finished, Travis turned to Steve.

"Steve, you should marry this lady! Anyone that can cook this good, you should not let get away!"

Felicia beamed with delight, and crinkled her nose at Steve.

"See? There is a second opinion that we should marry! And it is the opinion of a respected friend! You should listen to him! I like you, Travis! You should be Steve's best man at our wedding!"

"Whoa! Slow down!" Steve said. "Who said anything about getting married?"

"But Travis said…"

"He just said that as a way of complimenting you on the great job you did with dinner, and it *was* great! But I don't think he was implying that we should really get married!"

"Well it sounds like a good idea to me!"

"And we will save that topic for discussion at a later date, when we have put a lot more thought into it! But right now, I would like to hear the Lees tell exactly what caused them to seek asylum down here. Travis, you told me that there was an attempt on your life, and more attempts were likely to follow, so I'm curious to hear about it! For starters, *who* is after you?"

"At this point, I don't really know. It is either Al Qaeda, or the Muslim Brotherhood. Or it might be both."

"Wow. When you piss someone off, you aim for the big guys, don't you! I had to leave my work in Egypt ten years ago because of the Muslim Brotherhood. I hear they are primed and ready to take over the Mubarak government at any time. So what did you do to them? Or is it classified?"

"It was, before it made the national news. Most of it I can tell you." He went on to give Steve an abbreviated version of his mission in Egypt, and how it went off the tracks. This was when Janice first learned that Jim Deshler had been involved as well, but it didn't surprise her. When Steve had heard it all, he was bewildered.

"So the CIA thought the guy was Osama Bin Laden? How could they make a mistake like that?"

"As it turns out, it was a deliberate attempt by Al Qaeda to find out the capabilities of the CIA's spying network. Now that they know how he was being monitored, he will go underground and probably never be captured."

"Oh yeah, he'll slip up sooner or later! The Marines will get him!"

"However, in the meantime, no one knows where I have gone to. We told no one where we were going. We even forwarded our home phone to my cell phone, so if someone calls, they will think we are home Our farm and our phone is being monitored by the FBI, and the ATF, and who knows who else. The next time assassins try to hit me at home, they want to capture them alive, so they can squeeze information out of them. Then we'll know exactly who to strike back at. And hopefully, when this is all over, we can go back to our farm in Laurel Grove and feel safe again."

"Well, that's good, in a way, because you will be here to help get this eco-lodge up and running. I'll gladly take the help! I'm realizing just how much work is still ahead of us, and new problems seem to crop up every day. But we'll get past them."

"What about the schools here in Coca?' Janice asked. "Will Calvin be able to complete his senior year of high school here?"

"Hmm." Steve said. "I don't think the curriculum he was taking in the States will translate to here. The school system here is so far behind the U.S., that he might want to just wait and finish school when he gets back home."

"YES!" Calvin said, more enthusiastically than he intended.

"But who's to say how long it will be before we get back home." she said. "It could be *years!*"

No one wanted to think about that, because she might be right.

<hr />

As they got ready for bed that night, Janice sighed as she looked around at how small their bedroom was. She couldn't imagine having to live here for an extended period of time. But then, when their bungalow was finished out at the lodge, it was going to be so small and crude, that it was going to make this place look like a five star hotel! She didn't know if she could handle that.

She put her house coat on over her night gown, so she could go to the bathroom. She had been there earlier, before dark, and the place barely qualified to be called a bathroom. Yes, it had running water (which you had to be careful not to drink, or brush your teeth with), and it had a flush toilet, a porcelain sink, and a shower stall to bathe in, but no one even thought about installing hot water.

Stepping out the back door to the patio, she followed the stepping stones toward the little bathroom that was separate from the house. An outside bulb illuminated the door, and served as a night-light. As she approached, she saw the geckos scurrying to get out of her way, except one who was engaged in trying to swallow a bug bigger than he was. She opened the door, and clicked on the light, and screamed at the top of her lungs!

Spiders! As big as her hand, and everywhere, it seemed! On the sink, on the wall, one on the floor, and they all seemed agitated that she was disturbing them with her uncontrollable screaming. She couldn't seem to get away from them, so she jumped into the shower stall, only to see one on the inside of the shower curtains! She continued to scream!

She picked up a long handled scrub brush, and used it like a battle ax, swinging it, and smashing spiders right and left. They were so big and hairy, that they had to be poisonous! Steve and Travis arrived to the sound of the swooshing brush, and Janice hissing at the few that remained,

"DIE, YOU UGLY BASTARDS, DIE!"

"Whoa! What is it, Dear" Travis asked.

"You can't see? It's spiders! They're everywhere! They were coming after me!"

"Those are tarantulas." Steve said. "They're harmless to humans."

"Harmless my ass!" Janice cried. "They were coming after me!"

"They were probably just after the other small insects that were drawn by the light. They won't bite you, unless you try to grab one!"

"Well, don't worry about me grabbing them! They'd better get out of here!"

"They're running as fast as their eight legs can carry them." Travis observed. "Except the ones you already smashed!"

"I'm going to the store tomorrow, and getting a can of Raid!"

"Normally when we go to the bathroom," Steve said, "We turn the inside light on, then wait at the door for about ten seconds. That gives them time to get back to the safety of their hiding places, before you come in."

"Well, thanks for telling me that ahead of time! There's a lot of them that won't be going home tonight!" she said.

"Are you okay now?" Travis asked.

"I think so. I'll clean up these dead spiders and flush them before I leave. I think I'm okay now. Steve, are there any more surprises you haven't told me about?"

"Uh, well, just a precaution,…always look into the toilet before you sit down. Sometimes frogs or water snakes could be inside."

"Really! Yeah, that's nice to know! Is there anything else?"

"Uh, yes,…you should never come out here without shoes, because in the patio you could step on a scorpion, or a poisonous centipede."

"Uh-huh! Anything else?"

"When you come back from the bathroom, be sure to close the back door securely, to keep critters out of the house."

"Critters like what?"

"Well, the usual stuff. Mosquitoes, vampire bats,…"

"You have got to be kidding! Vampire bats? As in, *blood sucking vampire bats?*"

"Yeah, they kind of come with the territory. Part of the down side to living in a tropical paradise."

"Can I go home now, Travis?"

"Let's give it a little more time, Janice. We haven't even been here 24 hours yet."

"That's what scares me!"

The next morning after breakfast, Steve met with his foreman from the lodge site. He had a list of things they needed from town, so Travis and Calvin went with him, as they gathered items from all over town. First they went to a building supply store, where he picked up saw blades, and 50 pound box of nails. He also ordered twenty five 100 lb bags of Portland cement, and asked if they could deliver it to the lodge before noon. The store owner said he could, so he added the box of nails to the order, and several joints of various sizes of PVC pipe, with fittings.

Next they went by the Coca Police station, where Steve delivered a plain envelope of cash to the police chief. That looked suspiciously like a bribe to Travis, but Steve called it his monthly 'insurance payment'. It insured that there would be no legal 'complications', and swift action if they needed police protection.

"It is always best to make friends with the local authorities right from the start. They have the power to make your enterprise run smoothly, as long as you grease a few palms. In the long run, it's a small price to pay. Hey, you ought to see how much Exxon pays for preferential treatment! What I pay is peanuts! And down here it is not really considered to be 'corruption', it's just business as usual. The more you pay, the better an insurance policy you get."

They made a couple more stops, then went back by Steve's house before leaving for the lodge. They found Janice up and having coffee with Felicia.

"Janice, are you going out to the lodge with us, or staying here?" Travis asked.

"Well, considering that I am still in my house coat, and I don't know of anything I can do out at the lodge, I guess I'll stay here."

"Yes, you can stay here with me!" Felicia said. "We will go shopping."

"Okay then. You girls have fun." Steve said. "We're off to the lodge."

"Oh, one more thing." Travis said. "Here is my cell phone. Keep it with you, but remember when you answer it, that we are *at home*! Got it?"

"Of course I remember. How can I forget!" she replied.

"And you probably ought to put it on charge too. I forgot to do it last night. The charger is in my back-pack."

"Yes sir, I will do that right now. You boys have fun playing in the jungle!" She smiled because she was not going with them.

"Okay men, to the boat!" Steve said.

As they were getting in to the boat, Travis asked, "Do you think Janice will be okay, leaving her here in town?"

"She'll be fine! Felicia will entertain her all day long. You think she can cook well? Hey, entertaining guests is what Felicia is *really* excels at! She will take her shopping, and introduce her to her friends, and by the time you see Janice again, she will be speaking the local lingo! Nothing to worry about! She will take good care of her!"

"That's good." Travis said. "Then I won't have to worry about her. So Felicia doesn't have a regular job to go to?"

"No, like most Ecuadorians, she just has part time, services based jobs, and she can arrange her jobs around her schedule, so she can entertain Janice all day."

"What do you mean, when you say a 'services based' jobs?"

"Well, like occasionally doing someone's laundry, or ironing, or sewing, or cutting stove wood, or baby-sitting someone's kids, just jobs here and there to make a little spending money. And she does pretty well at it. She always has plenty of spending money, and I like that, because I never have to give her money."

The water taxi sped them up-river, and deposited them at the lodge, where everyone was busy doing their assigned tasks.

"One of the men I talked to this morning in town was a man who owns a boat mounted pile driver. He will be out here this afternoon to look at the location I have picked to put in the pier. I'm hiring him to drive in the piles for the pier, then my guys can get right on the pier construction. That will make access to the river a lot easier."

"You have so many irons in the fire now, I don't know how you do it all." Travis said.

"Hey, I love a challenge, and I love to stay busy with some kind of enterprise. So this project is right down my alley! Come on, let's check out the work."

Steve saw Ortega patrolling with his automatic weapon. "Senor Ortega, how is everything?"

"Bueno, Senor Meredith! No problems."

"Have you seen our 'friends' this morning?"

"No, not since yesterday. Sometimes we go days without seeing them. But I think they are always seeing *us*."

"As long as they stay in the jungle, and mind their own business, I don't care. They could be just harmless locals, who are curious about what we are doing. But we can't let them see us mining emeralds. That is my only concern with them being here!"

"Si, Senor."

"Let's go check out the lodge foundation." Steve said. "It looks like they are coming right along."

And he was right. Where there had been just a few stones laid for the kitchen floor the day before, now it was about half complete, and another mason was starting to construct the stone base for one of the cooking ovens. But there was also progress in the main lodge foundation as well. Five men were digging up local rocks, and chipping them down with big chisels and hammers, to make reasonably square shaped stones for constructing the stone supports for the floor beams to be laid upon. They had not started mixing cement and laying them though. One of the men said they were almost out of cement, and didn't want to delay the kitchen construction. Steve told them to go ahead and mix the cement, because more was being delivered from Coca at noon. The lead man came to Steve on the sly, and said, "Senor Meredith, I show you something over here." They walked over to the rock pile, and rolled over a big rock, and on the other side was a big emerald crystal.

"Wow, look at that! It's a real beauty!" Steve said.

"We dug it up with the other stones, and then covered it again, until you arrive."

"You did the right thing, Pedro. We don't want to make a big deal of it. Bring those chisels over here."

He directed them to cut most of the big chunks of rock off the emerald, leaving it embedded in a baseball sized piece, which Steve slipped into his pocket, to add to the collection later.

"Homer is going to flip out when he sees the emeralds we've already found. He didn't think we'd find much until after we got the lodge built."

"So he will be here tomorrow?"

"Yeah, him and Doc are coming in on the morning flight, like you did. He was surprised when I told him that you were already here. But don't worry, I told him not to tell anyone that you were here. I didn't tell him why. I thought I would leave that to you."

"Good."

"Hey dad, can I go see what kind of fish they are hauling in?"

"Sure, Calvin, go ahead." Travis said.

"The fisherman's name is Emillio, and he speaks some English." Steve called out after him. "I think Calvin is going to have a ball down here." Steve said.

"I think you're right. So when will we go to Quito to set up our accounts?"

"Whatever day Homer leaves, we will all go to Quito, to set up the accounts. And while we are there, it would be a good time to see some of the sights in and around Quito. Janice will like that, I think."

"Yeah, I'm sure. So what can I do to help here, Steve?"

"Well, anything that you think you can do."

"I have built rock walls before."

"Then pick up a trowel, and help these guys. They have a blueprint of the floor lay-out, so take a look at that first. I see they already have the first three floor supports laid out, and a line level set up. I think you'll be impressed with these guys' skill level."

According to the blueprint, the stone supports for the floor were to be 2'x 2' square, and as high as would be necessary to come up to the string level line. Because the site was already dug in to the hillside, and fairly level, the stone supports would all be about three feet high on this end, but progressively taller as the hill sloped downward.

"If you need a stone cut to fit, tell one of these guys, and they'll cut it for you." Steve said. "Otherwise they are going to cut all of them to standard sizes and shapes. Felipe, go ahead and mix up the mortar. I'm going over the hill to check on the saw mill."

They were using sand from the river to mix with the cement, to make the mortar, so there were small muscle and snail shells mixed in the mortar, which made it interesting. The first few stones he positioned, he noticed that there were small, sand-like crystals on the surface. On closer inspection, they looked like emeralds, so he asked Filipe.

"Si, estan emeralds, but they are very pequino,…too small to try to save, say Senor Meredith."

"Well, okay. I wanted to ask before I covered them with cement."

"Es bueno."

———◆———

As Travis began laying rocks, Calvin arrived at the side of the river to watch Emillio setting up two rod and reels.

"What are you fishing for?" Calvin asked.

"For lunch." Emillio replied. "I catch fish for the cook, to have for our lunch today."

"What kind of fish?

"First I catch bait fish, then I use that to catch good-to-eat fish. I show you." He baited a hook with a big grub worm, then he cast it far out in the lagoon, and allowed it to sink to the bottom.

"Big fish, full of blood, live on the bottom. No good to eat, but good for bait. You see."

"Can I help you fish, by using that other pole?" Calvin asked.

"Si, you help me, yes! But we must catch bait fish first. See? Watch the plug, when plug goes under water, then snatch the pole back."

"Okay. So, how long have you lived in Ecuador?"

Emillio drew back at such a question. "I was born here!"

"Oh, that's right." Calvin felt like a fool for asking such a question. Emillio returned a question.

"How long *you* live in Ecuador?"

"This is my second day."

Emillio burst out laughing, and said something in Spanish that Calvin had heard before, but didn't understand.

"So I must have said something funny?"

"Yes, very funny! But do you want to talk, or fish?"

"I want to fish."

"Then grab the pole! See, you have a fish!"

Sure enough, the float was bobbing under the water, as though he had a fish. He grabbed the pole and set the hook, then began to reel the fish in. Just like Emillio said, it was a bottom feeder. It looked like a big sucker fish. He pulled it out on the bank, and Emillio immediately began cutting it up, to make fishing bait.

"Okay, you use this to bait hook, and you can start fishing for good eating fish." He held up the hook, and the line connected to it. "You see this? This is steel line! You need this, because the fish will have very sharp teeth! Like razors! When you catch one, let me show you how to get it off the hook."

"Sure. What is the name of the fish we are trying to catch?"

"Piranha."

"Oh wow. I've never fished for piranhas before. So if I went swimming in the river, these fish would eat me up?"

"No, not unless you have a cut or wound, and the fish smell your blood. Blood makes them crazy! See this bait fish? It is a bloody fish, so it will make them crazy, you will see."

Calvin cast into the water, and in only seconds, he felt a snatch on the line, and he set the hook. "I got one already!"

"Pull it in! Quickly pull it in!"

Calvin reeled it in, but it felt like it got off the hook, because there was no more resistance. He yanked the hook out of the water, and saw something odd on the hook.

"Hey! There's a *fish head* on my hook, but no fish!"

"Si, Senor! That is because you were too slow to pull it in! You must snatch it out of the water very quickly, or the other fish will eat him! When you hook a piranha, the other piranha sense that he is in distress, and they turn on him! In only seconds, he is gone! Watch me! I show you how it is done."

Emillio baited his hook, and cast out in to the river. Almost instantly he got a strike, and he whipped the pole, snatching the fish out of the water, and on to the bank, where it thrashed and flopped violently, trying to get back in the water.

"Now I show you *this*, my friend!" He picked up a pair of needle-nose pliers, put his foot on the piranha, and used the pliers to grab the fish by the lower jaw. When he did, the fish opened its mouth, exposing the razor-sharp teeth, that looked as dangerous as sharks teeth. Emillio used a second pair of pliers to remove the hook, and then threw the fish into the bucket of water. "That is how you do it, my friend! You must be very careful. Even out of the water it will bite off your finger-tip with one bite!"

"Yeah, I see! Thanks for showing me that."

"Now you try again. This time, you snatch fish out of water quickly."

Calvin used the pliers to carefully remove the fish head from his hook. Even decapitated, the fish head was still snapping at him. He threw it in the water, and the water seemed to *boil*, as the other fish devoured it. He rebaited the hook, and cast into the river. As soon as he felt a tug, he snatched back, and a large piranha launched itself out of the water, and came straight toward him, hitting him in the chest. "Shit!" He slapped it down, sure that it was going to take a chunk out of him before he could get it off him. Emillio got another good laugh.

"See? That is the way it is done! We have two fish. To feed everyone for lunch, we need to catch 25 or 30 more. Be careful, and do not let him bite you!"

They fished for almost an hour, and got their needed number, then carried them over to a make-shift fish cleaning station, where he again showed Calvin how to grab the fish by the jaw, and cut off its head. Once the head was removed it became as harmless as any other kind of fish. They cleaned and filleted the fish, and carried them to the cook, who dropped them in a pan of white wine and lemon juice to marinate awhile before he fried them right before lunch.

"You are a good fisherman's assistant!" Emillio told Calvin. "You should help me every day!"

"I will, if I don't have another job to do. My dad likes to keep me busy."

"Tell your dad that I will keep you busy, but just between us, we will make our job easy! Tomorrow, instead of fish, we will have chicken. You can go with me down the river to buy chickens, and bring them back. You will talk to your dad?"

"Yeah, I'll see if he's okay with it. I'd like to do that."

≈ 13 ≈

While the guys were busy at the jungle lodge, Janice was getting along well with Felicia. It was nice to have another woman for her to relate to. Felicia had never been married, and had no children, but she took great interest in Janice's descriptions of her five kids, and all the shenanigans they had pulled over the years. Felicia said it was her dream to get married, and have a big family too, but it looked like for her, it was not to be.

"Have you and Steve talked about getting married?"

"I little, but he has been married two times before, and is not interested in getting married again, I think."

"Well, maybe you need to keep working on him! He might come around with time."

"I don't know. I would like to go to the United States though. That has always been my dream."

Travis' cell phone rang. The caller ID said Jim Deshler.

"Hello Jim!"

"Hello Janice! I thought I would be getting Travis."

"Well, he's not here right now. He left the phone with me, because he was going out to the lodge. Do you have a job for him?"

"Oh, no I don't. I just called to see how you are doing. How do you like Ecuador?"

"It's okay. It is going to take some getting used to for me. I would really like to be back at home, but we can't do that for awhile. I just have to make the best of it."

"That's the spirit! Well, just tell Travis that I called, but there's nothing urgent going on. Tell him to give me a call sometime, so we can chew the fat."

"Okay, I'll tell him. Bye Jim."

"That was someone from the United States?" Felicia asked.

"Yes, we had our home telephone forwarded to Travis' cell phone, which gets reception almost anywhere in the world! So if someone calls our house in Alabama, it will ring right here!"

"Aye! Dios mio! That is a really good phone!"

"I think it is a satellite link phone. Travis' employer provided it for him, because they work all over the world. That was him that just called, by the way."

"Steve says that more friends, *investors* in the lodge, will be here tomorrow. Do you know them?"

"Yes, that would be Homer and Doc, some of Travis' life-long friends. They want to see what kind of investment they have made. If you ask me, they threw their money away buying that land! It's so far out of the way, that who would want to stay there?"

"Many people come to Ecuador now to see wild animals, and the rain forest. Steve says that they come here to *get away* from civilization. I do not understand that either. I want to go to the United States where it is 'civilized', and Americans want to come here where it is not! That is *crazy* to me, but Steve says he will make a lot of money because of it."

"Well, what is going to make a lot of money, are the emeralds!" Janice said.

"Shah!" Felicia said, as she looked around, as though there was going to be someone else in her kitchen who was going to hear what Janice said. "Steve has told me very sternly, not to even *mention* anything about that! Not here in town especially!"

"You mean about the... 'stones'?"

"Yes! No one here knows about that, and it is good, because there are many desperate people here who are so poor that they would do anything to get their hands on the 'stones'. If they find out what is at the lodge, they would kill to take it."

"So this is all a great secret?"

"Yes. Everyone in town knows that Steve is building a lodge there, but no one knows what is *under* the lodge! You must never mention it in town, or around anyone who is not employed by Steve. I am surprised that Steve or Travis did not tell you that!"

"No, most of the time they treat me like I'm a mushroom. They feed me shit and keep me in the dark. But they should have told me about that! I thought everyone in town knew about it."

99

"No! Not at all! Well, I am glad that I told you, before you told someone else in town. Well, I must go to the market for a few things."

"Something for dinner tonight?"

"Yes, and other things as well. Would you like to go with me?"

"Sure. Why not?"

Felicia picked up her market basket and purse, and they headed out, but they were not headed toward the market.

"Isn't the market that way?" Janice asked.

"Yes, and we will come back that way. But first, I have somewhere else to go. Come along. You will see."

They walked down the paved highway, then turned off and headed into the poor barrios, where the houses were just shambles, built of cardboard and tin sheets. It looked like a really dangerous neighborhood, and she voiced that concern to Felicia, as they passed a suspicious looking young man.

"It is a poor neighborhood, yes, but it is not dangerous. This is where I grew up. I know everyone here, and everyone knows me. I want to show you something here."

A gathering of small children began to tag along with them. Poor children, most of them half naked, and all of them bare footed. It made Janice feel uncomfortable. It was like going to the chicken pen at feeding time, and seeing all the chickens following her, because they thought she had food. These children had the same hungry look in their eyes as the chickens. They were expecting something. Felicia stopped, turned to the kids, and said something to them in Spanish, and they hung their heads and dispersed. Felicia and Janice continued on their way alone.

They passed several shacks that all looked the same, and then stopped at one, and Felicia stooped over to go into the door opening, which was only about five feet high. She motioned for Janice to follow her. It was with trepidation that she did so. Inside the shack, there was the strong smell of wood smoke, and very poor lighting. As her eyes adjusted to the light that filtered in through the cracks in the walls and roof, she could see that there was someone lying in a bed. Felicia was speaking to her in soothing words, and trying to get her to sit up, to see her guest.

"Janice, this is my mother. Ma-ma, esa es mi amiga, Janice! My mother is not doing so well these days. I have two younger sisters who live here with her, but they are away most of the day, trying to earn money in town."

"Where is your father?" Janice asked.

"He was killed on the river ten years ago."

"Oh, I'm sorry."

"Our mother took good care of us, and now we try to take care of her. I am grown, and have moved out, but I still come by here once a day to check on her, while the others are away. Ma-ma, Nececita mi ayuda?"

"Si, para al bano."

"She wants me to help her get up to urinate."

"Where is the bathroom?" Janice asked.

"Outside." was the reply.

Of course, it had to be outside, Janice thought. *A shack like this would hardly have running water.*

Felicia helped her mother get up, and hobble outside, and over to a tin wall, where there was enough cover for her to relieve herself, then she helped her back to bed. She sat beside her mother and talked to her for ten minutes, then as she started to leave she pressed some folded bills into her hand, and got a package out of her purse, and left it on the table. Then she said good-bye, and they left.

"What did you leave on the table?" Janice asked.

"It was the left over fish filets, from our dinner last night. I always cook more than I think we will eat, so I can bring the left-overs to my mother and sisters. Okay, now we can go to the market." Felicia said, as they went back the way they had come. When the pitiful looking kids began to appear again, Janice dug in her pocket to get coins to give them, but Felicia stopped her.

"But I just want to help them." Janice said.

"Of course. But to *give* them money is not good, because it teaches them to beg from foreigners. It is better to *hire* them to do something for you. That teaches them to work for their money. Believe me, I know, because this is where I grew up."

"What do your younger sisters do to make money?"

"They are street vendors. They get merchandise from store owners here in town, and sell it out on the street."

"Merchandise like what?"

"Every day it might be something different. Cheap jewelry, candy, roasted nuts, fruit, socks or gloves. Whatever product they think they can sell. In the rainy season, they do well selling umbrellas and cheap ponchos. When they sell on the street, they get 10% of the selling price. Store owners like to use street vendors, because it gets their products out of their store, where customers can see them."

They exited the poor barrios, and re-entered the bustling part of town, where there was so many things to see. Felicia greeted almost everyone they met, and passed a few words with them, as they made their way through the crowd. They turned down a side street, and Felicia stopped to talk to women who were out on the sidewalk. Some, she introduced Janice to, and then they moved on.

"Those are some of the girls I grew up with. I like to keep in touch."

"I get the impression that some of them might be prostitutes." Janice said.

"Yes, they are 'working girls'." Felicia said, as they walked on. Janice felt that the least said about them, the better.

In the market, they gathered fresh vegetables, fruits, dry rice, and asked Margarita to select for them the meat for the day. "Do you like goat meat?" Felicia asked Janice.

"I don't know that I have ever had it."

"Then tonight, we will have goat meat!" Felicia said. "It is very good, and very cheap! You will like the way I will prepare it!"

Goat meat didn't even sound appealing, but if it was prepared as well as the fish she cooked the night before, then she was willing to try it.

⇥ 14 ⇤

Travis worked up a good sweat laying rocks on the lodge pillars, and was impressed with how good the pillars looked. Not that they had to look good, because they would be hidden under the floor, once the floor was laid. But he was satisfied that the lodge was going to have a solid foundation. He didn't see Steve again until lunch break, because he had been busy with the loggers, making sure the right trees were cut, and more importantly, the right trees were left. As they were washing their hands for lunch, Steve told him about an impressive and odd mahogany tree they had spared.

"It's got to be one of the biggest mahogany trees I have seen! It looks like it blew over when it was young, and so it grew sideways and branched oddly. I can visualize a tree house being built up in that sucker that will make the Swiss Family Robinson's house look like a doll house! In fact, we could build a special 'Honeymoon Bungalow' in it, and rent it out for a little more than the others. I'll show it to you later, to see what you think. And oh, by the way, the sawyers came across that big anaconda snake again! He's still hanging around here, and that's good, because that's what tourists want to see,…wildlife!"

"How big is it?"

"Well, they're not real sure. It's so big that they have never seen the whole snake at one time, and it's not like we can pull it out of the bushes and stretch it out and measure it. Although I did ask my men to try to do that the first time we saw him, and they basically told me where I could shove my measuring tape! But a conservative estimate of the big guy, is that he's over 40 feet!"

"That's one big ass snake! Are you sure it's a 'he'?"

"I got no idea."

"And are you sure it's safe to have it around? I mean, it could swallow someone's kid, and that would result in a lawsuit."

"Are you kidding? It could probably swallow some kid's 400 pound Dad for an appetizer, and then his lawyer! But that's the cool thing about it! It's so big, and potentially dangerous! Yet, tourists can come here and see it in its natural environment! You know, I bet we could feed it live goats on a regular basis and it wouldn't be hungry. I have heard that those big snakes are harmless when they are well fed. We could keep it well fed, and get it used to being around people, and our guests could have their pictures made with it! Wouldn't that be awesome? We could call this the 'Anaconda Lodge'! Yeah, that would be a cool name!"

"What about 'The Emerald Anaconda'?" Travis suggested.

"I don't know. The word 'emerald' might be too suggestive. What about: 'The Green Anaconda Lodge'?"

"That has potential. But if the anaconda decides to leave, then the name would lose some of the meaning."

"Yeah, but at least it's a few more ideas to kick around. We'll get Homer in on the naming contest too. He might come up with something good."

The sawyer crews were gathering for lunch, and someone asked where Atan was. Pablo said he saw him out flagging trees to be cut, but that was over an hour ago. He should be here by now.

"Where was he flagging when you saw him, Pablo?" Steve asked.

"Back near the perimeter, where all the mango trees grow. He is probably eating mangos for lunch!" This drew laughter from his fellow sawyers.

"I'll go look for him, while you men eat. Travis, want to go with me?"

"Sure, let me get a machete." He figured he might as well go with Steve, because all the lunchroom seating was filled up by the sawyers. Steve stopped by his tent and got an AR-15 rifle, and made sure it was loaded. "In case we see a jaguar." he explained. After they had gotten away from the camp, he confided to Travis,

"Seriously, if he was last seen in the mango grove, then there is the possibility that some large predator really *did* get Atan. Predators are know to hide near a food source to catch an unsuspecting prey."

"You mean a predator like a 40 foot anaconda?"

"Well, yeah, that's one possibility. But let's just hope that Atan lost track of the time. Most of these guys don't have wrist watches anyway.

We'll probably find Atan eating mangos. The mango grove is over that way."

Travis chopped through the underbrush and headed that direction, as Steve explained. "I had in mind to clear off a big flat area back here and plant it with centipede grass for a small scale soccer field, and a tennis court, and a net for volleyball. A high level Ecuadorian official told me that if we built a nice enough place here, they would recommend us as an off-season training camp for city league soccer teams. And that could be a big boost in publicity for us, in developing the eco-lodge aspect of our investment. If we get recommendations from the right people in the national government, that reputation will go a long way toward giving us credibility, in case the emeralds run out."

"Do you think the emeralds will run out, based on what you have seen so far?"

"At this point, I have no clue. I hope we can mine them for years, and build up a nest egg fortune for us all. But in case they do run out, we can have the eco-lodge to fall back on, if we promote it right. And I have had so many people in the government here express an interest in this place, that if we manage it right, and expand when we need to expand, we can eventually make big money, even at $50 per day, per person. The more bungalows we put in, the more potential for profit we have. The initial plan is for sixteen bungalows. If those sixteen bungalows have two guests each, that's 32 guests, and $1,600 per day! That's $11,200 per week! That's $48,000 per month, and $576,000 per year! Less the cost of maintenance and payroll, we still clear almost a quarter million bucks per year! And mind you, that is with just 16 bungalows! If we eventually expand to 32, or 64, or a hundred bungalows, the profits will only increase!"

"Sounds like you have been sitting up at night crunching numbers."

"Oh yeah! What else do I have to do? I have figured everything in, allowing for unseen problems that are sure to crop up, we are still sitting on a potential gold mine!"

"And that's in addition to the literal *emerald mine* going on behind the scenes."

"Yes, exactly! Admittedly, there will be a lot of unseen problems, but we can deal with them one by one. Okay, see those trees with the dark green leaves? Those are the start of the mango grove. Our plan is to cut out all the trees that are not mango trees, and have a ready-made mangrove orchard for stocking the lodge. We can also grow our own pineapples oranges, limes, papayas, bananas, and guavas."

"So in a lot of ways, the lodge can be self-sufficient?"

"Yeah, that's what I'm aiming for. The more we can do ourselves, the more profit we make. And we already have a loyal work-force to help us achieve that."

"Man! Look at all the mangos!" Travis said. They are literally falling off on the ground!"

"Yeah, but don't eat those on the ground, unless you saw it just fall out of the tree. If the ripe fruits lay on the ground for just ten minutes, they could already have parasites in them! There are these really bad-ass worms in the ground, and they quickly get in the fruit that falls on the ground, so don't eat those."

"I don't see any worms."

"That's because they are too small to see without a microscope. But you'll know when you get a dose of them, because you'll have the screaming shits for about two weeks!"

"So the fruit still in the trees are safe?"

"Yeah, the parasites are only on the ground."

"I don't see your man in the mango grove."

"Yeah, but we could easily have missed him, if he went back to the camp by another route. That's probably where he is, back at the camp eating lunch. ATAN! ALMUERZO AHORA!" he yelled into the jungle. "Oh well, we might as well head back and eat lunch too." Steve said.

"Would Atan have left his chain saw out here when he went to lunch?"

"No, he wouldn't. They are very protective of their tools."

"Then what's that?" Travis asked.

"It looks like a chain saw! Yeah, that's one of ours! It's not like him to leave it out here. Let's look around. He might have gotten snake bitten!"

"He might have got swallowed by that big ass snake you were making such a fuss about too!"

"Shit! Don't even think like that! Let's fan out from the saw and see if we can find him!"

"Either find him, or a snake with a big lump in his stomach!"

"Burr! Don't even say that, Travis! I don't even want to *think* that!"

They spread out in ever widening circles, but saw nothing, as they both called his name. Finally they returned to the saw to look for clues, and that was when Steve saw the rolled up paper stuck through the trigger of the chainsaw. It was a sheet of computer paper, which Steve himself had thrown away, but some of his workers would pull from the trash to use as toilet paper while out in the jungle. Atan probably had a wad of this paper in his pocket today, in case of emergencies. But this one had a message written on it.

"It looks like he left a message." Steve said. But after he read it, he said, "No, it's not from Atan. It's a ransom note! Someone captured him, and says if we want to see him alive again, we have to pay them $300 in cash!"

"$300 in cash? That seems like a pretty small amount for a ransom!"

"Well, not really, considering that down here, $300 is a lot of money, to people who may not make that much in three months! And besides, if they ask for too much, they know they won't get it anyway!"

"Has this happened to your men before?"

"No, not to *my* men, but it is fairly common down here. When I was with Exxon, they allowed so much per month, for ransoming their workers who were stupid enough to wander off from the work site. It's usually $500 though. But whoever grabbed Atan probably doesn't know if we have deep enough pockets to pay that much. But if we pay the $300, then next time it will be $400, and the next time $500, until they find out how much is more than we are willing to pay."

"So does the note say who grabbed him?"

"No, but I bet it was those strangers we keep seeing in the jungle. That's what they were doing. They were waiting to catch someone out by himself, and Atan accommodated them!"

"So what are you going to do?"

"What can I do? Other than pay the $300, and get Atan back. And then we will have stricter rules about working out in the jungle. No one is to wander off by himself any more! That's just one more cost of doing business in the jungle!"

"How do they want the money paid?"

"The note doesn't say, but it's almost universally understood that the ransom is to be left in the same place the note was found. I'll put the money in an envelope, and nail it to the tree right there. That's how it is usually done by Exxon, to get their workers back. This is no big deal. It happens here all the time."

"What would happen if we didn't pay the ransom?"

"The note says they will kill him, but I have never known anyone to be killed by their kidnapers down here. They would probably just keep him awhile, then turn him loose."

"So why pay the ransom at all?" Travis asked.

"Well, it's kind of like a tradition. If an employer doesn't pay the ransom for his workers, then he is looked upon poorly by the man's family. It's something that you just don't do, if you want the respect of your workers."

"Well, this is certainly a new twist on our business. If we don't pay it, we loose face with the locals, and if we do pay it, we'll be their 'cash cow' from that point on. They will probably kidnap someone different every week, just to keep the money flowing in. You know, that won't be good, when we start having guests here, and a few of them get kidnapped!"

"I know. That's why we are going to have to negotiate with them, and come to an agreement. We may have to pay them a flat rate up front every month, for them to leave our people alone."

That thought didn't set well with Travis. As they walked back to the camp, they discussed the options.

"So the military won't get involved?" Travis asked.

"Nope! Just ask Exxon. If the military was inclined to help, they would have helped Exxon. No, when we decide to go into business in the jungle, we just have to allow for things like this, because the government doesn't want to get involved, and show that they are powerless to stop it. They just take the easy road, and say it's not their responsibility. We are on our own, to deal with this. I'll go into Coca and get the $300. Maybe they will release Atan before sundown."

"I don't think we should pay it, Steve."

"Yes, we do, to show that we care about our workers."

"Okay, so we go ahead and pay *this time*, but I think we ought to look into finding out who these kidnappers are, and deal with them, so there will not be a second time."

"And by 'dealing with them' you mean exactly what?"

"The same way you deal with a fox that's raiding your hen house! You don't bribe him to not raid your hen house. You get your shotgun and kill him! End of problem!"

Steve grimaced. "Well, that might work in dealing with a fox raiding your hen house, but we're dealing with *people* here! We want to be good neighbors, and get along with everyone. We don't want to start a running feud that could turn into a jungle war! That won't help us any. It would draw unnecessary attention to our lodge, and if we plan to secretly mine emeralds, we don't need the extra scrutiny. Perhaps we can just pay them to stay far away."

"So you think we should just pay the ransom?" Travis asked.

"For now, until we find out who these people are, and where they come from."

"Wherever they are from, they are trespassing on our land!"

"And that's another thing that may be a touchy point with the locals, Travis. These people may have been squatters on this land long before we bought it, so in their eyes, they have every right to be here. In some cultures, the actual ownership of land is a very *abstract* thing."

"You're right. I guess we need to find out more about them, before we decide what to do."

"Yeah, we definitely need to find out more about them."

When they got back to the camp, Steve called everyone together and showed them the ransom note, and assured them that he was immediately going to Coca to get the money to pay the ransom. He also used the opportunity to introduce a few new rules. The first rule was that no one was to go off by himself to do anything, unless two more went with him. If they stayed in groups, they were not as likely to be kidnapped.

One sawyer asked, tongue in cheek, if that meant that they had to have two 'escorts', just to go 'relieve' themselves. Steve replied, also tongue in cheek, "Absolutely! One man to hold your hand, and the other to wipe your ass!" Everyone roared with laughter. No one seemed particularly up-set that Atan had been kidnapped, probably because they knew it was a commonplace thing, and there was probably no danger to him. When he returned, his co-workers would probably make fun of him, for allowing himself to be captured, so he could 'get out of work'.

After eating lunch, Travis and Calvin helped the masons lay rocks on the lodge foundation, while Steve went to town to get $300. Security officer Ortega organized everyone into three man work crews, so they could get back to work.

Travis noted that the construction of their bungalow was coming right along. The floor and roof were finished, but the walls were still being wired for electricity, and the bathroom pipes were being plumbed. That raised another question. Where was the piped water coming from? Eventually they were going to have a water tank, where they would treat the water, to make sure it was safe. Then they would pipe the tank water to the main lodge, and to all the bungalows. But the water tank was not built yet, so even if the bungalow was finished that day, it still wouldn't have running water. That meant no showers, and no drinking water, unless it was bottled, or boiled. It was doubtful that Janice was going to want to live in such a small and primitive abode, especially if there was no running water, and taking a bath meant swimming with the piranhas. Running water was something they took for granted in the States, but here it was a luxury.

The cement delivery from Coca arrived, about the time the pile driver specialist arrived, so Steve had to deal with them before he left for Coca. It was almost 4 P.M. when he arrived back at the lodge with the money. Immediately upon arriving, he got Ortega, and Travis to go with him, to nail the ransom to the side of the tree where the chain saw was found. They scanned the jungle, but saw no one, even though they were sure they were being watched. In the jungle, one was always being watched.

"There's nothing else we can do here." Steve said. "We'll have to leave before they can get the money. And as late as it is now, they probably won't release him until morning, so we might as well go."

"I'd like to hide out, and see who comes to get the money." Travis said. "I could grab him, and then instead of paying ransom, we'd just swap our men."

"No, we don't want to do anything that would jeopardize Atan. We just play by their rules for now, and see what comes next."

"Yes," said Ortega, "We should not do anything besides what we are told to do. It would not end well."

"Okay then," Travis said, "We'll see what happens."

≈ 15 ≈

Back in Coca, Janice was helping Felicia start dinner, and the goat meat was stinking up the whole house, as it boiled vigorously on the wood stove. But she didn't say anything about it, because she knew it would have to taste better than it smelled.

She went to lay out her clothes on the bed, when the phone rang again. It had been ringing all afternoon. Of course, everyone who called, thought they were calling the Lee home, not knowing that it was forwarded to Travis's cell phone. The Fraternal Order of Police called wanting a donation for their annual toy drive. Marla called again, but didn't talk long. Calvin's friend, Billy-Bob called, wanting to talk to Calvin. She truthfully told him that Calvin was not there. This time, however, it was General Morgan, which gave her hope that maybe things had changed, and they would be able to go back home.

"No Ma'am, there is no change in the status of our stake out. Is Travis there?" Morgan asked.

"No, but he should be back later."

"Will you have him call me when he gets back?"

"Sure." Janice replied, trying to sound as cold and impersonal as possible. She had no love for General Morgan, or the agency that had so often taken Travis away from her,...and oh yeah, caused this present situation. Well, she was partly to blame for the terrorists finding out where they lived, but that would be a moot point, if they had let Travis stay retired, and not dragged him into that mess in Egypt.

When she got back to her clothes sorting, she realized that they needed to wash clothes before they ran out of clean ones.

"Felicia, where is the washing machine?"

"Washing machine?"

"Yes, for washing clothes. Is it out back too?"

"We do not have a washing machine."

"Then how do you wash clothes?"

"Steve hires a woman from the barrios to wash clothes for us. Every morning she picks them up, and washes them, and returns them in the evening. Except when it is rainy season, then she brings them back the next day. So you have clothes to wash?"

"Yes."

"There is a big basket beside the back door. Put dirty clothes in that, and she will get them tomorrow morning."

"Just out of curiosity, how does she wash them?"

"She takes them down to the river, and washes them on the pier with a rub board."

"Oh." Janice replied. "Does she use soap?"

"Yes, certainly!"

"I just wondered, because the river is not what I would exactly call clean water."

"It sometimes is muddy, because of the rain, but it is not dirty."

Janice decided it was best not to argue with her. She just gathered up their sweaty clothes from the day before, and took them to the laundry basket out back. In doing so, she saw a *huge* scorpion scurrying across the patio, and had to muffle her urge to scream. At some point, the neighbors were going to get tired of hearing her scream, so she bit her bottom lip, and watched the creature disappear in the weeds. *Two days.* she thought. *I have only been here two days, but it seems like a month!*

She braved the odor of the goat meat, and returned to the kitchen to watch Felicia cook. It was amazing how she could cook four different things at one time, and regulate the temperature by adding wood chips to this fire, and letting another die down. Sometimes she used a spray bottle of water to cool down a fire that was getting too hot. There was an art to cooking over open flames, and it was learned by experience. And she did it with one hand, because the whole time, her left hand was holding her cell phone to her ear, as she kept up on the local gossip, jabbering in Spanish with her girlfriends. It was amazing watching her multi-task.

When the goat meat was tender enough to meet her approval, Felicia poured out most of the water it had been boiling in, and replaced it with boiling coconut milk. Immediately the *odor* changed to an *aroma*, as the coconut milk cooked into the meat. She began adding spices to this, and eventually goat milk, and flour, to make a rich gravy, and eventually the stinky main course became a delicious smelling entrée that she couldn't wait to try. Felicia seemed to sense her thoughts, and offered her a spoon.

"You would like to try this, no?"

"Yes, I would!" She took the spoon and dipped up a little of the rich gravy, and blew it to cool it off, then tasted it. Her taste buds went wild.

"This is *really* good! I mean it! I don't know how something that smelled so bad cooking could turn into something so good, but it did! You are going to have to teach me how you did it!"

"It is nothing. Just a matter of adding the right ingredients, at just the right time, and in just the right amount. And I tell you a little secret,…it is the coconut milk. Any meat cooked in coconut milk is much better! But surely you cook with coconut milk in America?"

"No, I have never heard of that before! Where do you get coconut milk?"

"Out of coconuts, of course!"

"We don't have many coconut trees in Alabama."

"Perhaps you should plant some there?"

"No I don't think they would grow there. It gets too cold in the winter."

"How cold does it get?"

"So cold that water freezes into ice."

"No! You are joking with me! Do you mean like the ice in the new refrigerator that Steve bought? It gets that cold *outside*?"

"Sometimes. Sometimes it gets so cold that the rain turns to snow, and piles up a few inches."

"I have heard of snow, but I have never seen it, except in pictures. Steve took me to see an old movie one time, and I saw snow falling from the sky in that movie! It looked so strange!"

"You should get Steve to take you to America in January, so you can play in the snow!"

"Oh, I don't think I will ever go to America. It costs so much money!"

"If you and Steve get married, he will have to take you there."

"But I do not think he will marry me. He says he will never marry again, after he divorced two times."

"But you would marry him if he asked you?"

"Yes, I will gladly marry him, if he will ask me!"

"Well, maybe I can *nudge* him that way for you."

"You think you can do that?"

"I won't know until I try."

———◆◆◆———

The men returned from the lodge much later than usual, so Felicia had to try to keep the food warm for them. Steve was in a bad mood, and told her what happened during the day. Janice picked up on the details, and was immediately alarmed. While Steve was gone to get his shower, she questioned Travis about it.

"One of the workers was kidnapped?"

"Yeah, well, they say it happens down here all the time, so there really isn't much to worry about, as long as the ransom is paid. And Steve already paid it."

The look on her face was priceless. It told him that something he just said didn't come out like he intended it to.

"It happens all the time?" she repeated. "Correct me if I am wrong, Travis, but in Alabama do we have to worry about strange people coming out of the woods and *kidnapping* our kids, and holding them for ransom?"

"Well, it could happen anywhere, Dear."

"But it doesn't happen just anywhere! It happens here! And you want me to move out there in that same jungle to live?"

"It's a problem we are going to work on." Travis said. "Any time you go to do something worthwhile, you're going to run into little snags along the way. But we correct the problems one by one, and before you know it, we have a really nice place here. It's just going to take a little time."

"Well, until you take care of those 'little snags' as you call them, I think I will stay here in town where it is relatively safe!"

"I agree. That would probably be for the best, as long as Steve is okay with it."

"General Morgan called, and wants you to call him back. And by the way, you are taking that phone with you tomorrow. I am tired of trying to convince everyone and their brother, that we are at home in Laurel Grove! Lying just rubs me the wrong way!"

114

"Okay, I'll take it with me. Give it to me now, and I'll call Morgan."

"The shower is free!" Steve announced, as he emerged barely wrapped in a towel.

"Calvin, go ahead and get your shower, while I make a phone call."

"Okay, Dad."

He got Morgan on the first ring.

"What's going on, General?"

"Nothing yet. But the reason I called is this: We need to get authorization from you, to monitor your home phone line. The reason, is that with your phone forwarded to your cell phone, we miss any potential probing by the terrorists who are trying to locate you. We have a trap set at your home, waiting on them to make a move. We have agents posing as you and your wife, actually living in your house while you are away, in case they try to monitor your house. And we really need to be able to monitor your phone, but we cannot do it legally, without your permission."

"Permission granted, General."

"Thanks. Now, even though we are monitoring your calls, you will still be getting the calls on your cell phone, just like you are doing now. It's just that we'll be listening in, and if it's a strange call, we will be able to trace it, and maybe get the heads-up that another attack is eminent."

"I understand, and I'm okay with that."

"Good! So how is Ecuador? Is your family adjusting well?"

"Somewhat. I don't think Janice will be happy here for long though. I hope the matter with the terrorists can be resolved fairly soon."

"So do I, Travis. Rest assured that we are diligently working on it from this end. By the way, should a really hot mission come up, that I think you would be the perfect man for, would you be willing to take it?"

"Is this hypothetical, or is there a real mission looming?"

"A little of both."

"Well, while my family is uprooted, and on the run, I can't even consider it. I have to look out for the welfare of my family first."

"I understand that."

"But the sooner you can resolve the matter at home, the sooner I can get back in the game."

"Rest assured, we will be doing all we can."

Travis had just hung up, when the phone rang again. The caller info said it was Janice's parents.

"Here, Janice, I think this one is for you."

"Hello?"

"HELP! HE'S AFTER ME!"

"Mom, is that you? Who is after you?"

"I DON'T KNOW! SOME STRANGE MAN IS IN THE HOUSE, AND HE'S TRYIN' TO GET ME TO TAKE MY CLOTHES OFF! CALL THE POLICE! YAA! HE'S GOIN' TO RAPE ME!"

"Mom! What is going on?" She heard the phone hit the floor, and scuffling in the background. Then she heard a familiar voice scowling:

"Come back here, you crazy old woman! I don't care if you want it or not, you are going to get it!" It was her dad, Herston. He picked up the receiver out of the floor and asked,

"Who have I got here?"

"Dad, this is Janice! What in the world is going on there?"

"Aw, your mother don't want to get her bath! I been chasin' her all over the house, trying to get her undressed, to get her in the bath tub! The stubborn old woman! She claims she don't know me, but I know she does! She jest don't want to get her bath! I got her clothes off her, but I can't get her in the tub!"

"How did she know to call my number?"

"I think she jest hit a number, and it happened to be your speed dial number. She's going to the doctor tomorrow morning, so she's *got* to have a bath! HERE, HERE! DON'T YOU GO OUT THERE! Dammit, she's done got the front door unlocked, and she's gone! The crazy old woman is naked, and running down the street! Listen, I got to go catch her before the police do!"

He hung up, and Janice dropped the phone on the bed and laughed so hard that she cried.

"What's wrong, Janice? Are you laughing or crying?" Travis asked.

"I'm laughing!" she finally said, after she caught her breath. "After what's happened the last few days, I *needed* something to laugh about! I wish I had a recording of that call! It was a classic!"

And whoever is monitoring our phone is probably getting a good laugh too! Travis thought. *And yes, they probably recorded it too!*

The dinner was once again great, though it was low budget. Travis couldn't believe that it was goat meat they were eating, because the only other time he had it, it was really bad.

Calvin told about the day he had, fishing for piranhas. "Emillio said he could use my help tomorrow too, if you would let me."

"What will you be doing?" his mom asked.

"He said we would go to the market to buy chickens. So I guess tomorrow we will have chicken for lunch."

"Homer and Doc are arriving tomorrow about ten in the morning." Steve said. "I really need to get out to the lodge early, and see what's going on. That will push me to get back to the airport by ten. Travis, can you stay here and pick up our partners in the morning?"

"Sure, if I can drive the Land Rover."

"It's yours. Take them to their hotel to drop off their luggage, then being them straight out to the lodge. If you hurry, we can get a half day's work out of them."

"What about me?" Calvin asked.

"You can go to the lodge with me." Steve said. "Emillio said you are a big help. But like everyone else, don't you wander off by yourself. Stay with someone, and watch out for strangers in the jungle."

Janice cringed.

"So what are you doing tomorrow, Janice?" Travis asked.

"I guess I will stay here with Felicia. We can have dinner ready when you come back from the lodge."

"Actually," Steve said, "I have made arrangements for all of us to eat dinner tomorrow night at a really nice place here in Coca. Just up the street from here. A place called Peppy's. Great food, and cold beer!"

"It sounds like Homer will love it." Travis said.

"Yes, Peppy's has very good food!" Felicia said. "It is better than my cooking!"

"I don't see how it could be better than your!" Travis said.

Felicia beamed with delight.

"Okay, so we are set on what we will do tomorrow?" Steve asked. "Good. Then I am going to bed. I am worn out! Janice, if you find a critter in your bed tonight, just rake it out and go to bed. It scares the neighbors when you scream like you did last night."

"I'm sorry, but I couldn't help it! It had *so many* legs!"

"That's why it's called a millipede, because it has a thousand legs, and they were all running as fast as they could go when you smashed him."

"I'll try not to yell out tonight."

"Good girl! Felicia, don't fix me breakfast in the morning. Just coffee, please."

"As you wish."

After everyone had retired, Calvin rolled out his sleeping bag in the living room. He missed not having a TV, but otherwise, he was having a blast.

≍ 16 ≍

Travis slept late, which was 8:30, then got up and ate breakfast, and listened to Janice's latest list of grievances, then prepared to go to the airport. Janice jumped at the chance to go with him.

A plane was landing as they drove up, which had to be their plane. There were only two flights a day to Coca from Quito. Homer and Doc were easy to recognize, because they were the only North Americans on the flight. They saw him in the crowd and waved.

"How are you two doing?" Homer asked.

"Well, we're supposed to pick up two Gringos and take them to their hotel!"

"That would be us!" Doc said. "And the sooner the better!"

"If you're wondering why he is green, I think he was about to get air-sick." Homer explained. "On the return flight, I'm not sitting by him!"

"What is the name of your hotel?" Travis asked.

"It's written down here somewhere. I'm not good with Spanish names."

"Hotel Caballeros." Travis read. "It means 'Gentleman's Hotel'."

"Maybe they'll let us stay there anyway." Homer said.

"Okay, so where is it?" Doc asked.

"How should I know?" Travis replied. "I've been here two days, and spent most of that time in the jungle."

"That's just great," Homer deadpanned, "They send a tourist to pick up tourists! I'm complaining to the city."

"Most reputable businesses are on the main road through town. It shouldn't take long to find your hotel."

As they drove, Homer asked the most obvious question first.

"Steve told me not to tell anyone that you were down here. What's the story about that?"

Without divulging anything of a top secret nature, Travis explained the situation, with the terrorists attempt on his life. In short, they were in hiding out for awhile.

"I'm sure I will read all about it in one of your future novels." Homer said. "With names changed to protect the innocent."

"It actually came at a good time, because Steve needs help getting the lodge up and running."

"So you have been out there?" Doc asked.

"Oh yeah, most of the two days I have been here, I've been at the lodge. It's really easy to get out there. Yesterday I was helping lay the rock foundation for the main lodge."

"How soon can we go see it?" Homer asked.

"Steve and my son Calvin are out there now. He told me to drive you to your hotel, then bring you both right on out there."

"Good deal. What will we need to take with us?"

"Bug spray, sun tan lotion, and boots. The site is a little muddy right now."

"I didn't bring boots." Doc said. "What about tennis shoes?"

"Are they snake-bite proof?"

"What!"

"I'm joking! The snakes down here don't bite, they just swallow you whole!"

"Don't worry, Doc, he's still joking!" Homer said. "You *are* joking, aren't you, Travis?"

"Well, to tell you the truth, they *did* see a 40 foot anaconda the other day."

"That's it!" Doc said. "I'm staying at the hotel! Take lots of pictures, Homer!"

"Nonsense! You came this far, you might as well go all the way and see the lodge for yourself." Homer said.

"I'll go ahead and tell you this, Steve is already finding emeralds everywhere they dig. He's trying to keep the emeralds under wraps while we get the lodge built, because the government sometimes sends inspectors out to make sure everything is done legally, and it wouldn't do for them to see us finding emeralds."

"What about his workers? Won't they tell?" Doc asked.

"Steve insists that everyone he has employed is looking at prospering along with the lodge, so everyone is in on the cover-up. From what I have seen in the two days I've been here, I think he's right. Everyone is on the same page."

Homer turned to Janice. "For a woman's prospective, what do you think about the eco-lodge?"

"Too many bugs and critters for me!" Janice said.

"You're asking the wrong person." Travis said. "She hates it down here!"

"You've got that right!" she said.

"But under the circumstances that Travis just told us about, you may have to be here awhile." Homer reminded her.

"But I won't be here a day longer than I have to be!"

Homer and Doc checked into their room, and were out again in five minutes. "Okay, let's go see what we invested our money in!" Homer said. They drove back toward the river, and parked outside Steve's house. Felicia was standing in the doorway smoking a cigarette, and waved as they got out.

"This is Steve's house, and that is Felicia, his girlfriend!"

"Wow, Steve certainly knows how to pick 'em!" Homer said.

"Quite a looker!" Doc commented.

"Did you call her a hooker?" Homer whispered.

"No, I said *looker*! Very good looking!"

"Well, if you men will excuse me, I'm going to stay here with Felicia, the 'looker'." Janice said. "I had enough of that lodge the first day."

"Okay," Travis said. "I've got the phone with me. See you later today. This way to the boat, gentlemen!"

"How convenient! He lives right here beside the dock."

Travis hailed a water taxi, and they loaded up to go.

⇥ 17 ⇤

When Steve and Calvin got to the lodge earlier that morning, Ortega informed him that the ransom money had been taken from the tree during the night, but Atan had not shown up yet.

"No big deal. He'll show us pretty soon. Their camp may be a long ways off in the jungle. But he should be here by noon. Is everything else going well?"

"Yes, everything. But it slows us down, because we must work in three man crews."

"That can't be helped for now. The pyle driver's barge will be here this afternoon, to start driving the pyles for the pier. If they need help, pull the rock masons off the lodge to help them."

"Si Senor!"

"So you're helping Emillio today?" he asked Calvin.

"I guess, unless you have something else you want me to do."

"No, Emillio needs help, and I think you'll like working with him. He is always hunting and fishing. I'm sure you'd rather do that, than mix cement, huh?"

"Oh yeah!"

"It looks like he's getting his boat ready, so go ahead."

Emillio was fueling up his outboard motor engine when Calvin hailed him.

"Ah! There is my assistant! Are you ready to go up the river?"

"Sure! So we are going to the market to get chickens?"

"To get chickens, yes, but not to the market. I show you."

They loaded ropes and nets, just in case they ran across something unexpected. A 12 gauge shotgun for protection, with extra shells. Empty buckets and a long handled frog gig.

"Where is your machete?" Emillio asked him.

"I don't have one."

"That is not good! Everyone needs a machete in the jungle! Look under the back seat in the canoe. There is an extra machete there that you can wear."

Calvin found the machete and attached it to his belt.

"Now all you need is a big straw hat, and you will look like a jungle man! Untie us, and shove us off the bank."

As they drifted away from the bank, Emillio started the engine, and they sped away from the lagoon, and out into the main river. Instead of going down river, toward Coca, he went up river, coursing the main channel, until they were several miles above the lodge. He slowed down and aimed the canoe toward a small cluster of thatched roof houses. Several small dark tanned boys waved at them as they approached.

"Throw them the rope!" Emillio yelled, and Calvin picked up the coil of rope, and hurled it toward the children. All of them grabbed the rope, and pulled them in.

"We start our shopping here!" Emillio said. They carefully stepped off the canoe, and picked their way up the steep dirt embankment by using toe-holds already dug in the bank. On top the embankment a crowd of children were gathering, along with a few adults, who came so see what the visitors wanted. Emillio spoke to them in Spanish, asking if anyone had extra chickens they wished to sell. He would pay $2 per chicken. Immediately children ran home to tell their mothers that strangers wanted to buy chickens. Emillio explained to Calvin, as he lit a cigarette.

"The best place to buy chickens, is in these little villages. Everyone raises chickens for their own use, but they always have more than they need, so they are eager to make a little money by selling them. It is difficult for them to take their chickens to the market, because it is a long way, and transportation is not always here when they need it. So when someone like us show up to buy chickens from them here, it is an easy sale, and they will sell cheaper than in town. In town they sell for no less than $3, but in the villages, you can buy them for $1.50. I offer $2, and have no problem finding chickens!"

"How many do we need?"

"I think fifteen to eighteen. That is allowing ½ chicken per man. Sometimes we have extra men to feed, so we always buy a little more than we think we need. Twenty will be good, I think. They may not have that many extra chickens here, so we buy some here, and some at other villages down the river."

In less than five minutes, children began arriving with chickens under their arms, and Emillio would check each chicken over good before he bought it. Some were too old, and some were too young, and one he rejected because it had a running sore on it's back. For each good chicken, he paid it's owner two dollar coins, and handed the bird to Calvin, so he could tie the legs together. They ended up with six good birds, and thanked the villagers, then hauled their chickens to the boat, and drifted down river. Before Emillio started the boat, Calvin asked him about the dollar coins he was using. Were they Ecuadorian coins?

"These? You do not recognize your own American money?" He showed them to Calvin, and he recognized them as being Sacagawea dollars.

"Oh, okay! Yeah these are U.S. coins, but I didn't recognize them, because I've never seen one that was worn slick like this! In the States, nobody uses these coins!"

"Do not use them? But why not?"

"We use paper dollars. The coins just haven't caught on yet."

"As you can see, we use them very much here!" He started the engine, and they eased on down the river about a mile, to another village, where he pulled over, same as before. He inquired about chickens, and this time they got ten suitable birds, and they moved on. As they puttered down the river, looking for the next village, Emillio suddenly saw something in the water.

"Look! Crossing the river!"

"What is it?" Calvin asked.

"I think, but I am not sure…we check it out!" He opened up the outboard motor, and they zoomed around to get in front of the large animal that was crossing the river.

"Yes, it is what I thought it was! This is very good luck, catching such an animal crossing the river!"

"Is it a wild pig?" Calvin asked.

"No, it is a tapir,…a large pig-like animal! It is very good to eat! If we can catch it, we will not have to hunt tomorrow!"

"How can we catch it?"

"We will try a rope around its head. It is usually a very quick animal, but in the water it is at a disadvantage. If we cannot rope it before it gets to shore, it will get away."

"Can't we shoot it?"

"No, if we shoot it, it will sink, and we will lose it! We must get a rope around its neck. Can you make a slip-noose with the rope?"

"I'll try."

They circled the animal as he swam, as they got the noose ready. Finally Emillio pulled right up beside the tapir, and Calvin slipped the noose over it's head, and tightened it up. There was a tremendous struggle, as the animal tried to get out of the noose, but it struggled to keep its head above water as well. The noose secure, they allowed it to swim on toward the shore. When it was almost there, Emillio jumped out in the shallow water, and attempted to rein in the animal before it got to shore. He was successful in holding him in the shallow water, and told Calvin to join him in the water with another rope.

"You want me in the water?" Calvin asked, no doubt thinking about the razor toothed piranha they were catching the day before.

"Yes, throw out the anchor, and bring me the other rope! We must tie his legs together, to get him into the boat!"

He certainly didn't want to, but he did it anyway. He threw out the anchor, then grabbed a coil of rope, and jumped in the water with Emillio. While Emillio held the animal with the first rope, Calvin made another noose, and slipped it over one of it's front legs, then proceeded to go around the animal, to pull it's legs together. Little by little, they immobilized the big animal, and got it lying on it's side in the water. They rested before attempting to hoist it into the mid-section of the canoe.

"It looks like a baby elephant, with that long snout!" Calvin said, and Emillio nodded. They got into position, and hoisted the big guy up and over into the canoe.

"Very good! Now we should get out of the water, my friend!" They climbed back into the boat and rested awhile. Emillio dried his hands, then got out a cigarette and lit it, then lit another one and handed it over the tapir to Calvin.

"No, thank you. I don't smoke."

"It is not to smoke, my friend! It is to burn off the leaches!"

"Leaches? You mean off the tapir?"

"No, from us."

"We've got leaches?"

"If you were in the water, then yes, you have leaches!" To illustrate, he pulled up his pants leg, and showed him two black slugs on his leg. "We were only in the water a few minutes, but it does not take long." He took a draw on the cigarette, to get it hot, then applied it to one of the leaches. A couple of seconds, and it turned loose, and he flicked it into the river, and went after the second one. Calvin rolled up his pants and was horrified to see *four* on his leg! He puffed on the cigarette, and burned the first one. It literally jumped off his leg, into the canoe. He used the point of his machete to flick it out into the river. They sat anchored there, ridding themselves of leaches for almost twenty minutes, before deciding that they were good to go.

"We were very lucky to catch this tapir. But we will have to cook it overnight to eat tomorrow, so we must continue searching for more chickens to cook today. We have sixteen. We need at least four more. There are several small villages close by. We will make one more stop for chickens, then head back to the lodge. We must hurry, if we will cook some of these chickens by noon."

Calvin pulled in the anchor, but he wasn't hearing what Emillio said, because he was itching all over, and imagining more leaches on his back, where he couldn't reach them. He wondered how many kinds of diseases leaches carried.

When they motored back up to the lodge, Emillio stood up and yelled for help in getting the tapir off the canoe. A crowd of workers quickly gathered on the bank to meet then when they arrived. Several strong men positioned themselves up the embankment, to pass the animal out of the canoe, on to shore. When they got it on shore, they gathered around looking at it for a few minutes, discussing the best place to put it until they needed it. Six men picked it up and carried it up toward the kitchen, and put it down in the shade, as Calvin, Emillio, and others, unloaded the chickens, and carried them over to the same where they had cleaned the fish the day before. They started right away, killing and cleaning half of the chickens. The other half they would save alive for the evening meal. The heads and entrails were thrown into the river, where the water seemed to boil with the underwater activity of the piranhas devouring chicken scraps.

"By 'feeding' the fish here," Emillio explained, "It keeps them expecting food here. Any time we need to catch fish to eat, we just throw in a hook!"

"So this would not be a good place to swim?" Calvin asked.

"No, not here." Emillio answered. "Not unless you want your bones cleaned!"

Every time they got two chickens cleaned, someone would carry them to the cook, who was cutting them up, seasoning them, and placing them on the grill. They had just barely gotten back in time to cook the chickens before lunch.

"We cut it close, but we got back in time my friend! It was stopping to capture the tapir that ran us close. But it will be quite a feast when we cook the tapir!"

"So we will cook him tomorrow?" Calvin asked.

"No, the cook said we will save him for Sunday! Saturday night we will dig the pit to cook him in, and Sunday we will feast!"

"We'll cook it in a pit?"

"Yes, in the sand! See those big sand dunes beyond the lagoon? That is where we will dig the cooking pit. We will cook it just like we are cooking a pig! You have never cooked a pig that way?"

"No, how do you do it?"

"We dig a big pit in the sand, and pile dry wood into it, and burn it down to charcoals. We cover the hot coals with sand and green banana leaves, then put the cleaned pig in on top the leaves, with all the vegetables and spices, then cover it with more leaves, then cover it with sand. You leave it there all night, and the next day you dig it up, and it is done! Sunday we will feast!"

"It looks kind of like a small elephant, like they have in Africa."

"Yes, I think it is closely related to the elephant. It is like the South American version of an elephant. If it had a longer nose, and bigger ears, it would be an elephant, no?"

"Yeah, that would make it look just like an elephant!"

A water taxi pulled into the lagoon, and slowed as it neared the shore.

"Ah, there is your father, and others."

"That's Homer and Doc." Calvin said, as he washed his hands off to go see them. The boat saddled up to the shore, and Calvin was there to help them off the boat. Steve also arrived from the lodge to meet them. Homer waved at them.

"Calvin, you are the official greeter?" Homer asked.

"I'm just here to make sure you don't lose your balance and fall into the water. The piranhas are in a feeding frenzy right now."

"Oh my god!" said Doc. "I hope you are joking!"

"Nope, we just fed them chicken guts, and it just made them more hungry!"

"You'll be okay, as long as you don't step in the water." Travis told him. "I don't think they jump out of the water to bite you! Or do they, Steve?"

"Don't get Doc freaked out!" Homer said. "You know he can't handle it."

"No, they don't jump." Steve said. "Welcome to the lodge, guys! I know things look chaotic right now, but this place will be nice when I get through with it."

"I can see a lot of potential here." Homer said, as he stepped off on the shore. A big blue Morpho butterfly fluttered across his path, and he stopped in his tracks. "Do you see that? That's a Morpho! They're just running wild here, aren't they?"

"Yeah, they're pretty much everywhere." Steve said. "And that's just one of *many* wonders that people are going to want to come here to see! The wildlife, the insects, the birds, the plants and flowers! This place is a tropical paradise!"

"We caught a tapir just this morning!" Calvin said proudly.

"Is that what you were loading off the canoe earlier?" Steve asked. "I was working on the main lodge, and I saw the commotion! Where is it now?"

"Over near the kitchen. Emillio said we're cooking it Saturday night!"

"No, no no! We are not going to *cook* a tapir! That is the kind of wildlife that people will want to see in the wild! Where is Emillio? I specifically told him *not* to put things on the menu that are indigenous wildlife!"

"Well, we didn't catch this one here." Calvin explained. "We caught it several miles up the river."

"It doesn't matter! We'll turn it loose here, and maybe it'll stay around here for the tourists."

"They're not going to be happy. Everybody was looking forward to having roast tapir Saturday night."

"Well, then tell them this: If they let the tapir go, I'll buy them five cases of beer, and a pig from town that they can roast on Saturday night. Go tell him that, Calvin, while I take these guys up and show them around."

"Sure." he replied, but he didn't think it was going to make Emillio happy. They all had their taste buds set for roast tapir. But roast pig might be just as good. He found Emillio at the kitchen, where he was cutting up the last of the lunch chickens, to get them on the grill. Calvin was right, he wasn't happy about it.

"Aw man! He wants him to turn it loose? That is messed up! The guys were already planning a Saturday night roast! I thought he would be happy that we caught it!"

"He is, but he says he wants it turned loose so tourists can see it in it's natural habitat."

"I have always thought that the inside of a roasting pit *is* it's natural habitat!"

"Well, you should probably talk to Steve about it then. I'm just the messenger. Oh, by the way. He said if you will turn it loose, he will buy you all five cases of beer, and a pig from town that you can roast Saturday night instead."

"Hey! Why didn't you say that from the beginning! That will be much better! Go ahead and set him loose. But do not cut the rope, it is my good rope. Just untie it, and put the rope back in my canoe."

"Okay." Calvin picked up a raw carrot to gnaw on, as he went release the animal. After all the trouble they had gone through to catch it, now he had to turn it loose. But he agreed that he would rather see it in the wild than actually eat it. It looked too much like a baby elephant anyway. The tapir cringed in fear, as he loomed over it. He held the carrot up to the animal's mouth, and his nose twitched as he smelled the offering, and then took a bite out of it. While the animal ate, he eased up to it and carefully untied the knots in the rope, until he was free. The tapir was so engrossed in eating the carrot, that he didn't seem to notice that he was free. Calvin rolled up the rope, and took it to the canoe, as he was told to do. When he turned back around, he bumped into the tapir, because he had followed him there.

"Git! You stupid animal! The jungle is that way!"

He just stood there, nose twitching, hopeful that Calvin had another carrot.

"No more, Dude! Now beat it! Get back in the jungle before somebody decides to roast you!" He reached out toward him, hesitant, in case he tried to bite him, but all he wanted to was smell his hand, to confirm that there were no more carrots. He patted him on the head, and the animal seemed to enjoy it.

"Okay, I've got to go, so you run along!" He turned, and walked up the hill to the kitchen, where he asked if he could help do something. There were potatoes to be peeled, and other vegetables to be chopped up and steamed. However, the cook and his assistant backed away from him, and Emillio laughed, and chided them in Spanish. Calvin turned around, and saw why. The tapir had followed him to the kitchen.

"Calvin, it look like you have a friend!" Emillio laughed.

"All I did was turn him loose!"

"And you fed him! I saw you give him the carrot. Now he is your friend for life,...which may not be very long, if the cook has his way!"

"I didn't know he was going to follow me!" Calvin said.

"Do you know what I think?" Emillio said. "I think this tapir may have been the pet of some local kid, when it was young, and that is why he is not afraid of us. I noticed that when we caught him, that he did not fight us as tenaciously as you would think a *wild* tapir would do. Yes, I think this fellow was once someone's pet!"

They watched, as the animal helped himself to the vegetable scraps that had been thrown out from the kitchen. He was seemingly oblivious to the presence of the same humans that were so recently intent upon roasting and eating him.

"Senor Steve said to release him, so the tourists can see him in his natural habitat. It looks like his *natural habitat* is going to be the *kitchen garbage pile*!" He repeated this to the cook in Spanish, who was not amused, and got animated, gesturing in no uncertain terms, for the animal to get out of his 'kitchen', as though his kitchen actually had walls.

"I tell the cook: 'It looks like you are going to have to keep your vegetables up off the ground from now on, or this guy will eat them'. See? He even eats onion peels! Just like a goat, he will eat everything!"

Calvin began peeling potatoes and dropping them in the boiling pot. The potato peels he threw to the tapir, who ate them as fast as they came his way.

18

Meanwhile, the investors were in Steve's tent, admiring the emeralds that Steve had accumulated since the construction had begun. Homer was more than impressed, he was excited. And it took a lot to excite Homer. He recognized the potential value of just what lay on the table.

"When are you going to take these to Panama City to sell?"

"I don't know." Steve replied. "That's not a priority right now, with all this construction going on. I need to be here to orchestrate things. I have enough cash in the general fund to take us a long way, before I have to sell more emeralds."

"Well," Homer explained, "I would like to see how the gem selling process works. I thought maybe you would be taking these to Panama in the next few days, and we would tag along to meet this Mr. Victor Carranza, from Colombia. Do you negotiate a price, or is there a set price per karat?"

"Well, first of all, the buyer we meet in Panama City might or might not be Victor himself. If he is very busy, he may send one of his gemologists to meet us, and evaluate our stones. He will sit down at a table with a magnifying glass, and carefully examine every stone, and then he will compute the size, clarity and color, and come up with an offer. In my dealings with him before, I have found him to be a very fair man. He knows quality when he sees it, and he will not offer a ridiculously low price for good quality. He doesn't mind paying well for quality stones, because he knows how hard they are to come by."

"That's good."

"If you want, I can call and set up a meeting in Panama. I'll tell Victor that my partners want to meet him personally, and I am sure he will make an effort to be there. What day do you plan to go back?"

"Doc and I planned to be here two days, then head back. So, today is Wednesday, we'll probably leave Friday."

"And on the way back, we need to stop in Quito, and let you guys each open a savings account in a major bank. That way, I'll have accounts to deposit your profits in."

"Yes, that's right. We need to do that." Doc said.

"We can fly from Quito to Panama in the afternoon, and be there in time to meet Victor Friday night with these stones. Then Saturday morning you guys can fly from Panama back home, and Travis and I can come back here."

"That will work." Homer said.

"Okay, I will call Victor in a few minutes, to try to set up the meeting for Friday evening, and if I can, then I will call to get the plane tickets reserved.

"Sounds like a workable plan." Homer said.

"Now, what I usually do with the emeralds is, I chip all the rock off the crystals that I can, and package them up in a sealed box in my suitcase, and it's usually well under the 85 pound weight limit. But I have not had time to chip these down, so we will take them 'as is', which is no problem for Victor, because he has the tools to remove the emeralds from the stone. The problem is the weight of the excess stone. Since there will be four of us, we will divide them up among us, and we should all be under 85 pounds each. If they ask us at the airport, we just say that we collect rocks. But usually they do not even ask."

Everyone nodded.

"Now, in other business news, there has been a disturbing subject come up recently. Travis may have mentioned it to you already coming from the airport. The kidnapping?"

"No, I didn't tell them about that." Travis said.

"Okay, yesterday one of our sawyers was kidnapped in the jungle by some unknown persons. Our security men have been seeing unknown people out in the jungle watching this place for two weeks now, but they always melt away into the jungle when we try to find out who they are. But yesterday they kidnapped Atan, and asked for a ransom of $300, which I have already paid."

"Wait a minute!" Homer said. "Should we be paying ransom to these people? Won't that just encourage them to keep on kidnapping our people?"

"Well, down here it is a common thing." Steve said. "Exxon pays ransom every week. It's just the cost of doing business here."

"That's what I mean!" Homer said. "If we are planning to have visitors to our lodge, we can't have them being kidnapped every week! Word will get around, and we will have no guests staying here!"

"We might have to work out a deal with them, if we can ever meet them face to face." Steve said. "Exxon makes monthly payments to them, and they leave Exxon's people alone. We may have to do the same thing, but to do it, we have to find out who they are."

"No!" Homer said. "We don't want to be extorted into paying ransom to them, just to keep them from kidnapping people! We need to call in the national police, and let them take care of it!"

"That is the problem. Ecuadorian government won't touch it! They say it is not their problem, and that we should work it out on our own."

"You've got to be kidding!" Doc said.

"No, this is not the U.S.A., it's Ecuador. Things down here are a lot different. So we need to co-exist with these people, whoever they are."

"I say we hire an 'exterminator' to take care of these 'pests'!" Homer said.

"It's not that easy a solution, Homer. We don't want to make them mad, or we could have a running feud on our hands, in addition to the kidnappings."

"We need to hire a professional to take care of this problem." Doc said.

"Hire one? Why hell, we've already got one right here on our staff!" Homer said.

Everyone looked at Travis.

"Wait a minute!" Travis said. "I don't like the way this is shaping up!"

"You are the best there is, at jungle warfare!" Homer said. "And you probably wouldn't have to kill anyone. Just give them a good scare!"

"I don't think so, guys. I'm trying to get out of that business, after what happened in Egypt."

"What happened in Egypt?" Doc asked.

"I'll fill you in later." Homer said. "So what did the kidnapped man say about his abductors?"

"He has not been returned yet." Steve had to admit. "I was hoping he would be back this morning, but it's almost noon, and still nothing."

"Say the ransom was $300?" Doc asked.

"That's right. We paid it last night. The money was picked up, but we've heard nothing else."

"$300 is a piddling small amount." Homer said.

"Well, that's what they asked for." Steve replied. "And down here it's a lot of money. And I think they were just feeling us out. Next time it will probably be more."

Homer cringed. "Next time, my ass! There had better not be a 'next time', or they might get more than they bargained for! I have run businesses for years, and rule number one, is that you don't let fringe groups intimidate, or interfere with the operation of your business. If they think you are afraid of them, they will go for blood!"

"More than likely, these are just poor people who have no other way of making money." Steve said. "They may have harvested timber and sold it in the past, but with international restrictions on wood harvesting, it has put a lot of them out of work. They turn to poaching wild animals, but then there are laws against that too. So many of them are bitter about the fact that they can no longer feed their families, the way they have always done. And then they see us 'rich' Americans come in and buy the land out from under them, and tell them that they have to go. We are treating them like, you know, the same way the U.S. Government treated *your* Choctaw ancestors, Homer! Remember the 'Trail Of Tears'?"

"Of course I remember, Pale-face!"

"Well, that's the same thing that is happening to the local indigenous peoples here, except that here, the government is not rounding them up and evicting them, like Andrew Jackson did."

"Andrew Jackson!" he spat. "That S.O.B. was a cold blooded murderer of my people!" Homer said. "I have never accepted a $20 bill in my life, just because it has that murderer's image on it!"

"So you must agree with me, that, ethically speaking, we cannot deal harshly with these people! They were here before we were, just like your ancestors."

Homer grudgingly nodded. "Okay, you have convinced me, Steve. So what do you recommend?"

"That's hard to say, until we can find out exactly who they are, and why they feel justified in extorting money out of us. Look, the thirty some-odd people we have working for us now, are *all* indigenous people. I hired them on good recommendations from my contacts in Coca. I intend to greatly improve their lives, by continuing to employ them, and their family members here at the lodge, because, after all, if it's a success, we will need a very large live-in staff to operate it. Now, if these renegades out in the jungle can be reasoned with, perhaps we can use them in some capacity as well."

"So what you are suggesting," Doc asked, "Is that we hire those kidnappers to work for us?"

"Sure! Why not? If they are jungle people, skilled in survival, which we think they are, they would make the best Security Force you could ask for! We would employ them to *protect* the lodge, and our guests, instead of *preying* upon them! I mean, if we are going to be paying them anyway, why not get a service back in return?"

"And we could take that a step farther." Travis added. "If they really are jungle people, then we can show them how to make even more money, by having them build a 'traditional Amazon Indian Village' back here somewhere in this virgin rain forest. They could actually live there, and put on demonstrations for our guests. They could charge us a fee for every time we bring a group of tourist there to see how they do things. It would be one of our planned 'Nature Walks', that we will advertise in our brochure, and on our web site. It would be a neat addition to the eco- lodge, and the whole 'back-to-nature' learning experience."

"Hmm,...not bad" Steve said. What do you think, Homer?"

"It sounds like another 'Buffalo Bill's Wild West Show', only the South American version." He replied.

"So is that a good thing?" Steve asked, because sometimes Homer's sarcasm was hard to interpret.

"It will be good for us. And if they agree to it, then it will be a good thing for them, financially. As long as they don't mind the degradation of living in primitive conditions, and being laughed at and made fun of, by the endless parade of stupid white folks! On one hand, I feel their pain, as a displaced and marginalized people. But on the other hand, I am an advocate of free enterprise, and have been all my life."

"So is that a yes, or a no?" Doc asked.

"Hell yeah! I say let's exploit the dumb savages!" Homer said. "It will be more humane than turning Travis loose on 'em!"

"All in favor of pursuing this course of action, say 'aye'" Steve said.

"Aye!" everyone said.

"Okay, we will try to befriend them, and offer them this proposition, at the first opportunity." Steve said. "So, let's get out and I'll, show you guys the rest of the set-up here. I'll show you the foundation of the lodge first."

They went out, and Homer had questions about everything they saw. When they went to the foundation of the lodge, Homer was excited to see that all the gravel under the foundation was emerald crystal bearing rock. In fact, he scratched with his boot heel and turned up a sizable emerald. At this discovery, he wanted to get a pick and shovel, and go to digging, but Steve and Travis had to restrain him. Steve whispered to Homer,

"Yes Homer, there are emeralds right here on the surface to be found, and when we do start the mining process, the results are going to be fantastic. But for now, while our ass is showing, we need to keep it under wraps, and concentrate on getting the lodge built. Once the main lodge is covering this site, we can start mining. But to do it now, would only draw attention to what we are doing."

"So we've got to keep it low key?" Homer asked.

"Yes, very low key. Especially with 'eyes' out in the jungle watching us! Those guys that kidnapped Atan are still out there, and if they find out that we are mining emeralds, they might decide it is more profitable to just kill us and take over our claim. We will build the lodge first, then try to *secretly* mine emeralds later, after the lodge is up and running."

"Yes, that makes sense. I understand. So after the lodge is up and running, I can come back down here and dig like a fool?"

"Hey, you're one of the owners of this place, Homer! After we get running, you can *stay* down here digging if you like! But we have to keep it quiet for now, and even then too."

"Yeah, you're right. But I'm putting this one in my pocket!"

"No problem."

Security officer Ortega approached the men.

"Excuse me, Senor Steve. Can I have a word with you in private?"

"Certainly, but everyone here is a partial owner in this place, so you can speak freely. What is it?"

"Well, I hesitate to bring this up, but you need to know that the men, they are talking. They are saying that you did not really pay the ransom for Atan, because he is not back yet."

"Well, that's absurd, because you were with me when I dropped off the money."

"Yes, I told them that, and so now they are talking that we should stop work, and send out parties of armed men to find Atan, and find out once and for all who is out there. I know that you are the owners, and what you say is the final word. But these men working here, are not just working for a paycheck. They are working for a secure future for their families for many years to come. And they know that having a group of people out in the jungle *preying* on this lodge will not be good for business. They feel, and I do as well, that we should go no farther with the construction here, until we have settled this thing. Every man here is willing to arm himself, and help search for Atan."

The four investors looked at one another, trying to decide if this would be a good thing. Finally Steve spoke.

"What do you think guys?"

"Doc and I are leaving for Quito tomorrow, so You and Travis need to decide on this." Homer said.

"Yes," Doc said, "You and Travis handle this any way you think is best."

Steve turned to Travis. "What do you think?"

"Well, we're leaving for Quito tomorrow too, and we won't be back until the next day. Why don't we give it until then? If Atan is not back by the time we return day after tomorrow, then we look at beating the bushes for him."

"I think that is a sensible course of action." Steve said. "It will give this thing a chance to resolve itself. If Atan shows up, then maybe he can tell us how to contact the kidnappers about a possible deal, like we discussed before."

"So we will do *nothing* before you get back, day after tomorrow?" Ortega asked.

"Yes, I think that would be the best course of action. Just keep the construction going, but be safe, and no one go out in the jungle alone, until we get back. Then we will discuss how to go forward."

Ortega clearly had something else on his mind, but he kept it to himself. He would abide by Steve's decision, even if he didn't agree with it.

Travis answered his cell phone four times during the day, three of them from people he knew, who thought they were talking to Travis at his home in Alabama, and he said nothing to indicate to them that he *wasn't* at home.

But the fourth call was a strange one. It was a caller with a Middle Eastern accent, who asked if he would like to make a donation to the Christian Children's Fund. The caller may well have been who he said he was, but Travis was suspicious.

"Say you are with the Christian Children's Fund?"

"Yes, sir."

"Do you have a similar fund for Muslim children?"

"Uh,… not that I am aware of."

"A fund for Muslim children, whose parents were killed by strapping on suicide bombs and blowing themselves up? Is there a fund for those children?"

"I don't think so, sir."

"There probably should be." He told the caller that he did not have time to talk further with him right then, because he had to go out in the back yard and feed his chickens, but he encouraged him to call back later. As soon as he hung up from him, he called General Morgan, and told about the call.

"Okay, I haven't heard it, but the men out at your house are monitoring and recording all your calls, and should already know about that one. But I'll call them to make sure they are watching and alert. If he called from somewhere near your home, then there might already be hit men on the way to your house, as we speak."

"Good, I hope you can catch them. Janice is already tired of the jungle."

"Even if we do catch them, it still might not be safe for you to come home just yet, because there will very likely be others coming after them."

"I know," Travis sighed.

"But there might be a way." Morgan said. "If you are interested."

"Not if it involves changing my identity, and moving to Arizona! The government's witness protection program sucks!"

"Well, yeah, that was going to be my suggestion, to fake your death, and give you a new identity, but you don't have to move to Arizona. You could stay in Alabama."

"No, right now that's not an option. I want to continue to live in my own home, on my own property, and I want to be able to go to town, or anywhere I want to go, without worrying that someone is going to recognize me. If I have to go into hiding, then it means that the terrorists have won! I would rather be killed by an assassin, than have to hide like a rat the rest of my life."

"What about the safety of your family?"

"That's the problem. The only reason I would even consider the Witness Protection Program, would be because of them. The people that are after me would kill anyone that gets in their way. What I want to do, is strike the person who is giving the orders to kill me. We can kill and capture hit men for years, but until we get the guy with the fuzzy nuts, who is running the organization, it will just be a waste of time."

"I agree."

"So, are there any leads yet?"

"No, but if there were, I wouldn't tell you, because I know what you would do. And we can't have a 'loose canon' screwing with our foreign policy right now. It was bad enough what you did in Egypt, and that still hasn't died down completely. But rest assured, if it comes down to something that I think you can handle, you'll be the first to know."

"So, until then, we're going to give it some time, and see how things shake out?"

"That's right."

≠ 19 ≠

That evening they all returned to Coca, and Steve took Homer and Doc to their hotel, so they could get cleaned up for dinner at Peppy's Restaurant. Travis and Calvin showered at Steve's house. As he was waiting to take his shower, Travis asked Janice what she did all day.

"I hung out with Felicia. We went by to see her mother again, then went to town for some things. I think she goes to town to socialize more than to shop."

"Well, that's the culture. At home, you socialize with your friends by phone. She does it by going to town."

"And she has some odd friends too!"

"Well, if you want to talk about *odd friends*, let's just take a look at some of *your* friends!"

"I know. I have some real losers as friends, but some of the people she knows are just,...I don't know! To me, it seems like some of them are just a little *inappropriate* for her to be associating with."

"At least in your opinion?"

"Well, yes, in my opinion."

"So what is inappropriate about them, in your opinion?"

"They're *men*! If she is Steve's girlfriend, she shouldn't have so many *male* friends!"

"She is a beautiful woman. Men are attracted to beautiful women. What is wrong with that?"

"Oh, you don't understand! Men don't understand about women, the way *women* understand about women!"

"You lost me there."

"Travis, you have *always* been clueless about women!"

"I can't argue with that."

"I might as well be talking to that wall!"

"I know! I am just as dumb as a rock! And that's one of my *good* points."

"Will you shut up and stop agreeing with me!"

"You don't like me arguing with you either, so what else can I do?"

"You can just shut up and listen when I tell you something! You don't have to have an answer for everything! Sometimes I just want you to listen, and let me blow off steam, without offering any snide remarks, or solutions!"

"Okay."

"I said *shut up*!"

(A few moments of silence.)

"Okay, so what are you thinking, Travis?"

"I'm thinking, 'how can I get off this merry-go-round'! I'm starting to get dizzy!"

"I'm sorry, I didn't mean to bite your head off! I'm just tired of this place, and the people here, and want to go home."

"I can understand that. It's called culture shock. But you know the situation."

"I know."

"Just try to make the best of it. When we finally do get back home, you'll be wishing you were back down here!"

"Humph! Don't hold your breath on that!"

"Did Calvin tell you about the tapir he made friends with today?"

"The what?"

"Tapir,...that's an animal. It looks kind of like a pig, and kind of like an elephant. He had that thing following him around like a pet today. Ask him about it when he gets out of the shower."

———◆◀———

Peppy's Restaurant was within walking distance, so they set out walking, while Steve went to pick up Homer and Doc with the Land Rover. They all met outside, and went in to a large table on the patio out back, under a mango tree that occasionally dropped mangos. Steve ordered them the house specialty, a combination of seafood (or actually river food), that was expertly prepared. There was fish, fresh-water prawns, shellfish of all kinds, frog legs that were so large, they mistook them for chicken legs. The side dishes were rice, potatoes, yucca, palm heart, and 'jungle salad'. A platter of various fruits was the dessert.

After such a sumptuous dinner, they hung out and talked for hours, which meant that eventually they ordered a pitcher of beer, and then another one, as the story-telling shifted into high gear. Steve was like the *master* of story-telling, once he got wound up, and properly saturated with alcohol. He kept them laughing for hours into the late evening.

At some point in the evening, the cock-roaches started coming out to clean up the crumbs dropped by the restaurant's patrons. Everyone at one point, felt something crawling up their leg, and would wait until it got to knee level, and then slap it off. The locals all agreed that the cock-roaches were just a part of their night out, and seemed to accept it as par for the course. Janice was horrified, but after a few beers, she just slapped them away like everyone else.

Steve was in the midst of an intense tale, when he saw a huge cock-roach on *top* their table, lapping up spilled beer. Without letting it interfere with his tale, he picked up a glass beer pitcher, and set it down heavily on the cock-roach with an audible 'crunch'. Though the pitcher was empty, it was heavy enough to ruin the cock-roach's day. Or so everyone thought, until the empty pitcher started to rock from side to side, and then actually start inching across the table on the back of the wounded cockroach.

"Would you look at that!" Doc said in amazement. "No wonder those suckers out-lived the dinosaurs!"

Steve grabbed the pitcher right before it inched off the edge of the table, and the big cockroach fell to the floor, flipped himself upright, and ambled away.

"I hope I didn't make him mad." Steve said. "He's likely to go home and recover, then come back looking for me."

"And he'll bring some of his gang members with him, to whip your ass!" Travis said.

"That is one bad-ass cockroach!" Homer said. "We should hire them as security guards out at our lodge!"

"I'm sure we'll have plenty of them out there, without hiring extras." Steve said. "In fact, the local jungle people eat them. They stir-roast them in a skillet until crunchy. They thrive in the thatched roofing of their huts. Any time they want a snack, they just poke a stick into the thatch to stir them up."

"That's gross!" Janice said.

"No, actually they are pretty good." Steve said. "They are kind of like crispy fried bacon."

Steve noticed that Calvin had not said a word all evening.

"Calvin, how do you like working with Emillio?"

"I love it! Always something interesting to see!"

"I noticed that the tapir was following you around today."

"Yeah, he's like a pet! I can't get rid of him! Emillio said he thinks he was once the pet of some local kid, because he is so tame."

"Yeah, that's a possibility. I have seen the local kids with pets of all kinds! Baby sloths, parrots, monkeys, snakes, spiders,…you name it, I've seen them as pets down here!"

"I was watching a nest of ants that was cool. They were cutting pieces of green leaves, and carrying them back to their nest. It looked like a river of green, as they headed toward their nest! And some were carrying bugs and seeds."

"Those were leaf-cutter ants. They carry all that fresh green stuff underground, where they stash it away and let it mold. The mold is what the ants eat, and feed to their young ants. They know exactly what kind of leaves to cut, to grow the kind of mold that makes the best food."

"I put my foot down on their trail, and in seconds, they started a new trail over the top of my shoe!"

"Yeah, there's not a whole lot that stops them. Tell you what, tomorrow ask Emillio to take you to see a nest of Army Ants, if he has time. There are not any near our camp, but I'm sure he knows where there are some up the river somewhere. But you have to be careful around Army Ants, because they are so big and voracious, that they can actually be a danger to humans. They have been known to cut up and haul away human babies, in a matter of a few minutes."

"Wow, they sound dangerous."

"They are, but they are a wonder to see. They call them Army Ants, because when they 'march', they clear a swath through the jungle sometimes five feet wide. They cut up and haul away literally everything in their path! I have seen them strip a straw hut down to just the bamboo pole frame. Any slow moving insect or animal in their path is a goner. I saw them overtake an anaconda snake, and strip it down to just the bones in about ten minutes! I have heard some of the locals call them 'land piranhas', because they work so fast! They are mesmerizing to watch, but be sure to stay out of their way!"

"Before we get too drunk," Steve said, "And while we have all the owners here together, we have to decide on an official name for our lodge."

Homer raised his hand and said, "Homer's Hideaway!"

"No! That sounds more like biker's bar!" Doc said.

"Ideally, the name should evoke an image that we are trying to project about our lodge." Steve said. "Something that sounds exotic and perhaps a little mysterious!"

"Shangrala!" Homer sang out, off he top of his head.

"Well, yeah, if this were the Himalayan Mountains, that might be an appropriate name, but this is actually the rain forest, Homer, and I think the name should reflect something along those lines."

"Homer's already drunk!" Doc said.

"Good one!" Homer said. "The Homer's Already Drunk Lodge! I like it!"

Steve just hung his head.

"How about the 'Biting Insect Lodge'?" Janice suggested.

"Actually, that is the best suggestion I've heard yet." Steve said. "But I think we can do better! Come on everyone! Brains in gear! Think *past* the margaritas, people!"

"The Green Jungle Lodge!" Felicia said.

"The Emerald Lodge!" Travis said.

"The Anaconda Lodge!" Calvin said.

"Yes, all of those are good!" Steve said.

"What about the 'Green Anaconda'?" Doc suggested.

"Good! Now we are getting somewhere!" Steve said.

"What is *your* suggestion?" Homer asked Steve.

"What about the 'Napo Lodge'? since it is on the Napo River."

"Too boring!" Homer said. "I like 'The Emerald Anaconda'!"

"Yeah, I like that too." Doc said.

"It does have a ring to it!" Steve said. "Any more suggestions?"

"I like it too." Travis said. "I think that's the winner!"

"Is everyone in agreement?" Steve asked. "Does anyone not like it?"

No one spoke up against it.

"Okay then, the name is, 'The Emerald Anaconda Lodge'. All in favor, say 'aye'!"

In unison, everyone said, "Aye"!

"Anyone opposed?" No one spoke up. "Okay then, 'The Emerald Anaconda Lodge' it is!"

Of course, they had to celebrate with another round of drinks.

"So what time is our flight out in the morning?" Homer asked.

"8:40 flight to Quito. That will get us there in time to go to the America Del Sur Bank, and set up your accounts, then we will eat lunch, and head back to the airport for a 2:30 flight to Panama City. Our meeting with Victor Carranza is at 6:00 in the evening. And if he is true to form, he may insist on taking us out to dinner afterward, to a restaurant that he owns on the beach there. So eat a light lunch, because his dinners are extravagant."

"So I guess I'm not invited to go?" Janice asked.

Steve made a pained expression, and said, "Victor is a funny man, and by 'funny' I mean, he is very set in his ways. When you conduct business with him, it is all business. He generally frowns upon a business partner bringing a wife and family with him. He doesn't like distractions. And we want to make a good impression on him, so I suggest just the four of us go, because that was all I told him were coming. Sorry, Janice."

"Oh, that's all right. I'll just hang out with Felicia, *again*." she said, smiling toward Felicia, who smiled back at her and raised a beer glass.

≈ 20 ≈

They were up early, to catch their flight to Quito. Calvin got up early too, and told his mom that he was going to the lodge to help Emillio. She didn't like it, especially with people being kidnapped from the lodge, but Steve assured her that he would be fine as long as he stayed with Emillio, and the other workers. "Besides, what am I going to do here in town?" Calvin asked. Finally she gave her approval, and he ran down to the dock to flag down a water taxi.

When Calvin got to the lodge, he knew right away that something was up. Instead of separate crews working on their particular projects, there was a mass meeting. Everyone was gathered at the kitchen, and the talk was low and serious. He found Emillio, who was listening to Ortega give out instructions to the men. That was when Calvin noticed that all the men were armed with some sort of weapon. The guns were few, but axes and machetes were in abundance. One man was armed with bow and arrows.

"What's going on, Emillio?"

"Good morning, Calvin. Perhaps you should not be here today."

"Why? We're not hunting today?"

"Yes, I will hunt, and the cook will cook, but everyone else will be doing something else. Atan, who was kidnapped, has still not returned, and his family is greatly concerned. Today, because Senor Steve is away, everyone has agreed to stop work, and search for Atan. We will search the jungle all around our camp, and if we encounter the strangers,... well, that is why everyone is armed."

Calvin jumped, because something touched him on the back of the leg. He turned to see the tapir nuzzling him, no doubt looking for a free hand-out.

"Ah, your friend has found you!" Emillio said. "She is your constant companion now! You should name her!"

"Is it a girl? I thought it was boy."

"I think it is a girl."

"What is a good girl's name?"

"I like Loretta!"

"Sounds good to me. Hello Loretta. Are you hungry?"

"Loretta is always hungry."

"So everyone is going out to find Atan?"

"Yes, this is what Steve should have done, instead of running off to Quito. Atan's family is very upset. They want to know where he went. Some of the men are angry, because they say that Steve did not really pay the ransom. But Ortega has told them that he knows the ransom was paid, because he himself nailed the money to the tree. So the fault is not with Steve, but with the worthless people who took the money, but did not release Atan. Jungle people are people of their word! When they do not do as they say they will do, then to others, they are *worthless,* and their words are empty!"

"So where will we be hunting for food today?"

"Today we hunt for caymen, and I know just the place. There is a swamp up the river, where caymen are as numerous as frogs!"

"Exactly what is a caymen?" Calvin asked.

"A giant lizard, similar to a crocodile or gator. I will show you! Come, we will prepare the canoe."

Meanwhile, back in Coca, Janice and Felicia drove the men to the hotel to get Homer and Doc, and they all went to the airport. Their flight left on time. The girls went back to town, because Felicia said she had some business lined up for today.

Arriving in Quito before noon, the guys got a taxi to El Banco De Americana Del Sur, where they explained what they wanted to do, and the banker gleefully opened accounts for the three Americans, with initial deposits of $25,000 each. Of course, with deposits of that amount, they could apply for dual citizenship in Ecuador, so all three of them went ahead and did the paperwork for that as well.

All paperwork complete, they checked the time, and saw that they had just enough time to eat a quick lunch at KFC across the street, and then hailed a taxi back to the airport.

On the flight to Panama, Travis and Doc sat together. This gave Doc the opportunity to ask Travis some personal questions.

Travis, how are you doing?"

"Pretty well, Doc, but that's not what you're really asking, is it?"

"No, I'm referring to that little matter I helped you with. What was it? Five years ago?"

"Yes, right after I came back from Greece. The matter with the sorcerer?"

"Yes, has that been a problem?"

"Nope! You did a good job, Doc. I've kept it buried pretty well, I think. Not one incidence since!"

"That's great. So I guess the least said about it, the better?"

"That's right. I came close to calling it forth when I was in Egypt last November, but I resisted."

"That's real good! You have a sound psyche, Travis, or else you couldn't suppress it like that. I am still amazed at the details of that case. Never seen one like it before, or since."

"Like you said, the least said about it, the better, Doc."

They landed in Panama City at 4:35, claimed their suitcases, and grabbed a taxi, which took them to their hotel, then they immediately set out, with their rock collection, for the Institution de Gemology, which was like a co-op for the buying and selling of raw gems and precious metals that were mined anywhere in South or Central America. This was where Steve had met Victor Carranza the first two times he met with him. The place was known for its high level of security, and for maintaining the anonymity of the dealers and producers who bought and sold there. There were no sales receipts, or records of sales or purchases. All transactions were conducted behind closed doors, in cash, or precious metals, so there was never a paper trail for any tax agency to use as evidence. It was sort of like a high level flea market. As they got out of the taxi, Steve gave them a few pointers.

"Victor does not get in a hurry. When we lay the stones out for him to look at, just stand back and be patient, and let him do the talking. We start at six, he might study the stones uninterrupted for two hours, before he comes to a conclusion on their value. Don't rush him, or try to help him evaluate the stones. He doesn't like that. As I say, just lay out the stones, and be patient.

"So we could be here until eight, waiting on him to evaluate the stones?" Doc asked.

"Yes, maybe even later than that." Steve replied.

"Maybe we should have eaten dinner before the meeting."

"There's no time now. Besides, I told you that after the evaluation, Victor will want to take us to *his* restaurant to eat."

"My stomach will be growling by then!"

"Tell your stomach to cool it! Stay close to me as we go through security."

They had to pass through a metal detector, and submit to a physical pat-down. They also had to open their bags to show what items they were bringing into the building. Carranza had already reserved a lab for them to meet, and show their treasures. When they got there a little early, they found Victor already there, with a bald headed nerd, and a big man who stayed back in the shadows,...presumably his security man, who could have passed for a hit man for the Chicago Mob.

"Steve! How good to see you again!" Victor said. "And I see that you have brought your partners this time! Good, I think it is prudent that I deal with all of you, because of the unpredictable nature of the rain forest. People have been known to disappear there! It would be a shame if you disappeared, and I had no one else to deal with!"

"Fortunately, I'm still here!" Steve said. "Let me introduce you to my partners."

"Yes, and please, let's keep it on a first name basis. I have a hard time remembering last names anyway. All of you may call me Victor, and this very bald gentleman with a magnifying glass is Alberto, he is my chief gemologist. And the big man in the shadows is Gustavo. Now your partners?"

"All four of us are equal investors in this venture. This is Homer, a businessman from Alabama."

"Howdy." Homer said.

"This is Doc, he is a doctor of psychiatry from Birmingham."

"Good to meet you, Victor."

"Likewise, Doc."

"And this is Travis. He is an insurance investigator."

"Hmm, that's an interesting occupation."

"It keeps me busy." Travis said.

"Well, now that we have been introduced, I can't wait to see what you have brought me!" Victor said. "If they are anything like your last offerings, they should be very interesting!"

"I think you'll be impressed!" Steve said. "Especially with *this* one!" He pulled a large crystal out of his pocket, and set it on the examination table in front of Victor.

"Madre de Dios!" Victor exclaimed. He resisted the temptation to touch the stone, before he got the magnifying glass away from Alberto, and closely examined the gem. He finally turned the stone in the light of the evening sun that pierced through the window, to see how the light illuminated the stone.

"I am speechless!" Victor finally said. "This is crazy to believe that an emerald this big could also be a trapiche emerald! I have never seen anything like this before! Yes, yes, I will let you examine it, Alberto!" He stepped back and handed the glass back to his gemologist, as he asked a few questions about their mine site.

"I know you are not willing to divulge the exact location of your mine, and I respect your privacy. But I must know, one thing: Is there evidence of any unusual geological conditions in connection with this site? There has to be something similar to my site, but also something very different."

"Well," Steve said, "There are some unusual conditions that I have documented, but I am not ready to release my findings yet."

"I respect that! Perhaps when you have confirmed your findings, you will share them with me?"

"Yes, I will do that." Steve said.

"You know, the formation of emeralds is in fact, an *accident* of nature." Victor said. "Very rarely do all the right minerals exist in one place, in just the right amounts, and under the right conditions, at just the right time, to produce emeralds, so it could be true that emeralds are the rarest of gem stones! And trapiche emeralds are the rarest of the rare! You know, emeralds have no industrial value. They are not as hard as diamonds. Rubies can be used to produce lasers. But emeralds are just *pretty*! Their value is determined by the demand of the market, and the market is demanding trapiche emeralds. You are sitting on a gold mine my friends!"

"That's good to know." Homer said.

"Please, let me see the rest of your stones!"

Steve hefted a big white linen bag up on the table. (Actually it was a bed sheet he had 'borrowed' from their hotel room.) He rolled out the linen, displaying 134 pounds of rocks, all of which contained at least one emerald. Victor was like a kid in a candy store, as he browsed past the stones, pausing to closely examine every one. He was in a state of ecstasy as he spoke lovingly about the stones.

"You know, emeralds are like, the *queen* of gemstones! Emeralds were one of only three precious gemstones that adorned the crown and jewelry of Queen Cleopatra, and many other Egyptian pharaohs dating back to antiquity! Why were emeralds so coveted by ancient kings, and are still coveted even today? I am told that there is a psychological reason for emeralds being so coveted, which you might find interesting, Doc."

"Really?"

"Yes! It is said that the human eye is more sensitive to the color green, than any other color. Therefore, the color green conveys comforting, soothing images to the brain. And since emeralds come is so many different shades and deep hues of green, that it is inevitable that one could get *lost* gazing into the depths of the stones! Like being mesmerized by gazing into the deep green eyes of a beautiful woman,… or a wild Bengal tiger! It is a green that can be hypnotically soothing, and exciting at the same time! Do you not agree, Travis?"

"I'm not allowed to say, Victor. My wife's eyes are blue."

"Ah! Then you should be excited by blue sapphires!" He paused at one emerald, picked it up, and studied it closely. "Alberto! Here is another exceptional stone! I will set it out from the others."

Alberto was already beginning his evaluation of the stones, by applying small adhesive pre-numbered stickers on each stone, for future reference. He then looked closely at each stone, and wrote in a notebook, the number of the stone, and the approximate estimated karats of each stone. These numbers would later be translated into dollar values, when they attempted to negotiate payment for the stones.

"I will tell you the truth, my friends. I have long believed that my mines in Colombia were the only sources of emeralds in the New World, but I am seeing now that I was wrong! Not only are my mines not the only ones, but neither are they the *best*! I think all of you should think seriously about selling your mine to me! From what I have seen, I must give you a very good price for your claim, because the emeralds from there are exceptional!"

"That is something that my partners and I have not discussed, but perhaps before our next meeting, we will do so." Steve said.

Homer started to say something, but then decided against it. If there was one thing Homer understood about business, it was that you don't want to lay all your cards out on the table at the start of a hand. There was still a lot he didn't understand about the emerald business, and so he kept his mouth shut. Later, he was glad he did.

Steve was right, in that the evaluation of the stones took over two hours But once Alberto had examined each stone, and recorded it in his notebook, Victor suggested that they go to dinner. They left the stones in the locked room with Alberto and Gustavo, and requested a guard to watch the door while they were gone. They took two taxis across town to the fancy seafood restaurant that Victor owned, called appropriately, 'Victor's Place'. Steve rode with Victor and Alberto, while Travis, Homer and Doc rode in the second car. As they rode to the restaurant, Homer made a confession.

"I almost said something I shouldn't have, when Victor suggested that he buy us out."

"And what was that?" Doc asked.

"I almost said, 'we can't sell you the mine, because we don't own the mineral rights to it'."

"I'm glad you kept that to yourself." Travis said. "We can't sell the mine, because technically, and legally, it's not really a mine."

"Yeah, I realized that, right before I opened my mouth. In fact, he might not even want to buy our emeralds, if he knows where they came from."

"No," Travis replied, "I think if he knew we were mining them illegally, he would still want to buy them, but he would say, 'don't tell me where they came from'. I think he is so impressed with the quality, that he *has* to buy them. But he would most likely tell his buyers that they came from *his* mines in Colombia. But as long as he pays us for them, who cares?"

"I know I don't!" Doc said. "And by the way, how much does Steve estimate those stones are worth? How are we to know what a fair price is? Did he tell either one of you?"

"Not me." Homer said.

"Well," Travis said, "The day before you guys arrived, he told me that what was on the table was probably $200,000 dollars worth, but I don't know if he meant wholesale or retail value. And that big emerald that Victor went ga-ga over wasn't part of what he showed me. I guess we'll depend on Steve to know the value, and trust him to get the right price."

They arrived at the restaurant, and the matra'd came out to meet them, and told Victor that they had prepared his personal dining room for them. Victor said he wanted to give his guests a tour of the kitchen first, so they followed him back through the kitchen, and met the head chef, and saw how clean the kitchen was. When they finally went to their reserved dining room, Alberto was already there with his notebook and calculator, still crunching numbers. Victor said,

"Gentlemen, you are my guests, so I encourage you to order anything from the menu that you desire! Drinks included! After we have eaten, we will see what Alberto has come up with as to the value of your stones. Then I will make an offer, and we will reach our agreement."

Homer thought: *Yeah, and him treating us to dinner is going to influence us to take his offer, even if it is a bit low.* He understood how shrewd businessmen operated.

They looked over the menu, noting that there were no prices on anything. Not that they were having to pay for it anyway, but it spoke to the kind of clientele that Victor's Place catered to. Those who were so rich, that the price was not a factor in their choice of what to eat. This was probably the most expensive place that any of the Alabama natives had ever eaten. So they did as Victor instructed, and ordered what looked good. Almost every choice included lobster in one form or another.

The dinner was incredibly good, and the after dinner drinks were even better. Steve was kicking his story-telling into high gear when Alberto approached Victor, and slid a folder in front of him. Victor opened the folder, studied Alberto's evaluation, and made a few notes with his pen, then announced that he had an offer.

"I depend on Alberto's expertise in evaluating stones. He has an uncanny ability to recognize value with just one look. Considering that most of the emeralds you brought me today are trapiche emeralds, their value is very great. First I will give you the projection of their value retail, which is what I will try to sell them for, then I will give my offer for the stones.

"The retail value of the stones, after they have been cleaned, cut, polished, and advertised, is roughly 2.6 million dollars. My offer to you, for the rough stones is slightly less than half that, at 1.2 million."

Everyone's jaw dropped, even Steve's. This was much more than even he had hoped they would get.

"Is that an acceptable offer?" Victor asked.

Homer almost blurted out 'we'll take it!', but they all waited on Steve to respond for them. He finally collected his wits and said,

"Yes, Victor, that is an acceptable offer!"

"Great! Gustavo! Bring the money."

Gustavo came forward with a big brown leather satchel, and set it in the chair beside Victor.

"Count out 1.2 million, Gustavo."

Gustavo emotionlessly reached in the satchel with his big hands, and brought out four bundles of new U.S. $100 dollar bills with each handful, and slapped them solidly on the table. "Forty,... eighty,... one-twenty,...one-sixty,...two hundred,...two-forty,...two-eighty,... three twenty..."

The partners watched in wide-eyed amazement as the stack of cash grew larger and larger. They had never thought of it before, but 1.2 million in cash was a *big* pile of cash! They were starting to wonder how they were going to travel with such a sum in their possession.

"Five-sixty,...six hundred,...six-forty,...six-eighty,...seven-twenty,...seven-sixty,...eight hundred." He stopped because the satchel was empty. He took it and placed it beside the wall, and hefted another satchel into the chair, and continued counting. "Eight-forty,... eight-eighty,..."

The cash just stacked higher and higher, and Doc couldn't help letting out a slight giggle at the insane sight. It was unbelievable.

"Nine-sixty,...one million,...one million-forty,...one million-eighty,...one million, one-twenty,...one million, one-sixty,...one million, two hundred thousand dollars!" Gustavo stood up, brushed his hair back, then picked up the satchel and returned to his place against the wall.

"Thank you, Gustavo! Well gentlemen, here is your cash. I always seal a deal with a hand-shake." He stood up, and shook hands with all four men.

"It was a pleasure doing business with you men." Victor said. "Steve, just let me know when you have another shipment ready for me, and I will arrange to meet you again at the Institute. Remember also, that I have a Western Union branch here in this restaurant, for your convenience. I bid you gentlemen a good night, and a safe trip home!" With that, he, Alberto, and Gustavo left the restaurant, and left them staring at a big pile of money. They sat down to admire it. Doc asked the obvious.

"How are we going to get all this back home?"

"You heard what Victor said about the Western Union." Steve said. "He had a Western Union office put right here in his restaurant, just for the convenience of his business associates. We can wire all this money into your accounts in Quito, now that they are set up. That's what I did with the money from the first two times I've been here."

"What if I want to wire mine to my account in the States?" Doc asked.

"You can do that," Homer said, "But it would be stupid, because then you could be taxed on it."

"But I thought you said the money we made would be tax free?"

"Yeah, on the Lodge. But this is like, money under the table." Homer said. "This money should go into your account in Quito, and no one in the States needs to know about it."

"So let's divide it up first." Steve said.

"It feels like we robbed a bank!" Travis said.

"Doesn't it though?" Homer agreed.

"Okay, we have 1.2 million,…split five ways, that's two hundred, forty thousand each…" Steve began.

"I thought we were dividing it four ways?" Doc said.

"The fifth cut is the building fund for the lodge." Homer reminded him. "And it is only temporary, until the building expenses are paid for, and it starts making money itself."

"Oh yeah, I forgot about that." Doc said.

Travis smiled and said, "Guys, do you realize that we each invested $121,000 of our money to get this project started, and even before the lodge is *built*, we have made $240,000? Guys, we have *doubled* our investment in the blink of an eye!"

"Now that's what I call a great investment!" Homer said, as he sipped his drink. "I'm glad I got in on it!"

"So am I!" Doc said.

"But you guys realize that there is still a lot of work to do." Steve said. "You've been to the lodge, and you see what all there is to be done. I would appreciate you guys helping out any way you can."

"It looks like I'll be right there with you for awhile, Steve." Travis said.

"Yes, and I appreciate that. But you two, if there any way you can get away and spend some time down here, it will help."

"Before I came down here," Homer said, "I put out notice that I was looking to hire a school teacher, and a doctor, both fluent in Spanish, for the lodge."

"That's good. Maybe by the time we get the school and medical clinic built, we can find someone. Tell you what, let's wire this money out, then go to our motel and lay out a few plans. You two are going back home tomorrow morning, and Travis and I are going back to the lodge. We need to do some serious partner planning tonight while we are still together."

"Yes, we do." Homer agreed. They recruited a couple of waiters to help them gather up their mountain of cash, and carry it to the Western Union desk. Money sent, they hailed a taxi back to their hotel.

⊰ 21 ⊱

When they arrived back in Quito the next morning, they had about an hour to wait for the flight back to Coca. Steve went to get a hamburger, while Travis watched their bags at the boarding gate. That was when his cell phone rang, and it was General Morgan.

"Hello, Travis."

"Good morning General. Anything to report?"

"Yes, and I am afraid that it is not good news. Are you sitting down?"

"Yes, go ahead."

"I won't beat around the bush, Travis. Your house burned to the ground this morning."

Travis was stunned. Morgan waited for him to comprehend the news, and say something. Finally he said,

"So what happened? Did an assassin use a fire-bomb?"

"No, I'm afraid it was nothing as dramatic as that. Remember I told you that we had agents in your home, posing as you and Janice?"

"Yeah."

"Well, they were cooking breakfast, when your dog started barking. The agent thought it might be an assassin, so he turned the stove off, to go see about it. At least he *thought* he turned it off. He actually turned *on* the back burner, which had a skillet of oil on it. By the time he got back from checking out the disturbance, the kitchen was fully engulfed in flames. He called 911, saying he was Travis Lee, and requested the fire department, but by the time they got there, it was too late. All they could do was stand back and watch it burn."

Travis sighed. "The Laurel Grove Fire Department has never been accused of being competent."

"I'm sorry, Travis. That's about all I can say."

158

"This is really going to up-set Janice! Actually, I'm pretty pissed off myself!"

"Apparently some of the volunteer firemen know you, and when the agent told him that he was Travis Lee, well, there was a lot of explanation that had to be made. The agent told them that he was house sitting for you, which is technically the truth. So now the cat is out of the bag, about you being out of the country. Our stake out is blown. You might want to come back home to deal with your insurance agent."

"No, I will call him later. He can go out and assess the damage without me being there."

"Don't worry about securing the property. I have agents here to make sure nothing is disturbed. You'll probably want to pick through the ashes for personal items."

Yeah, personal items, Travis thought. *If the house burned to the ground, there probably isn't much left to recover.* "Yeah, I'm sure we'll want to do that when we get home. Can you make sure the chickens and the dog are fed until we get back?"

"Oh absolutely. Don't worry about any of that. So when do you plan to get back?"

"Well, I'm kind of in the middle of a project down here, so it still might be awhile."

"No problem! I'll keep my guys here as long as you need them. It's the least I can do. And listen, I know you have insurance that should cover this, but if it doesn't, I'll make sure it's covered. I am privy to several undercover 'slush funds', stocked by senators who don't ask questions, when it is ear tagged 'covert military'. So I can replace anything that was lost, except things of sentimental value."

"I'm thinking about all those unfinished manuscripts I had there. This is going to be a big blow to my writing career. Damn! The more I think about it, the more I realize how much I lost!"

"I'm sorry, Travis!"

"I know. You already said that. What's done is done though. Let me think about how I'm going to break this to Janice. Is there anything else, General?"

"No, but if anything comes up, I'll pass it on to you."

"Thanks."

He put his phone away, and slumped back in his chair. He knew there were a lot worse things that could happen in life, than loosing their home, but right now, this seemed pretty bad. He honestly didn't know how he was going to break the news to Janice. Since she got here, she has said nothing but how she can't wait to get back to her own home, and her own bed! This was going to totally devastate her world. And considering all he had lost in that fire, it was devastating to him as well. For the next month he was going to think of *something else* he had lost in the fire, and be devastated all over again.

Steve showed up with a bag-full of McDonald's burgers, and offered him one. He slowly unwrapped it, while Steve miraculously talked and ate at the same time, babbling on and on, about their deal with Victor. Finally he realized that Travis was not as happy as he was, and asked why. Travis told him about the fire, and that sobered Steve's mood as well.

"Wow. Have you told Janice yet?"

"How can I? I have the only phone."

"Oh yeah. So she doesn't know yet?"

"Nope!"

"Well, I don't want to be the one to break it to her, because she really has her heart set on going back home!"

"I know."

"So how are you going to tell her?"

"I am open for suggestions."

They sat munching on hamburgers, deep in thought. Finally Travis spoke.

"I think I'm *not* going to tell her for now. If I tell her, she will want to go home immediately, and I think I need to be here, helping you get the lodge up and running."

"So how are you going to keep something like that from her? She's bound to hear it from someone back at home."

"I've got our only phone, and you heard her the other day. She doesn't like having the phone, because she is afraid she will accidentally 'spill the beans' that we are not really at home. So as long as I have the phone, how will she find out?"

"Good question. But you know you'll have to tell her eventually."

"Yeah, but I'll put it off as long as I can. I'm going to see if the insurance will replace the house, and try to get it re-built before we get back home."

"Wow, that could take six months!"

"Then that's how long we'll be here then. Hey, I just thought of something. If my house burned to the ground, then any calls to my home can't be forwarded to me down here. The only ones who can reach me, will be the ones who call my cell phone number, and very few people have that number. So I should get a lot fewer calls because of that."

"Yeah, that makes sense."

"I need you and Felicia to help me find some way to make Janice happy to be down here. Some reason to stay and accomplish something, that will take her mind off wanting to go home. Got any ideas?"

"At the present time, my mind is drawing a total blank. But let's give it serious thought on the way back to Coca."

"Yeah."

<hr>

It was mid-morning when they arrived back in Coca, and they were surprised that only Janice was there to pick them up.

"Where is Felicia?" Steve asked.

"She said she had 'business' in town, and for me to pick you up," she said coldly.

"Is there something wrong, Dear?' Travis asked.

"Why would anything be wrong?"

"Well, I just thought that you sound a little ticked off about something."

"Your son did not come home last night!"

"What?"

"He sent word to me by way of a boat driver, that he intended to spend the night at the lodge!"

"That's no problem!" Steve said. "I spend lots of nights at the lodge, so I can get an early start the next morning."

"He didn't even come tell me himself! He sent word with a man that could barely speak English!"

"Oh, that must have been Pepe!" Steve said. "His English is getting better though."

"I don't see any problem, Dear. Calvin seems to be having a great time!"

"I'm glad someone is! One of you drive! I am too upset!" Janice said.

"You drive, Travis. I need to get off on main street, to order supplies for the lodge."

"Okay." It was a very short drive. They were almost home, when Steve said, "Let me off here, at the hardware store. Don't wait on me. I'll walk home."

As soon as Travis pulled away, Janice unloaded on him.

"I am not so up-set about Calvin spending the night in the jungle, Travis, because I know he can handle it! No, what really upset me was something I didn't want to say in front of Steve! It's something I found out about Felicia while you were gone!"

"What did you find out about her?"

"Did you know that she is a *prostitute*?"

"A prostitute? Nah, I think you are just letting your imagination get out of control."

"Imagination, nothing! She *told* me that she is a prostitute, and that Steve *knows* all about it, and is *fine* with it! It's like, her home business! That's how she makes money to support her mother and two younger sisters! She said she has never asked Steve for money!"

"Are you sure that's what she said?"

"Of course I'm sure! You think I imagined all that?"

"Steve hasn't mentioned a word about it. He just introduced her as his girlfriend."

"So is that creepy, or what? I mean, she's been turning tricks since you left yesterday morning! I haven't seen her since yesterday afternoon! She came back to get something, but then she was gone again!"

"Wow, I never saw that coming. But then, if it's true, it's not really any of our business, is it dear?"

"What do you mean, none of our business! I feel like I was lied to! I thought they were in love! I thought,…I don't know what I thought! All I know for sure, is that I am ready to go home, and I mean right now! I have had enough of this place, and these people, and the rain forest! I want to go home and sleep in my own bed, in my own house, and go to the mall, and get a kid's meal from McDonald's!"

"But you don't even like McDonald's, Dear."

"Well I do now! Anything from home is better than eating goat meat, and roaches, and who knows what else! I don't care if I can't go to our house right now. I'll go live with my parents, or even *Marla*, if she will take me in! I just want to get out of here!"

"I know you're upset, but you know you can't go home right now. It's too dangerous."

"I know, but I can't bear to be in this place another day!"

Travis gritted his teeth, because he knew that they had no home to go back to. He couldn't bring himself to tell her that her home, along with all her memories, had burned to the ground. He had to come up with something that was goods news.

"I tell you what, Dear, since we can't go home right now, why don't we take a vacation, just the two of us? And maybe when we get back, you'll have a little better outlook on things."

"What kind of a vacation did you have in mind?"

"Well, why don't we go to Quito, and just take our time seeing things? There are a lot of historical things to see around Quito. It is an old Spanish colonial city. There is a whole lot to see."

"What about Calvin?"

"We can leave him here. He's having such a good time that he camped out in the jungle last night. That must mean he likes it pretty well."

"Do we have enough money to be able to do that? I mean, we didn't bring much cash with us."

"We have our debit account back at home. And oh yeah, you haven't asked me about what we got for the emeralds!"

"How much did you get?"

"My part alone was $240,000 dollars! I had it wire transferred to the account I just opened in Quito. So we have plenty of money, to do whatever we want to do!"

"Wow! In that case, can we do something I have wanted to do since I was a little girl? I've never asked you before, because I knew it was expensive to go there. But since we've got all that money…"

"Just tell me what it is."

"I want to go to the Galapagos Islands, and see all those strange animals that I've seen on those nature programs! Can we do that? I mean, the Galapagos are islands owned by Ecuador, so we might as well see them while we are here!"

"If we do, will you promise to try to endure our stay here as long as we need to? To put up with Felicia, and the critters, and the poor living conditions, and who knows what else that might pop up?"

Janice had to think about that awhile. "I'll let you know. Are you going out to the lodge with Steve?"

"Of course. I need to make sure Calvin is okay."

"Then I'll let you know tonight, when you come back to Coca."

"Fair enough."

They were parked on the curb at Steve's house. They got out to unload the suitcases before Steve got there. In the house, they realized that Felicia still was not there.

"See? She's still gone!" Janice said.

"Well, let's not judge her. After all, this is a different culture, and their business is *their* business. We are just their guests. And keep in mind that us being here is a great imposition on them too, but they are not complaining. So please try not to get bent out of shape over anything you hear or see, because what you are experiencing is a different culture. And we should be tolerant of other cultures, especially when we are visiting them. This is their home."

"Okay, I'll try. Have you heard anything from home?"

"I called General Morgan from the airport in Quito. He didn't have much to report. No second attack yet, but it could come at any time. Did I tell you that he has agents living in our house, posing as us?"

"Yes, you told me that. I hope they don't bother any of our personal stuff."

"I'm sure they won't. Everything will be right where we left it." *Or at least everything's ashes will be right where we left them,* he thought. Then as an afterthought he said, "Janice, didn't you copy all our computer files about a week before we left?"

"Yes, once a month, like I always do. Why?"

"And that would include all of my writing files as well?"

"That's right. All your writing files, as well as all my files, I copied them and put in the safe in the basement, like I always do. Why?"

"Oh, just in case they try to get on our computer, and lose my writing files. I forgot all about those before we left, or I would have brought a copy with me to work on. I'm glad you thought to back them up."

He was REALLY glad she had backed them up, or he would have lost a lot of irreplaceable manuscripts.

"I like to think that I do something right every once in a while." she said.

164

"You do, Janice, and I appreciate that."

"Hello! Is anyone home!" Steve yelled from the front door.

"We are in here." Travis replied from the kitchen.

"Hey, so Felicia is not back yet?"

"No," Janice replied.

"Well, no problem. I'll leave a note for her to have dinner ready for us tonight, unless you are going to be here, Janice."

"Are you going to the lodge with us, or staying here?" Travis asked.

"Oh, I might as well stay here." She said, even though facing the jungle seemed preferable to facing Felicia, after she found out what she did about her. "I'll tell her that we need to fix dinner. When you see Calvin, tell him that I want to talk to him!"

"Will do."

"So are you ready to head to the lodge?"

"Yeah, let's go."

They went down to the riverfront and flagged down a water taxi, and headed up river. As they rode, Travis carried on a conversation with Steve, over the whine of the outboard motor.

"I didn't tell Janice that the house burned."

"I wondered if you did."

"But she was already up-set about something else she found out while we were gone."

"What was that?"

"She said that Felicia told her that she is a prostitute!"

"You mean Janice didn't know that already?"

"I guess not, but neither did I, so it was a shock to me too."

"It must have slipped my mind, I guess." Steve said. "I told someone, I guess it must have been Homer. But I thought surely Homer would have told you."

"Nope!"

"Sorry about that, but I thought you and Janice knew. I met Felicia 'professionally' three years ago. When I bought the house in Coca, I offered to let her stay there rent free, if she would maintain it for me, even when I'm out of the country. It's been a good arrangement. My only stipulation was that she not bring her work home with her, and so far, she takes her dates elsewhere. You know, I was wondering why Janice was asking about me and Felicia getting married! Now I understand. She didn't know that we don't have that kind of relationship!"

"Well, she does now."

"I didn't mean to traumatized her."

"I think she'll get over it. This whole trip has been one really big culture shock for her. She has traveled before, but she never had to *live* among the people in another culture, and that is what's so shocking to her. I'm sure she and Felicia will still be good friends."

"Well, for what it's worth, prostitution in this part of the world is a pretty respectable profession. Not that Janice will change her mind about it, but it is, what it is. A woman with Felicia's beauty can make a lot of money in the profession. I have encouraged her to invest some of her profits in stocks and about a year ago she started an IRA at the bank I use in Quito. The first year, she invested the maximum amount they allowed, so she is making really good money, for a part time job. Since she moved into my house, I have not given her a dime of my money, because she always has plenty of her own. I know there is a social stigma attached to having a girlfriend who is a prostitute, and such a thing in the States, especially Alabama, would be scandalous. But hey, I've been married two times, and both times the divorce was like the most excruciating pain you could imagine! I lost everything I owned twice! I'm just glad there were no kids involved. But with Felicia there is no pressure, no binding commitments. It's like getting free milk, without having to buy the cow!"

"I'm sure Felicia would be flattered to know she was being compared to a cow!"

"She probably wouldn't understand the analogy."

The boat had to swerve to miss a big log in the water. They had to hang on, and lean into the turn.

"I don't think I will ever get married again. For me, there just aren't enough reasons to justify it."

"It's not for everyone, I guess."

The pilot cut his engine to turn and enter the crescent shaped harbor of the lodge. It was not the rainy season, so the shallow places in the river were starting to show. One of them was entering the harbor from the river. Boats larger than the shallow draw water taxis were going to have trouble entering in the dry season.

"I'm going to have to get a dredge out here to deepen the entrance to our lagoon, if we plan to get bigger ships in here."

Travis nodded.

They knew something was wrong when they got out of the boat, because there was no one working on the foundation of the main lodge. In fact, they saw no activity anywhere, except the kitchen area. Only the cook, and a young assistant were there, preparing vegetables for the noon meal.

"Where is everyone?" Steve asked the cook.

Reluctantly, he replied, "They are not here."

"I can see that! Where is everyone?" Steve asked again.

"They go to find Atan's killers!"

"His killers!"

"Yes, they find Atan yesterday, in the jungle. He was shot in the back with a shotgun."

"Where is my son?" Travis asked, almost afraid he would find out that he was in on the man-hunt.

"Your son up river, with Emillio,....fishing I think."

Steve was so flustered that he didn't know what to ask first. Finally he asked, "Who authorized this man-hunt?"

"It was no one, and it was everyone! When Atan was found, everyone was very angry! They say, 'this cannot happen', and everyone get a weapon, and they go into the jungle!"

"Was Ortega with them?"

"Yes, everyone was angry. They said to tell you, when you get back, that this is something they must do. If bad people live in the jungle, then no visitors come here, and no one will have a job."

"Well, that's probably so, but I wish they had waited to talk to me first! We might want to be more diplomatic in our dealings with those people."

"Hey, if they killed Atan, there's not much to talk about." Travis said. "And your people realize that."

"Yes, they do what they have to do!" the cook said.

"Where is Atan's body?" Steve asked.

"They took it to Coca yesterday, to his family there."

"When did they leave here today?" Steve asked.

"They leave at sunrise. They think they know where the killers are. They intend to kill them all."

"Oh god! That's all we need, is to have a massacre associated with our lodge!" Steve lamented.

"But you have to admit that they're right." Travis said. "Something like this needs to be nipped in the bud, before it becomes a bigger problem. The future of out investment here rests on it."

"I know, but I didn't want to start a war with those guys!"

"Hey, they kidnapped and killed Atan! The war has already been declared!" Travis said.

"But we still don't know who we are dealing with! It could be some cut-throat drug smugglers from across the border with Colombia. Those guys are not someone to trifle with!"

"Well, it looks like we'll know something soon, if all our guys went to get them."

"I just hope they don't walk into an ambush! They should have waited to discuss this with me!"

They heard another boat entering the lagoon. It was Emillio and Calvin. Travis met them at the landing and caught their tie off rope.

"Dad! You're back!"

"Yeah."

"Look what we caught! A 55 pound catfish! I know, it doesn't look like a catfish, but that's what Emillio said it is. Catfish are orange and black down here." They hauled it out on the landing with a rope, where it flopped and slapped its massive tail.

"This should be enough for lunch and dinner." Emillio said. We used a baby anaconda for bait!"

"I hope the mama anaconda doesn't find that out." Travis said.

"Did you hear that they found Atan?" Calvin asked.

"Yeah, and I heard that everyone is gone looking for his killer. Steve is angry about it, because they didn't discuss it with him first."

"The security chief didn't want to wait for Steve, because he said that Steve didn't have the stomach to do what was needed to be done." Calvin said.

"You mean Ortega?"

"Yeah, that's his name."

"So what did he mean by that?"

"I don't know, but everyone agreed with him. You ought to have seen them leave! They were armed with every kind of weapon you can imagine!"

Steve was still at the kitchen when someone came out of the jungle and approached the kitchen. Steve spoke to him, then immediately ran down to the landing.

"Emillio! I need for you to go into Coca right away, and get the doctor from the main street clinic, and bring him here! And he needs to bring a nurse with him, and plenty of dressings for wounds! We have a lot of hacked up people on their way here. The doctor needs to be here when they arrive!"

"Is it our people that are hacked up?"

"Yes! We need dressings and antibiotics! And go by the herbalist and get a liter of sangre de drago! Quickly!"

"Si, senor! Calvin, take the catfish to the kitchen! I must go!" He untied his boat, and shoved away from the bank, started his outboard, and headed to Coca.

"This is what I was afraid of!" Steve said, as the messenger arrived from the kitchen, drinking a bottle of water. He had blood spattered on his face and arms.

"Rondo, tell me the truth," Steve said. "Was anyone killed?"

"Si! Many were killed, but none of ours! We attacked them with machetes, as they were waking up. They did not have time to get their guns! Ortega shot anyone who tried to escape. We killed the others with machetes and clubs, but they fought back fiercely, and we have many wounded, but none are killed. We killed them all, and burned their camp!"

"Was there any women or children there?" Travis asked.

"No, it was all men. We think they were smugglers from Colombia."

"What were they smuggling?"

"Drugs. Coca base. We burned that too!"

"Oh god! That's all we need, is to get on the toes of a drug cartel! They'll send their hired army to wipe us out!"

"No, they were not cartel. They were farmers,...local people. Not connected to any cartels." the messenger said.

"How do you know that?" Steve asked.

"Because we know some of them from town. Indios."

"You killed people that you knew from town?"

"Yes, they were the ones watching us here. Up to no good! Ortega said that we kill them, and their families think that they were killed by the cartel. Cartels do not like farmers making coca base on their own!

It cuts into their profits. That's why we burned their camp, and their product, to look like a cartel hit."

Steve just hung his head. He obviously did not approve of what they had done, but he would save the lecture for Ortega, who seemed to be the ring-leader of this pre-emptive strike.

"How long will it be before the others get here?" Steve asked.

"Probably thirty minutes behind me. Maybe longer for some of the wounded."

"Maybe I shouldn't have sent for a doctor." Steve mused. "If word gets out in Coca that the drug producing farmers were massacred, and then they learn that the doctor was called out *here*, they will put the two together, and know that our guys were the killers!"

"But *they* drew first blood, by killing Atan." Travis said.

"I don't think that will make any difference in the court of public opinion. Those people that were killed most likely have relatives in Coca, and this is going to cause hard feelings, something I was trying to avoid."

"So what can we do?" Travis asked.

"We need to talk to Ortega, to see what really went down, and what condition their camp was in when they left it. I hope they didn't leave any evidence of who did it. Not that there will be any kind of scientific forensics examination of the site, but we need to go there and plant evidence that will point to someone else."

"Someone like who?" Travis asked.

"Like maybe FARC, that para-military drug smuggling organization in Colombia. It would be reasonable to put the blame for this massacre on them, because it would be along the lines of something that FARC has been known to do. That's it, Travis! That's what we need to do! We'll get Ortega to take us back to the camp, and we can make things look like it was FARC that did it!"

"Maybe we should discuss it with Ortega first, and see what he says."

"Yeah, right. And I'm sure he will agree that we need to deflect blame for this away from us. Come on, let's go to the kitchen to wait on them to arrive."

When they got there, they found Calvin, and the cook's assistant hoisting the big catfish up on a tree limb, so they could clean it. Loretta, the pet tapir was all in the way. Every time Calvin turned around, he tripped over her.

"Hey Calvin, I wonder if the airline will let you carry your pet home with you?" his dad said, smiling.

"I'm not carrying *this* thing home! I don't know why she picked me out of the crowd of everybody here to hang around with, but I'm tired of her already!"

"Because you feed her!" the cook said with irritation. "If you feed her, then she becomes yours!"

The cook's assistant used a sharp knife to gut the fish, dropping its entrails into a plastic bucket. Then he cut the tough skin around the head of the catfish, and used a pair of pliers to grab the skin, and strip it down to the tail, exposing the raw flesh of the fish. Within a few minutes, the meat was filleted off the bone, and battered, ready to be fried.

"Here they come," Calvin said, pointing to the jungle with a bloody knife, as a stream of armed men somberly approached the kitchen. Just like the messenger, most of them were spattered with blood, but not their own. The first wounded man had a machete slash to his arm, but he had already treated the cut with 'dragon blood'.

Ortega was among the first to arrive, and Steve went out to meet him. Travis wanted to hear what he said, so he went out as well.

"Senor Ortega! What have you done?" Steve asked.

Without flinching, Ortega replied, "We did what needed to be done!"

"But you should have waited and talked to me first!"

"What we did, we would have done with your approval, or without! We responded the only way we *could* respond! Now, if you want to fire me, then that is your right."

"No, I'm not going to fire you. But we need to know exactly what happened."

"Yesterday we sent out search parties, looking for Atan, and we found him, about a quarter mile into the property. He had been shot in the back with a shotgun!"

"He was executed?" Travis asked.

"No, it looked like Atan was trying to escape. He was running away when he was shot, and the shooter was about 30 to 40 feet away, I guess, by examining the shot pattern. They did not intend to bury him. They left him in the jungle to rot! We were angry, so this morning before dawn, we left to attack their camp. We caught them unprepared, and killed them all. So now we have solved our problem!"

"Who were these people?" Steve asked. "Rondo said they were farmers that had produced coca base, but did you know them from town?"

"Some, yes. But most were strangers." Ortega replied.

"How will it be seen, when they are found?"

"What do you mean?"

"I mean, how will the people in Coca respond to them being killed? Will they blame us? Will their relatives seek retribution?"

Ortega scratched his stubbled chin with a hand covered with dried blood. "That is hard to say. It depends on who finds the camp, and reports the attack."

Steve explained to Ortega the plan to go back to the massacre site, and try to make it look like a FARC attack. Ortega thought this over and agreed that it would be worth the effort. If they could convince those who would find the wiped out camp, that FARC had done the deed, than that is where it will end, because there was no one stupid enough to go after the FARC for something like this.

"If we are going to plant evidence, then we'd better go there right now, before someone else finds the camp." Steve said. "Do you feel up to going back there right now."

"Yes," Ortega replied. "Their camp is about two miles in, so we had better leave right away. Let me get water, and we will go."

"Are you going with us, Travis?"

"Sure. That's the plan."

"We need a can of spray paint. I have one in my tent. I'll be right back."

While Steve was gone, Ortega returned with two more AK-47's, one for each of them. Travis checked the clip, to make sure it was loaded. When Steve returned with a small back-pack, Ortega handed him the third gun.

"What is that for?" Steve asked.

"You might need it."

"I'm not going to fight. I'm just going to plant evidence at the scene of the killings."

"You'd better take it, Steve. It might save your life, or mine!" Travis said.

"Not likely, but I'll take it with me. Someone should show me how to use it though."

After a quick explanation of how to use the gun, Steve thought about something else.

"We can't go until the doctor gets here."

"Why not?" Travis asked.

"Because I need to make sure he understands that the wounds he is here to treat, have nothing to do with the massacre that he will hear about later."

"But it will be natural for them to put the two events together, later when the massacre becomes known." Travis said. "Anyone with half a brain will assume that the two events could be related, and then there will be that suspicion."

"I know. That's why I need to be here when the doctor gets here, to convince him that it is not related."

"How will you do that?"

"Leave it to me. Senor Ortega, you and Travis go the camp, and do whatever you need to do, to make it look like a FARC attack. Can you do that?"

"Yes, Senor Steve! We can do that!" Ortega said.

"Then here, take this." Steve said, as he handed Travis the can of spray paint. "Ortega will know what to do with that. Be careful, and good luck!"

Travis and Ortega slipped into the jungle, and were on their way.

⊰ 22 ⊱

Meanwhile, back in town, Janice was sitting in the patio swing out back, waiting on Felicia to return from her two days of working the streets of Coca. Although she was shocked and somewhat angered by what she found out, it helped that Travis had put things in perspective for her. No, it wasn't her place to judge Felicia, and she had no right to impose her sense of morality on someone from a different culture. She was just a visitor here, (or at least she *hoped* she was just visiting,) and soon she would be going back home where things made sense. And then she could look back at this whole living nightmare, and maybe even laugh about it, as she told her friends about it. It would be kind of neat to look back on all this later, from a different perspective, and laugh, yes *laugh* about it.

Her eyes grew big, as she felt something large crawling across her shoulder. She couldn't see it, but she imagined it was one of those big hairy tarantula spiders, with their big venomous fangs, about to sink them into her jugular, and drink her blood. She jumped up and slapped at the same time, and felt some big insect detach from her blouse and hit the ground. She picked up the nearest weapon she could find, which was a dead limb from the overhead tree, and began smashing the large critter to pieces on the ground. "DIE! DIE! DIE, you @#%&$ bug!"

"I think you kill it, Senora." came a female voice from the corner of the house. It was the laundry woman, who had come by to pick up the dirty laundry. She walked over to Janice, who was still breathing hard from the bug mutilation she had just committed. The laundry woman looked down at what remained of the bug, just a spatter of yellow goo, surrounded by large harmless looking insect limbs.

"I think it was a large 'stick bug'," she said. "They are harmless."

"I know *that one* is harmless!" Janice replied. "It shouldn't have sneaked up on me like that!"

"I come to get your laundry." the woman said.

"Yes, yes, go ahead. I'm okay now." She looked all around for more 'stick bugs' but didn't see any, so she gingerly sat back down in the swing. The giant bugs were one of the many things she wasn't going to miss about this place. She couldn't believe the ugly word that she had uttered when she was killing that bug! It would have been embarrassing if someone she knew had heard he say that! Oh well, it was just a measuring stick of how out of her element she was, being down here where everything was creepy-crawly and hideous! She was going to feel so much better when she got back to good old Alabama, where the worst things she would find were ticks and chiggers! And well, fire ants and gnats too. But those were nothing compared to the critters they had here!

Her blood pressure got back to normal as she swung gently in the shade. She was wishing that she had gone with Travis to the lodge now, because it was getting to be boring here in town. Yes, there were lots of things to do, but not when she didn't speak the language. And she would rather do things with Travis anyway. All those years when Travis was gone to some exotic places, doing all kinds of neat things, and she was stuck at home with the kids. Now she was gone to an exotic place with him, and she was still *stuck at home*, as it were. Why didn't she opt to go to the lodge with him? It was clear that she could be assaulted by bugs here or there, so why not be there, where she could at least irritate her husband?

"I'm going to do it! I'm going out there with Travis and Calvin! I don't know what I'll do when I get there, but at least I'll be doing something!"

She went in the house and got her sun glasses and insect repellant and hat, and walked across the street to the dock, where there were always boats for hire. The first person she saw was a fellow who had just tied up his boat, and was coming ashore.

"Excuse me! I need a ride up river to the new lodge being built there. What is the rate? Fifty cents?"

"I am sorry, Senora, but my boat is not for hire. Wait, you say you need to go to the lodge?"

"Yes, I am Mrs. Lee, Travis's wife."

"Ah, then your son is Calvin?"

"Yes, he is my son!"

"I am Emillio! Calvin has been working with me! You stay here. I will return very quickly, and we will go back to the lodge, and I will take you there."

"Okay, great. I'll wait here."

That was easy, she thought, as Emillio rushed on into town, and left her waiting on the pier. She noted that Calvin's back-pack was in Emillio's boat, so that made her feel better about riding with him, that he was really who he said he was. He was probably in town to pick up something for the lodge. She was surprised that Calvin didn't come with him. After what seemed like thirty minutes, she saw Emillio returning, carrying a large white bag, and right behind him, were two people, a man and woman, and they seemed to be in a hurry.

"Okay, we are ready to go now. On the boat, please!" Emillio said. "move to the back, so the other passengers will have room!"

After they were seated, and Emillio was maneuvering the boat out to open water, Janice struck up a conversation with the other passengers.

"So you are going out to the lodge too?"

"Yes." the man said. "We have been told that there are many injuries there."

"Injuries? What kind of injuries?"

"We do not know. Only that it is urgent that we get there to care for the more severe injuries."

"So you are a doctor?"

"Yes, and this is my nurse."

"Emillio, what is this about injuries?"

By this time the boat was accelerating in open water, and Emillio signaled that he could not hear her over the engine, so she would have to wait. She settled back to enjoy the ride. It was a sunny day, and was going to be a hot one as well. She noticed grey logs lying on the sand and gravel bars as they made their way up river. *Peculiar*, she thought, *that all those logs are about the same shape. Some large, and some small, but all the same shape.* But then they passed close to one, and a large, toothy mouth gaped open, and then she realized what all those logs were! She turned around in her seat, and yelled at Emillio, while pointing at the crocodile-looking monsters, and Emillio yelled back,

"They are caymen,…sunning themselves!"

They look like crocodiles to me! Janice thought, as they sped past them on both sides of the boat. Any time they passed too closely to one, the Cayman would suddenly gape his mouth open as a warning. They didn't have to worry about *her* messing with them! She suddenly became concerned about the speed Emillio was driving the boat. If he crashed or capsized, they would surely be devoured by those hideous creatures! She did not know that in spite of their dangerous look, they were usually harmless to humans. Just big lizards. She noticed a lot of things that were different today, from the first time she visited the lodge. She concluded that the river was an ever-changing thing.

When they slowed their speed, and turned into the Lodge's protective lagoon, she noticed the group of men gathered at the kitchen area, and she assumed that it was lunch time, but it wasn't. When they pulled up to the landing, Steve was there to meet them.

"Good morning, Janice! I didn't know you were coming out here too."

"It was a spur of the moment decision. Where is Travis?"

"Uh, he's here somewhere. Calvin is up there at the kitchen, helping them cook lunch. Hello! Doctor Ramos! Good to see you again! And Regina, how are you?"

"We heard that you have a lot of injuries" Ramos said. "What happened here?"

Not wanting to discloser the exact cause of the injuries just yet, he said, "There was some disagreement among the men, and it came to blows, and from fists it graduated to machetes. But no one is seriously injured, like I first thought. In fact, we probably could have treated them ourselves."

"But now that we are here, we might as well examine them." Ramon said.

"Oh sure, sure! And I will certainly pay you well for this visit, so come on into the camp. Here, let me help you with that bag, Regina."

"Thank you."

"Janice, why don't you go on ahead and find Calvin, while I discuss something with the doctor?"

"Sure."

When she was out of hearing, Steve confessed to the doctor and his nurse, "The injuries my men have were not self inflicted."

"No?" Ramon asked.

"No, the truth is, we had a run-in with a camp of drug smugglers back in the jungle, and we killed most of them. Unfortunately, some of them were related to people in Coca, and we fear reprisals from local people."

"That is bad business! The drug trade has ruined a lot of good people!"

"Yes, and we are trying to open a lodge here that will bring in a lot of tourists, and in turn, a lot of tourist money to Coca. So we need to keep an untarnished reputation here. Do you know what I mean?"

The doctor stopped. "I assume that you want me and my nurse to keep the details of this from public knowledge?"

"Yes, it would be best for all involved. If anyone asks, just say it was a construction accident you came out here for. The men had a few bruises and cuts, but nothing serious."

"And why should my nurse and I lie for you?"

"Because if you do, I will make a $10,000 donation to your health clinic. You can use the money, I assume?"

He looked at his nurse, and said, "Yes, we can use the donation. That is very generous! Regina, when we get back to town, if anyone asks, we treated bruises and cuts from a construction mishap."

"Yes, Doctor."

Steve and the doctor shook hands, and then went to the kitchen to begin sewing up machete cuts.

Meanwhile, Janice found her son, sitting on a bucket, scratching the tapir behind the ears. The animal grunted with satisfaction.

"Calvin, what is that?"

"Hi, Mom. This is Loretta! She's a tapir. We were going to eat her, but Steve decided to keep her around as a pet."

"She looks like a cartoon of an elephant!"

"Well, Emillio said it is related to the elephants. Here, scratch behind her ears. She likes that."

"So you have her named already?"

"Yeah, well, Emillio did. He said she reminds him of his ex-wife. Want to pet her?"

"No thank you. Where is your dad?"

Sensing that he shouldn't tell her the true nature of his dad's hike into the jungle, he said, "He and Ortega went on a scouting trip, into the jungle. You know, to kind of mark out hiking trails for the Lodge? They'll be back soon. So what are *you* doing here?"

"I got tired of sitting in town with nothing to do. Is it safe for them to be hiking in the jungle? Didn't somebody get kidnapped a couple of days ago?"

"Yeah, but they found him, and now the people that kidnapped him are gone, so it's safe now." (By 'gone' he meant, of course, that they were dead, but he figured that was something that she would be better off not knowing.)

"How can they be sure?"

"They're pretty sure."

"And what's up with all these people with cuts?"

Calvin didn't have an answer for that. "Dad can explain all that when he gets back. I'm not sure how it started. Lunch will be ready in a few minutes. We're having fried catfish!"

≈ 23 ≈

When Ortega and Travis closed in on the smugglers camp, they advanced cautiously, not knowing what they would find. Had someone else been here since the massacre, or was it still as they had left it? They stalked around the perimeter, then entered the camp, to the smell of burning cocaine, and spilled blood. Travis was aghast at the carnage, and he had certainly seen his share of it in 'Nam. Some had been shot, but most had been brutally killed with machetes and clubs. It was easy to see the anger that had been unleashed here.

"Was all this done in retaliation for Atan?" Travis asked.

Ortega, standing in a puddle of drying blood, with his AK-47 slung close to his chest, took out a cigarette and lit it, as he gazed far off and replied,

"No, this was not in retaliation for Atan. This was done for our future! You see, Travis, the success of the lodge for you, represents an investment of your money. If it fails, you lose your money, but that is all. As an American, I am sure you have more money than what you invested in this lodge. Is that not so?"

"That's true. I would not have invested *all* my money in something like this. That would be foolish of me."

Ortega nodded and said, "That is what I thought. But for the 38 Ecuadorians working on the lodge, including myself, whose future depends on the success of the lodge, we have no *money* to invest, but we invest with our *lives*! The promise of a good life for us, and for our children, was put in jeopardy by these want-to-be drug smugglers, who were always watching, and always waiting to prey on us, and any future visitors to the lodge. That is why we killed them! To protect the future welfare and success of our people! Steve would not have understood that, which is why we got together and decided to act, while Steve was gone, so he would not try to stop us."

"Well, I've got to hand it to you, Ortega, you and your guys did an efficient job!" Travis said, as he kicked a severed hand across the ground. "And out here where there is no law, I guess you have to sometimes take the law into your own hands."

"That is exactly the way it is. So you understand the reason we did this, and approve?"

"I don't think it could have been handled any other way." Travis replied.

"Good. Now we must work quickly to make this look like a FARC hit, and get out of here before we are seen. The last thing we must do, is walk around and shoot everyone, one shot in the head with the AK-47. That is a 'signature' of a FARC hit job. But first we will put up a sign. Here, this canvass will work. Let's stretch it out, and tie the corners, so that it spreads out like a banner."

They quickly made a banner out of the canvass tarp, and then Ortega got out the can of red spray paint and shook it up. He wrote 'MUERTE A TODOS QUE SE VENDE COCAINE DE NOSOTHROS', then stood back to make sure it looked right.

"Are you going to sign it FARC?"

"No, no! The FARC would never sign their name to a hit, but the way I worded the sign, it will leave no doubt that it was a FARC hit. Some things you do not need to spell out, to get your message across. Yes, that looks good! Now we will do as I said, and shoot everyone in the head, and we will be done here."

They went around and performed their morbid task, and in doing so, kept a body count. When they finished, they combined their numbers.

"There were sixteen in this camp. That is a very big operation. But the message from 'FARC' should scare the others into not returning here. There are almost surely others involved that were not here when we attacked. Also, I found one who was not dead, but he is now."

"You are an efficient man, Ortega."

"Yes, but we must leave now. The shots may have alerted someone else that we are here. Come, my friend."

Travis picked up the paint can, to take with them. When they left, they deliberately did not leave the same way they had come, in case someone tried to track them. Ortega stopped a few hundred feet away, and made a prognosis. "It will surely rain this afternoon. That should erase most of the evidence, in case someone tries to track us."

"Even the tracks left by your people who attacked this morning?"

"Time will eventually erase that as well. Let us hope that the killings will not be found for over a week. By then, there will be no evidence."

"After a week in this jungle, the bodies will be a mess!"

"Yes, the wild animals, insects and maggots will work quickly to confuse the evidence. But I do not think it will be a week before they are found. I think some of their companions will find them before sundown today. But that should be no problem for us, if they believe the sign we left them. They will be so scared to be there, that they will likely shit themselves in their haste to get away! Drug smugglers who operate outside FARC fear them greatly."

"What would FARC do if they found out that we used the fear of their name to intimidate other drug producers?"

"They would be flattered I think! But would they be angry, and retaliate against us, assuming that they knew we were the ones who had done it? No, I do not think so. Such a thing as we did, would only spread their fame. It would be for them, like free publicity."

"Did any of your men take weapons away from here, after the killings?"

"No. I was very emphatic that we should take nothing from their camp. We did not want to appear to be thieves."

"So the weapons we saw on the ground were the only weapons these people had?"

"Yes, and good for us! If they had been better armed, we could not have over-run them so easily!"

"So the only guns they had was a rusty shotgun, and an old pistol that was falling apart?"

"Yes. The only other weapons they had were machetes and knives. What that tells me, is that these were not professional smugglers. Professional smugglers would have been armed with military assault weapons, like FARC. No, these were not professionals, nor were they backed by professionals. I think it is just as I thought before. They are just farmers, who thought to supplement their meager income from farming, by producing a batch of cocaine base, and selling it without FARC having knowledge of it, because FARC gets a better price, by monopolizing production."

"So why did they kidnap Atan?"

"Perhaps they thought they could scare us off from the lodge, by kidnapping someone, just like other groups do. They wanted to intimidate us into thinking they were a much bigger operation."

"And why did they kill Atan?"

"I think that was an unplanned turn of events. I think Atan saw an opportunity to escape, and tried to run. But whoever was guarding him with that rusty shotgun, panicked, and over-reacted, and shot Atan as he was fleeing. That was unfortunate, and I am sure they felt bad about it, and were probably still trying to decide what to do, when we attacked them early this morning. If we had known that they were just poor farmers, we would not have attacked them as fiercely as we did. But we had to assume that they were well armed, and would fight back more than they did."

There was a few moments of silence, as they both contemplated this, then Ortega said, "But what is done, is done. I regret that it happened as it did, but we had to protect our interests. By making this look like a FARC hit, we can deflect the blame from us, to them. But the fact is, the real blame lies with those dead farmers, who got into a business that was over their heads."

Travis felt a buzz in his pocket, and at first thought it was a bee. But then he remembered that his cell phone was in that pocket, and he had the ringer off, on vibrate. He retrieved it and answered it.

"Hey, Travis! Am I calling at a bad time?"

"No, Jim. I'm good. What's up?"

"Well, I have a job for you, if you can take it."

"Where?"

"Mexico. Thirty miles west of Mexico City."

"Is it a quickie?"

"It should be. But hey, if you are busy, I can take it. I just thought that since you were down that way, you might want it."

"Actually, I think I might take it, then swing back home for a brief visit, before coming back down here."

"You're still in Ecuador?"

"Yes. Have Helen book me from Quito, to Mexico City. And the test kit, have her ship it to Mexico City as well, for me to pick up at the airport."

"Will do."

"What are the case details?"

"I'll send a whole packet of information. But the skinny of it is this: A Cessna exploded after take-off from a local airport. Debris is scattered over a ten acre area, fortunately an open field. Rumor has it that the passenger was a Mexican Federal Prosecutor, who has been vocal in trying to crack down on the local drug cartels. Foul play is suspected. According to what local witnesses saw, an RPG might have been used. All four people on the plane were killed, including the pilot."

"It sounds intriguing."

"So are you interested?"

"Sure, I'll take it. I can probably be in Quito by four this afternoon. Helen can base her bookings on that."

"Where are you right now? I hear birds singing."

"Right now? I am crouching in the jungle with an AK-47 across my lap."

"Sounds like a story might be accompanying that."

"Yes, there is a story to tell, but it will have to be later. Okay, I need to go, so I can get back to Coca, and catch a flight to Quito."

"Call me from Quito."

"I'll do it." He hung up, and told Ortega. "I have to get to Coca, to catch a flight out."

"An emergency?"

"Yes, but that's part of my job."

"So then we go back to the lodge."

⊰ 24 ⊱

When Travis and Ortega emerged from the jungle, about noon, everyone was congregated at the kitchen area. Steve saw them, and came out to meet them halfway.

"How did it go, guys?"

Ortega said nothing, but gave him a 'thumbs up' sign, which said it all. Travis handed over the remainder of the can of paint.

"Great! So everything went as planned?"

"If anyone finds their camp, they will think it was the work of FARC." Ortega said with pride.

"It looks very convincing." Travis assured him.

"That's really great! I think we dodged a bullet this time. Just another hurdle to clear in getting this place up and running! And lunch is ready, so come and eat."

"Si, Senor!" Ortega said.

"Uh, I got a phone call." Travis said. "It was Jim Deshler, wanting me to do a small job in Mexico. I told him I would do it."

"Okay, so when do you leave?"

"I need to be in Quito this afternoon, no later than four."

"Ouch! Then you'd better get your lunch to go! I'll have someone take you to Coca right away. How long to you figure to be gone?"

"Possibly four or five days. I'll leave Janice and Calvin down here. But part of that time, I plan to go back to Alabama and assess the fire damage to my home, and get a contractor working on it. But don't tell Janice about that part, because she doesn't know about the fire yet. I'll tell her later, when the time is right."

"Okay. Well, listen Travis, I know that what we did to that camp was kind of cold, but it was necessary."

"Hey, no problem. I understand the situation. You have some really dedicated people in your employment here, and you'd better make sure that they stay satisfied. If anyone gets disgruntled, they could cause problems for us. That's all I have to say about it."

Janice was ticked off when she found out Travis was leaving them down there, to go on a job for FBN Investigations.

"Couldn't Jim have handled that job?" she asked.

"Well, it *is* my job, Janice. I told him before I came down here that I could still do jobs for him, as long as they were close, and Mexico City is pretty close."

"But I thought we were going to take some time for ourselves, and go to Galapagos Islands?"

"We still are. When I told you that, I didn't mean right away. When I pass through the Quito airport, I'll gather travel information on the Galapagos, and might even go ahead and book a trip for us. From what I understand, travel in the Galapagos is regulated, so that means we might have to wait for an opening with a tour group. It has been rumored that the Ecuadorian government might start limiting the number of people that can visit the islands, because of the negative environmental impact on the wildlife. Because of that rumor, tour groups to the Galapagos have been booked up solid for months. It might take weeks, or even months to actually get to go there."

"Well, okay then, let's plan to go somewhere else while we are waiting. Seriously, Travis, I need to get away from this place awhile, if you want me to keep my sanity!"

"Okay, when I get to Quito, I will book a trip for the Galapagos as soon as possible, but then I'll also ask about other sights to see in the meantime. How does that sound?"

"It sounds like be best offer I'm going to get. How soon to you have to leave for Mexico?"

Travis looked at his watch. "Steve is getting Emillio to run me to town right now. I'll go straight to the airport when I get there.

"Then I'm riding back to Coca with you. I'll have to put up with Felicia until you get back."

"She likes you. Try to get along. Is Calvin staying here?"

"I guess. I think he's found his second home."

"When I get back in a few days, our little bungalow should be finished and ready to move into. Are you going to be adventurous and move into it with me?"

"I don't know. Living in Coca would be a luxury compared to moving into that bungalow. No electricity, no running water, no toilets! Don't ask me now. Wait until later."

"Okay. I see Emillio waving, so our ride is waiting."

Steve met them at the boat.

"I'm going to town too. I got word that our 1500 gallon water tank is completed, and ready for shipment. I'm going to the welding shop that made it, and inspecting the pieces, to be sure it's what I ordered. It is fabricated in six pieces that will be assembled up on the hill there. The pump and filtration systems are already here, but we don't plan to get them out until the tank is assembled."

"I wish I wasn't leaving so soon. I'd like to see how it was made."

"By the time you get back, we'll probably have it assembled and ready. We'll probably already have the supply line installed as well. It will require us to dig a ditch to bury the 4 inch line. And if we dig a ditch, you know what we will find! Cha-ching!"

The boat pulled out into the lagoon. Before they got to open water, Steve leaned over to Janice and said,

"I hear you didn't know that Felicia was a 'working girl'?"

"Is that what you call it?"

"I wasn't trying to deceive you, but I thought you and Travis already knew about her. I told Homer the situation, and I thought he was a big enough gossip that he would tell Travis, but I guess not. Looks like in the future, I need to spread my gossip through someone else! So now you understand that Felicia is not really my 'girlfriend'. I use that term in a very loose way. I give her a place to stay, in exchange for her looking after my house while I'm gone."

"She is a very attractive house sitter!"

"Isn't she, though? But there's nothing wrong with that! I've always said, why have a house sitter that's as ugly as home-made sin, when I can have one that's drop-dead gorgeous? It boosts my property value too!"

"I'll bet it does."

The outboard opened up, and made further conversation impossible, as the sped down river toward Coca.

———◆◆◆———

Felicia greeted them with a smile when they got to the house. Janice felt obliged to smile back, and asked if she needed help with anything around the house. Meanwhile, Travis threw all his necessities in his suitcase, and took it to the Land Rover. Then Steve took him to the airport, where he just barely caught the afternoon flight to Quito.

———◆◆◆———

Travis made the plane change in Quito, and was on the way to Mexico City before he realized that he was in the same clothes he had worn in the jungle, to the massacre site. Were there any spatters of blood on his pants? Was there blood soaked mud in the treads of his shoes? He hadn't even thought to check, or change clothes, because he was so focused on catching his flight. He would take a shower and rinse out his clothes when he got to his hotel in Mexico City.

How did he feel about the way Ortega and his men had handled the attack on the farmer/smugglers? Well, it was certainly efficient. They were expecting a far more formidable foe, so they went in with brutal resolve, and the result was over-kill. But in the absence of government law enforcement, they had done about the only thing they could have done, and he couldn't fault them for that. It just seemed that such a start to the founding of the lodge might taint its legacy. Their profits made at the lodge, either from the emeralds, or the lodge itself, would seem like 'blood money' from now on, and though he had not actually been in on the initial attack, he had helped cover it up. According to Ortega, those who carried it out, thought it was a necessary evil, to secure their future well-being. In a country where there are not a lot of really good opportunities for the common man to *legally* make a good living for his family, it was seen as acceptable to kill off a few 'malos' who they perceived as threatening their opportunity.

No he couldn't hold that against them. If he did, he would be a hypocrite himself. Why? Because in Vietnam, he had done a lot worse things, to a lot more innocent people, under the guise of '*it was war, and they were the enemy!*' And now, looking back at that war, through the clarity of time, he realized what a fool he had been. To do such horrible things, in such a bad war, for reasons that now seemed so petty and hollow, seemed almost criminal. He had really gotten into the war, and the justifications for it, and in his young, impressionable mind at the time, he didn't believe that he could have done anything that was too far off the charts, as long as his cause was right. But as the years rolled on, he realized more and more how his cause was not as pure as he thought it was, and therefore, the things he had done looked worse and worse.

Seeing the massacre that morning in the jungle brought all that back. He hoped the justification for the massacre would still be seen as necessary years from now. He hoped that those who participated in it, would keep the reasons clear in their mind, and those reasons would be magnified to prove them as having done the right thing.

At the airport in Mexico City, he claimed his suitcase, then went to the Fed-Ex office there and claimed the test kit that Jim had sent him. The file on the crash was supposed to be inside. As much as he had traveled, this was his very first time in Mexico City, so he had no past reference to go by. He got a taxi to the hotel that Helen had reserved for him, which was way out of the city, in a suburb near the crash site, which was convenient. When he checked in, the desk clerk exhorted him to be vigilant, and keep his doors locked at all times. It sounded like a rough neighborhood.

Once in his room on the fourth floor, he got out his cell phone, and went out on the balcony to check in with Jim. A sea of low rent shacks were all he could see from his vantage point. Just as Jim answered the phone, a bullet ricocheted off the stucco wall behind him, and he hit the deck. Three or four more bullets glanced off the stucco, as he heard Jim's voice, saying, "Hello? Hello Travis! What's going on?"

"Hello Jim! Right now I am crawling back into my hotel room! I was in the balcony, and someone was taking pot shots at me!"

"They were shooting at you?"

"Yes! Tell Helen she put me up in a real winner of a neighborhood,... again!"

"I'm right here!" Helen said, on speaker phone. "I put you up there, because it is near the crash site, and convenient for you!"

"Well, the hotel is nice enough, but the neighbors are probably drunk and celebrating something. I thought hand guns were illegal in Mexico?"

"They are," Jim said, "But nobody goes by the law there, so just watch yourself. How do you know it was a hand gun?"

"I could tell by the inaccuracy. They were probably firing from two blocks away. They were probably just trying to see if they could scare the Gringo. They did! He and his amigos are probably down in an alley laughing their asses off right now!"

"I'm glad you're taking it so well. Did you get the folder I sent you on the crash?"

"Yes, I have it right here. Hold on, while I get it out."

For ten minutes he and Jim went over some of the chemical tests he was going to have to make, to determine if an RPG was actually used in the downing of the Cessna. Jim went over a whole list of things to look for, and test for, and how to get it right, because there was most likely going to be a criminal investigation by the Mexican Bureau of Investigation, because one of the victims of the crash was a Federal Prosecutor.

"When you are promoted to the status of Federal Prosecutor in Mexico," Jim said, "It comes with a safety vest with a reflective target on your back."

"Did you fax the MBI that I would be here in the morning?"

"Yes, they are expecting you at their headquarters at 8A.M. Said they would be responsible for getting you to and from the crash site. Unless there are complications, I see no reason for your investigation to go beyond tomorrow. So the day after tomorrow, you can be back on vacation in Ecuador."

"Vacation? You think that's what I've been doing down there?"

"I'm sure you and Steve are staying busy."

"Yeah, we are. But when I finish here, I'll be going home to Alabama."

"Yeah, I remember you saying something like that."

"The reason I'm going back home is because I've been informed that my house burned down."

"Mercy!" Helen said. "How did that happen?"

"That's one of the things I'll be checking on. I have not told Janice about the fire yet, because if I tell her, she'll want to go home. and we can't go home yet. I intend to get my insurance agent out there, and make arrangements to re-build."

"I wish you luck with that. Is there anything we can do to help?" Jim asked.

"Not that I can think of right now."

"I can go ahead and book you a flight to Birmingham." Helen said.
"Yes, that will be a help. Thanks."

≈ 25 ≈

Back in Coca, Janice was making a real effort to overlook Felicia's profession, and just be the friend she had been before she found out, but it was hard for her to do. Felicia was just the same as before, and was starting to see Janice as an older sister. The fact that Janice knew she was a prostitute didn't seem to phase Felicia at all. But why should it? It was not only legal in Ecuador, but it was socially accepted as a legitimate profession.

When she got the word, from a water taxi driver, that Steve was staying at the Lodge that night, Felicia told Janice that they were going out for dinner.

"Janice, tonight we will go out on the town! We will have a 'girl's night out'! We have dinner, and drinks, and maybe we dance all night long!"

"I don't know. I'm not much of a 'party person'. You wouldn't have much fun with me."

"Yes! We have plenty of fun!"

"Will there be men involved?"

"Who needs men to have fun? The entire night is on me! I treat you to lots of fun! Trust me!"

"Well, I can pay for the dinner, at least."

"No, no! I said it is on me! Besides, we will go to a place where the owner owes me money! The entire evening will be free! Calvin is staying at the lodge tonight?"

"Yes, that goes without saying. He loves it there."

"Good! Then it will just be you and me! Do you have a party dress?"

"No, just these plain clothes I brought with me."

"That is okay! I have lots of nice dresses that you can wear! We pick one out later. I show you how to party Ecuador style!"

The day after the lodge workers got together and wiped out their perceived threat to the lodge, everyone was in high spirits, and laid into their work with a renewed vigor. The Lee's bungalow was almost finished. The main lodge foundation was finished, and the craftsmen were laying out massive slabs of timber, to select the ones that would serve as the main floor supports, that would rest on the stone foundation pillars. The slabs were measured, cut, notched and fitted, and then the massive foundation began to take shape.

In the afternoon, a small cargo ship arrived in the harbor, having negotiated the sand bars to get there, it had a heavy load,…the pre-fabricated water tank, that would store the lodge's fresh water. Steve called everyone off their jobs, to help unload the six large steel pieces, with the help of the ship's crane. Once the pieces were on shore, it was going to be a matter of human muscle, to get the parts to the highest point of the site. Calvin couldn't believe that no one suggested that they use one of the logger's bulldozers to move the pieces. But once he suggested it, they quickly and cleverly made temporary skids to put the parts on, and pull up the hill to the assembly site. The bags of galvanized bolts, and rubber gaskets were carried by hand.

The bulldozer quickly scraped off a flat area for the assembly, an area that did not need a concrete foundation, because it was almost solid rock. The site was leveled with picks and shovels, then covered with a layer of sand to cushion the tank, and the bottom piece was set in place. A strip of self-adhesive rubber gasket was placed around the joint, Then, with sheer manpower, the second piece of the tank was lifted and set into place, while Calvin got inside the tank with a spud wrench to align the holes. Everyone who was not holding the piece in place, was assembling and screwing nuts on the bolts. When all the bolts and nuts were in, but not yet tightened. The third piece was hoisted into place, bolted together, and then all the bolts were tightened.

With the bottom three pieces together, the top three were going to be trickier. They would have to erect a primitive hoist of some kind, to hang a shield wheel from, and hoist the tank parts up with a steel cable, pulled by the bulldozer. Everyone scattered to gather the materials needed. Calvin helped build a wooden scaffold inside the tank, so they could continue to align the holes from the inside.

Within an hour, everything was ready, and the fourth piece went up flawlessly, and was bolted in place. It took most of the afternoon, but finally the last piece was in place, and bolts assembled, it was finally all together. All that remained, was for someone to go around with a big turn handle, and tighten all the bolts. Then the scaffold inside was disassembled, and hauled out in pieces through an access port in the bottom.

Calvin stood back and admired the assembled tank, and marveled that it only took 40 men five hours to construct it. It was a lesson in what could be accomplished when everyone was motivated and working together. Steve was amazed as well.

"Yeah, once we get it piped up and operating, we will plant banana trees all around it, and it will hardly be noticeable by our guests."

"Do banana trees grow that tall?" Calvin asked.

"Not quite, but we can paint the top to camouflage it. No one will notice it!"

With the tank in place, Steve marked out where the purification unit and pumps would be located, and was then able to determine exactly where the ditches should be dug to bury the fresh water pipe, which would arrive from Coca the next day. The crew that had completed the lodge foundation was assigned to dig the ditch, from the river, up to where the pumps would be. This confused Calvin.

"You are going to use river water to supply the lodge? I thought you'd drill a well, or dig one by hand, like in the old days."

"No, I weighed the cost of drilling a well, as opposed to buying a filtration system, and the later was the cheaper way to go. Besides, there might not be a suitable aquifer under the ground here to tap anyway."

"But if you dug a well by hand, straight down, like in the old days, then you could have a legitimate excuse to sink a shaft,…to look for emeralds."

Steve looked at him blankly. He had absolutely not thought of that. Here he was, a professional geologist, and it took a kid with no college education to point out the obvious. He cracked a wide grin.

"Of course! Why didn't I think of that? We can get our water from the river as planned, but we can say we are digging a well, to tap into a *better* source of water! Calvin, you are a genius! That way, I can tell a lot more about where to look for the emerald veins, by digging a test shaft straight down! But that will be a lot later, after we have put in the infrastructure of the Lodge itself. There is still a whole lot to do before that."

"How can I help?" Calvin asked.

"You already are helping! By helping Emillio hunt and fish. By helping erect the tank, like we just did. Just be here willing to help with anything we need to do, and you will be a great help. Are you good at fitting pipe?"

"I don't know."

"Well tomorrow you'll find out, because the pipe is arriving from Coca. We will lay the big supply pipe, from the river to here. Then we will pipe up the pumps and connect to the tank. And then there will be the water main that will run from the tank, down the top of this ridge. From that water main, we will branch off and run a ½ inch line to each of the bungalows, and a line back the other way to the kitchen and Lodge restrooms."

"When will the pumps and filtration system arrive?" Calvin asked.

"They are already here! See those plastic-covered crates over there? Those were delivered two weeks ago. I was waiting on the tank to arrive before I un-crated it, so now we can go ahead with that. I wish we had a forklift to move stuff like that, but a forklift wouldn't be practical with all these steep hills and ridges. But we have a lot of man-power. I'll get those moved over here and we can un-pack them. I tell you what! This has been quite a day. We've got a lot done."

⊰ 26 ⊱

Travis woke up the next morning thinking, *Wow, what a smell this city has! And it's not a good smell.* Travis had noticed in his travels that every major city has it's own smell. That was not exactly a new flash, because anyone could notice that. But Travis, with his *heightened* sense of smell, could literally tell one city from the others, just by its smell. He could be blindfolded, and identify most major cities just by their smell. And *this one*, was one he was certainly going to remember, because it was very particular.

Oh well, so much for the smell. He went down to breakfast, then gathered his test kit, and caught a taxi to the MBI headquarters. They took him out to the fields where the plane debris was still scattered. The body parts had already been removed, but little flags marked the spots where they had been. The flags were written on with a marker, giving a number, and a description. The first one he looked at said, '064- braza izquerda - no mano'. (left arm with no hand). He didn't think he wanted to read any more of them. *Just look for pieces of the plane that will tell you what you want to know. Leave the scattered body parts for the medical experts.*

The Mexican investigators helped him locate the plane ID number, which checked out as the same plane that was insured. He couldn't help noticing the condition of the metal pieces scattered over the field. The condition certainly seemed to indicate that some sort of external explosive device had taken the plane down. He found several prime pieces, and swabbed samples of explosive residue from them for his chemical tests. He carefully sealed the samples in separate zip-loc bags, and labeled them. He also took samples from the remains of the fuel tank, as well as items that had been in the cabin when the explosion occurred. Every tiny detail would provide another piece to the puzzle.

The fact that witnesses said that the plane exploded, and then the fuel tank ignited, was a sign that something had externally hit the plane.

And then the investigators found something else. Pieces of the planes aluminum skin that had *bullet holes* in it. They would be examined by ballistics, to determine caliber of the bullets, but to Travis, they looked like some kind of fully-automatic weapon, because there were just too many holes, for such a fast-moving plane.

It was absorbing work, and before he knew it, it was afternoon. He went back to his hotel, where he unloaded his samples, then went downstairs for lunch, then went back to the crash site about three, and stayed with the investigators until dark. He had carefully examined everything he knew to examine, and was satisfied that he had all he needed. He went back to the hotel to start testing the samples he had gathered during the day. He went up to his room, and opened the door. When he turned the light on, he was startled to see a man with a black beard, sitting on his bed, pointing a 9mm pistol at him.

"Come in and close the door." The dangerous looking man said, waving the 9mm, fitted with a silencer. That did not look good.

"I don't have much money." Travis said, assuming this was a robbery.

"You need no money. Are you investigator Travis Lee, of FBN Investigations?"

"Yes, that's right." Travis said, as he entered the room, and closed the door behind him. "And you are…?"

"I am your *executioner*."

"For doing what? My job?"

"For killing Muhammad Nasser Hassan! Our holy man! You came into our town at night, like a dirty, filthy thief, and *murdered* our beloved cleric! And now, you will die! And I will also mutilate your body, just as you did Hassan! *Allah Akaba!*"

Travis dove into the bathroom, as two bullets splintered the door facing. In the darkness of the bathroom, he reached down to his calf and removed his kabar from its sheath. When the man appeared at the bathroom door, he flung the knife at him, as he dove into the shower stall. If the knife missed, he was going to die in the shower stall, because he was out of weapons. He thought about removing the shower rod to use as a gouging tool, but he got tangled in the shower curtain.

The man fired into the dark bathroom. The porcelain toilet shattered, as well as the mirror above the sink, and then he heard the gun discharge one more time when it hit the floor, the bullet ricocheting off the tile floor, and hit the ceiling. And then, silence.

He climbed up out of the shower, and looked around the corner. His assassin was sitting in the floor, slumped against the wall, with a far-away, glassy look in his eyes. His kabar was buried up to the hilt in the man's chest.

Travis exhaled raggedly. He realized that his fling of the knife had been just plain lucky. *Damn lucky!* He could have thrown that knife another hundred times, and not hit the target like he did on the first throw. *Right through the heart.*

His first thought was, *where is this guy's partner? I know they always attack in twos.* He picked up the gun, and checked out the closet. No one there. Under the bed? No one there either. If he had a partner, he was probably in the lobby, or outside in the car waiting on him. He locked the door, while he decided what to do.

This was Mexico, so there probably wasn't much that Morgan could do for him, so far as cleaning up this mess. If he called the Policia, there was no telling what they would do. Probably throw him in jail, and not let him call anyone, so he had better do all the calling he needed to do now. He took out his cell phone, but stopped. *How did this guy know to find me here? Are they somehow listening in on my phone calls? How did he get into my locked room? And where the hell is his partner?* That was the troubling thought. Where was his partner? He thought it best to keep quiet awhile, and see what happened.

He checked the clip in the pistol, and saw it had plenty of bullets for what he would need. He pulled his kabar out of 'Omar's' chest, and went to the bathroom to wash it off, and return it to his sheath. 'Omar' was a big guy, for an Arab. He checked his pockets, and of course, found no identification on him. A hit man never carried an ID. He left 'Omar' slumped against the wall, while he waited. He turned out the light, and went to sit on the bed to wait, and think about what he needed to do.

How would he explain this to the police? *'I went to dinner, and when I came back, this dead man was in my room.'* Yeah, that sounded real convincing. The officers would probably laugh all the way to the jail cell they were going to throw him into. *'The man tried to rob me, and I threw my knife at him.'* No way would they believe that he threw his knife at him. That was just too far out to believe. *'Right this way, Senor Rambo!'* as they would shove him into a cell with fourteen degenerate

Mexican criminals. The Alpha criminal says, *'Hey amigos, what have we here?'* The Beta criminal says, *'Looks like a Gringo that has lost his way! Hey Gringo! Hey Gringo! You got a cigarette?* Alpha criminal: *'I think we should welcome him to Mexico! What do you think, Amigos? Gringo! Drop your pants, bend over and grab your ankles!'* And then he would have to kill one or two of them, and then he would never get out of prison here. How to best avoid all that? Step one: avoid the police. Step two: get out of the country as soon as possible. Step three, if he is caught: Lie like a rug. But first, where is this guy's partner?

He waited for about 25 minutes, then he heard a light rap on the door, and a muffled voice whispering through the door. Most likely, it was 'Omar's partner, coming by to admire his handiwork. He got up and rapped on the door in return, then unlocked the latch. The person on the other side whispered something in Arabic, and then slowly opened the door. When he turned on the light, he was looking into the barrel end of the 9mm.

Two quiet shots, and the thin, mustached man dropped in his tracks. Travis did a quick glance both ways in the hallway, saw it was clear, then dragged the thin man in to the room and let him drop, while he re-locked the door.

"Ahab, meet Omar!" Travis said, though he suspected that they already knew one another. When he dropped 'Ahab', face-down, his face happened to fall on 'Omar's crotch. He thought that was as good a place as any to leave him. Travis gathered his things, which weren't much. His suitcase and test kit. He swept the room, to make sure he had not left anything. He wiped his fingerprints off the gun, and placed it in 'Omar's right hand. He found a large wicked-looking knife on the bed, no doubt the knife that 'Omar' in tended to mutilate him with. He took the knife, and jammed it into the wound in 'Omar's chest, made by his kabar, then wiped off his fingerprints, and wrapped 'Ahab's' hand around the handle, to put his fingerprints on it. He went around the room, wiping his off fingerprints off anything he might have touched, thinking that might help. Then he unlocked the door, hung the 'No Moleste' or 'Do not disturb' sign on the door, locked it, and went down to the lobby.

To the receptionist he said, "I have reserved room 423 for only one night. Can I extend it for another night?"

"Yes, let me check, Senor." He flipped through his reservation book. "Yes, you can have it for three more nights, if you wish."

"No, just one more will do. Just add it to the credit card."

"Si Senor."

Travis went outside and hailed a taxi, and told him to take him to the international airport. At the airport, he hunted a U.S. airline that was departing in the next two hours for Atlanta. He saw a Delta flight, and went to the gate to see if there were any available seats. He was in luck. An hour later he boarded the flight, sure that he would not be able to return to Mexico in this lifetime, because he was pretty sure the police would be looking for him as a 'person of interest'. When the plane took off, he finally felt safe.

"What a day!"

• ◆ •

From the Atlanta airport, near midnight, he used a pay phone to call Jim Deshler, as he waited on the connecting flight to Birmingham.

"Hey! It's about time you called!" Jim said. "Did you complete the investigation?"

"I have all the data gathered, but I have not run the tests yet. I'll do them when I get back home. I am in Atlanta now, calling from a pay phone."

"What happened to your cell phone?"

"Nothing. It's in my pocket. But it might not be safe to use it." He explained what happened to him at the hotel in Mexico City, and shared his suspicion that the enemy had somehow tapped his phone, because they knew he was going to be in Mexico City, and even where he was staying.

"That is not good," Jim said.

"Tell me about it! My fear is that they know I took my family to Ecuador, although there is no indication of that. Do you think they might have tapped *your* phone?"

"If they did, then they could be listening to us right now."

"Crap!"

"I tell you what. Finish the crash results, and fax them to Helen, and I will catch up with you later. I'll call you from a secure phone."

When Travis hung up, he realized that made more sense, that they were listening in on *Jim's* line, because they knew that he worked for FBN Investigations. If they monitored Jim's phone, they would sooner or later find out where *he* was,…and it worked. They almost got him. But the troubling part was, he just told them that his family was in Ecuador, and that he was heading to Birmingham, which they would naturally assume that he was headed home. But now that he understood that they didn't have a tap on *his* phone, he used it to call General Morgan, even if it *was* midnight.

He obviously woke the General, but Morgan was glad he called. He told him what happened in Mexico City, and the General agreed that the tap was most likely on Jim Deshler's phone.

"But that's good, because we know they are doing it. Do you remember the Patriot Act that congress passed right after 911?"

"Vaguely. Refresh my memory."

"The Patriot Act allows us to get a warrant, and tap into any phone conversation, if it involves catching terrorists, and safeguarding the country. And I think this definitely qualifies. I'll call the judge tonight and get the warrant, and while the terrorists are listening to you, we'll be listening to them!"

"Is the technology really that good?"

"If you only knew, Travis, you would be amazed at what we can do. Big Brother can do a lot of things that John Q. Public doesn't even suspect!"

That's scary, Travis thought. *Shades of George Orwell, 1984.*

———◆◆◆———

Not wanting to rouse anyone at three in the morning, he got a rental car to use for the couple of days he was going to be there. He drove to Laurel Grove, and went to his parents house to crash and sleep a few hours before daylight. He knew his Dad was usually up and drinking coffee at 4:30 every morning, so he might catch him already awake. The kitchen light was on, so he assumed he was. They never locked the front door, but their dog was their real security system, and he did his job. Before he could get out of the car, he saw his Dad in the doorway, naked, except for his Fruit of the Looms, and weilding his double barreled shotgun.

"It's me, Dad!"

"Travis? I thought you was gone off to who-knows-where?"

"I was, but I'm back now to see about the house."

"Hmp! What house? It burned right down to the concrete slab! I was going to see what I could salvage, but those guards won't let nobody near it!"

"Military guards?"

"Yep."

"Well, we'll go look at it in the morning. Right now, I just need some sleep."

"Your old bedroom is still there. I won't tell your mother that you're here, until you get up."

"Thanks, Dad."

"I don't reckon you want coffee."

"No, just sleep."

"We'll talk in the morning, son."

⊰ 27 ⊱

Janice was apprehensive about going on a so-called 'girl's night out' with Felicia, because she was afraid of what Felicia would call 'fun'. Her idea of a night out, was going out to a nice restaurant with Travis, so this was going to be a new experience for her.

She was wearing one of Felicia's 'party dresses', which fit her pretty well, except that she was shorter than her host. When she looked at herself in the mirror, she couldn't help but laugh. Not surprisingly, she looked just like an Ecuadorian prostitute.

"So, you like the dress?" Felicia asked.

"Yes, it is certainly...colorful!" She imagined herself with a fruit basket balanced on her head, like the Chiquita Banana girl.

"I think you will be the prettiest lady at the party!"

"Oh, listen to you! I haven't been out like this since,...well, I don't think I ever have! I was seventeen when I got married, and I went straight to raising kids! I missed out on the party stage of my life."

"Well, tonight you can start to catch up on what you missed!"

Oh god! What am I doing? Janice thought, as she continued to scrutinize that strange woman in the mirror. *I am too old to be doing this crap! But I'll go through with it, just to try to fit in with Felicia and her friends, because I might be here for awhile. I might as well assimilate into the local culture. I'll try to have fun, but not too much!*

"We need to be going, Amiga! The sun set an hour ago! The night is wasting!" Felicia urged her.

"I need my purse."

"Here it is, so let's go!"

Out the front door, and down the street they went. The orangish street lights gave a surreal glow to the tropical night, as moths swirled around the lights. *Oh gosh! I probably look like a prostitute walking down the street!* Janice thought. Especially when they passed a garage, where a half dozen men, probably mechanics by day, were hanging out, drinking beer, and transforming into wolves in the moonlight. When they saw the two women walking by, they hooted and howled, and called out to them. Janice was mortified, but Felicia just hurled teasing insults back at them in a good natured way, as they walked on by. Janice was glad she didn't speak Spanish, because she really didn't want to know what they had said. But once they were past, Felicia said, "Do you know what those guys wanted?"

"Not really." Janice replied.

"They wanted sex! And I told them they had each other!"

"Didn't that make them angry?"

"No! That's just the way the game is played! I know most of them, and they are all losers! They wouldn't know what to do with a hot senorita if they had one!"

They turned down a dark alley, and Janice hesitated. "Are you sure it's okay to go down there?"

"Yes! This is a shortcut I use all the time to get to Calle Presidente, that is where the place is we are going. Come, it is safe. You will see."

A cat screeched when Janice stepped on it's tail in the dark, and she almost ran out of the alley.

"Relax! It is just a gato!" Felicia said as they emerged on to a well lit, and more populated street. They passed a tall man who said,

"Felicia! Que pasa?"

"Tardes, hombre!" Felicia replied, as she kept walking.

"Who was that?" Janice asked.

"I don't know his name, but I think I have danced with him before. See the bright sign there? That is where we are going! It is called 'La Rumba'. I think you will like it there."

"It certainly is a crowded place!" Janice said, slightly panicked by the crowd. Large crowds of strangers scared her, and she hesitated to go any farther, but did anyway.

"Yes, it is very popular with the local people. Everyone knows me there!"

Especially the men! Janice thought, as they walked up to the door. A stout bouncer guarded the door, but Felicia just patted him on his massive chest, and walked on in. Janice hesitated, but Felicia said,

"Come on in! It's okay, you're with me!" She slipped past the bouncer's intense glare, and entered another world.

Inside, she could not hear anything for the loud music, being cranked out by a live band, and amplified with massive speakers. Everyone was drinking and smoking, talking and laughing, though she didn't see how anyone could be understood with the music so loud. She guessed that they read one another's lips. She followed closely behind Felicia, not wanting to lose her in the crowd. And Felicia was ever stopping to exchange a few words with people in the crowd. Finally they made their way to the back of the room, where there was a door leading out to a large patio. There were a lot fewer people out here, as this was the open-air dining area. The tables were scattered among the trees and hedges, and well lit with strings of what Janice would have called Christmas lights, but instead of colored bulbs, they were all clear, and illuminated the dining area very romantically. Felicia picked a table under a tree, where they had a good view of the whole patio.

"So, how do you like this place?"

"I was scared to come in the front door, through all those people, but back here, this is really nice! I like this. The music is better from back here,...not as loud."

"And you will love the food! The owner of this place employs two very good chefs. Anything on the menu is good!"

A waiter in a white coat approached and handed each of them a menu. "Buenas tardes, Senorita Felicia! And who is your friend?"

"This is Janice. She is from the United States. She has never been here before."

"Ah, then she is in for a real treat! What will you Senoritas be drinking?"

"You know what I want!" Felicia said.

"Yes, a lime margarita, and for you?"

"I'll have the same thing." Janice said.

"Very good."

"And bring us a sampler plate too." Felicia added.

"Ah yes!" He hurried away to get their drinks.

"You will like the sampler plate. It is just an assortment of appetizers, to snack on before we order the main course. It goes really good with a margarita!"

"So is this like, one of your favorite places?" Janice asked.

"Yes, I like to come here. Steve comes here with me a lot, because he likes it too. But these days he is so busy with that lodge…"

"That's the way Travis is! He gets wrapped up in his work, and sometimes I don't see him for weeks!"

"What is it about North American men? They all seem to be *driven* to succeed! They should take a lesson from Ecuadorian men, and slow down! They are too busy to enjoy life!"

Two young waiters arrived. One delivered the margaritas, and the other, the sampler plate. Janice had to do a double take at the sampler plate. There were three or four samples of a half dozen things. All of them were unidentifiable except one.

"Are those *bugs*?"

"They are roasted *cucarachas*." Felicia replied. "Steve calls them cock-roaches. But they are very good!"

"What are the other things?"

"Well, that is fried cayman,…that is fried cheese sticks,…this is plantains, like a fried banana,…and those are things on the skewers are roasted grub worms."

"And those?"

"I think those are smoked turtle eggs. So what would you like to try first?"

"The only thing I recognize is the cheese sticks."

Felicia smiled and sipped her margarita, then said, "You must prove your *courage*, by at least *trying* all these things!"

"I'm good with being a coward then."

"No, no no! This is our girl's night out! You must do something new! You must do something wild and different! Be brave, Janice! To pass the test, you must try all of these things! But you will not have to try them alone. I will also eat everything that you eat!"

Janice pulled her margarita toward her and had a drink. "I'm going to have to be pretty drunk to try some of those things!"

"No problem! I will keep the drinks coming! Now, what will you start with?"

"Easy ones first. A cheese stick."

"Okay, a cheese stick! mozzarella, I think."

"It doesn't taste like mozzarella."

"Ah! I think it is goat cheese, but it is still good, no?"

"Probably better than those other things."

"Oh no! you will see! So what is next?"

"You say that is bananas?"

"Yes, plantains, a kind of banana."

"Hey, this tastes good!"

"Of course! I told you everything is good here!"

"That's all I recognize. What did you say this is?"

"Cayman. It is a big lizard. Kind of like a crocodile. You will try it next?"

"Sure, why not." She broke open a piece and tasted it. "Hey, this tastes just like chicken. I can handle this."

"See? You are halfway there! You are doing good!"

"But I don't think I can handle those last three."

"Try the turtle eggs. They are just like chicken eggs, only smoked."

She cut one in half with her knife, and Felicia was right. They looked just like chicken eggs inside. She popped half in her mouth, and passed the other half to Felicia.

"Hey, this is pretty good too,…but a little chewy. Rubbery is more like it, but it tastes good."

"Okay, you have only two things left. Roasted grub worms, or cucarachas?"

"Are you sure those are grub worms? They don't look like worms."

"They are the big plump white worms, that come out of the heart of dead trees. See? That is the worm's head."

"Okay, you didn't have to show me that!"

"First pull him off the skewer, and hold him by the head, and bite the back end."

"You want me to bite his ass?"

"Yes, bite his ass."

Janice grimaced, took a big drink of margarita, then picked up the worm and bit off a small piece. It was tough like jerky, but she was surprised by the taste. "It tastes just like bacon!"

"Yes! Good, isn't it?"

"Yes it is! That might be my favorite one yet!"

"Ah, but you have not yet tasted the cucaracha! To me, they are the best!"

"Well, I must say, I am pleasantly surprised so far! This is opening up a whole new world of food for me! Okay, I am ready! Let's try the roach!"

Felicia showed her how to peel back the folded wings, to bite the large abdomen of the bug. Thinking this was going to be the grossest thing ever, she took a bite of the crunchy roasted bug, and then reported, "It's good! Wow, it's really good! Nothing like I expected! I'll never look at bugs the same again!"

They talked and laughed, as the sipped their margaritas, and divided up the remaining appetizers, then ordered their dinner, which was something light, after all those bugs and stuff. Janice got a salad, and crispy fried fish, with a small side order of stir-fried fish eggs. Felicia ordered something that was exotic and different for her. A cheeseburger with potato fries.

After dinner, they ordered fresh margaritas, and watched people dancing out on the patio floor. For Janice, the margaritas were causing the room to spin around, as she was getting a really good buzz. This was about the time two pretty teenage girls arrived at the table, and Felicia introduced them as her two younger sisters. "Janice, this is Maria, and this is Verona!"

Janice bit her tongue just in time to keep from asking, *Are they prostitutes too.* Instead she complimented them on their beautiful dresses, and invited them to sit with them and order a drink.

"No thank you." Varona said, and Maria added, "We can't stay long,...we're working tonight."

"So you are out selling merchandise on the street?" Janice asked.

Maria looked at Varona and smiled. "Yes, you could say that!"

"Well, don't work too hard!" Janice heard herself say, as she suddenly realized what it was they were selling. She and her big mouth! The girls left, giggling to one another. Felicia smiled and ordered two more margaritas.

She and Felicia talked non-stop on into the night, ordered more margaritas, and at some point in the night, Janice realized that she was up on the dance floor with a large group of young people, doing the 'Macarena' dance. It must have looked hilarious, because Felicia was sitting at their table about to die laughing. Later, while she was ordering yet another margarita, she saw Felicia up dancing with one of her female friends, and she wondered how anyone could dance with the entire patio spinning around like it was doing. Though she was very drunk, she was having a great time.

Janice had no idea how late they stayed out, nor how she was able to get back home, but she woke up the next morning at Steve's house, in her bed, with an incredible hangover. The margaritas were good, but she vowed that she would never do that binge drinking thing again.

The next morning Travis got up to look at the site of his burned out house, but decided to wait on the insurance man to arrive. He really dreaded seeing his home it in that condition, but he knew he had to deal with it sooner or later.

"Ain't much left, is there, son?" His dad said.

"I don't know. I haven't seen it yet."

"The guards you've got there wouldn't let me get close enough to see it. But as hot as it burned, I don't think there's much left at all."

"There should be a few things. Non-burnable things. But I don't have the time to sift through all that right now. I'm going to leave the guards here, until I get through with what I'm doing in Ecuador."

"Just what *are* you doing in Ecuador?"

"We're building an eco-lodge. You know, like that place we stayed in Peru a few years ago? Remember, I took Jenny down there, and you went with us?"

"Oh yeah, I remember that place! And I wouldn't have given you two cents for it! So why are you building another one, after what happened at that one? You got a death-wish or something? You didn't get enough abuse from those jungle injuns?"

"This is an entirely different situation, Dad. It's a different part of South America. There are no hostile Indian tribes at this place. Steve and I are going in together with a couple other friends to develop it, and we can make a lot of money off it, if we do it right. And once we get it built, you and Mom can go down there and stay for free."

"For free? You couldn't *pay* me to go stay there, if it's anything like that other place! With all those malaria carrying mosquitoes floating around, and a million other things, just waiting to take a bite out of your ass! No thank you! I'll stay right here in Alabama, where I belong!"

"Suit yourself. But there are a lot of people willing to pay a good price to stay at a place like that. If it makes you feel any better, Janice feels the same way about it as you do."

"I bet she was tore up when she heard about the house burning down."

"Well, actually, she doesn't know about it yet. I was kind of planning to keep her busy in Ecuador, while I get the insurance man out here, and get a new house started."

"You ain't told her?"

"I'm hoping that she will be so impressed with the new house, that it will soften the blow of loosing the old one."

"The house ain't the main thing. It's the stuff *in* the house that's going to up-set her. All her family pictures, and sentimental stuff. That's what's going to get her. And she's going to be pissed off that you didn't tell her about it sooner."

"Well, she's been pissed off before, and got over it. I'm the one that has to live with her, and I say take the chance. Well, I need to get the insurance man out here. What is the agent's name?"

"Bob Butterworth. Your mother has him on speed dial."

———•◆•———

Travis called the insurance man, and had him meet him at the house at 10 A.M. Though he had a Homeowner's Policy, he had never met the agent, because he had bought the policy from his predecessor, Mr. Wesson, who retired several years ago. When Mr. Butterworth got out of his car, Travis shook his hand, and asked how his wife, Mrs. Butterworth was doing. "Is she still selling syrup?" He asked with a smile.

"Mr. Lee, if I had a dime for every time someone made that joke about Mrs. Butterworth, I would be a rich man!"

"Sorry. I couldn't resist."

"It's good to see that you still have a sense of humor, after loosing your home. Most people would be devastated by such a loss."

"It's just stuff, and stuff can be replaced, to an extent."

"That's a healthy way of looking at it. I heard about the fire, from a member of the fire department. I wondered why you took so long to call me."

"I have been out of the country for awhile, in Ecuador."

"Oh! Vacation, or working?"

"A little of both. I went in with some friends on a land deal down there. We've been making improvements to the land. I had someone house-sitting at our home here in Laurel Grove, when the fire happened."

"I see. Well, your policy is for full coverage, so lets take a look at the damage." As they walked, they continued to talk. "This person who was house sitting for you, is he a relative of yours?"

"No, I don't even know his name. He was appointed to look after the house by a trusted friend. I was told that it started as a grease fire in the kitchen, and it got out of hand. Also, there was some delay in the fire department getting there, which didn't help. I have not actually seen the house yet. I'll be seeing it for the first time when you do."

As they walked to the top of the hill, they were met by an armed soldier.

"Halt! This is a restricted area."

"Stand down, soldier. I am Sergeant Travis Lee, and this house you are guarding is *my* house."

"Do you have a photo ID sir?"

"Yes. Here is my passport. This man with me is Bob Butterworth, my insurance man."

"Do I need a photo ID too?" Bob asked.

"No sir, not as long as you are accompanied by Mr. Lee. Okay, you both may pass."

When they got out of hearing, Bob asked, "What the hell? Why are soldiers guarding your house?"

"I'm kind of in the reserves. When 911 happened, I volunteered to return to active service, to train snipers. As a part of the deal I struck with the military, they have to watch over my property while I am gone."

"So this time you were spending in Ecuador was more than just improving a land investment. It was also related to your training of snipers?"

"That is actually classified information, Bob. Sorry."

"And if you told me what you are really doing there, you would have to kill me, right?" Bob said smiling.

Travis gave him an intentionally fake smile, and replied "Something like that."

"Then please don't tell me anything about Ecuador! Oh man! Is this your house?"

"Apparently, this is what's left of it." Travis replied, shocked himself at the total destruction. His dad was right, there was virtually nothing left but a concrete slab. The fire had been so hot, it had reduced the entire home to ashes. The only thing left standing in place, ironically, was the porcelain toilet. He had read many a book and newspaper sitting on that throne. The epiphanies of some of his best ideas were inspired while sitting at the 'oval office'. It was once a private refuge. Now it was a relic for all the world to see. Large blue tarps had been spread over most areas of the burned house, and weighted down with bricks, to preserve what might be left of their personal effects. He didn't even bother to raise the tarps, to look under them. He didn't really want to see what little was left. He would wait and let Janice look for surviving items.

"It looks like a total loss, Travis. I'm sorry." Bob said.

"This is a little overwhelming." Travis said. "I lived here most of my life. All five of my kids were born and raised in this house. To see it just…gone, is hard to take."

"I understand." Bob said. "In my line of work, I see this all too often. But fortunately, you were insured. I know I can't replace your memories, or sentimental items, but at least I can put you back in a home! How long will it take you to comb through the ashes, so we can bulldoze the site, and start re-building?"

"Actually Bob, Janice and I have talked for years about how we should have built the house on top the hill, instead of on the back-side, like this. When we got married, the house site just sort of evolved. Is there a chance that when we rebuild, we can have it built over there, on top the hill?"

"I don't see why not. The site would be easier to prepare than this one. So you intend to just leave this burned house back here covered with tarps?"

"Yes, for the time being. You see, Janice doesn't even know the house burned yet, and I'd like to have the new house built before she finds out."

"So your wife is where?"

"Ecuador. We are temporarily living there."

"Okay, so we should go back to my office, and wade through all the paperwork, and get this project rolling. Do you have a preferred contractor in mind, to re-build your house?"

"Yes. I'll have to look them up in the phone book. And I know where I can get a copy of the original floor plans for my house. Though I might want to scale it down some, since most of my kids are gone now."

"No, don't go smaller. Your kids might be gone, but think about the grand-kids! The insurance goes by cubic feet of floor space, so we will pay for building it back at original size. You can even use a new blueprint, and design an entirely new house, as long as you do not exceed the original floor space."

"That sounds good. Janice might want some changes. But how do I ask her that without telling her about the fire? I tell you what. I'll go ahead and get you the floor plans, and line up a contractor. In about three days, I can call you with any modifications to the blueprint. But as far as I am concerned, they can start today, clearing off the spot, and pouring the foundation."

"You said top of the hill? Won't those fruit trees be in the way?"

"No, they can take them out. They're old trees anyway."

Mr. Butterworth got Travis to mark off exactly where he wanted the new house to be built, then they went into Laurel Grove to do the necessary paperwork that was required to get the project started. It ended up taking all morning, but when he was done, he had also personally spoke to the building contractor, and they were on the same page as to what he wanted.

That afternoon, he went back to his parents house, and spent the afternoon conducting the chemical tests that were required for his investigation of the Mexico City plane crash to be completed. The process was prolonged by the fact that his Dad was right there watching him, and asking questions about every step of the process. He never knew his Dad was interested in such things. By dinner time, he had everything completed, and the results were ready to fax to Jim. After dinner, he drove over to the University of Central Alabama Library, to fax the information, and he was done. But along with the faxed information, he included a note to Jim, to not communicate with him via cell phone, because his phone had been compromised.

Before heading back home, General Morgan called, wanting to meet with him somewhere to discuss something of importance. He was already en-rout from Fort Benning, and would be in Laurel Grove within thirty minutes. They agreed to meet in the city park.

Travis went to the park, to pick out a picnic table for their meeting. Morgan arrived shortly after.

"You say you have something of importance?" Travis asked.

"Yes, I think you will find this interesting." He sat down at the concrete table beside Travis and opened his briefcase.

"Remember me telling you that I could use the leeway provided by the Patriot Act, to intercept phone calls?"

"Yes."

"Well, I got an injunction to record any calls in and out of FBN Investigations, and what that does, I am told, by the experts, is that it also permits us to access any kind of wire-tap that may have been placed on their lines. True, we were just 'fishing', but guess what?"

"What?"

"We got a bite! We detected an older style wire tap on their phones, the kind used back in the '70's. Not only that, but with our sophisticated system, we were able to back-track their system, and find link-ups to three separate cell phones, which we also got injunctions on, to legally access them, and guess what else we found?"

"Tell me."

"All three phones were registered to Muslim clerics, one at a mosque in Charlotte, North Carolina. One in Atlanta, Georgia, and the third in St. Louis, Missouri. We have records of their calls back and forth with a person in Cairo, Egypt. We have gained a wealth of information from tapping these guys! Information that we never would have gotten otherwise. You see, our surveillance technique is not to actually listen in on all phone conversations. That would be literally impossible, given the millions of calls made every minute. So we use the computer to flag certain words and phrases, such as 'bomb', or 'Al Qaeda', or 'attack', or any other words that our specialists think that terrorists might use in their communications. However, it didn't take the bad guys long to realize what we were doing, so they changed their wording. The word 'bomb' might be substituted with 'potato', or 'Al Qaeda' might be substituted with something like 'Girl Scouts'. So then their conversations go unnoticed, because there are no 'red flag' words to stand out. But when we back tracked these three cell phones, we were able to focus in on them, and easily interpret their ambient and docile code words.

Of course, they were in Arabic, but our translators had no problem with that. What I have here, is a printed out record of conversations between their operatives in this country, and the cleric in Cairo, who is apparently directing their actions. According to their conversations, they were not sure what happened to the two hit men they sent to Mexico City, because they did not call in at their appointed time. But later, as you will read there, after you called Jim Deshler, they knew that you had killed them. And they heard you say that you were headed home to Alabama, and that your family was still in Ecuador. I'll give you a few minutes to read over the transcript. Start with page three."

Travis settled back on the bench and read the back and forth conversations between the people who were trying to kill him. It was very enlightening. It didn't fill in all the gaps, but it was enough that he was able to understand how they were doing what they were doing. When he finished, he slapped the report back down on the table.

"So their substitute word for me is 'little boy'?"

"Apparently so."

"And these guys are in no way affiliated with Al Qaeda?"

"No, it is the Muslim Brotherhood that is after you. Al Qaeda is too busy on the run in Afghanistan right now to be concerned with something as petty as this. Yes, they were using your phone calls to Jim Deshler to tell them where to find you. They knew you were going to Mexico City, and even knew what hotel you would be staying in. They thought it was going to be a simple thing to catch you there and kill you."

"And they almost did. A hit man was the last thing I expected to see when I opened my hotel door."

"You didn't read the last page of that transcript, did you?"

"I thought I did."

"You'd better go back and look again." Morgan said.

"Oh, yeah, I *did* miss the last page." He read the last page, and realized that the last page was by far the most important.

"So they have already sent two hit men to Ecuador, and two here! What time was this phone call made?"

"Before ten this morning."

"So if they were sent out from Atlanta this morning, Atlanta being the hub of the South, they probably flew out this afternoon to Quito.

And according to this transcript, they know I went to Coca. Which means they will catch the morning flight to Coca tomorrow morning!"

"Did you tell Jim exactly *where* in Ecuador you would be?"

"I told him Coca, and it's not a big place, so it won't be hard for them to find me, or my family there."

"That can be a problem then." Morgan said. "Do you have any ideas?"

"Yeah, let me call Steve down in Ecuador."

"I'll go for a walk."

"No, you can stay. You might want to hear what I tell him."

He punched out the number, and waited. Finally Steve answered.

"Hey Travis! What's up?"

"How are things going down there?"

"Really good. We got a lot done today."

"Great. But I've got some not-so-good news. We have found out that two hit-men have been dispatched to Coca, to try to find me, or my family. They are likely to arrive on the morning plane tomorrow from Quito."

"What do they look like?"

"No idea. But they could be Egyptians."

"So you want me to 'greet' them at the airport?"

"No, I want you to try to get my family out of there, before they arrive."

"The best place in the world to hide them is at the lodge. There we can see anyone coming or going. We have pretty good security."

"Is Calvin still out there?"

"Yes, and he is a big help."

"Well, let him stay at the lodge with you. But I want you to put Janice on the morning flight to Quito. Tell her I will meet her at the Quito airport, at say…the McDonald's restaurant in the food court. If she wants to know why, tell her that it is a surprise."

"Okay, I can do that. So the hit men will get off the plane, and then Janice will get on. You do know that there is only one flight, Condor Express, and it makes a morning run both ways?"

"I didn't realize that, but if that's the case, then you need to keep Janice out of sight until the bad guys get out of the way."

"Oh yeah. No problem. Do they know her by sight?"

"I don't know."

"No problem. I'll take care of it. Uh, what do you want us to do with the hit men?"

"Be creative. And thanks, Steve. I'll square up with you later on the plane ticket."

"No problem."

Travis put his phone away. "That is taken care of. Now I have to get to Quito, as soon as possible."

"According to their phone conversations, they want to get you and your family! You really stirred up a hornet's nest when you killed that cleric, and they are determined to get you. I mean, you have already killed four men they have sent to get you. I wonder how many more they will sacrifice to get you?"

"I guess we'll find out."

"I can take you to Fort Benning, and get you on a military transport to Atlanta."

"Even better, I can go to the Arlington County airport, and charter a flight small plane to Atlanta. It will probably get me there quicker. And besides, I can leave my rental car at the airport."

"Okay, let's go." Morgan said. As they walked to their cars, Morgan asked, "Where are you going to take Janice from Quito?"

"I promised to take her to the Galapagos Islands, and this might be a good time to do that."

"Well, while you are gone, we can follow the leads here in this country, and see where they go, and who they associate with. The 'sleepers' here will be rounded up in no time. Unless the Justice Department wants to watch them awhile, and see how many others they can catch. This is a golden opportunity for them to identify sleepers, and secretly monitor their actions and movements. But I don't know if we can get the contacts in Cairo. It's like a hornet nest there. Without getting the nest, the hit men will continue coming until they get you."

"So let's go to Egypt, and clean out the nest."

"That might be a bigger job than it sounds like."

"Bigger than the VC headquarters at Doc Chow?"

Morgan smiled. "You certainly cleaned out *that* nest, didn't you? But we were at war with North Vietnam at the time. Egypt is our ally, so to speak. We couldn't do something like that to them. We'll have to drop that as an option. The CIA was pushing their resources to get you in the last time."

"No, if you remember, I was the one that made the in-roads to get in and make that hit. The CIA didn't have a clue. And they still don't."

"Well, we're not going to do it again, because we have orders to stand down on this matter. We can get them if they come over here, but we're not allowed to go back over there."

"Oh well. Let's see how things shake out. I'll call you in a couple of days."

"Yes, you do that."

Travis got in his car and headed to the Arlington County Airport. He called ahead to book a charter flight to Atlanta.

The sun was going down when he got to Atlanta, and there were no flights to Quito that late in the day. But he was able to get a connecting flight to Miami, then a red-eye flight to Quito from there. That would get him to Quito before Janice was due arrive there. He sighed. It seemed like he spent half his life flying these days.

He had not taken the time to go back home to get his suitcase, so he was going to be traveling light. But he could shop for clothes later. He wondered what kind of clothes they would need for the Galapagos? Clothes for hot weather, or cool weather? He could read up on it on the way.

⇥ 29 ⇤

Janice was delighted to find out that her husband had a surprise for her. She was hoping it was a plane ticket back home to Alabama, but Steve burst her bubble by assuring her it wasn't that.

"No, I think it is something else. I swear, I don't know what it is, but it's got to be something nice, because he 'owes you'."

"He owes me?"

"Yeah, he said he hates that he had to put you through all this, but of course, it was necessary. Yeah, he owes you something nice!"

"I hope you're right. So do I need to take my suitcase?"

"I don't know. He didn't say. If you needed it, I'm sure he would have said so. No, I would leave it here."

"What about Calvin? Is he supposed to come too?"

"No, he specifically said to leave Calvin at the lodge. And in fact, you probably couldn't drag him away from there with a team of wild horses! He really likes it there.

"So I fly out in the morning?"

"Yeah, the plane will arrive from Quito about ten, then returns about 10:45. Travis said he will be waiting for you at the McDonald's restaurant in the airport at Quito."

"I can't wait! This is so exciting." Janice said.

———◆◆———

After informing Janice of her surprise, Steve went about making plans for their two 'uninvited guests', that would be arriving with the 10 o'clock plane. Two of his lodge workers were in town with him, to gather supplies. Reading between the lines of what Travis told him, he called his guys together for a strategic meeting.

"Pablo, you and Carlos will have special assignments tomorrow. For those assignments, both of you will need cell phones, so here are your cell phones. You know my number?"

"Yes, Senor Steve!"

"Okay, here is what is happening. Tomorrow two foreign men will get off the 10 A.M. plane from Quito. Those two men are assassins sent here to kill Senor Travis, and his family."

"Dios Mio!"

"Say it is not so!"

"Now, we are not going to let that happen. Travis and his wife will be gone tomorrow, so we are going to take care of this problem while they are gone. The assassins will not know that their targets are gone, but we will try to lead them to the lodge, where we can deal with them. Carlos, does your cousin still drive a taxi?"

"Yes, Senor Steve."

"Good. Then tomorrow, you will borrow your cousin's taxi, and pick up the foreigners at the airport. Talk to the other taxi drivers, and make sure that you are the one to pick them up. You will take them where they want to go, and then call me."

"Si, Senor!"

"Pablo, you are to be a water taxi driver tomorrow. Get our boat from Emillio, and use it as a water taxi. Stay at the dock near my house and wait on Carlos to bring the guys to you."

"Si, Senor."

"Carlos, if they need a water taxi, be sure to direct them to Pablo. And Pablo, you let me know where they are at all times."

"Yes, Senor Steve."

"If we can get them on our boat, and headed out to the lodge, be sure to let me know, and we will have a 'welcoming party' ready for them, when they arrive."

───── ◆ ─────

Calvin's role at the lodge had changed somewhat. Instead of being just Emillio's assistant in procuring food, he was now used more in different aspects of the construction. He liked that, because he was learning new skills every day. After helping assemble the water tank, he fitted and assembled all the pipe connecting the tank with the pumps, and the pumps to the river. Others were doing the hard work, of digging the ditches, and having to pick through the rock. His job was to fit and assemble the pipe, and then turn on the pumps, to be sure the pipes did not leak before they were covered back up.

And of course, in the process of digging all those ditches, they found emeralds at every turn of the shovel, it seemed. All 'rocks of interest' were collected in a bucket, and sent to Steve's tent at the end of each day.

The first bungalow was completed, and Calvin moved his sleeping bag into it right away. The last thing to be completed was to connect the water. Calvin helped them do that, and then they had a mock ceremony, in which everyone gathered at the bungalow for the official 'turning of the spigot' that meant the bungalow was now livable, and had 'running water'. After the dirt and spider webs blew out of the faucet, and cleared the lines, and it ran with (relatively) clear river water, they all cheered. Later the filtration system would be put on line, and they could actually drink the water…maybe…after testing it. But for the time being, Calvin proudly called the new bungalow his home.

The construction of the main Lodge was progressing slowly, but very impressively. The massive mahogany slabs were notched and fitted together with great skill and care, and the graceful, yet durable frame was starting to take shape. The floor boards were being cut and fitted in geometric designs that would be a delight to the eye. While the heavy-duty woodwork was going on, some crews were busy with already cutting bamboo poles that would be used to construct the massive thatched roof. The number of poles needed had been carefully calculated, and daily quotas were set, so that they would have enough material gathered by the time it was needed. Once they went up with it, it needed to all go up together. The same method was used to collect the thatching. Daily quotas built up an enormous pile of thatching after just a couple of days. Calvin found it hard to believe that the thatching could actually repel a torrential rainforest downpour, but he became a believer after the first rain fell on his small bungalow. It repelled the rain perfectly. The men who constructed it came by to see if their handiwork held up, and it did. Calvin's conclusion was, these men really knew what they were doing.

In the early morning, he liked to watch the monkeys swarm around the small feeding tower over next to the jungle. The cook would stock it with green bananas every morning before he started breakfast, and by the time breakfast was served, the monkeys had arrived. Ropes had been tied from the tower, to the trees in three directions, so the monkeys never had to touch the ground. They shimmied across the rope like acrobats, and put on quite a show. Even the baby monkeys made it to the tower. After about forty minutes, they had depleted the bananas, and returned to the jungle, via the ropes.

That evening, after a long day of hot, tiring work, they all met at the kitchen, for dinner, and then relaxation afterwards they sat around their fire and talked. Most of the conversation was in Spanish, but as a group, they were trying to gradually get more comfortable conversing in English. They knew that once the Lodge opened, many of their guests would be English speaking, so everyone had to get proficient in English eventually. They would try to tell stories in English, just for practice, and Calvin would sometimes help them word what they wanted to say, even though he did not speak Spanish. He was a good sounding board for them.

While they were around the fire, a water taxi arrived, and Steve came into their camp with two bottles of rum to pass around. He called everyone together for an important meeting.

"Tomorrow we anticipate having two visitors." he started.

"More government inspectors?" Someone asked, then there was a smattering of laughs. The joke was, one could hardly turn around at times, without bumping into an inspector.

"It is *always* possible that we could have inspectors! But no, the two strangers we are expecting are bad men, *malos*. They are coming here looking for our partner Travis, and his family. Calvin, I am taking your mom to the airport in the morning to send her Quito, where your dad will meet her, and take her somewhere safe. He said for you to stay here, because this is the safest place for you, right now."

"Who are those men?" Calvin asked.

"Do you remember the attack at your home in Laurel Grove?"

"Yes."

"It's the same people that tried before. Your Dad got word that two more are headed down here to kill him. But we will not let that happen, will we, Men?"

"NO!" was the unanimous reply.

"Okay, here is what will happen, I think. Carlos will be driving his cousin's taxi tomorrow in town. He will try to bring these men to the dock, where Pablo will bring them here. Once they get here…" Steve didn't have to finish the sentence. Everyone thought they knew what would happen then. There was serious chatter in Spanish, and a clear difference of opinion over what would happen then. Steve participated in this back and forth banter, until he raised his hands in the fire-light, and said,

"Listen, it might be best if we *do not* kill them, at least not right off. These men are terrorists from Egypt, and the U.S. authorities might want to beat some information out of them first. So we will capture them here, and tie them up, and we will let Travis decide what to do with them when he returns."

He laid out further instructions on how to deal with them, because he didn't know if they would be armed or unarmed. He tried to verse his men on what to do, no matter what the situation. "If these men are armed, we will take no chances. Comprendemos? We do not risk our own people, if they are armed. We kill them, but only in self-defense!"

When he was sure that his men knew what to do, he turned to go back to Coca, and saw Calvin.

"Calvin, when this goes down, I want you far away from the action. I told your dad I would make sure that you stay safe."

"It sounds like you have everything taken care of."

"I hope so. But if you see the boat arrive with two men tomorrow, you stay up there at the water tank, or somewhere out of the way."

Steve went back to the boat to return to Coca. When he was well out of hearing, Calvin shook his head.

"Stay out of the way, *my ass*!" he sneered.

⇥ 30 ⇤

Travis arrived in Quito at sunrise the next morning. He slept some on the plane, so he was not totally wiped out. He was cautious in getting off the plane, by pulling his hat down over his face, because he was sure that the assassins were already here, waiting on the flight to Coca, which would leave at 8:00. And he was fairly sure they had seen a picture of him, so they might recognize him. Travis, on the other hand, had no idea what they looked like.

He walked down the concourse, went to the men's room, then went to a vendor for a cup of coffee. The girl was perplexed when he asked for ice to cool down the coffee. "Asi mi gusta," he smiled at her.

He slowly walked back down the concourse to the Condor Airlines gate. There was only one. He wondered if one plane was all the company owned. He found a stray newspaper, and sat among a crowd of travelers across the aisle from Condor, where he could peer over his paper and try to identify his assassins. There were two pair of men sitting on the other side, and either one could fit the profile, so he kept an eye on them. Soon one of the four men got up and went to the men's room. As he went past him, Travis could clearly see that the man had Egyptian features.

For a fleeting moment Travis started to get up and follow him into the men's room. If there were no witnesses, he could take him out easily, and leave him locked in a stall. Sooner or later, his partner would miss him, and go looking for him. Then he could take out the second man too. He felt in his pocket. Yes, there was his trusty nylon cord! It would make no mess, spill no blood, and choke off any cries for help.

But that was still too risky. This was a busy airport, and men were constantly coming and going from the men's room. Chances were, he would be seen. And then of course, there was the chance that these were not the assassins. Best to lay low and watch.

At 7:15 there was a call to board the plane, and he watched the two pairs of men get up and go to the boarding door. After they got up, he could clearly see that the other pair were local men from Ecuador, so the two he originally suspected were most likely the guys. He would wait a half hour, then call Steve with a description of the two men, so he could spot them when they landed.

With the plane departing, he had about a five hour wait for it to return with Janice, so he used the time to hunt the Tourist Information desk. They, in turn, referred him to a travel agent near the main entrance to the concourse. He knew they would have brochures to make plans with. He asked for information on trips to the Galapagos Islands, and other things to do in Ecuador.

When the girl heard he was wanting to go to the Galapagos, she asked when he intended to go.

"I was hoping to go there later today, with my wife."

"I'm sorry, but there is a three day waiting list to visit the Galapagos."

"Why is that?"

"Because there are so many tourists wanting to go there. I was told just minutes ago that you must make reservations now, to go there by this coming Wednesday."

"Well that throws a kink in my plans. I was hoping to go there today."

"Well sir, I can go ahead and sign you up on a small ship, to visit the main five islands of the Galapagos, departure Wednesday morning. But in the meantime, I can recommend a lot of things to do around the Quito area for the next three days before you leave. Would you be interested in something like that?"

"How long will the five island tour be?"

"Five days. One day will be totally devoted to each of the five islands. You will be amazed at how all five islands are so different from one another."

"So three days touring around Quito, then five days in the Galapagos, that's eight days."

"Is that a problem?"

"No, that will be fine. Sign me up, and my wife also."

"Okay I will have to get some in formation from you."

He spent almost an hour there, signing up, asking questions, and gathering information on what to do the first three days. Afterward, he went and ate a light breakfast, to wait on Janice. As he waited, he called Steve, with a description of the two Egyptians.

"You should have no problem spotting them. They stick out like camels at a rodeo. Both are wearing the same color kaki pants, but one is wearing a brown button-up shirt, and the other is wearing a drab olive tee shirt. Both men have thin black beards. They are thin, but muscular. Both of them boarded wearing dark sunglasses."

"You didn't get fingerprints too?" Steve asked, tongue in cheek.

"No, but I almost followed one to the men's room for a blood sample though."

"I should have no problem spotting them. But let me ask you this: Are you as *sure* that these *are* the assassins, as you were that the Egyptian cleric was *Osama Bin Laden*?"

"I get your point. And yes, there is the possibility that these men are not the assassins. But you decide for yourself, once they get to Coca. Watch them, and what they do. But don't take any chances, Steve. If these really are who I think they are then I think they could be very dangerous men."

"Don't worry about that. I'll have lots of people with eyes on them, once they get here. Do you have any preference of what we do with them?"

"You're not thinking about trying to capture them, are you?"

"Do you have an objection to that? It's either capture them, or kill them. What do you want us to do?"

"I don't think they know where to look for me after they get to Coca. So they will be asking around town, and probably showing a photo of me to the locals. If no one has seen me, they have no reason to go out to the Lodge. Just watch them, but don't do anything. If they can't find me, and nobody has seen me, then maybe they will go back to the States."

"Okay Travis. Don't worry about a thing. Call me in a couple of days for an update."

"I will."

Steve had no intention of playing that silly game for days. He had work to get done on the Lodge, so they needed to handle this situation as quick as possible. He looked at his watch. It was almost time to take Janice to the airport.

━━━◆◆◆━━━

As Steve drove her to the airport, she was too happy to contain her anticipation.

"I'm so excited that Travis wants me to meet him in Quito! Steve, are you sure that you don't know what this big surprise is?"

"Honestly, I don't know, Janice. He did not confide in me what the surprise is."

"You are lying! I'm sure that you know!"

"Scout's honor, I don't know!"

"Steve, you probably never were a Scout!"

"Yes I was! In fact, I made it all the way to Eagle Scout! And on my honor as a scout, I swear that I don't know what it is."

"You're lying!"

"Okay, you're right! I *do* know what it is! The surprise is, he is going to tell you the truth about himself. He's been gay all these years, and he has decided to finally come out of the closet! And yes, he and I are romantically involved!"

Janice crossed her arms and stared daggers through him. "Now I *know* you're lying! Some Scout you are!"

"I think he wants it to be a surprise, so he didn't tell me what it is, because he knows I can't keep a secret. But it's got to be good."

"Is that my plane coming in?"

"It almost has to be. Yeah, it has the Condor logo. Looks like it is right on time. We need to go to the Condor counter to get your ticket. Come with me and show them your passport."

Actually, he wanted to get her out of the way of the disembarking passengers. Not that the assassins would recognize her, but he didn't want to take any chances. So as she was getting her ticket, he watched the passengers getting off, and recognized the two men Travis had described to him. He took out his cell phone and called Carlos, to make sure he was in position to offer them a ride, and also gave Carlos their description.

Carlos was parked in front of the terminal. A couple of tourists exited the terminal, and tried to hire him, but he said he was waiting on someone, and referred them to another taxi. This happened three times before his targets appeared, and he approached them and offered his services. They accepted, and got in the back seat.

"Take us to a motel." one of the men said.

"Which one?" Carlos asked.

"The cheapest one." he replied.

"That would be 'La Sonrisa'. My name is Carlos! Where are you gentlemen from?"

"America."

"Ah yes! I love Americans! All of Coca loves Americans! You will have a good time here, no? Are you here on business or pleasure?"

"Business." the other man said.

"Ah, then you work for Exxon?" Carlos asked.

"You ask a lot of questions, for a taxi driver." the brown shirt said.

"That is because I know that you are new to Coca, and I know where everything is! I can find anything for you! If you want to fish, I can take you to a bait and tackle shop! I can tell you all the good restaurants! You want to hunt? I take you to get guns and ammo. You want 'weed' or prostitutes, I can fix you up there too! We have beautiful women here!"

The two men looked at one another.

"You can take us to buy guns?"

"Yes, no problem! You want shotguns or rifles?"

"What about hand guns?"

"Ah, you see, hand guns are illegal to own in Ecuador, except for the police, of course. But that does not mean I cannot find them for you! It is more difficult, and more expensive, but I know someone, who knows someone. I can make a few calls."

"Yes, do that. But take us to our motel first."

"Si Senor! After I drop you there, I will call around."

As soon as he dropped them at their hotel, Carlos called Steve, and told him that they were looking for guns. Steve gave him his instructions, and said he would call Pablo for him. Carlos waited for the men to return to the taxi. When they emerged, Carlos had good news.

"You are in luck, my friends! I call around, and find out that a gun dealer up the river has just received a new shipment of guns!"

"He is not here in town?"

"No, he cannot sell guns inside the city limits. His place is 12 miles up the river. And with him, you must pay in cash. It is no problem to get there, because we have water taxis to take you there!"

"Can *you* take us there?"

"Me? I must operate my taxi! This is my living! But I take you to a good friend who has a water taxi. I will tell him what you want, and he will take you there. No problem! And the water taxi only costs a dollar, both ways!"

"Okay, take us to your friend. But this had better not be a trick! We are not fools! We were sent here by very important people."

"I am honest with you, my friends! You want guns, and this man up the river is the man to buy them from."

The two men put their heads together and quietly discussed things in Arabic. By the time they got to the dock, they had come up with a better idea. Carlos got out of the taxi and waved in Pablo, and his boat.

"This is my friend Pablo. He can take you up the river, to the gun dealer. Pablo! Venga, venga!"

Pablo tied off his boat and jumped up on the dock, to come see the men. When he got there, Brown Shirt had a better idea.

"Let us do this: I give *you* the money, and you go up the river and buy the guns for us."

This was an unexpected turn of events. Things were going exactly as planned until this. Pablo pretended he did not understand, because he was not sure how to respond to it. Carlos answered for him.

"Pablo's English is not so good. But it would be bad for *us* to go purchase the guns for you. As Ecuadorians, we cannot be caught with a hand gun! Many months in jail! But for you, a foreigner to get caught with a hand gun, you just pay a small fine."

"This gun dealer, is he Ecuadorian?"

"No, he is North American. He can smuggle things in, because he knows the officials here. He knows how to 'grease palms' to get things into Ecuador."

Brown Shirt pointed to Pablo, and said, "Send him to the American gun dealer. Tell him that a customer will pay him well for two 9mm hand guns, and two boxes of bullets. Tell him to bring them to town, so we can see them. We will pay his price. Tell him!"

"I can call the American, and save Pablo the trip." Carlos said. "Excuse me, while I call."

"Why not call the American, and let me speak to him?" Brown Shirt asked.

"Yes, I can do that." He took out his cell phone, and called Steve. "Hello, Steve! I call you back about the guns. I have a customer here who wants hand guns, but he does not want to go up river to your shop."

"Let me speak to him!" Brown shirt demanded.

"Here, he wishes to speak with you himself." He handed off the phone to Brown Shirt.

"Hello."

"With whom am I speaking, please?" Steve asked.

"Do you need to know my name to sell me a gun?"

"No, but I *do* need to have some assurance that you are not working for the national police."

"I just arrived here from the United States."

"You can say anything over the phone."

"I need you to bring me two 9mm guns with ammunition, to town, so I can examine them."

"Perhaps Carlos did not make this clear to you. I cannot legally bring these guns into town. In fact, I am greatly stretching my legal boundaries by selling them *outside* of the town. For you to insist that I come to town, that sound like a set-up, to me. So either you come to me, or you find guns somewhere else."

"It sounds like a set-up to me as well, for me to go up river to meet you." Brown Shirt said.

"Well, Slick, take it or leave it!" Steve said. "You're the one wanting to buy a gun. I'll sell it to someone who is willing to come to me."

Brown Shirt sighed, and spoke to Green Shirt in Arabic, then got back on the phone to Steve.

"Okay, we come to you. How much for two guns and ammo?"

"You said 9mm? I assume you'll want extra clips too?"

"Yes, extra clips."

"I think $1200 will cover it."

"What! That is robbery! I pay $800 and no more!"

"This here ain't the U.S.A., where there's gun stores on every corner, Slick! I had to smuggle these babies in, and that involved great risk to me! I think $1200 is a real good price. Take it or leave it!"

"Okay. We will be there. Within an hour." He hung up, but he wasn't happy. He and Green Shirt had a discussion in Arabic, then he told Carlos, "We need to go back to our hotel, and then to an ATM, then back to our hotel again."

"And then back here to the dock?"

"Yes."

"Okay, I will tell Pablo to be here waiting on you."

On the way back to the hotel, Carlos tried to carry on a conversation with the two men, but they were not very talkative.

"It might be none of my business, but why do you need hand guns anyway?" Carlos ventured.

"You are right," Green Shirt replied, "It is none of your business."

But Brown Shirt added, "For personal protection."

"Yes, it is good to have protection, if you go into the jungle. But here in town it is very safe. You will like Coca, because the people here really friendly."

"This Steve that we are buying guns from, he is an American?"

"Yes, he is a *North* American, from the U.S.A."

"Are there many North Americans here?"

"Yes, most are here to work for Exxon, but some are tourists."

"We have a friend here in Coca, from the United States. Perhaps you can help us find him." Brown Shirt said.

"What is his name?"

"Travis Lee."

"Mmm, the name does not sound familiar."

"Perhaps you have seen him? Look at this photo." He handed a photograph to Carlos, and he looked at it critically.

"You know, I think I *have* seen this man!"

"Where?"

"I drove him and his wife and son from the airport a few days ago."

"Where did you take them?"

"To the expensive hotel here in town."

"Is he still there?"

"I do not know."

"Did he go anywhere else?"

"I am just one of many taxis here. He could have gone anywhere with another taxi. I do remember that he and his son were talking about fishing on the Napo River."

"Where?"

"They did not say. But I tell you what, if I see Mr. Lee, I will tell him that you are looking for him."

"No, do not do that. We want our visit here to be a surprise to him. But if you see him, please contact us at our hotel. I will make it worth your trouble."

"Okay, I will be on the lookout for him. Perhaps we will happen to see him in town, while we are gone to the ATM."

He took them by their hotel, then to an ATM. While they were both withdrawing money, Carlos made a quick call to Steve, conveying that they had asked about Travis, so they had to be the right men. Steve told him to proceed with the plan as rehearsed, and to be vague about what he knew about Travis.

Carlos took them back to their hotel, so they could leave their identifying documents there, then he took them to the dock, where Pablo was waiting. When he saw them speed away, Carlos called Steve again.

"They are on their way."

<hr>

Pablo sped his guests up-river, weaving to dodge logs and other floating debris in the water. He waved as he passed another water taxi, then slowed up as he passed a canoe of Indian fishermen who were letting out their gill nets. He sped up again in the open water, until he neared the lodge's natural lagoon, then he slowed and picked his way around the gravel bars, and then up to where the giant pyle driver machine was busy driving piles for their new dock. A crew of lodge workers were busy grading out a level walk-way, and inlaying it with flat stones from the river. Steve was there supervising them, and watching for the arrival of their 'guests'. As they off-loaded on to the bank, he came forward to meet them.

"Good morning, gentlemen. How was your boat ride?"

"It was good. Where are your guns?"

"That's what I like! A man who gets right down to business! I am Steve, and this is my landing here. See the big tent on top the hill? That is where you can look over my inventory. I hope you brought cash?"

"Yes, we have $1200."

"You should have brought more, because once you see my inventory, you are going to be like kids in a candy store! You'll want to buy more than just a couple of 9mm hand guns!" As they walked up the hill, Steve impressed them with what he had for sale. "I have AK-47's, M-1's, AR-15, .308, the latest in military assault rifles. I have grenades, smoke canisters, Claymores, MRI's, bullet-proof vests, laser sights, night vision goggles. And for the right price, I can make you the proud owner of four rocket propelled grenades, and a sidewinder anti-aircraft missile!"

"You have all that in this tent?" Brown Shirt asked.

"Some of it. If it's not here, it's in one of my storage facilities close by."

They stopped at the entrance to the tent, and Steve said, "Please, after you!"

They left the bright noon sunlight, and entered the dark tent, and it took their eyes a few moments to adjust to the dim interior. Finally when they were able to clearly see, they knew they had walked into a trap. A dozen men with guns surrounded them.

Steve doled out plain instructions to them.

"Face down on the ground, gentlemen! Hands behind your backs, and do it now! You are about to be hog-tied!"

As he complied, Brown Shirt asked, "Are you CIA?"

"Nope!" Steve answered. "I am an Eagle Scout, with the Boy Scouts of America! You two are under arrest."

"Why are we under arrest? We have done nothing!"

"You were trying to buy guns illegally."

"But we did not buy them! You have no evidence!"

"Get those ropes good and tight, Ortega. We don't want our guests to get away and give our lodge a bad review."

"Where will we keep them?"

"Let's try the storage shed, until I can make other arrangements. Someone search their pockets. Put everything on the table. Someone go tell the blacksmith that I've got a small job for him, and to meet me at the storage shed in 15 minutes. What have they got?"

"Not much. $1200 cash, pocket change, and a hotel key."

"No passports?"

"No."

"They don't even have a knife?"

"No knife.

"Well, that is just plain embarrassing! Everyone should carry a knife in the rain forest! Pablo, take that hotel key, and go to town. You and Carlos go to their hotel room, and get all their stuff, and bring it here. They have to have some ID with them somewhere."

"Si Senor Steve."

≒ 31 ≒

Janice's plane was right on time, and Travis met her with a hug.

"Okay, what is the surprise?" she asked.

"We are about to start a three day tour of the sights around Quito, and then we will go to the Galapagos Islands for five days! How does that sound?"

"Are you serious?"

"Of course I am! I already made reservations, and I have a rental car waiting outside!"

"But I didn't even bring my suitcase!"

"That's okay. We'll go shopping first, and then start seeing the sights."

"Did Steve know about all this?"

"No, I just told him to get you here. I didn't say why."

"How was your job in Mexico?"

"It was easy. The hardest part was the paperwork."

"So what is there to see around Quito?"

"Well, there's museums, and old cathedrals. Spanish colonial architecture."

"Anything else?"

"Well, there is the Middle of the Earth monument, just out of Quito, to the north-east."

"What is that?" Janice asked, as the left the airport, for his rental car.

"The middle of the Earth? Well, the way I understand it is, on the equator, there are actually four magnetic 'corners', and all four are equally spaced out around the equator. Have you ever heard someone refer to the 'four corners of the earth'? Well, that's what they are referring to. In navigation, sailors realize that there is more than just the magnetic North. There is also the magnetic 'four corners' of the earth, that they have to take into account when navigating. Of the four magnetic corners, only one falls on land. The other three are in the ocean. But the one that is on land, is the one right here in Ecuador, and it is called the 'Middle of the Earth'."

"So is it just a marker, or what?"

"No, it's actually a big deal, they say. Even the Incas realized that the place was special. With their knowledge of astronomy, they realized that it was a special place, and they built a rock alter to mark the exact spot. And then in the 1950's a group of French engineers decided that they could go one better than the Inca, and they used modern surveying equipment to locate a more accurate 'Middle of the Earth' marker. By their calculations, the true marker was a quarter mile from the Inca marker. To celebrate the fact that they had out-done the Inca, they built a big, elaborate marble monument, complete with marble statues of the French leaders and everything. But then guess what?"

"What?"

"Just a couple of years ago, the Ecuadorian government engineers brought in this new GPS technology, to check and see how accurate the French surveyors really were. The French were a quarter mile off. The GPS pin-pointed the exact same spot marked by the Inca, 600 years ago! Boy, since Napoleon Bonaparte, those French haven't been able to beat anybody! Even the ancient Inca put them to shame!"

"So where did you learn all of this?"

"I read up on it while I was waiting on you."

"That's good. You can explain things to me while we're traveling. I am really excited to be going to the Galapagos though!"

"We'll leave Wednesday going there. Until then, I think we can find a lot of things to do around here."

"The first thing I want to see is a nice restaurant! I'm tired of home cooked jungle food!"

"How does KFC sound?"

"If I were back home, I would laugh. But that sounds pretty good right now."

"So what have you done while I've been gone? Are you getting along any better with Felicia?"

"Oh yeah. The day you left, she said she was going to treat me to a girl's night out, and *was it* a night out!"

"Did you enjoy it?"

"Oh yeah, it was a lot of fun, but I don't remember most of it! I had a hang-over the next day, and a head-ache the whole day after that!"

"Sounds like alcohol was involved."

"Ugh! Don't even mention *margarita*! I don't remember how or when I got home."

"You've got to know when to say no. Those margaritas will sneak up on you!"

They got into his rental car, and they left the airport, heading into the business district of Quito, where they saw several familiar signs besides KFC. Taco Bell, McDonald's, Longhorn Steak House, and plenty of Chinese buffets.

"That Longhorn Steak House sounds better than KFC." she suggested.

"I think so too." Travis pulled into the steak house.

"This is going to be like going out to eat back home!" Janice beamed. They were seated, and ordered iced tea, then looked over the menu.

"Have we gotten any calls from home lately?" she asked.

"Why do you ask?"

"Because you have the only phone. I'm just curious to know if anything is going on there. Any calls from our kids?"

"No, not lately."

"Who was the last one that called?"

"I think it was General Morgan."

"So have there been any more attacks at home?"

"No, everything is quiet there."

"Good! Then we can go back home?"

"No, not quite yet. He said they were able to tap into the terrorist's phone records though, and they are still plotting to get me, and they suspect that I have left the country."

"Do they know you are down here in Ecuador?"

"To be honest with you, yes, they do."

"Then we need to leave!"

"No, let's not panic. You see, the reason they knew I was down here, was because they know that I work for FBN Investigations. So they tapped Jim's phone line, and have been listening in every time I called him."

"Oh my! That means they know all about where we are!"

"No, actually all they know is that I was going to the town of Coca. They have no idea where I went after that. In fact, we know that two hit men arrived in Coca this morning on the same plane you flew out on."

"You knew all this, and didn't tell me?"

"I'm telling you now. Steve and some of his men are luring them out to the Lodge to deal with them."

"But Calvin is out at the Lodge!"

"It's okay. Steve knows what he is doing. I'll call him later to see what's happening."

"So this whole trip to the Galapagos was just to get away from those terrorists?"

"No, we were planning this trip before that even came up, remember? I wish I *was* in Coca right now, so I could deal with the terrorists personally, like I did the ones in Mexico City."

"What?"

"That's right, you didn't know about that, did you? What happened was this: The bad guys were listening in when Jim sent me to Mexico City to cover that plane crash. So, they sent two hit men to the hotel that Helen put me up in, intending to kill me there."

"What happened?"

"Let's just say that the Mexican Bureau of Investigation would like to question me about two Egyptian men found dead in a room rented by me. So I probably will not be going back to Mexico any time soon. Do you want the details of what happened there?"

"No, I'd rather not hear about it."

"So, the bottom line is, we *know* that terrorists are listening to all of Jim's conversations, but the *good* thing is, they don't know that *we* know about it. The FBI traced their tap, and are now monitoring all their calls, to sleeper cells all over the U.S. If we want to catch some of their hit men, all I have to do is call Jim, and tell him where I will be, and they are sure to send men there to try to get me. And then we get *them*. Morgan is supposed to be paying a personal visit to Jim and Helen, to explain what's going on, and how we can use this to benefit us. So in the near future, I may be setting a trap for them."

"My goodness! I didn't know all this was going on! We really need to get away to the Galapagos for awhile."

"At least there I won't have to be watching over my shoulder every minute."

They ordered their lunch, then Janice went to the ladies room. While she was gone the cell phone rang.

"Hello."

"Travis?" His heart sank, because it was Janice's sister, Marla. But it was good that she called while Janice was in the restroom. He was sure that it was about their house burning, which Janice didn't know about yet. "Yes Marla. How are you?"

"Well, I called to speak to my sister. Is she there?"

"No, she is not. Is there anything I can help you with?"

"When did your house burn down? I went by there this morning, and saw it! I couldn't believe my eyes! Is everyone okay?"

"Yes, we were not there when it happened."

"What caused it to burn down?"

"The insurance investigator is looking into it."

"So, where are you now?"

"We are still on vacation,...out of the country."

"I would really like to talk to Janice. When..."

"Listen Marla, I'd love to chat, but I am busy right now, so I've got to go."

"You are not going to let me talk to my own sister?"

"She is not here." (He saw Janice emerge from the ladies room.) "Good bye, Marla!" He hung up, and immediately called Steve, because she saw him on the phone already.

"Hello?" Steve said.

"Hey, this is Travis. What's happening there?"

"What's happening here is, we have two 'guests' hog tied, and stashed away in a safe place. I was just about to call you, to see what you want to do with them."

"Was anyone hurt?"

"Nope! It went slick as snot! They walked right into my trap. So what do we do with them?"

"Where do you have them?"

"At the Lodge. We left no trail, so no one will miss them, in case that point figures in to your decision of what to do with them."

"It might be useful, if we can get them turned over to the U.S. military. They might have useful information that we can use. I will Call Morgan, to see if he can arrange to pick them up."

"So until then, we will do what with them?"

"Feed them pork and water, and make sure they hear nothing from the outside world. I'll have General Morgan contact you."

"Sounds like a plan."

He hung up as Janice rejoined him.

"Who was that?"

"Steve. He said everything went well. The two assassins are in custody, and will be there, until we figure out what to do with them. Excuse me, while I make a call to Morgan."

Morgan finally answered. "Travis, how are you?"

"Great. I called to inform you that the assassins sent to Ecuador have been captured."

"Good! You mean you didn't kill those too?"

"Well, I didn't catch them. My buddy Steve did. He asks, what do you want to do with them?"

"I would like to get them back to the States for questioning, if possible. Or even better, to the U.S. Naval Base, at Guantanamo Bay, Cuba. There, we can employ whatever means necessary to get information out of them. But we'd like for the Muslim Brotherhood to think they never left Ecuador."

"How will you get them out of Ecuador?"

"The U.S. and Ecuador are presently conducting a joint training operation, to help out the Ecuadorian military. I think in the midst of this controlled chaos, we can smuggle out a couple of prisoners. We have transport planes going in and out of Guayaquil for the next week. What I need is info on where to pick up the prisoners."

"Okay, then here is Steve's cell phone number. Get with him, and he can tell you where to pick up your cargo."

He gave him Steve's number, then hung up.

"It doesn't sound like you are on vacation, Travis."

"No, it doesn't." He turned the ringer off on his phone, in case someone like Marla tried to call back. "There, how is that?"

"Great. Are you ready to order? Here comes the waiter.

⊰ 32 ⊱

Marla was greatly put off by not getting to talk to her sister. She was sure that Janice was there, but Travis just didn't want to let them talk. It wasn't right, that he wouldn't let her talk to her own sister! True, she had lost a bet to Janice, and agreed to never again meddle in their personal affairs, and she had reluctantly stuck to her promise. But there was nothing in that agreement that prohibited her from just *talking* to her sister! All she wanted was to discuss the possibility of committing their Mom to a nursing home.

And she wanted to get Janice's reaction to loosing her home to a fire. That had to be traumatic for her, and she wanted to see if there was anything she could do to help out. But that vindictive husband of hers wouldn't even let her talk to her! That sounded suspicious to her.

She wondered if Janice was okay. Didn't Travis have a big insurance policy on her? It just didn't feel right that he would take her out of the country, and then not let her talk to her own family! She suspected that there was something wrong with that picture. She was sure that Travis was up to no good, but she couldn't really speak out, because she had promised not to meddle. But was it meddling, to look out for her little sister's welfare? Was it meddling to make sure that he didn't kill Janice for the insurance money? He would probably kill her, and make it look like an accident, so he could marry that 'other woman' that sneaked off to Colombia with him that time! It was so clear to her! Why couldn't anyone else see that? It was so plain to her, yet no one could see it! But what could she do? She didn't even know where in the world they had gone! But she could look up Janice's grown children, and see if they knew where they had gone. Surely one of them would know something. And what about Travis's parents? They lived down the road from them.

They should know something. She was already in Laurel Grove, so she decided to drive out to see them.

Mr. Lee's old hound dog alerted everyone in the neighborhood when she drove up, but she was sure the dog was harmless, so she intended to walk right past him, to get to the front porch. Nothing doing. The old dog was enthusiastically protecting the porch steps like an all-American linebacker protecting his end zone, and so she backed off. The door opened, and the elderly Mr. Lee appeared with a shotgun.

"Who are you, and what do you want?"

"Mr. Lee, I am Janice's sister, Marla. Remember me?"

"I sure do! Sic her, Boy!"

The hound erupted with vicious barking and snarling.

"Wait a minute! I need to talk to you!"

"About what?"

"I just want to find out where Travis and my sister have gone. I have family matters to discuss with Janice, but I can't get in touch with her."

"Call them. They have a cell phone with them."

"I tried, but Travis wouldn't let me talk to her. Can you at least tell me where they went?"

"First of all, I don't know where they are. He didn't tell me yesterday when he was here. And secondly, if he didn't want you talking to Janice, he must have a damn good reason."

"He was *here* yesterday?"

"That's what I said."

"Can I talk with your wife?"

"Nope! She's gone to the store. Now, if you're done, you need to get on down the road."

"What are you going to do? Shoot me? Sic your dog on me? That wouldn't look so good on the police report!"

"Well how about this?" He propped his shotgun up against the house, and picked up some fossil rocks from the window ledge. "You get off my property, or I'll hit you up side the head with a rock!" He lazily heaved one at her, and she easily side-stepped it.

"I'm leaving! Don't throw your back out, old man!"

Stung by the insult, he wound up and showed her how well he could really throw, and threw a strike that zipped past her chin, and glanced off the side of her car. Her jaw fell open, and she ran for cover behind her car.

"Now get on out of here, and don't you let the gate hit you in the ass!"

She got in her car, and left quickly. Now she knew where Travis got his demeanor. It was a family trait.

"We got rid of that bitch, didn't we, Boy?"

The hound just yawned and flopped down for another nap.

———◆———

As Marla's car zipped past a parked car on the side of the road, one of the two men inside lowered his binoculars, and said in Arabic,

"It is her!" He held up a photo of Travis Lee, and his family, and pointed to Janice in the picture. "Follow *her*, and she will take us to *him*!"

They pulled out on the road, and perused the red sports car, from a respectable distance.

⊰ 33 ⊱

After lunch, Travis and Janice drove around the city of Quito for awhile, to get the feel of driving in Ecuador. Most of the street lights were either out of order, or if they did work, the other motorists ignored them. Stop signs were apparently mere suggestions. But though the rules were ignored, at least the other drivers were courteous. They stopped at a couple of street markets, to check out the colorful textiles and crafts. Janice found a woven llama hair blanket, with a village scene, and she had to have it.

"This will look great on the wall in the living room!" Janice said. Travis agreed, though he knew that the living room didn't exist any more. But the new house was being designed from the old floor plans, so hopefully she would have a *new* wall to hang this blanket on, by the time they returned home.

This also reminded Travis that if he wanted any revision in their new house, he had to call the builder very soon. So he tried to get ideas from Janice.

"Our house is so full of stuff now, I don't know where you'd put much more. How would you feel about building a new house? A bigger house?"

"Bigger house? With all the kids gone? If we built a new house, it should be smaller! Less to clean and take care of! No, what I need to do, is clean out the entire house. Closets, back rooms, everything! By the time I throw away five truck loads of junk, and let the kids get what they want, we'll have a lot more room in our existing house. It will be so different that you'll think it's a new house! Wait and see!"

No, you wait and see, Travis thought. *The 'cleaning out' phase was already done.* "Well, if you are going to clean out all that, you might as well go ahead and shop for a few more new things to decorate the house with. Something to remember this trip by."

"Can I really?"

"Sure, why not. But remember, whatever you buy, you have to carry through the airport, to get it home."

"No, *you'll* have to carry it!"

"Yeah, you're probably right. So let's buy stuff that is light-weight, and takes up little space. Like that wall hanging. That's perfect. I like that. But before you buy anything else. Remember that we're going to the Galapagos, and anything we buy now, we'll have to carry with us."

"Ooh, I forgot about that."

"So let's not buy anything else right now. We can browse and look, but wait until we return from the Galapagos before we buy anything."

"I think you're right. But if we find something, we can write down the place we found it, and come back."

"Yes, that'll work."

⇥ 34 ⇤

Back at the Lodge, there was a flurry of activity, after Steve talked to General Morgan. He gathered a crew of men, and hurried down to the partially cleared area that would soon be their tennis courts, to prepare an emergency landing pad for a helicopter.

"Cut that row of palm trees, and make them fall that way, toward the river, because we need to keep this area clear. Calvin, do you have those bed sheets?"

"Yes, right here."

"Okay, you and Miguel take them to the middle of the field, and spread them out. Make a big white 'X' with the sheets, and then weight them down with rocks. That will make a very visible landing pad. Hurry! Hurry! The chopper will be here any minute."

The chain saws whined, and one by one, the palm trees fell, creating a wide open space for the chopper to land. Calvin was still in the dark as to why the chopper was coming, because no one told him, and he didn't ask. Miguel had no idea either. They laid the sheets out to form an 'X', and carefully weighted them down, then got out of the way.

"Why are we doing this?" Calvin asked.

"I told you, a helicopter landing pad." Steve replied.

"But why is the helicopter coming here?"

"They are taking away our prisoners. It will probably be a military helicopter."

As they spoke, they heard the distant sound of an approaching vehicle. They couldn't tell if it was a small plane, or a chopper, until it got closer, and they saw that it was, in fact, a state-of-the-art Apache helicopter, that appeared to be fully armed. It was flying low over the trees, to avoid detection, until it came to the river, then it turned south, and easily spotted the big white 'X' near the Lodge. It wasted no time zeroing in on the pad, and setting down. As soon as it touched down, a dozen armed men jumped off and approached them. One of them addressed Steve.

"I am Major Hurst, sent here by General Morgan."

"Yes, and I am Steve Meredith. Your prisoners are up here in that tent." They all moved swiftly to the tent, where soldiers went in and brought out the two Egyptian men. Real handcuffs were snapped on them, in addition to the home made bindings that the locals had put on them. As they slipped cloth hoods over their heads, one of them said,

"We have rights! We want a lawyer!" Brown Shirt demanded.

The Major got in his face and said, "This is not the United States of America, and you are considered enemy combatants. Therefore, you have no rights. Sergeant!"

"Yes sir?"

"Tape this man's mouth shut!"

"Yes sir."

"You will talk later, when we want you to talk!"

Calvin watched as a liberal amount of duct tape was applied to both men, over their beards. He knew *that* was going to be painful to get off. Both prisoners were herded toward the waiting chopper, which had never turned its engine off. They packed back on it, and were up and gone in less than a minute. When they left, one of the sheets blew free, and drifted toward the river. Miguel ran to retrieve it.

"So what are they going to do with those guys?"

"Questions. They will be answering lots and lots of questions." Steve replied. "Be very glad that you are not in *their* place."

"Why were they coming here to buy guns?"

"Because they couldn't bring their weapons on the plane with them. Thanks to their fellow terrorists, no one can carry a gun on an airplane anymore. So the first thing they tried to do, was buy guns once they got here. Carlos pointed them down here, by telling them that I was a gun smuggler, and could sell them guns. And they believed him. Those two men were sent here to kill your dad, but I assume you already knew that?"

"No, I didn't."

"The same people that attacked your home, somehow they tracked your dad down here. But those two will probably never be heard from again."

"Where are they taking them?"

"I don't know, other than somewhere to pump information out of them. Probably to Guantanamo Bay, Cuba. That's where a lot of the Al Qaeda prisoners were sent from Afghanistan."

"Why there?"

"I think because it is not technically U.S. soil, and so they don't have to extend to them the same rights and privileges as U.S. citizens. And because Al Qaeda does not recognize the Geneva Convention, the U.S. is under no obligation to extend to them the rights or protections of the Geneva Convention. Which means that they can torture them in any way necessary, to get information out of them. But those guys are more dangerous than enemy combatants, because they are like spies, infiltrating the U.S., waiting on the perfect time to strike. Yeah, capturing and interrogating a couple of those guys is a really big deal."

"So we should get a reward or something for catching them?" Calvin asked.

"Our reward, is making our homeland safer. Okay guys, time to get back to work. We are burning daylight here."

⊰ 35 ⊱

The next morning, Travis and Janice left their hotel to put their little rental car to the test, by driving out the Pan American Highway, to visit the Middle of the Earth monument. It wasn't hard to find. They followed one of the school buses that was hauling students to the monument for the day. It just happened that this was the same day that Quito grade schools were let out to have a field trip, so they knew the place was going to be crowded.

The French monument was certainly impressive, covering several acres, with marble and concrete stones marking this or that, and the extensive trimmed hedges made it look impressive. But it's grand scale was a little hollow, considering that it was constructed at the *wrong place*. The Inca monument, just a pile of stones, could be seen on a hilltop to the west of the French monument. The equator itself passed through both sites.

Beside the Middle of the Earth monument, a private land owner had taken advantage of the large crowds, to open a restaurant, and mini museum. The sign invited tourists to come visit his personal collection of relics, and also to explore the wonders of physics, through a series of science experiments. That looked interesting, so they paid a dollar to see what it had to offer.

The museum, though small, was very interesting. There were relics there from all over Ecuador, including the rainforest. A collection of authentic shrunken heads, hanging by their hair, attracted Janice there with morbid curiosity.

"Are those really human heads?" she asked.

"Of course they're real! Don't they look just like the one Jenny and I brought back from Peru?"

"You mean that one is real too?"

"Of course it's real."

"Then why are they so small? A human head is bigger than that."

"Well, what they do, is they skin the head. They take out the skull, then sew the head skin back up, with herbs inside it. Then they smoke it with a wood fire, to preserve it and dry it out. The result, is this little dried up ball of skin, that amazingly retains some identifiable features of the individual. They were once easy to buy down here, but the government had to make it illegal, because it was encouraging the jungle tribes to kill rival tribesmen, just to shrink their heads to sell to tourists. It also encouraged cannibalism, because there was no sense in letting all that human meat go to waste."

"Wait! You are making that up!"

"No I'm not. It used to be the common practice in the jungle. Do you know what those are?"

"Some kind of animal."

"Yeah, it's a mummified llama fetus. Almost every Indian house you go into, here in the Andes Mountains, you will find one of those for good luck."

There were also a lot of stone tools and weapons that had been accumulated over the years. It was an interesting mix of items. Ancient items mixed in with modern day crafts. When they emerged from the other side of the museum, they were in a nice patio-like area, with neatly trimmed hedges, and well manicured lawn grass. Down the middle of the patio was a strip of concrete about 15 feet wide, with a white stripe painted down the middle of it. They were approached by a young, man, who turned out to be one of the sons who owned the land. He introduced himself, and offered to give them a guided tour of the science experiments they had set up there.

"There are many strange things that take place on the equator, that do not occur anywhere else. And so we have set up a few simple experiments here, to illustrate those things." the guide said. "One of the most fascinating things is this first one."

"What is it?" Janice asked.

"This is just a sink, mounted on a rolling table, to illustrate the fact that water flows differently in the north and south hemispheres. Where are you people from?"

"The United States." Travis said.

"Ah! And in the United States, when you run water out of a sink, which direction does the water swirl? Clock-wise, or counter-clockwise?"

Travis and Janice looked at one another. They had never really noticed.

"In the northern hemisphere, and in the United States, the water always flows *counter-clockwise*." the guide said. "Let me show you."

He rolled the sink five feet on the north side of the equator, then used a garden hose to half fill the sink. He threw in a few leaves from the hedges. "The leaves are just so you can easily see which direction the water is flowing. Are you ready? Now I will pull the plug."

They watched the water flow out of the sink.

"Which way did it flow, my friends?"

"Counter-clockwise." Travis said.

"Yes! Remember that! Now we will re-fill the sink, and roll it five feet south of the equator. Again, I will throw in a few leaves, just to see more easily which way it flows. Here we go."

Again the water flowed out of the sink.

"Which way did it go, Senora?"

"It went the opposite way,...clockwise." Janice said.

"Yes! That is amazing, no?"

"It certainly is!" Janice said. "You wouldn't think that just five feet would make that much of a difference."

"I can see it in your eyes, Senor! You are wondering to yourself, '*which way will it go* on *the Equator*?' Am I right?"

"You're right. That was exactly what I was thinking."

"Watch, and I will show you!"

He refilled the sink a third time, and rolled it directly over the Equator, threw in a few leaves, and then pulled the plug. They watched in fascination, as the water did not swirl either way, but sucked straight down.

Travis laughed out loud. "Well, I never would have believed it! That really is amazing!"

"Okay, now for the second experiment. See the set of scales on the north side? Stand on them, and see how much you weigh."

Travis got on the scales. "It says 251 pounds."

"Okay, now carry the scales south of the line, and weigh again."

He did so, and reported, "Still 251."

"Okay, now put the scales on the equator and weigh yourself."

He did so, and reported, "I lost weight! I'm 248 on the equator!"

"Yes!" The guide said. "What that shows, is that anything on the equator weighs about 1% less than anywhere else on the Earth!"

"How can it do that?" Janice asked.

"It is simple. The centrifugal force of the Earth's rotation, tends to sling things off at the equator, therefore causing it to weigh less. Look here at experiment number three. It will graphically illustrate what I mean. This ball mounted on an axle is a perfect illustration. See? It is a representation of the Earth spinning on it's axis. I will spin the ball, then pour a glass of water on the ball as it spins. Where does the water sling off the ball?"

"Around the middle." Janice said.

"That's right! It slings off in the middle, where the equator is! That is the centrifugal force! That is why you weigh less on the equator."

The next experiment involved balancing a fresh chicken egg on the head of a nail. On either side of the Equator, the egg would not balance. But on the Equator, if you balanced it properly, it would stand up on either end.

They went down the line, trying each of the twenty-something experiments, and each one did not fail to amaze them. When they left, they had to admit that this was the best part of their visit to the Middle of the Earth. When they left, Travis drove east on the Pan American Highway, and they had gone quite a ways before Janice said something.

"Didn't we come from the other direction earlier?"

"Yep."

"So we're not going back to Quito?"

"No, we brought everything from the hotel, didn't we? No, we will fly to the Galapagos Islands from the city of Guayaquil, in the south. So instead of hanging around Quito for a couple more days, then flying to Guayaquil, I thought we would drive to Guayaquil, and see the sights. We should have plenty of time to get there to catch our flight on Wednesday. We take the Pan-American Highway all the way. They say it winds through some beautiful country."

"But is it safe to do that?" Janice asked with concern.

"Safety is relative, Dear. Remember, I almost got assassinated in my own living room! It can't be any more dangerous than that."

"But we've never driven in a foreign country before. We don't know what to expect!"

"And that's what makes it so exciting! You never know what's beyond the next hill, or around the next bend."

"I don't know, Travis. It seems awfully dangerous!"

"The travel agent I talked to assured me that it is perfectly safe to drive the Pan-American Highway. Besides, it is widely known that I am the badest man alive! I am badder than anything we will encounter!"

"Yeah, right!" Janice laughed. "You just dream on!"

The highway went from east, to southeast, as they began to climb up into the highest parts of the Andes Mountains. And the higher they climbed, the thinner the air got. The trees disappeared, and were replaced by grass and cactus-like plants, and then even those disappeared when they reached 16,000 feet. The engine in their rental car was struggling to run in the thin oxygen as well, and near 17,000 feet, they pulled over to let the engine rest, and to look around at the alien landscape. There wasn't much grass here, mostly lichens and moss, that was fed by the moisture from passing clouds. They walked only a few feet, and were out of breath.

"Best not to go too far." Travis said. "We'll be too tired to get back to the car."

"What are those?" Janice said, pointing to a ridge far above them. "It looks like some kind of animals."

Travis zoomed in with his camera, and took several pictures, then enlarged them.

"They look like deer." Janice said.

"I think they are called vicuna. They are a relative of llamas and alpacas. They only live at high altitudes like this. Their fur is so fine and expensive, that the government has made it illegal to hunt them, or else there wouldn't be any left.

"I don't see how anyone could hunt them up here. I can hardly breathe!"

"If we stayed at this altitude very long, we would acclimate to it. Our bodies would produce more red blood cells, and that would convey more oxygen to the brain, and then you could breathe normally."

"I don't want to stay that long. I'm ready to leave."

As they walked back to their car, Travis pointed out a tall peak to the north. "That must be Mount Chimborazo. I read about it in the airport. Did you know that they claim it is taller than Mount Everest?"

"No, it can't be that tall!"

"Yeah, it is! The article I was reading said that if you measured from the center of the earth, to the top of the mountain, it is actually about 200 feet taller than Everest. You see, the Earth is not perfectly round. It's like a balloon, you squeeze it on the top and bottom, and the sides bulge out around the equator. Everest is considered to be taller, only if you measure from the sea level. But 'sea level' is not the same all over the Earth."

"It's not?"

"No, and the first time engineers realized that, was when they were surveying Panama, in preparation for digging the Panama Canal. They were astonished to learn that the Pacific Ocean was several feet lower the Caribbean side."

"Why was that?"

"Well, they determined that it was caused by the Earth's rotation. It rotates from west to east, therefore the land pushes into the Caribbean, and pulls away from the Pacific, causing the difference in sea level. That's one of the reasons they had to build locks, to elevate ships to the higher sea level on the other side. And because the sea level is higher around the equator, it makes more sense to measure the height of a mountain from the center of the earth, to the top of the peak. And if you do that, then this mountain, here in Ecuador, is 200 feet taller than Everest."

"Okay, if you say so. I'm getting cold! Is that snow on the ground over there? Yes it is! No wonder I'm cold!"

"Okay, we'll move on. The engine has had time to rest."

They drove on, and climbed a little higher, and actually saw a little snow falling, but then they began the descent on the other side. It got warm so quickly that the windows fogged up. The road began winding around like a snake, and then like a cork-screw, as it hugged the steep contours of the mountain sides. In places, the asphalt turned into gravel and dirt, and then back to asphalt again. Pot holes were big enough to get stuck in, and Travis had to slow down to a crawl, to avoid the worst ones.

"Travis, are you *sure* that this is the Pan-American Highway? I have seen logging roads in Alabama that are in better shape than this!"

"Yeah, it's pretty bad in places, but I'm sure that this is the Pan-American Highway. I think the really bad spots are where the road washed out, and was temporarily repaired. But they may never get around to re-paving those spots. After a few years, and a few more landslides, the whole highway will be graveled again. It's an international road, but I'm not sure who is responsible for repairing it. Probably the country where the damage occurs."

They met a lot of supply trucks on the road, and in places, the road was barely wide enough for two trucks to pass without folding in their side mirrors. And there were very few guard rails on the narrow curved roads, which made them very dangerous. The slightest moment of distraction could send a trucker down a mountainside to his death.

As they descended on the winding road, the foliage was rapidly changing from the sparse moss and lichens, to bushes, then trees, and finally vines and banana trees. Dense clouds of mist enveloped them, as they were literally descending through clouds.

"This is a type of rainforest called a 'cloud forest', because the jungle gets its moisture from these misty clouds, instead of actual rain." Travis said.

"Visibility is so bad, I wish you would slow down a little!"

"I'm going 35 now! If I go any slower, we'll get run over from behind, by one of those big transport trucks." But Travis had to admit that it was scary when they passed on-coming traffic. They literally could not see the on-coming vehicle until they were only 20 feet apart. They were like apparitions that suddenly appeared from out of nowhere, and they *hoped* that the 'ghost' was not on their side of the road.

Finally they came down out of the mountains, to Travis' relief, and the driving got much easier, as they cruised through lush green farming country. Travis realized that his shirt was soaked with sweat, from that intense drive down the mountains. It was getting to be late evening, and they could see families gathering to eat their evening meal, and to socialize around bonfires, or in some cases, burn barrels. That was a big difference between how families passed the evenings in the U.S. and here. Evenings in the States, everyone would be gathered around the TV, or on their computers, with very little family interaction.

"We're not going to make it to Guayaquil before dark, are we?" Janice asked.

"No, we're still a hundred miles from there, but there is a large town about 20 minutes ahead of us. I'm sure they will have motels. If not, we can probably just pull over at one of these houses, and ask to spend the night. I bet they would be glad to put us up."

"No! We can't do that."

"Sure we can. It's customary for them to put up strangers that come to their door at night. They think nothing of it. Of course, it is also customary to offer to pay the host for their hospitality, but most times they will refuse to take it. So instead of looking for a motel, do you want to pick out a family, and…"

"No, I don't. Let's just find a motel."

"So you're afraid to interact with the locals?"

"It would be uncomfortable for me, okay?"

"Okay. I guess you had enough 'mingling with the locals' in Coca, right?"

"It was scary at first, but then I got used to it. I like Felicia now. She's okay. I know that you like to get out and mingle with strange people, and learn about their strange customs and all that, but that's just not my idea of a fun vacation. I don't like the unpredictability of trips like this."

"So you don't like adventure?"

"Adventure, that's one of those words you could just as easily substitute with 'danger'! And no, I do not think that danger is exciting, the way you do! I want to quietly and peacefully live out the rest of my life in the comfort of my own home! If I want adventure, I will find a good movie on HBO!"

"So after all these years of marriage, now I find out that I'm married to a stick-in-the-mud?"

"That's right! Deal with it, because I'm not changing!"

"No, I think *you're* going to have to deal with it! We're on our way to the Galapagos! It doesn't get more adventurous than that!"

"If it's dealing with strange animals, I can handle that."

"You just can't handle strange people?"

"That's right."

"It looks like it will be dark by the time we get to the next town."

"That's okay, as long as we get there. I *am not* stopping out here at someone's house!"

They drove on in silence, noting all the curiosities along the way. As they neared the next town, they noticed that it was lit up more than usual, and there were a lot more people walking the road.

"What's going on here?" Janice asked.

"I don't know. It looks like some kind of festival."

"Look how colorful the women are dressed!"

The road went straight through town, but there was something big going on up there in the town plaza. The road was blocked off with wooden saw-horses used as barricades, to prevent anything other than foot traffic.

"Well, we're in luck. There's the motel right here, if I can find a parking place."

The party-goers eventually parted, so they could park the car in front of the hotel. Travis went in to see if they had a room. While he was gone, Janice turned around in her seat to watch the crowd moving toward the center of town. She was struck by one thing: everyone here were indigenous Indians. There were no foreigners at all. No Europeans, no North Americans, no Asians or Africans. They were all Ecuadorian Indians, descended from the Inca. The men wore cowboy hats, and the women wore those funny little derby hats that were so common in the Andes. Passing by their rental car, they hardly seemed to notice her there. *I'm not as strange to them, as they are to me,* Janice thought. *What in the world am I doing here? If Travis wasn't here with me, I'd be as lost as a goose!* That presented a worrisome scenario. *Suppose Travis drops dead with a heart attack? (Well, it* could *happen!) What if I was suddenly here on my own? What would I do? Where would I go? I can't even speak the language! I can't even ask for help!* She was very near having a panic attack when Travis returned.

"We're in luck! They had one room left! It might not be what you are used to, but at least it's a room."

"Can we go now?" Janice asked.

"What do you mean? Didn't you hear me? I said, we have a room!"

"Didn't you hear *me*? I want to get out of here! I don't like this place!"

"What do you mean? We just got here, and I just paid for a room!"

"I'm not kidding, Travis! Let's go down the road and look for another place."

"No, we are staying right here! The next town big enough to have a motel is probably 50 miles away! Get your bag, and let's go in!"

She didn't want to, but she did it anyway. He was right about the accommodations being not quite up to par, but they couldn't afford to be choosey. They were lucky to get this room.

"Get things situated, and we'll go down to the plaza to see what's going on."

"You mean out in that crowd of people?"

"Yeah, down to the plaza. There is some kind of festival going on, and it looks interesting."

"Do I have to go?"

"No, I guess not." But then he thought about it. "Yes! Yes you *do* have to go! We are in Ecuador, not Alabama! We may never be here again, so yes, you are going to get up and go with me! You are not going to be sitting in a nursing home when you're 95, and say that you had a boring life! Now let's go!"

"In other words, let's go see what kind of trouble we can get ourselves into? Is that how you stay in trouble all the time, Travis, by being curious, and having to know what's going on all the time?"

"Janice, it's just a festival. Probably something to do with the harvest. Bring your camera too, you might see something unique."

She grumbled, but complied. This was what she didn't like about traveling. Always going and doing something, and in this case, among a crowd of strangers. Travis seemed to thrive on it, but she would be just as happy watching TV. As they got out on the street, and mingled with the locals, she began to get scared. It was the on-set of another panic attack. She didn't know what caused it, other than being around large crowds of people.

Once while on vacation with Travis and the kids, they were driving west from the Grand Canyon, trying to make Las Vegas before sundown. As they came over the hill and saw the lights of Las Vegas stretched out across the horizon, she was hit with the same kind of panic-attack. She couldn't explain it, but it was very real to her. The thought of all those people, and all those light was overwhelming. She told Travis they *couldn't* go to Las Vegas! They had to turn around and go somewhere else. *Anywhere* else! But of course, Travis ignored her phobia then, just like he did now, and they drove on into Las Vegas. She was terrified for two days, until they finally moved on.

That was the same kind of panic-attack she was having now, and just like before, Travis was ignoring her phobia completely. If Travis could have known how terrified she was, he wouldn't have made her come, but obviously he didn't think it was that serious. Outwardly, she was composed and holding it together, but inside, she was so terrified that she was about to scream.

No, it made no sense, but then, phobias seldom do.

"It must be something really big, because people are here from all over. And they are all Indians, descendants of the Inca."

When they got to the plaza, it was packed solid with people, yet there was room to navigate between them, and get closer to the center of the plaza, where there was a ceremony of some kind going on. Travis wanted to get close enough to see what it was. In passing through the crowd, they were brushing the clothing of people and llamas, and Janice didn't even want to imagine how dirty and germ-laden they were. These were, for the most part, farmers and animal herders, all decked out in their newest hats for the occasion. As they brushed through the crowd, Travis heard them talking among themselves, but not in Spanish, the language of the Conquistadores, but rather, in their native Inca tongue. He had no idea what they were talking about.

When they got near the center of the plaza, they could see that there were what appeared to be eight or ten very old people, wrapped in brightly colored blankets, and seated in chairs, and there was a procession of peasants filing past the elders, offering them flowers, bits of food, and even a sip of corn beer. It was a very festive atmosphere. Everyone was laughing and talking, as the line slowly moved up. That was when Travis realized that where they had stopped to take a photo was in the slowly advancing line. When he realized it, he apologized, and tried to get out of the line, but the old man behind him said, "No, no, esta bien! Su estascion aqui! Si, por favor!"

"What did he say?" Janice asked.

"He said we are welcome to stay in the line."

"What line?"

"The line of people who are filing past those old people, paying homage to them."

"But we don't even know them."

"It doesn't matter, Janice. When in Rome, do as the Romans!"

"But we don't even know…"

"It doesn't matter. Just watch what everyone else is doing, and do the same thing when we get up there!"

"Well, if the 'Romans' are eating cow dung on crackers, I think I would not be 'doing as the Romans', as you put it!"

"Just be respectful of their culture, and do as they do!" A bit curious himself, Travis turned to the old man behind him and asked who the old people were. In response, he got a long explanation of lineages, and complex Inca names, and somewhere in the midst of it all he couldn't follow everything he was saying. But the bottom line was, the 'old people' as he called them, appeared to be the ancestors of all these people who were here to honor them. Travis therefore had a sneaking suspicion that these 'old people' might not be alive. He had heard tales about the Inca, of how they worshiped their ancestors, and even on special occasions (like today), they would go up into the mountains and remove the mummified remains of their long dead ancestors, and bring them down into their villages. They would set them up, in places of honor, and allow them to enjoy the party with their living descendants. They would be offered food and drink, just like they were alive. And after the ceremony, they would be taken back to their mountain-top crypts, where they would reside until the next ceremony. He had never seen this ceremony in person, but he suspected that he was about to.

Yep, Janice was going to be in for a shock when she offered a drink to the 'old people'. It would be neat to meet a mummy face to face, but with Janice's phobia about crowds of people, it might not be a good idea for her to meet the ancestors.

"You know what, Janice? You might be right. We don't know those people, so maybe we should get out of the line."

By now, Janice was starting to feel the festive mood of the crowd, and was getting more comfortable. "What about 'doing as the Romans'?"

"Yeah, well…"

"It's okay, Travis! I'm going to show you that I can immerse myself in other cultures, just like you can!"

"Well, these old people are *really old*!"

"Which is why everyone is treating them so special! I bet they are just *adorable* old people!"

"I'm sure they are."

"What was that man telling you about them?"

"Uh, he was telling me their names, and how they are related to the people here. I can't even pronounce their names. Something with fourteen syllables."

As they got closer, an Indian woman was handing out bread, and clay bowls for the corn beer to the people in line. The beer was in a barrel, and required someone with a long arm to dip it up.

"You get the bread, Dear. I'll get the beer."

"Okay."

Travis noticed that the people ahead of them were nibbling a piece of the bread, and sipping the beer, before they offered it to the ancestors, so he told Janice to do likewise. She nibbled the bread, and he sipped the beer, which was horrendous tasting. One sip was enough. As they neared the first ancestor, he got ready with the camera, to catch Janice's expression when she saw that the 'adorable' old people had actually been dead for a few hundred years.

Janice neared the ancestor, and for the first time, saw the grotesquely dried out face inside the brightly colored blanket. Her jaw fell open, and she dropped her bread and screamed!

Travis snapped the picture, then rushed to catch her before she hit the cobblestones. Too late. She had passed out dead as a wedge.

"Yep, that was a Kodak moment! he thought, as he tried to revive her.

———◾◆◂◾———

When Janice regained consciousness, she was looking up at a starry night sky, surrounded by a ring of unfamiliar faces. She was about to panic and scream again, when she recognized one of the faces as her husband, Travis.

"Janice, are you okay?" he asked.

"I…I want to get up!"

"Okay, here grab my hands." He slowly pulled her up to a seated position, where she took a deep breath.

"Oh my god, did I throw up?"

"No, you just passed out. Everyone came rushing to help you, but you were out cold."

"If I didn't throw up, then what is that awful taste in my mouth?"

"Oh, that's probably the corn beer. Someone tried to revive you by giving you a sip of the ceremonial beer." (He saw no need to tell her that it was him.)

"Yuck! I need some water."

The Indians gathered around her were asking in Spanish, if she was okay, and Travis told them that she was. She just needed some room, and fresh air. They helped her to her feet, and he began to lead her away, toward the plaza fountain.

"Travis, that old person was *dead!*"

"Yeah, somebody told me that she has been dead for about 500 years. She is one of their ancestral mummies that they honor every year, by taking her out of her crypt, and bringing her to the party, so she can party with the living."

"And you don't think that's strange?"

"Oh yeah, I think it is very strange, but it's their custom. They kind of worship their ancestors."

"And you *knew* this, before you let me give her some bread!"

"No, I didn't *know* it, but as we got closer, I began to suspect that it might be the case."

"And you didn't see the need to give me just a little warning?"

"I thought about it,…but that would spoil the surprise. It made a great photo!"

"I don't even want to talk to you! Get me out of here!"

"Here, let me buy you a Coke, to get the taste of that beer out of your mouth."

"Sure."

He reached down in a refrigerated box and found her a Coke, and paid the vendor. As she drank the Coke, she began to feel better.

"So they prop up these dead people and *feed* them?"

"It's just a ceremony. They know the ancestors are dead, and it's their way of showing respect for them."

"Could you imagine us doing that back in Alabama? What would folks think of us if we dug up our ancestors and had a party with them?"

"It would be different. The corpses would probably be the talk of the party."

"How did they preserve the bodies like that? Don't they rot?"

"From what I understand, the mummies are kept high in the mountains, where the cold dry air naturally mummified them over the years. That's why they take them back to the mountains after they have the ceremony,…so they will stay mummified. I think these Indians used to live up higher in the mountains than they do now. But they still have the ceremonies. They just have a long haul, in bringing the mummies down, and then afterward, taking them back up. You know, we have something similar to this. We have Decoration Sunday, when we clean up the graves of our family, and decorate the graves with fresh flowers."

"Well yeah, but we don't dig them up and drink beer with them! This is a little morbid!"

"It is all relative to the culture, Dear. They are just continuing the customs of their ancestors before them. Customs can be neat!"

There was a whole section of the plaza occupied by food vendors, selling every kind of food imaginable. Some had set up portable grills, roasting ears of corn, and potatoes. Some were grilling various kinds of meat. Fresh baked breads, candies and cookies. Fried and salted nuts, and lima beans, as well as a lot of nuts and seeds they had never seen before. The aroma of all these goodie cooking, along with the sweet smell of wood smoke, made them hungry, so they tried to decide what to buy. Travis bought a roasted ear of corn, and great-smelling meat and veggies on a skewer. Janice went more for the cookies and breads. They went to sit on the side of the fountain to eat, and watch the crowds file past the ancestors. A band playing flutes and drums set a rhythm for some to dance by.

"What kind of meat is that on the stick?" Janice asked.

"I don't know. I didn't ask."

"You didn't ask?"

"No, it looked and smelled good, so I bought it. Want some?"

"I might try a little. Want some of this bread? It's baked with raisins inside."

"Are you sure they are raisins?"

"It's something small and fruity. Maybe not raisins, but it's good."

"This ear of corn is good too."

"Hey, this meat is really good! You should try it!"

"I will, after I finish my corn. So what does it taste like?"

"I don't know. The heavy smoke flavor makes it hard to identify. But it is really, really good!"

"Chicken?"

"Not unless it is dark meat."

"Pork?"

"I'm not sure. It is just a little greasy, but in a good way."

"Beef?"

"No, I'm sure it's not beef. Wrong texture."

"Want me to go ask what it is?"

"No, don't spoil it for me. I'm probably better off not knowing."

He agreed, because he really knew what it was, and yes, it was best that she didn't know. They bought a bag of cookies and roasted nuts to carry with them as they left the plaza, headed back to their motel. Janice had to admit that, with the exception of meeting the mummy face to face, she had enjoyed the outing.

36

Travis and Janice rose up the next morning and got back on the road to Guayaquil which took them straight through the center of the plaza where they had gone walking the evening before. But now the crowds were gone, as well as the mummies of the ancestors. The only indicator that something had happened here were the presence of sanitation workers sweeping up the debris left from the day before. The mummies no doubt were already on their way back up the mountain to their eternal resting place, where they would rest until the next year's ceremony. Janice could just imagine those tortured remains being slid back into their nitch in a rock cliff somewhere.

She had said nothing about it, but she had had one troubling dream after another during the night, and all of the dreams involved grotesquely grimacing mummified faces, and even one in which she was eating a roasted meat skewer, that turned out to be made with reconstituted mummy flesh. (Yuck!) Travis never did tell her what kind of meat it really was. As they passed through the town, and out the other side, she asked Travis,

"What was the name of that town we stayed in last night?"

"I don't know. I didn't ask, and I don't think I saw a sign with a name on it. I can find it on the map though, if you want to know."

"No, it's not important."

They drove out of the foothills of the Andes, and into the flat, humid rain forest of the Pacific side of the mountains. It was plain to see that this area got a lot of rain. The rivers they crossed were gushing with rain water, and the lush jungle steamed in the sunshine. The variety and abundance of road-kill testified to the healthy bio-diversity of the jungle around them. But the farther south they went, the more signs of human encroachment they saw. Soon large patches of slash-and-burn fields appeared, planted with mostly sugar cane. Houses appeared, and then shanty-towns, as the human population increased. Most of the people here were blacks, descendants of the African slaves brought over by the Spanish, to labor on the sugar plantations. Now a large percentage of the population Ecuador's southeast coast were descended from African slaves. As they passed through, the sights they saw could well have been images from a West African village instead of Ecuador.

Soon they entered the industrial region of Guayaquil, and then saw the high-rise buildings of downtown, where they were headed. Travis had reserved a room for that night at the Guayaquil Hilton, which was downtown, on the edge of Guayaquil Bay. They had no problem finding the hotel, and checking in. As they rode the elevator up to their room, Travis explained a few things, and made suggestions.

"Our flight to the Galapagos leaves out in the morning at eight. So we have the rest of today to explore the city."

"What is there to see?" Janice asked.

"Well, this is an old Spanish colonial city, founded as a strategic port in the early 1500's. There is probably a lot to see, depending on your interests."

They got off the elevator on one of the upper floors and found their room, which turned out to be very spacious and luxurious.

"Wow, I am impressed with the room." Janice said, and then rushed to the balcony. "And look at that view! Is that the ocean?"

"Yes, the Pacific Ocean."

"Oh Travis! This is so nice!"

"Well, don't get too attached to it, because we will only be here for one night. And when we come back from the Galapagos, we will fly directly to Quito."

"So today will be our only day here?"

"That's right."

"I could stay right here on this balcony, and be happy! This is a beautiful sight!"

"Well, there is no reason we have to get out. We will leave the rental car at the airport in the morning. But you might want to go out tonight to a nice restaurant. I hear the seafood here is really good."

"Yes, that sounds good."

"And it might not be a bad idea to just stay here and rest today, because from what I hear, this visit to the Galapagos can be an arduous adventure. Probably a bit more than you are used to. I could go for a nap myself."

They were both more tired than they realized. They stretched out on the bed and slept most of the afternoon.

———◆◆◆———

Meanwhile, back in Alabama, Marla went down to Bruno's to pick up a few grocery items. She parked her red sports car, and went inside. As soon as she was in the store, a plain white rental van pulled into the parking spot beside her car, and the two men waited. When she came out of the store thirty minutes later, the two men looked around, to be sure there were no police, or other witnesses. One got out and opened the back door of the van. The other got out and opened a bottle of chloroform, and soaked a rag with it. When Marla walked between her car and the van, the man turned around and slapped the rag over Marla's face, and held it there. She struggled briefly, then went limp, as her groceries clattered to the pavement. The other man came around and grabbed her, and together, they hauled her to the back of the van, and threw her in. One man got on the back with her, and the other got in the driver's seat, and quickly drove them away.

———◆◆◆———

At three, Travis woke up and took a look out the balcony, then called the front desk. He was hanging up as Janice woke up.

"I didn't mean to sleep this long. Who were you talking to?"

"The front desk. He said there is a very good seafood restaurant just three blocks from the hotel. We'll go there this evening. He also said there is a very interesting city park right next to the hotel here."

"What makes it so interesting?"

"Iguanas! He said there are thousands of wild iguanas there, because the city feeds them twice a day. At 9A.M., and 4P.M. I thought you might want to go down at four and watch them feed the iguanas, before we go to dinner."

"Sure, let's do it. I wonder what they feed them?"

"I'm not sure what they eat, but we'll find out."

They dressed appropriately for dinner, then set out, calculating to get to the park by four. As they went down, Janice asked, "Have we gotten any calls from home lately?"

"I don't know. I've had the ringer turned off."

"What? We might have had an emergency call from somebody!"

"If we did, I can call them back. I'll check it later." (What he didn't tell Janice was that they wouldn't be getting any calls through their house phone, because it had burned up with the house. Any calls he got would be from someone who dialed his cell phone number, so there would not be many calls at all. Only from Steve, General Morgan, Jim, and anyone else who had his cell phone number.)

When they got down to the street level, they saw that the hotel clerk was right. The city park was right there adjacent to their hotel. It was a very exotic park, because Guayaquil was in a tropical zone, practically anything they planted grew well. There were palm trees, as well as all kinds of tropical fruit trees, like mangos, avocados, guava, and some kinds he had never seen before.

But the one thing they noticed, anywhere they looked, were the iguanas. The tree branches were full of them. And not just one tree, but *all* the trees. Everywhere they looked, there were iguanas. The feeding had not started yet, but already the iguanas were starting to move down out of the trees, to where city workers were unloading large black garbage bags of what they presumed to be the iguana food.

"Travis, this is scary! Look at all of them! And look at how big they are! Some of them are five feet long! I hope they aren't carnivores!"

"I was just thinking the same thing. Know what this reminds me of? All these big lizards coming down out of the trees, and converging on the food?"

"No, what?"

"Remember those old Tarzan movies? When they showed a river scene, and somebody fell in the water? All the crocodiles would slide off the riverbanks and converge on the food! That's what this feels like!"

"Ooh! Don't say that!"

"Really though, they can't be dangerous, or else they wouldn't have them in a city park, and they certainly wouldn't be encouraging them to stay by feeding them!"

"But see how mean they look!"

"They're ugly all right! But being ugly don't make them mean. Look, they're opening the bags and dumping out turnip greens. So I guess the iguanas are vegetarians."

"Wow, look at them go after that stuff!"

They dumped out lettuce and cabbage leaves, and then a variety of vegetables, like squash, tomatoes, and the iguanas went after it with reckless abandon. Some of the large males got into fights over the prime veggies. They noticed that some of the visitors to the park were picking up the greens and feeding the iguanas by hand, even the kids, so this had to be a pretty safe thing to do. As they watched the feeding, Travis wondered out loud where the city got all the vegetables to feed them. A man standing beside them spoke up.

"It is old things from the farmer's market. This is where they dispose all their old vegetables. But not just to the iguanas, but also to the poor people. They have learned to come here to scavenge for food. See that boy with the bundle of greens? He is not feeding the iguanas. Watch, he will take it and give it to his mother on the park bench…"

"…And she put it in her bag." Travis finished.

"Si. That is why there are so many people here to feed the iguanas," the man said. "There are visitors like you, and then there are those who survive by getting a share of the iguanas food. The city knows this goes on, but they look the other way. The poor must eat as well."

"Do you live here?" Travis asked.

"Yes, I work at a law firm down the street. I come here when I get off work, more to watch the people, than the iguanas."

"So there are a lot of poor people in the city?" Janice asked.

"Oh yes. Every city has them. Was it not Jesus who said that we would have the poor with us always? And the poor will survive the best way they can. At least here, they get food without robbing or stealing from anyone. And sometimes they get more than vegetables, I am told. Sometimes iguana skins are found in the park, where someone has butchered an iguana for it's meat!"

"Oh, that's awful!" Janice said.

"Not really. As you can see, no one will miss an iguana now and then, because they are so many! It is good to thin them out, I think. And when the poor people thin them out, they feed their children as well. It is a good thing. I have concluded that the city feeds the iguanas here, so that it will draw the poor, who in turn help curb the iguana population by eating them. And this takes the pressure off the city in another way as well. They do not have to provide welfare money for the poor, the poor take care of the iguana overpopulation, and it also lessens the crime rate. A man who can provide for his family, without having to beg or steal, can hold his head high, and keep his self esteem intact."

"What does iguana meat taste like?" Travis asked.

The man smiled at them. "I am told, that it is sweet, like the meat of a lobster. And then others say it tastes like chicken. I can not say, because I have never eaten iguana myself. Well, I must be going on my way. Peace be to you, my friends."

"That was a nice man." Janice said, after he was gone.

"I think he was a pick-pocket." Travis replied. "He was waiting on an opening, but I have my wallet in my front pocket, with my hand on it."

"No! You're just saying that!" Janice said.

"Well, see there? He had to be going, but he stopped to strike up a conversation with those two women tourists. He's looking for an opening to steal something, I betcha! He's looking for an easy target, and he does that by being kind, and helpful. He probably 'works at a law firm' about like I do!"

"You're just paranoid!"

"Paranoid of what?"

"Of strangers! You think everyone you meet who is nice, is a pick-pocket or a thief!"

"No I don't. I meet a lot of nice people who are not pick-pockets, but *that man* is a pick-pocket, you can bank on it! I can tell."

"How can you tell?"

"I have ways."

"Yeah, right!"

Travis let it drop, because he wasn't going to convince her. He couldn't tell her how he knew the man was a pick-pocket, because he would have to tell her about his heightened sense of smell, and he already knew that she wouldn't believe that either.

He had learned that every emotion had a corresponding smell. As the man had talked to them, he could smell the *nervous anticipation*, which griped the man. That was the emotion that seized a thief right before he tried to steal something. The anticipation of gaining something of value, while at the same time, trying to overriding the fear of getting caught. It was that exhilarating feeling of taking the chance, that motivated some thieves. And it was that emotion that Travis could smell. But he couldn't tell Janice that. He had tried years ago, but she thought he was joking. But then he realized that it was probably better to keep such an ability a secret. Many was the time it had gained him a tactical advantage.

Janice stepped forward and picked up a head of celery. She broke off a stem and held it out to a two foot long iguana. He instantly came forward to get the prize, and was standing on its hind legs to chew on the leafy end, when he suddenly bolted away. Janice didn't know why, until she turned and saw a *huge* iguana bearing down on her.

"No, don't run!" Travis exhorted her. "He won't hurt you. Just stand there and hold the celery, and I'll get a good photo!"

The huge iguana was one of the biggest in the park. His spine bristling head was almost as big as hers, but she stood her ground, and let the iguana eat out of her hand. Then she held out the whole celery head, and he went after it voraciously. Without realizing it, she was drawing back from the giant lizard, and in response, to continue reaching the food, the iguana stood up on it's hind legs and stretched. To keep it's balance, it grabbed her leg with it's front claws, and Janice was about to freak out, and Travis knew it.

"Don't get scared! He's just going after the food!" Travis said. "Hold still and I'll make a video!"

"I don't want a video! I just want this monster off me!" She screeched, as she was unwittingly holding the celery farther and farther away from it, which caused it to just try to climb farther up her side reach it.

"Travis! Get this thing off of me!"

"Hold on! I'm getting some great pictures!" And he wasn't the only one. A crowd of tourists were gathering to see and photograph this brave American woman, who was letting this monster climb up her side. When the iguana's head got up level with hers, and they were looking eye to eye, she was about to 'lose it', Travis yelled,

"Just a little longer! Hold on, Janice! Hold it together!"

"I'm trying!"

"Hold the celery out away from you!"

She did, and the iguana climbed on up her shoulder, and across to her right arm, which was upraised with the celery. Standing with arm raised, like the Statue of Liberty, the iguana brushed over her head, and was stretching for the elevated celery, and began to climb her right arm.

"It's too heavy! I can't hold it up!"

"You're doing great!"

"Nooo!" She dropped the celery and threw the big iguana off her shoulders, and scampered to get away from it. The iguana hit the ground and pounced on the celery, then began devouring it. The crowd of spectators gave her a round of applause for her performance.

"That was great, Dear! What are you going to do for an encore?" Travis asked.

"I am going to go back up to our room, and take a shower! That iguana stinks!

"Yeah, I was going to suggest that. I can smell it from here. But I got some great pictures!"

"I'm glad you did!" she said, as she walked back toward the hotel. Travis went with her, but not walking too closely. They went back to their room, where she took a shower, and put on her other set of clothes. Travis left her smelly clothes soaking in the sink, while they went to dinner.

They passed through the park again, but by this time, the food had been devoured, and the iguanas were once again retreating to the safety of the tree branches. The crowd of spectators had dispersed.

"Well, that was fun." Travis said, but got no response from Janice. "And you will have loads of fun showing off those pictures when you get back home."

"That was terrifying, Travis! I hope you know that!"

"Hey, I wasn't the one who made you feed them! You did that, and deep down, I think you enjoyed that giant reptile climbing on top of you!"

"It was creepy!" Don't let me do something like that again!"

"Well, just put it behind you. Let's enjoy a nice dinner, in a nice restaurant, because after today, we'll be living on a boat for five days, as we explore the Galapagos Islands. There's no telling what kind of food they will serve on the boat."

"Living on the boat? Travis, have you forgotten how easily you get sea-sick? You didn't even think about that, did you?"

Travis didn't say anything, as he thought about it. No, she was right. He had not given a moment's thought to that aspect of the trip. And yes, he did get motion sickness easily. Twice he had tried to go deep-sea fishing, and both times it ended in disaster, as he had heaved his guts out the entire time. So why was it that he thought this trip would be any different?

"Did you hear me, Travis? I said, you didn't even think about you getting sea-sick, did you?"

"Remind me when we get finished with dinner, to go to a pharmacy and get some of those motion sickness patches to put behind my ears."

"Do those things work?"

"I certainly hope they do. And you'd better hope so too, because you will be within close proximity of me at all times."

"Not if you start blowing chunks, I won't!"

"Well, let's not think about that right now. Let's just enjoy dinner, and be grateful that our feet are on solid ground!"

It was a really nice restaurant, and expensive too. Janice suggested that they might want to go somewhere less expensive, but he assured her that with the emerald money coming in, they could certainly afford it. A waiter wearing white gloves brought them the menu, and served them a complimentary glass of white wine. When they looked over the menu, they were impressed.

"I have never seen such a variety of seafood offered by one restaurant!" Travis said. "Look at this! Every kind of fish you can imagine, prepared every way you can imagine! And they also have oysters, clams, octopus, squid, shrimp, lobster, sea urchin, sea cucumber, scallops, ...am I seeing correct? Does that say jellyfish?"

"Yes it does." Janice replied.

"Shark steaks, eel, sea snakes. What is that?"

"I can't even pronounce it!"

"They have all different kinds of sushi. I think I'll pass on that whole page!"

"Me too. Oh, they have more than just seafood! See? Steaks, chicken, pork, lamb, cuya,...what is that?"

"Cuya is a favorite meat in the Andes. It's guinea-pig!"

"Oh, that's what Rose came back talking about, when she went with you and Chris to Peru!"

"Yeah, want to try it?"

"I don't think so!"

"Ah! Now here is something I *know* you'll want to try! Iguana steaks, grilled over mesquite wood!"

"No, I don't think so!"

"Actually, that doesn't sound bad at all. I might come back to that."

"I'm thinking that I want to stick to something that I know. Fried fish, or chicken. The grilled sea bass sounds good too."

"How about an appetizer of fried popcorn shrimp, with ranch sauce?"

"That sounds good. I think I will go with the grilled sea bass."

"And I'll have the mesquite grilled iguana steak."

They were brought a small salad, and then the appetizer. They nibbled shrimp as they waited on the main course. Travis got out a brochure explaining what they would be doing for the next five days.

"We fly from Guayaquil, to tiny Baltra Island, which has the only airport in the islands. The airport there is actually an old U.S. Military Base. It was constructed quickly, in December 1941, after the Jap attack on Pearl Harbor. Military planners felt the need to protect the Panama Canal, in case Japan tried to seize it by force. A squadron of U.S. fighters were stationed there to fight off the Japs until the Canal Zone could be reinforced and better armed. But fortunately, the Japs had no plans to attack the Canal so soon. So the landing strip on Baltra Island was turned back over to Ecuador near the end of the war. Now it is where most all tourists to the Galapagos fly into. The island is bare, except for cactus, grass, and an assortment of lizards.

"After we land, we will be ferried across to Santa Cruz Island, then we will get on a bus and ride to the other side of the island, where our tour ship will be waiting. But this is also the island that has the Giant Galapagos Tortoises! The guide said that we would be looking for the giant tortoises as we drive across the island. At the port where we embark the ship, there is the Charles Darwin Tortoise Hatchery, where baby tortoise are hatched, and raised until they are big enough to release into the wild."

"Ooh! I bet that is interesting!"

"There is supposed to be a lot to see there, but I don't know how much time we will have. Well, here comes our dinner. I'll tell you about the rest later."

The iguana steak was actually two slices of the meaty iguana tail, kind of the same way he had seen gator tail served in Louisiana. It looked and smelled great. Janice's sea bass looked even better.

After dinner, they walked around awhile in the downtown area of Guayaquil, until they found a pharmacy. They bought a bottle of

Dramamine for seasickness, and asked about the patches. Travis was finally able to get the pharmacist to understand what he wanted, and he bought a box of 12 patches. That was better than one patch a day for each of them, even though Janice said she had never been sea sick in her life. He suspected that this trip might be a first for her, and that certainly didn't bode well for him either. Especially when he told the pharmacist where they were going.

"Oh! Pacific Ocean is very bad this time of year! Very bad! Waves from El Nino sometimes get twenty or thirty feet high!"

Something audibly *lurched* in Travis' stomach when he heard that. The two most nauseating times in his life, were the two times he tried to go deep sea fishing. A close third was when he was on a Marine gunboat, screaming down the Mekong river. The driver had the 'peddle to the metal', and was deliberately weaving erratically, to dodge the mortars and machine gun fire. The only reason this wasn't his #1 most nauseating time, was because he was busy returning fire with a .50 caliber machine gun. He didn't get as bad sick that time, because he didn't have *time* to get sick.

As they quietly walked back to the hotel, Janice knew what he was thinking. "We don't *have* to go to the Galapagos, Travis. We can always change plans and do something else." she suggested.

"What? Nonsense! You said you have been wanting to go to the Galapagos all your life! There's no way we are going to back out the night before we go there!"

"But I know how easily you get sea-sick. I can't do that to you! Let's change plans and do something else."

"It ain't gonna' happen! I already paid for the trip, and by-golly, we are going! Full steam ahead!"

"Do you mean that you love me *so much*, that you are willing to go, *knowing* that you are going to get sea-sick?"

"Well,...yeah, that too!"

"Oh, so that's not the only reason?"

"Hey, I have always wanted to see the Galapagos too! We are going to get on that ship, and give no thought to getting sick! We are going to have fun!"

If they had only known where they were going to be in 24 hours, they *both* would have gladly bailed out.

≈ 37 ≈

Somewhere in a remote area of Arlington County, the white rental van was parked, and the two men had Marla bound hand and foot with duct tape, as they prepared to interrogate her.

Marla was greatly disappointed when she found that these two tall dark haired, dashingly handsome kidnappers had no intention of raping her, and had even suggested that the only way she would cooperate with them was if they *forced* her. To her dismay, the two Arabic men seemed disinterested.

"Where is your husband!" the lead man demanded.

"Which one, the drunkard, the psychopath, the child molester, or the fool?" she replied.

"Your husband! Where is he?" he demanded.

"I don't have a husband! All I have is four ex-husbands, thank god!"

"Your present husband! Where is he?"

"What are you, stupid or something? I just said as plain as I know how, that I *do not* have a husband! So whatever it is you have in mind for me, you don't have to worry about my husband interfering! I am single, and totally unattached, and I have no problem with threesomes! It would be a real challenge to entertain two guys at one time. Know what I mean?"

The two men conversed in Arabic, then the lead man asked again. "Where is your husband, Travis Lee?"

"Travis Lee? He isn't my husband! He's my brother-in-law! But what has he got to do with what we are about to do?"

The second man pulled out a photo, and held it up, and both men compared the image with Marla, and spoke in Arabic among themselves. Then the lead man showed her the photo. It was a family photo of Travis and Janice Lee.

"This woman is not you?" the lead man asked.

"No! It most certainly is not me!"

"So this is not you? You are not Janice Lee?"

"Why, hell no! Anyone can see that I am much prettier than my little sister! And I might add that I am a lot more fun in bed too! She doesn't have a tenth of the experience that I've…"

"Shut up, you stupid woman! What is your name?"

"My name is Marla. So what is yours?"

"I ask the questions! Where is your brother-in-law, Travis Lee?"

"Is he in some kind of trouble?"

"I said where is he?"

"He *is* in trouble, isn't he? What did he do to piss you off?"

"I said, *I will ask questions!* You will answer! Where is Travis Lee?"

"So you are going to like, kill him, or at least beat him up?"

"Where is he?"

"Because if you are, I will *gladly* tell you where he is!"

"Then tell me where he is!"

"He is out of the country somewhere."

"Where? Where is he?"

"They didn't say where they were, but they are definitively not in the United States! Does that help you at all?"

The two men discussed the matter in Arabic, and they were clearly not happy.

"Okay, so I wasn't much help in finding Travis. Does that mean we can't salvage the evening by having a little fun? What about it, guys?"

The men grabbed her and pulled her to her feet outside the van. The second man went to get in the driver's seat, while the lead man pulled out a large, wicked looking knife. His deep, dead eyes looked darkly at her.

"Wait now,…you don't have to do this! I won't tell anyone, I swear!"

The lead man slashed two, three, four times, as Marla gasped in disbelief as she fell. The man put up his knife, got in the passenger side of the van, and they drove off, leaving Marla crumpled on the ground in the darkness.

———◆◆◆———

Their early morning flight to Baltra Island was routine enough. The weather was good. The sea below looked calm. What did that pharmacist know about the condition of the sea anyway? He was probably just trying to scare them, and though Travis wouldn't have admitted it, he really had. Sea-sickness was *his* phobia.

When the big plane set down on the small island, he saw that the brochure was right. There really was nothing there but scrubby cactus and grass. But even as the plane taxied to the terminal, he could see large lizards lying on the edges of the runway, sunning themselves.

At the terminal they met a guide, who checked their names on his clip board, and pointed them to a shuttle. The shuttle carried them just a short distance, down to the rocky south coast of the island, where a pier took them out to a waiting ferry. The ferry transported them just across the strait, to the much bigger, Santa Cruz Island, where their tour would begin. As they crossed the strait between the two islands, large flocks of Blue-footed Boobies dove into the ocean beside them, and came up with fish. The mangroves that grew all around the edges of the island were teeming with life of all kinds. The most obvious were the bright red crabs, which came in all sizes.

On the bus, they were able to meet some of the others who would be on the same trip with them. Most were ageing American couples, who all said that this trip to the Galapagos was their 'trip of a lifetime'. As they headed out across the island, everyone had their eyes on the surroundings, to locate animals. It didn't take them long to meet the island's primary resident, the Giant Tortoise. One was slowly lumbering across the highway in front of them. As they neared, the tortoise stopped, as though to say, '*this is my island, and I can stop in the middle of the road if I want to!*'. And of course the tour bus stopped, not only because they wanted an up-close look at the giant tortoise, but also because he literally had the road blocked.

"Would you look at that!" Travis said. "Back at home, the tortoises are in danger crossing the road. Here, they *own* it!"

"As you can see," the guide said, "The Giant Galapagos Tortoise has no fear of the highway, because he is as big as a small car. And because they are a protected species, we cannot interfere with him. If he sits there all day, blocking the road, then we must wait, because here, all wildlife has the right of way. Our driver would be heavily fined, even if he *accidentally* hit's a wild animal. So you can be assured that we take all precautions to protect the wildlife."

The 94 year old man on the front row made a suggestion. "You mean we can't all get behind it and push it far enough out of the road to get by?"

"No, it is illegal to do that." The guide explained. "We would be charged with 'interfering with the normal migratory route of the Giant Tortoise', and that is illegal. Even the residents of this island, whose families have been here for generations, must respect the giant tortoise. A lot of cattle is raised here, but if a rancher builds a fence to contain his cattle, the bottom wire on the fence must be no less than 42 inches above the ground, to allow clearance for the tortoises to pass under them. But it is a law that is not needed, because the tortoise is like a small armored tank. If an obstruction is in its way, it will bulldoze it down. A low fence it will easily tear down to get through. The residents tell me that there is nothing they can build to keep a giant tortoise out, if he wants in!"

Since they were stopped anyway, they got off the bus and got close up photos of the tortoise, and also explored the vegetation at the side of the road. Travis used his zoom lens to get photos of flowers and birds, and a few insects. In twenty minutes, a small traffic jam developed, as traffic both ways stopped for the giant tortoise.

Their guide continued to tell them about the giant tortoise. "Back in the 18th and 19th centuries, ships would stop here to load up on these giant tortoise for food. They would catch 40 or 50 of them, and haul them to the hold of the ship, where they would be stored on their back, until needed. The tortoise could survive for months in the ship's hold."

"That seems to be so cruel!" one woman said.

"Yes, but one of these tortoise could feed the whole crew, and fresh meat was hard to come by on the open sea. No one knows how many thousands were killed in this way. But that was nothing compared to what happened in the early1900's. A well known soup company came here and built a cannery, for the sole purpose of canning turtle soup! There was no government regulations, and everyone seemed to think that there was an unending supply of tortoise. They slaughtered literally *hundreds of thousands* of giant tortoise, to make canned soup. At the Darwin Center, there is an old photograph from that time, showing an *acre* of empty tortoise shells, discarded from the cannery.

It was heart-breaking to see such slaughter! On a neighboring island, the tortoise were almost totally wiped out. Today, only one old tortoise survives from that island, a male named 'Lonely George'. He is a slightly different species of tortoise from the ones on this island. Since he is the last of his kind, researchers have been trying to get him to breed with a female from this island, but so far, with no success. If he dies with no heirs, then his whole species will die out. That would be sad."

"How old is lonely George?" Janice asked.

"He is thought to be around 200 years old."

"Have the researchers tried giving him Viagra?" an old man asked. "It works miracles for me!"

Everyone laughed.

Meanwhile, the giant tortoise continued to block the road, as though he liked all the attention he was getting. Finally a tour guide from another group had a solution. (Apparently this had happened to him before.) He unwrapped a head of lettuce and placed it on the side of the road, in plain sight of the tortoise. When the tortoise saw it, he slowly lumbered toward it, and took a big bite out of it. But his movement opened one lane for traffic, and they quickly got back on their way.

Halfway across the island, they stopped at what looked like a giant sink-hole, but the guide told them that this was the island's ancient caldera. This was where the volcanic eruptions had come from, that had built the island, thousands of years ago. The last time the volcano erupted, the cone collapsed in on itself, creating this giant caldera. But now it was overgrown with vegetation, and the edges of the caldera, which dropped off with rocky cliffs, were inhabited by thousands of cliff-dwelling birds. Several species had developed on this island alone, and many there on the cliffs of this dead caldera.

They stopped every time someone wanted to see something, but that was good, because that was what they were there for, to see the Islands strange and exotic variations of wildlife. But as a result. It took all day to cross the island, something that should have taken only a couple of hours. By the time they reached the southern end of the island, they only had a short time to see the Charles Darwin Research Center, where baby tortoises were hatched. They also visited 'Lonely George'. The sun was setting as they left the Center, and they got some great photos of the sunset.

"Our dinner this evening will be aboard our ship." their guide informed them. "Our ship's chef is one of the best I know. You will love the food."

Travis got concerned. "You mean we will eat dinner on the ship, then come back ashore to sleep?"

"No, no. We will go to the ship now, and get you settled into your rooms on board, then dinner will be served."

"So what you are saying is, we are about to go to our ship, and we will basically be there for five days straight?"

"Yes. Except, of course, for the times during the day, when we will be exploring different islands. Every day we will go ashore a different island, to explore the different species of that island. But at night, we will come back aboard the ship to enjoy the luxury accommodations! At night, while you sleep, our ship captain will take us to the next island, so that you will have a different sight greet you every day. But all this was explained in the itinerary you should have received when you signed up."

"Yes, it was. I just forgot. Thank you." Travis said.

Janice knew that her husband was about to get stressed, knowing that they were going to spend the night on the ship. He had the impression that they would spend the night at an on-shore hotel, then board the ship the next day. But this was a bit unexpected.

"Are you okay, Travis?" she asked.

"Yeah, I'm okay!" he replied, but she knew he wasn't. But it was too late to back out now. They loaded up on rubber speed boats, and were run out to their ship, a 70 foot, two story ship.

"It looks like a new ship!" Janice yelled over the wind, as they sped toward the ship.

"Yes, it is!" their guide said. "It is only a year old! It is very nice! You will see!"

As they climbed aboard for the first time, Travis noted how blue, and *bottomless* the sea looked. He also noted that the ship was rocking back and forth, and instantly his mouth began to water. That was the first thing that happened when he started to get motion sickness, and it was not a good sign.

They were assigned a cabin, and theirs was one of only two cabins on the second floor. *Great,* Travis thought, *when the boat rocks, the top level swings twice as much as the bottom level! I'm done! I'll be barfing all night!* As soon as he and Janice got to their cabin, he got out his bag from the pharmacy. He took a sea-sick pill, then opened the box of patches.

"Which ear do I put this behind?" he asked Janice.

"I don't think it matters. Why don't you read the directions?"

"Yeah, the directions! Where are they?"

"Right here. Travis you are going to have to calm down! You are going to make yourself sick just thinking about it! Get your mind on something else!"

"I will, after I get the patch on."

"It says here that it doesn't matter which ear."

"What about if I put one behind *both* ears?"

"Well, it doesn't say to do that, but if it makes you feel better…"

"No, I'd better follow the instructions."

"It says to use a tissue to wipe away any sweat or oils on your skin, before applying the patch. I guess so it will stick better."

"Yeah, yeah, what next?"

"That's it. That's all there is to it. Maybe you should lie down before dinner, to settle your stomach."

"Sounds like a good idea. Which bunk do you want?"

"It doesn't matter. You choose."

He flopped down, face-up, spread eagle on the bed, and closed his eyes. "Good. You rest there, and I'll go down to see when dinner will be ready." Travis didn't reply. He closed his eyes and tried to think about something else, which was almost impossible.

Down on the main deck, Janice found everyone going about their usual routine. No one seemed in the least bit concerned that they were on a ship. There were free 'welcome aboard' drinks before dinner, so Janice got hers and mingled with the other travelers ant talked about their families. Since Travis wasn't there, she drank his drink as well. When dinner was announced, she said she was going upstairs to get Travis. She found him snoring loudly.

He doesn't like to miss a meal, she thought, so she woke him up.

"How do you feel?"

"I'm okay."

"Well, dinner is being served, if you think you can eat something."

"Sure. I might as well try." He got up slowly, and was impressed that he didn't feel a thing. He got downstairs and still felt okay. It was a pleasant dinner, and he was starting to think that the patch was really working. The dinner was really nice, and colorful too. Travis mused about this as he ate, and wondered if it would be this colorful the second time he saw it, while leaning over the handrail blowing colorful chunks.

After dessert, the guide gave them the bad news that there was a violent Pacific storm moving into the islands from the south-west, so instead of them setting out right away for Isabella Island, the captain decided that they would best weather the storm there in the harbor. At about four in the morning, when the storm was expected to pass, they would set out on the open sea, to reach their next day's destination. Travis raised his hand.

"You have a question, Mr. Lee?"

"Yes. Since there is a storm coming in, can't we go ashore and spend the night?"

"We have no accommodations reserved on the shore." he replied.

"Well, I'm good with just sleeping on the beach."

"No, there will be torrential rain with this storm. You might drown before morning, or you might be eaten by something large during the night. Or killed by a bull seal. They are very territorial."

"Okay, it was just a thought. I'm good with staying on board." Travis replied.

"We will have no problem weathering the storm anchored here in the harbor." the captain said. "With the rocking of the boat, you will sleep like babies!"

Travis could envision a different sort of night, but he said nothing. As everyone retired to their cabins, he and Janice climbed the spiral stairs to get to their cabin. The ship was already rolling with the waves, and to the west, where there should have still been somewhat of a glow from the sunset, there was only the ominous darkness of the looming storm headed their way.

"What do you think, Travis?"

"I think I am going to stretch out on my bunk and hang on for dear life. And leave me a clear path to the toilet!"

"Where are those patches?" Janice asked. "I think I'm going to need one myself."

They retired to their bunks, to wait on the storm.

⊰ 38 ⊱

Marla couldn't believe that she was still alive. The man had slashed the duct tape binding her hands, and in the process, has inadvertently slashed the side of her left hand to the bone. In the darkness, she couldn't tell how bad it was. She ripped the sleeve off her blouse and wrapped it around her cut hand, then drew her legs up, and picked at the duct tape binding her feet together. She finally felt the end of the tape, and began to unwrap her feet.

She had no idea where she was, other than some remote dirt road. There were hundreds of those in Arlington County, so she could be anywhere. Prior to this, her only knowledge of dirt roads was during high school, when she let her dates take her out on dirt roads like this one, to engage in undisturbed sex. And she was expecting that the two men who abducted her from the grocery store parking lot, had the same thing in mind, but instead, they were looking for, of all things, her stupid brother-in-law! They had apparently mistook her for her sister, Janice, which was an embarrassment itself. She was plainly much prettier than her younger sister! And now, she had been dumped, like discarded trash, on the side of a dirt road!

She got her feet free and stood up, looking both ways down the dirt road. They had left her and gone that way, so that was probably the way back to the main road. She held the cloth tightly on her cut hand, and began walking slowly that way. As she walked, she thought about how lucky she had been, actually. They could have just as easily killed her, and left her here. She didn't get a good look at them, in the darkness, except that they both had dark beards, and spoke with a heavy accent. It was probably good that she didn't get a good look at them. If she could identify them later, the might have killed her as well.

The only thing that she was certain of, was that this was all Travis' fault! They were looking for him, and she really would like to know why. Most likely he was involved in some kind of shady drug deal or something, and had made a few enemies! And it really was a good thing that she didn't know where he was, or she would have certainly given him over to them!

She had promised Janice that she would no longer interfere in their marriage, but this changed things! She had almost been killed, just because she knew Travis. She felt like she deserved to at least know why! She was going to demand to know what was going on.

Travis was hoping that he could close his eyes and fight off the nausea long enough to go to sleep on the ship. But he would not have time to go to sleep. When the first winds from the storm arrived, they both knew it. The bunks were so small that they could grab on to the mattress on both sides, to keep from being slid off one side or the other, as the boat began to pitch violently.

"I'm glad these bunks are bolted to the floor!" Janice yelled over the storm. She wasn't even sure that they were, but something was holding them in place, as well as the other furniture, as their back-packs and shoes could be heard sliding back and forth on the floor.

"Are you asleep, Travis?" She had to wonder, because she had not heard a word from him since the storm hit. No, he wasn't asleep, but he wasn't in any mood to engage in conversation at such a stressful time as this. He was as wide awake as he had ever been, listening to the wind howl outside, as the ship violently pitched from one side to the other. He could envision a monster wave crashing into them, and smashing the ship to bits. He wondered if these mattresses could be used as floatation devices. And he wondered if Great White sharks fed during violent storms, or if they waited until it passed, then went around chomping up survivors clinging to floating debris,...like maybe this mattress?

A few times the ship rolled so far over that he felt the mattress starting to slide off the bunk, but then there was a crash, and then it lurched far in the other direction. This happened dozens of times, before the inevitable happened; a perfect lurch and crash that was so violent, that he was flung completely off his bunk. The mattress came with him only because he had such a death grip on it. He crashed into the floor, and went under Janice's bunk. While there, he realized that it was probably safer there, because he could grab on to the frame of her bunk, and not be flung all over the room.

He heard Janice in distress, but didn't know what happened, or where she was. She yelled first on one side of the cabin, and then on the other side. He felt a splash of water flowing across the floor, and finally called back to her.

"Janice! Where are you?" In response, the ship was thrown violently to one side, and he felt a large debris pile wash up against him, and it was moving. "Janice! Is that you?"

"Yes! How did you get in the floor?" she asked, as she grabbed on to him.

"I guess the same way you did!" he yelled back. "Where is all that water coming from?"

"One of the port holes came open! I got up to close it, and haven't been able to stand up yet!" she yelled back.

"Here, hold on to your bed frame! I'll try to close it!" He let go of her, and the next wave knocked him out from under the bed, and crashed him into the dresser, which had no drawers in it. They were all pulled out and were part of the debris he could hear being flung from side to side in the cabin. With the next lurch toward the wall with the port holes, he grabbed something that felt like the wood trim on the walls, and pulled himself up. In the simi-darkness, he reached for a port hole, but that one was closed. He moved down to the other, and felt that it was open, but before he could leverage himself to close it, a wave hit that side of the ship, and sea water blasted him in the face, and washed him to the other side of the cabin, where he found himself almost on the dresser. He recovered, and with the next roll, slid back across to the port hole, and this time quickly slammed the window shut, and latched it.

But then he noticed that their cabin door was blown open, so he fought his way over to it, and closed it too, but it wouldn't latch. He felt the door frame, and realized that the latch assembly was ripped out, probably by a colossal wave smashing into them. With no way to close the door, he made his way back under the bunk, where Janice was still clinging to the bed frame for dear life.

"Did you get it closed?" she yelled over the storm.

"Yeah, but the door is smashed open! All we can do is hang on!"

"Do you think we can make it downstairs, where it's safer?"

"No, the waves would wash us off the ship! Just hang on and ride it out! That's all we can do!"

Travis held on to the bed frame, and Janice held on to him, for what turned out to be one of the longest nights of their lives. There was no chance for sleep, with water and debris washing back and forth on their floor. Every time Travis loosened his grip on the frame, they were almost washed out from under it. The struggle was never-ending.

About four in the morning, the sea calmed, and the ship went back to the gentile rolling of the evening before. The storm had passed, finally. They could hear the crew stirring below, as the engine started up, and they began moving. When the ship began moving, it stabilized, and it was a smooth ride. Travis breathed a sigh of relief. They got up and found their wet mattresses, put them back on their bunks.

"Are we having fun yet?" he asked Janice. She didn't even acknowledge the remark with a reply. She flopped over on her bunk and slept like a zombie.

By nine the next morning, the ship was anchored in a pretty little cove with sparkling white beaches. The calm waves lapped gently on the desolate shore. With not a cloud in the blue sky, there was no hint of the previous nights storm. What a difference a few hours made.

With their cabin door smashed open, everything in their cabin got wet. They assessed the damage, and tried to get things back in order. Fortunately, their passports and cameras were inside a zip-loc bag, inside their soaked back-pack. They went to eat breakfast in wet clothes.

Others were telling their horror stories about the previous night, but their horror stories could not compare with the Lees. A deck hand was sent to their room with a tool box, to repair their cabin door while they ate breakfast. When they got back, they found their mattresses dragged out and drying in the sun. They had mopped up most of the sea water, and did their best to get everything back in order. One of their dresser drawers was missing, and it had presumably washed out the door during the storm.

"I'm just glad that *we* didn't wash out the door!" Janice said, then turned her attention to Travis. "And I am so proud of you! You survived a storm at sea, and didn't barf a single time!"

"I was too busy hanging on for dear life, to barf. But don't get too happy about it. We still have five days of this."

"Hopefully, this was the worst part."

"Yeah, so do I."

⇥ 39 ⇤

Their first expedition to the island was at ten, so they were getting their things together for that. Camera, batteries, insect repellant, sunglasses, hats, bathing suits and sandals. They were going ashore to explore an inland tidal pool, where flocks of pink flamingos nested.

The same motorized rubber raft that brought them to the ship the previous evening, was also the craft that would take them ashore. There were no landing piers on this island, so they would be deposited in shallow water, and have to wade ashore.

Cormorants dotted the mangroves, and Blue-footed Boobies crowded the top of the embankment as they came ashore. As they followed the guide up the embankment trail, to the interior of the island, the boobies never moved, but rather looked up at the tall invaders with curiosity.

"They don't seem to be afraid of us at all." Janice said. "They must be used to humans coming here."

"To the contrary," their guide said, "They are not afraid, because they *are not* used to seeing humans. Thousands of years of living here on these islands has taught them that they are not in danger from anything. You see, they have no natural predators here, so they don't know to be afraid. That is why we are careful not to intentionally, or accidentally introduce anything to the islands that are not native to them."

"So there are no cats or dogs here?" Travis asked.

"On this island? No. Nor are there any humans living on this island. Nothing but indigenous animals live here, and that is the way we intend to keep it."

"But you said there were cattle ranches, that made allowances for the giant tortoises with their fences." one of the other travelers said.

"Yes, that was on Santa Cruz Island. Many years ago, settlers made claims on Santa Cruz Island, as well as San Cristobal Island, and so those islands have human inhabitants, and domesticated animals. We can't do anything to change that, because they were here before the Galapagos were set aside as a wildlife sanctuary. But the rest of the islands, that still are not touched by man, are protected and preserved. One of the smaller islands had goats introduced to it back in the 1930's, and the goats multiplied so fast that they were quickly turning the island into a bare rock, because the goats would eat everything, including the cactus. But a few years ago, the Ecuadorian government brought in hunters and soldiers, to sweep the island, and kill every goat they saw. They killed almost 200,000 goats, and have since gone back and killed many that they missed the first time. The island is now goat free, and many of the indigenous plants are starting to come back. But introduced species on other islands, both plants and animals, continue to be a major problem."

"So the flamingos we are coming here to see, were they introduced?" Travis asked. "They seem out of place here."

"The flamingos were here before the first explorers discovered the islands. Speculation is that they were probably blown here from South America, by storm winds, hundreds or even thousands of years ago, and then they couldn't get back. Or perhaps they made no attempt to get back, having found plenty of food here. And there are some subtle differences between these, and their cousins in Venezuela, but those differences are evidence of their adaptation, and evolution to their new environment. And those differences alone tell us that they have been here for quite awhile."

"What are those boobies doing?" Janice asked.

"That is a courtship dance." the guide said. "They raise one foot, then the other, left, right, left, right, and then they shake their wings, and clack their beaks together, and then repeat the whole thing. I have seen them do that all day long."

After a trek through eight foot tall bushes, they came out in a clearing beside a large tidal marsh. The tide was out, so the marsh was mostly exposed mud, but it was covered with a large flock of pink flamingos, who all craned their necks to see the tourists, then turned en mass, and promptly walked away. The young flamingos, the white fuzzy ones, were herded together in the middle of the flock.

"The flamingos are shy, and do not like to be photographed." the guide said. "But with a zoom lens, you can still get good photos."

They stayed there for over an hour, before the guide suggested that they go. "We are on a peninsula here, just a narrow neck of land. If we walk across this ridge, we will be on the beach again, but on the other side of the peninsula. If we are lucky, we will see sea turtles digging their nests, and laying eggs there. It is one of their ancestral nesting areas."

They topped the hill, and could see the broad, white beach, and were expecting to see it dotted with turtles laying eggs, but they saw only one turtle, and she was heading back to the water. They crowded around her, as she continued her clumsy crawl, and made it to the surf. Once in the water, she propelled herself away very quickly.

"Let us follow her trail and see where she laid her eggs." the guide said. The trail was not hard to follow. It led up the beach, past the first dunes, to a pile of freshly dug sand.

"The female turtle digs a hole, then lays from 200 to 500 eggs in the hole, then covers them. The sun will heat the eggs during the day, and incubate them. When the baby turtles hatch, they will emerge from the sand, and scamper as fast as they can go, to reach the security of the ocean. Many do not make it. They are eaten by sea birds, as they dash for the water. But even after reaching the water, they are not safe, because they are so small that they are eaten by fish, sharks and seals. It is estimated that one out of 300 turtles that hatch, live to adulthood. That is why they lay so many eggs at one time, so that the chances are greater that a few will survive."

"Can we dig up the eggs to look at them?" a woman asked.

"No, absolutely not! It is strictly illegal to disrupt a sea turtle's nest."

"So is the turtle population down?" one man asked. "We only saw one turtle."

"No, the population is doing well. It was just by chance that we saw this one turtle. Most of them come ashore at night to lay their eggs, and are back in the sea before sunrise. The one we saw was lagging behind."

"So is there an 'egg laying season', or do they lay all year round?" Travis asked.

"We are here, very near the Equator, so there is very little difference in times of the year, and the turtles come ashore all during the year. Their arrival is unpredictable. If you wish, we could come here again tonight with flashlights, and we might see two or three, or we might see hundreds of them! No one can predict how many. Remember, we had a storm last night?"

"How can we forget?" Travis said.

"Well, look at the sand. The rain smoothed out the sand, but after the rain, there were quite a few sea turtles here on the beach after the storm passed. See those disturbed areas in the sand? Those are where turtles returned to the sea from laying their eggs. Notice that you do not see tracks coming from the sea, only going back to it. That means that the turtles were on the beach when the storm arrived, or got here during the storm, but did not leave until the storm passed."

"What is going on down there?" Travis asked the guide, pointing down the beach, where a swarm of sea gulls had gathered, and were swooping down to the beach, then back up in the air.

"Oh! We must go there right away! I think it is baby turtles hatching!" He took off running toward the gulls, leaving his group behind. Everyone looked at one another, then began running to catch up with the guide. When they caught up with him, he was shooing the birds away, and yelling for them to hurry. When they got there, the guide had his shirt tail full of baby turtles.

"Hurry everyone! Gather up what is left of the baby turtles, before the birds can get them, and we will release them in the sea!"

Most of the babies had already been snapped up by the hungry birds, and the ones that the guide had saved, he had gathered them as they emerged from the sand. Travis arrived, and saw a turtle coming out of the sand, and bent over to pick it up, it's little flippers working wildly, as it instinctively knew it had to reach the sea. Janice was lagging behind, so he held the turtle up for her to see.

"Look, Janice! Baby turtles! Come help catch...Hey! You son-of-a-bitch!"

In the blink of an eye, a gull had swooped down and snatched the baby turtle from his hands! Travis watch helplessly, as it carried its meal away, the turtle's flippers still moving.

"There are still more here to save!" the guide said, as he grabbed another turtle. Travis got down on his knees, and gathered up six turtles as they came out of the sand. One of the older women in the group had a tote bag with her things in it, She dumped her things out on the sand, and offered her bag. "Here put them in this!"

They gathered 25 or 30 turtles, before they stopped coming. As well as they could tell, none of the turtles made it to the water on their own. All were snapped up by hungry predators.

"At least we saved some of them!" he said. "It was really bad luck that these babies hatched in the daytime. Hardly any make it to the safety of the ocean in the daylight. Most of those that survive, hatch out at night."

"What are we going to do with these?" someone asked.

"We are going to release them into the ocean, of course. However, I must ask that no one take photos of us catching and releasing these turtles. If you have photos already, please delete them."

"Why?" someone asked.

"Because what we just did was illegal. We are never supposed to interfere with the natural order of things, here in the Galapagos. We are allowed to come here to observe only, never to interfere with the wildlife."

"But if we hadn't interfered, the birds would have eaten them all!" the woman with the bag said.

"Yes, they would have." the guide said. "But that is what we were supposed to let happen. But I myself could not stand by and watch the babies be eaten! We interfered, and saved a few of the turtles, but please do not tell anyone what we did, or else I could lose my job!"

"That's a stupid rule!" Travis said. "If I could have gotten my hands on the bird that snatched that turtle out of my hands, it would have been a dead bird!"

"That is the whole point." the guide said. "The birds did not kill the turtles out of meanness. They are feeding themselves, and *their* babies. It is the natural order of things. So please do not tell anyone what we have done. Now let's go release these turtles into the water!"

They all waded out into the ocean, about chest deep, and submerged the cloth bag under the water, then opened the top, and one by one, the baby turtles darted out of the bag under water, and headed out to sea.

"These babies are very fortunate." The guide said. "They may still be devoured in the open ocean, but at least we gave them a chance to survive, when before they had none."

Since they were already wet, they stayed there and swam awhile, noting the many curiosities. Travis found a walrus skull with 12 inch long ivory tusks still intact. He was going to keep it, but was informed that such things could not be taken from the islands. He also found a few odd seashells, which he kept.

They returned from their morning shore expedition, and got back on the ship. Travis was slightly dizzy, but at least he wasn't feeling sea sick, and no one was more surprised than he. When he got a shower before lunch, he noticed that his patch had washed off, probably when they went swimming. So after he dried off, he applied another one. He didn't know if the patch was responsible for him not getting sick, but why find out? He had plenty of patches, so why not use them?

They were served a really nice lunch, complete with wine and artistically arranged dessert. It was like dining in a fine restaurant. Afterward, Janice said she was feeling a little dizzy, so she went and lay on her bunk, and was asleep in minutes. Travis looked at his phone, and saw that General Morgan left a message for him to call back. He started to ignore it, and take a nap too, but then remembered that Morgan didn't usually call unless it was something important. He left the cabin, and went up on the sun deck on top the ship, to have privacy when he called. He was glad he returned the call.

"Hello Travis! I am glad you called me back. I have some news that you are going to like!"

"Good news for a change? I won't know how to act!"

"Do you remember that I said we were going to get a warrant to wire tap, and seize the phone records of suspected Al Qaeda operatives in the U.S.?"

"Yes."

"Well, it has led to a treasure trove of information about the terrorists, and how they operate in our country."

"Great!"

"I've got guys that listen in 24/7, and they have learned something I thought you ought to know. This isn't exactly a news flash, but the people who put the death warrant out on you, are definitely Muslim Brotherhood leaders. But the hit-men they have been sending to kill you are on loan from Al Qaeda. The reason for that, is that the Muslim Brotherhood does not have operatives outside of Egypt. And according to what chatter we are hearing, Al Qaeda is getting exasperated over the fact that they have lost six sleepers operatives trying to make a hit on you. They know that four are dead, and the two that went to Ecuador looking for you, have disappeared without a trace, and are assumed to be dead."

"Those are the two that you sent to Gitmo?"

"Yes, and they have already yielded valuable information about other operatives in the States. But the thing that you will find interesting, is what Al Qaeda told the Muslim Brotherhood, when they requested more operatives to go after you. They said they would send no more, because it was considered to be a waste of resources. Al Qaeda has bigger fish to fry. So unless the Muslim Brotherhood sends operatives of their own, which is unlikely, you and your family should be safe."

"So why would the Muslim Brotherhood not send their own hit men?"

"Like I said, they don't have the resources. They are not a very sophisticated operation, as you probably saw when you were in Egypt. They have only gained notoriety outside Egypt because of their affiliation with Al Qaeda. And Al Qaeda is using them as canon fodder in this war on terrorism. That was brilliantly illustrated in the way they nudged the CIA into sending you to kill that cleric. Al Qaeda knew exactly what they were doing!"

"Well, enough about that. It was a low-light of my career. So in your estimation, their attempts on my life have ended?"

"I am cautiously optimistic that they have ended."

"Is there any chance that they know that we are listening to them, and they are cranking out bogus information?"

"I really don't think so. From the tone of the messages, they are the real thing. And there was something else we learned, that didn't make sense, because I knew that Janice was down there with you."

"What?"

"We recorded one conversation, from an operative in Alabama, who reported to the Brotherhood that he had kidnapped your wife, in an attempt to find out where you are."

"No, Janice is here with me, as we speak."

"Okay, so that was a false report. The operative reported that they had captured a woman who they thought was Janice, but obviously it was not her."

"Who did they capture?"

"I have no idea."

"Are they still holding her?"

"I don't know that either. I have no independent reports that they captured anyone, so I am going to classify it as false information. But if that other information is true, very soon, you can go home!"

"Well yeah, if I had a home to go to!"

"My guys guarding the place say that your new house is going up really well."

"I hope they are feeding my chickens."

"Oh yes, they are taking care of everything there. I think they said they shot a coyote the other day. It was trying to get your chickens. They said they may have used 'overwhelming force' in neutralizing the critter."

"What does that mean?"

"It means that some of your trees might be shot to hell."

"Please tell me that they did not use a .50 cal. machine gun to kill the coyote."

"Okay, I won't tell you. But they got the critter."

"Well, that's good, ...I guess."

"Have you told Janice yet about the house?"

"Not yet. Right now, and for the next four days, we are touring the Galapagos Islands. As we speak, I am bobbing up and down on a ship off the coast of the islands."

"And you are not sea-sick?"

"No. I think I found a solution for that. Have you heard of the patch, that goes behind your ear?"

"Oh yes. The Navy Seals have been using those for years."

"And you didn't tell me about them?"

"I didn't know you were going to be on the water."

"Travis?" Janice called out from their cabin.

"I have to go, General. Thanks for the information."

"Have fun, and I will call you if anything else comes up."

"Yes, keep me informed."

The tropical sun was beading down on him, but it felt good, for a little while. The sea was calm, so he went to his cabin to lie down for a nap.

"Where did you go?" Janice asked.

"I was up on the sun deck. It is nice, but there's a little too much sun."

"I'm going to check it out." she said as she picked up her hat going out the door, as Travis laid out on his bunk.

It was like a giant weight had been lifted off of him, to find out that there would be no more assassins coming after him. *Maybe*. There was always that *maybe*. He wasn't about to let his guard down though, because there was a chance that the information was bogus. He had not lived this long by making assumptions, and there was no reason to start now.

He wondered who the woman was, that they had supposedly captured, thinking that she was Janice. And more importantly, what did they do with her? It wasn't likely that they would just release her with an apology. Most likely, they had killed her, so she couldn't identify them. That was too bad, but there was nothing he could do about it.

"Travis! Bring the camera! There are dolphins out here!" Janice cried. He got up, grabbed the camera, and went back to the sun deck.

⇥ 40 ⇤

That night at sunset, those who wished to do so, loaded into the rubber landing craft, and were shuttled to the shore, so they could re-visit the beach where the green sea turtles were likely to be coming ashore. Travis and Janice jumped at the chance to set foot on solid ground again. They and another couple were the only participants. Those who stayed on the ship were enjoying happy hour at the bar.

Being ashore the island after dark was like stepping off a space ship on to another world. When the sun went down, all those strange creatures that had been hidden during the day, suddenly came to life. For them, the darkness meant *feeding time*. It was a good thing these alien visitors were much too big to be taken down, or else they would have been just another meal.

"Look at that funny little crab," Travis said, as he shined his flashlight down at their feet. "He thinks he is going to eat my sandal!"

"Yes," said the guide. "That is why I said for everyone to wear shoes to the shore tonight. Those little crabs are notorious for biting on the feet. No matter how big you are, they will attack, and try to bite out a chunk of your foot. Their eyes are bigger than their stomach! Actually they are scavengers, they come out at night to clean up anything dead that washes up on the beach."

"And from their prospective, we just washed up on the beach?" Travis asked.

"Exactly. And they can be a nuisance, because they will follow you around, and try to bite you every time you stop. But I have found the solution for that problem. Watch this."

He deliberately stepped on four or five of the crabs, crunching their shells under foot.

"Now we will move on, and they will not follow us, because they are too busy cannibalizing their next of kin. Because these crabs only patrol the beach, we can move inland now, and not be bothered by them."

"So if you hadn't crushed a few of them, they *would have* followed us inland?"

"Yes. And again, do not tell anyone that I showed you that, or else I could lose my job. It is our policy to always protect the creatures here. But I have been here all my life, and I can tell you this: There is no shortage of those biting crabs! Sometimes I wish there were! Okay, let us move on, and cross the peninsula. Did everyone bring insect repellant? If not, you will soon wish you did! The mosquitoes from the tidal marsh can be very aggressive."

"Do you mean that the mosquitoes breed in salt water?" the other guy asked.

"Yes, and when they bite, it is as painful as a bee sting! So take caution."

They were startled by a sudden commotion in the bushes near them.

"What is that?' Janice asked.

"I don't know. Let us see." the guide said. They cautiously parted the bushes, and saw two large lizards facing off. The sudden appearance of flashlights caused them to pause, but only briefly, then they were right back at it, trying to rip one another's heads off.

"Those are two males fighting for dominance. The females are likely to be very close by, watching."

They left the lizards to their bout, and they walked up to the top of the sandy ridge, where they stopped, overlooking the beach on the other side.

"I will show you something." the guide said. "As your eyes adjust to the darkness, watch the beach over there, and tell me what you see."

As their eyes adjusted, the white beach became lighter, and then gradually, they began seeing other things. Large black spots dotted the beach. They looked like rocks,...except that they appeared to be moving.

"Turtles?" Travis asked.

"Yes, we are in luck! There appears to be many coming ashore tonight, so you will have the privilege of watching them lay eggs! Everyone leave your lights off and follow me!"

With their eyes adjusted to the darkness, they could see well enough to see where they were stepping. The light colored sand would betray the presence of any critters that might cross their path. While they were descending the path, and still among the sparse bushes, Janice noticed something out in the water.

"Is that a boat out there?" she asked.

The guide stopped, and motioned for them to stop as well. He took out a pair of binoculars from his bag and scanned the dark object.

"Yes, it is a boat, and I think it is someone up to no good." he said.

"What do you mean, no good?" Travis asked.

"I think it is someone attempting to steal turtle eggs, or perhaps someone who has come to butcher a turtle. Turtle meat and eggs bring a good price on the black market. And this is not the first time poachers have been seen here. They come here often, because they know that the turtles come ashore here almost every night. There are no lights on the boat, because they do not want to be seen. We must get back to our ship quickly, and use the radio to call the Ecuadorian Coast Guard. If they have a patrol boat near by, perhaps they can catch them before they get away."

"So why don't we catch them ourselves?" Travis asked.

"It is too dangerous. They are probably armed."

"Yeah, you're probably right. So what will the Coast Guard do to them?"

"If they catch them, they will go to prison. But that is a big if, because these poachers will not be here long. They know haw to get what they want, and leave quickly. By the time we get back to the ship and call the authorities, and by the time they respond, those poachers will be long gone. It is the same story every time. And the poachers know that, and that is why they strike so randomly. They know the Coast Guard cannot be everywhere at one time. They just do not have the resources."

As he was talking, Travis was feeling in his back-pack to see if he still had his roll of duct tape.

"So we will go back to the ship now." the guide said.

The other man asked, "Can't we shine our flashlights toward them, and at least scare them off?"

"We could, but if they are armed, they might shoot at us. And it is my responsibility to keep you safe, so it is best that we do not let the poachers know that we are here. I will take you back to the ship when I go to make the call, then I will return to this hill to watch them until the Coast Guard gets here, to tell them which way they went."

"Why don't I stay here and watch them?" Travis said. "You take the others back to the ship, and I will watch, in case they leave before you get back."

"Are you sure you want to do that?" the guide asked.

"Sure, why not? I mean, I'll just be watching them until you get back."

(Janice rolled her eyes. She knew Travis better than that.)

"Okay, we can do that. I will be back as quickly as I can."

As they were leaving, Janice said, "Travis, be careful."

"Don't worry. I will." But he said it with *that look* of his, that spoke volumes.

As soon as they were out of sight, Travis took off his sandals and left them beside his back-pack. The only thing he took with him was his kabar, and the roll of duct tape.

He slipped down the side of the sandy ridge, staying to the left side, where a row of boulders broke up the smooth landscape. He wouldn't be as likely to be seen there. When he got to the water, he waded out, until it got deep enough to get down and do the breast stroke. He went out to the deep water, then approached the dark boat from the ocean side. As he was doing this, he wondered, *Do great white sharks patrol these waters? With the abundant wildlife here, I bet they do!* But he had to put that thought out of his mind, as he focused on the business at hand. Besides, he was already out here now.

It was a relatively small boat, only about a 24 footer, but it was a fairly new boat. As he swam up on the ocean side of the boat, he could hear two men talking in Spanish, but not well enough to make out what they were saying. On the back end of their boat was a metal ladder, where he could climb onto the boat. He pulled himself up just enough to see across the deck, and identify the forms of two men, propped up on the side facing the beach, talking low, and puffing on cigarettes. They never suspected that a visitor had just come aboard. One of them looked at his watch, and asked the other if he wanted a beer. He then left, and went down below deck to get them out of the refrigerator. As soon as he disappeared below deck, his partner was yanked down from behind, and had a knife so tightly to his throat, that he didn't dare swallow, let alone cry out. Travis grabbed the first thing he could find. A sponge out of a cleaning bucket, and crammed it all into to the man's mouth, then rolled him over and taped his hands behind him. The other man was still below deck, so he also wrapped a strip of tape around the man's head, sealing the sponge in his mouth.

When the number two man came up the stairs with two cold beers, Travis knocked him down, and put the knife to his throat. He handed the startled man another sponge, and said "En su boca! Ahora!" The man did as he was told, and poked the sponge into his mouth, then Travis rolled him over, and taped his hands behind him. Then he taped the man's mouth shut, like his buddy. He dragged both men around where they could not be seen from the beach side of the boat.

He sighed in relief. There was no one else on the boat, a fact that he verified by picking up a hand-gun and looking below. It looked like there were at least two men on shore with a small rowboat. They were still busy around the turtles, so Travis retrieved one of the cold cans of beer off the deck and popped the top. He had drank both of them by the time he saw the rowboat returning from the beach. He wondered how this was going to play out. He didn't want to have to shoot them, but it might be necessary, if they both saw him at the same time. He needed to lure one away from the other, long enough to subdue them one at the time. If he couldn't do that, then he would have to use the gun. He checked to make sure it was loaded.

It seemed to take the two poachers forever to row back to the ship with their booty, because the waves kept washing them back toward the shore. But finally they got past the breakers and quickly approached the ship. In the moonlight Travis didn't see much in the boat that they had poached. He expected that they would have a whole turtle in the boat with them, but all he saw were a few five gallon buckets. When they pulled up beside the boat, they yelled to their partners on the boat to throw them the rope. Travis saw a coiled rope at his feet, so he threw it over to them. They tied the rope to the handle of a bucket, and yelled for him to pull it up. He did so, without hanging over the side, so they could not see who was pulling up the bucket. When he got it up, he saw that it was half full of turtle eggs. He untied the rope, and threw it back to them.

When he threw it back, he saw that one of the men was climbing the netting on the side of the boat, to come aboard, while his buddy was staying in the row boat to send up the buckets of plunder. That would never do. He left that side of the boat, and went to hide with the two captives. When the man got on board, and saw no one, he yelled out for them, assuming that they had gone below deck for some reason. Travis was ready to ambush him, if he tried to go below deck looking for them. But instead of doing that, the man turned back to getting the buckets of plunder on board. He pulled up the last three buckets, the last of which came up as the fourth man also came on board. Both men were discussing the five buckets of plunder they had gotten, then they angrily yelled out for their partners, who they assumed were below deck.

That was when Travis came out of hiding with the gun. The men were startled, and one went for his pistol, but Travis fired a shot past his head, and the man did as his buddy, and raised his hands. Travis ordered them to *carefully* drop their guns to the deck, which they did. One of the men was pleading with Travis to let them go, because he had eight children, and he was doing this, not for money, but to simply feed his children. That might have been true, or might not. Travis would let an Ecuadorian judge decide.

He threw him the roll of duct tape, and told him to securely tape his buddy's hands behind his back, which he did. He told the bound man to lay down, and when he did, he had his buddy tape his ankles together. He then told the only man left standing, to lay face-down on the deck, with his hands behind him. Travis then taped his hands together, and he had all four men immobilized. He had a fourth of the roll of tape left, so he went back and re-taped all four men, hand and foot, and also taped their mouths shut. He then dragged all four out on deck, and laid them out like hunting trophies. He gathered all four guns, and threw them overboard.

The five buckets of plunder consisted of three buckets of turtle eggs, and two buckets of freshly butchered turtle meat. He wondered if that was worth these four men going to jail. If not, they should have considered that beforehand.

Before he left for shore, he thought about one more thing. He went down below deck, and opened the engine compartment. He used a hammer to smash a few of the engine components, just in case one of the poachers worked the tape loose, and tried to start the engine. They would be dead in the water here until the Coast Guard arrived.

He stepped over the bound men, as he prepared to go back in the water, but then he thought, *why not use their row-boat? They won't be needing it, and I don't want to be a Great White treat!* So he borrowed their boat, and rowed ashore.

He walked past where the poachers had butchered the turtle, and saw the mess they had made there. Fortunately, they had only killed one. The little red scavenger crabs were already at work, climbing all over the turtle carcass, cutting off chunks to eat, and doing what they did best, recycling the turtle's remains.

He walked up the ridge in the moonlight, and finally found his backpack and sandals. The crabs were all over it, trying to find out if it was edible. He tried to shoo them away, but they retreated, then charged back toward him, with their menacing claws. They probably envisioned themselves as a hunting party of cave-men, attempting to bring down a mastodon, relying on their superior brains to out-wit the beast, and have him for dinner. However, Travis shattered their vision, by smacking a couple of them with his sandal. They then turned on their fallen brethren, and started to feast, as Travis put on his sandals, gathered his things, and headed back toward his ship. He had only gone as far as the top of the ridge, when he met the guide, who was coming back for him.

"So the boat has already left? Which direction did it go?" the guide asked.

"It is still there. Are the Coast Guard on the way?"

"Yes, but it will take them almost an hour to get here. They will be gone by then!"

"No, I don't think so." Travis replied.

"Why are you wet?" the guide asked.

Travis told the guide what he had done, and that the Coast Guard would find the four poachers neatly bound up, waiting on them. And they would also find enough evidence on the deck to incriminate them.

The guide shook his head. "You did all of that by yourself? It was a very foolish thing to do! It was very dangerous! They could have killed you, and then it would have been *my* fault, for leaving you here!"

"Hey, everything worked out. No one was hurt, not even the poachers!"

"Aside from that, it is very dangerous to swim out to that depth of water after sunset, because there is the threat from sharks!"

"For real?"

"Yes! No one swims off shore of the Galapagos after dark, because the sharks are looking for an easy meal! You are very lucky that you were not eaten!"

"Well, thanks for telling me that now. I sure won't do it again."

"So you say there are four poachers?"

"That's right. And they killed one turtle, and it looks like they got all of her eggs. But all that is on the deck. the Coast Guard will find it all there."

"They will probably photograph the eggs, to use as evidence, then take the eggs back to the beach and bury them. They will still hatch. So let us return to the ship. I can call the Coast Guard, and let them know what to expect."

When they got back to the ship, it appeared to be 'happy hour' in the lounge. Everyone was there with drinks, except for Janice, who was outside by the rail, waiting for their return.

"Are you okay?" she asked.

"Why wouldn't I be okay?" he replied.

"I was just afraid you might do something stupid."

"Nah, not me!"

"How did you get wet?"

"I went for a swim. No big deal."

"Well, let's go to our cabin and change your clothes then, so I can wash those. Remember that we only have two sets of clothes each."

"I remember."

"And you lost the patch behind your ear again. So after you shower, dry off, and put another one on. Have you felt sick yet?"

"Not since last night, during the storm."

"I think the patches might be working."

He didn't want to jinx himself, by agreeing with her. He just wanted to make it through the next three days, as barf-free as the first two.

⇥ 41 ⇤

Marla was crying as she gathered up the scattered contents of her purse, where they had dumped it on the graveled road, while searching for information. In the moonlight, she began walking in the same direction the van had gone, assuming at was the way back to civilization. She walked for what seemed like hours, until she finally came to an asphalt County road, but at that time of the night, it was just as desolate as the dirt road. She walked the paved road for almost an hour, not knowing where she was, nor if she was walking toward town, or away from town, or even if there *was* a town nearby. She still did not recognize where she was. When she saw a car coming in the distance, she was undecided on what to do. Should she hide, assuming it was someone who was up to no good? Or should she flag them down and get a ride? She was paralyzed into inaction, and so the car approached her as she stood on the shoulder of the road, their headlights blinding her as they slowed down. She was relieved to see that it was an Arlington County Deputy's car, and she rushed to the driver's side, and immediately tried to explain her situation.

"I am *so* glad to see you! I was kidnapped by two men, who abandoned me out here in the middle of nowhere! I think they were terrorists, because they spoke a foreign language!"

"Good evening to you too, Ma'am!" said the young officer. "Have you been drinking this evening?"

"No, I haven't been drinking!"

"Where is your car, Ma'am? In a ditch somewhere?"

"I can't remember exactly! I think it might be at Bruno's. I was coming out of Bruno's in Laurel Grove, when these *terrorist-looking* men kidnapped me and brought me out here!"

"Really? Did they attempt to sexually abuse you?"

"No! That was the strange part! They wanted to find my brother-in-law!"

The officer picked up his radio and called dispatch. "This is Arlington 0114. I have a 9-12 and am requesting back-up, on Arlington County 52, six miles east of Land-fill Road."

Dispatch replied: "Copy that. Back-up en rout."

"I would really appreciate a ride into Laurel Grove." Marla said. "All I need is to get back to my car."

"We should probably check out your claims of terrorists, Ma'am. Can you step away from the car, please?" He got out of his patrol car, and shined his flashlight around at the surrounding woods. "Ma'am, I need for you to take a sobriety test for me. Have you ever done that before? I bet you have."

"I told you, I haven't had anything to drink!" Marla protested.

"Then what kind of drugs have you been taking?"

"Nothing! I don't do drugs!"

"You say two men abducted you from the Bruno's parking lot? What time was that?"

"It was just after sun-set! I came out of Bruno's, and a man grabbed me from behind and slapped a rag over my face, and I passed out. The next thing I remember, it was well after dark, and I was way out here, up one of those dirt roads. I was in the back of a van, and there were *two* men, and they were asking me all kinds of questions about my brother-in-law."

"What does your brother-in-law have to do with this?"

"That's what *I* would like to know! I think he is up to no good, because he won't even let me talk to my own sister! I think he might be planning to kill her for the insurance money!"

"That's a pretty serious allegation. Do you have any proof of that?"

"Well, no, but…"

"Let's get back to you, and why you're out here. Oh, wait a minute, here comes my back-up. He might want to hear this too."

The second officer arrived, so he asked her to stay right there, while he went and spoke to the other officer, then both of them returned to her. The second officer was an older, with graying hair, and he immediately noticed her bleeding left hand.

"Ma'am, how did you cut your hand?"

"They had my hands tied together,…the terrorists, I mean. Before they left me, one of them slashed the rope with a knife, and accidentally cut my hand."

"Are you right-handed?" the older officer asked.

"Yes, but what does that have to do with anything?"

"Because that cut looks like it might be self inflicted."

"Why would I cut my own hand?"

"Have you ever tried to commit suicide before this evening?"

"What are you talking about? I was abducted by two strangers! They were speaking a foreign language. They looked like Arab terrorists to me!"

The two officers looked at one another. Since 9-11 there was no shortage of reports of 'terrorists' lurking everywhere. The crazies used 'terrorists' to explain away all kinds of bad decisions, and stupid mistakes they had made, thinking that it would somehow lend credibility to their stories. However, the officers found it highly unlikely that there would be international terrorists lurking out here on a dirt road in the backwoods of Alabama. It was more likely that this woman got into an argument with her drunk boyfriend, and he abandoned her out on the side of the road. She was too humiliated to admit what *really* happened, so she blamed it on 'terrorists'.

"Ma'am, we are going to take you to the hospital, to let them tend to your cut hand," the elder officer said, "And afterwards, we will take you by the police station, so you can file your report on this incident. So by that time, try to come up with something more believable than 'terrorists'!" (He winked at his fellow officer.) "We will disregard that tale you just told us, if you will simply tell the truth about what really happened in your report."

Marla became livid.

"Do you think I would *make up* a story like this! Do you think I would do *this* to myself?" (holding up her cut hand.)

"Ma'am, we see all kinds of strange things on Saturday nights." the elder officer said. "Believe it or not, your story is not as far out as some of them. But you obviously have an injury there, so we are going to take you to the emergency room at Arlington Memorial Hospital, to get treatment. But before we leave, we want you to breathe into this device, to prove that you have not been drinking."

"No! I told you I haven't been drinking, and it is insulting to me, to ask me to take a test! You might as well be calling me a liar!"

"So prove me wrong, by taking the test, please!" The elder officer said.

"No! I know my rights, and you can't make me!"

"That's right, we can't make you, but if you haven't been drinking, it is in your best interest, to prove it, by taking the test. Otherwise, we have to assume that you *have* been drinking."

"Okay! I'll take the stupid test, if it will make you happy!"

She passed the test, of course, then allowed them to take her to the Arlington Memorial Hospital, to have her hand looked at in the emergency room. She needed six stitches. Afterward, they took her to the police station, where she filed an official report on her abduction. They could find no reason to hold her, so she was told that she was free to go. But with no one to call to come get her, she had to call a taxi to take her to her car. Her sports car was right where she left it, in the Bruno's parking lot, and her car keys were right there where she dropped them when she was grabbed.

⤞ 42 ⤝

The morning of the third day, the Lees woke to see the shore of a different island. The white beach was only a 50 foot strip, separating the blue ocean from the rocky interior of the island. But that narrow strip of sand was the daytime resting place for a huge colony of seals. They could be seen laying out on the sand in clusters of 15 or 20, but there were hundreds of clusters scattered as far as they could see in both directions on the beach. They couldn't wait to go ashore and see them up close.

At breakfast, their guide came and sat with them.

"How are the Lees this morning?" he asked.

"Still dizzy, but at least I don't feel like barfing." Travis replied.

"Then it is a good day! You will enjoy the shore visit today. And by the way, I wanted to tell you that the Coast Guard found the poachers right where you left them! They were surprised to find them packaged and ready to go!"

"Well, good."

Janice didn't even ask, because she didn't really think she wanted to know what they were talking about.

After breakfast they were instructed on how to approach the seals, and get photos without upsetting them. The big male seals were regarded as the most dangerous, because he might see the visitors as a threat to his harem. Fortunately, they could not move very fast on land, so as long as they stayed a safe distance from them, they could easily retreat if the bull seal took offense and charged them. They donned their life jackets, and loaded the rubber raft to go ashore.

It was overcast, and threatened to rain, but everyone was prepared to get wet. When they landed on the beach and waded ashore, Janice marveled at how much bigger the seals looked up close.

"I don't know if I want to get close to them, Travis. They look scary!"

"Yeah, but you heard what the guide said, they are clumsy on land."

"So am I! And in this sand? You think I can out-run them in this sand?"

"I don't think they'll get after us. Look, they're all asleep!

"Ooh! There's a baby one!" Janice said.

"There are a pair of twin babies over here!" another woman said, and most of the group moved to get a look, and take photos. The twins' mother looked at them, yawned widely, and rolled over toward her babies, as though to say, *you can look, but don't touch.* They were amazed at how seemingly tame the animals were. Just like all the other animals on the Galapagos, they had very few natural predators, and they seemed to know that the humans they came into contact with were only there to observe.

The group moved up the beach, past several groups of seals. In each group, there were several females, and one dominant male, and usually three or four baby seals. The only aggressiveness they witnessed was when a lone male got too close to a dominant male's harem, and he immediately attacked. The two males squared off growling, with heads raised to display their teeth. The lone male apparently didn't like his odds, so he backed away, and avoided a fight.

"That is too bad," the guide said. "A bull seal fight can be very entertaining, if you do not mind the sight of blood." He then pointed out something that he had been watching for a few minutes.

"I do not intend to alarm anyone, but look out in the water. See that shark fin?"

"Where?" someone asked.

"It can only be seen occasionally. See? There it is again! That is a Great White shark, and he is here because he thinks he might catch a single seal in the water. He is hungry, and looking for a meal!"

"Do the seals know he is there?" someone asked.

"Probably not. A seal's eyesight is not that good out of the water. But I am sure they are aware of the constant danger from sharks. The seals feed mostly at night, and they go out in groups. Seals may be clumsy and slow on land, but in the water they are like guided missiles! They are faster than sharks, and more agile, so they can easily out-maneuver a shark. A group of seals can actually harass and toy with a shark, until it gets frustrated and goes elsewhere. That is why the seals hunt in groups, for protection. Many eyes watching are better than two. A shark can only catch a seal when it attacks suddenly and without warning. But with the tide coming in right now, these seals should be moving farther up on the beach. Yet they are not doing so."

"So as the tide rises, the seals move up higher, to be safe from the sharks?" Travis asked.

"Yes, and the way that shark is patrolling back and forth here, I would say that he is planning an attack. If you want to get a really unique video, I suggest that we wait and watch right here for a few minutes."

"How can he attack?" a woman asked. "The seals are safely out of the water. Is he waiting on one to go for a swim?"

"You will see. Everyone watch the shark. I will tell you when to start your cameras. In fact, let us move up on the beach a few more feet, just to be safe, and get a better camera angle. Okay, yes…this should be far enough. Like I said, everyone watch the shark!"

"Is this some kind of joke?" one of the men asked. "The water looks too shallow for a shark that big to get anywhere near those seals."

"Oh no, I am not joking. I am serious. I have seen this many times, and I can tell that the shark is about to attack. With the tide coming in, and the wind driving the waves, it creates just the right conditions for a shark attack. Watch him as he swims back and forth. Occasionally he will raise his head up out of the water slightly,…see? He did it just now! When he raises up like that, he is spotting his target on the beach! He is trying to gauge whether he can reach them or not!"

"So you are saying that *that shark* is about to come ashore?" Travis asked.

"Very possibly!" The guide replied.

"Oh bull!" the other man said. "You are *so* pulling our leg! There is no way that shark is coming up on this beach! Folks, he is just joshing us!"

"Yes, he will! I will tell you what to watch for. See, he is swimming back and forth now, occasionally raising his head out of the water. He is picking his target! Soon you will see him stop pacing, and he will seem to disappear. Actually, he is heading out to deeper water, to get up enough speed to propel him up on the beach, far enough to grab a seal!

I have seen it many times, but have not been able to catch it on film. Watch and see! You will be amazed!"

"He seems to be having second thoughts." Travis said. "He's just cruising back and forth."

"He is calculating the waves." the guide said. "He knows he can get more momentum, if he times his attack with a big incoming wave, so he is calculating the rhythm of the waves. Everyone keep watching, and be ready with your cameras."

"This is crazy!" the man said, as his wife added, "Where did he go? I don't see him any more."

"Get ready!" the guide said. "You are about to see him come in like a torpedo!"

Everyone was watching intently.

"There! There he comes!"

From the deeper water they saw the shark fin break the water, headed straight for the shore. When it reached shallow water, it *really did* look like a torpedo coming in, and it was not slowing up. When it got to the most shallow water, nearest the shore, they saw that the 'torpedo' had a large dorsal and tail fins. As the big wave crashed into the beach, the big shark abruptly burst out of the sea, and came sliding up on the beach with his mouth open, snapping at the seals! Instantly, the seal herd panicked and scattered, but not all of them were quick enough. One of the seals closest to the water was running as fast as her flippers could carry her, but the shark slammed into her with such force that she, and two other seals were sent tumbling like bowling pins. The shark chomped down with its razor sharp teeth, missing one seal, but not the second one. Blood sprayed out in all directions, splashing the sugar-white sand with crimson. With prey in mouth, and the wave gone back out, the shark seemed to be hopelessly beached. But he had his prey, and he continuously flopped, and gravity did the rest, pulling him back toward the water, where the next big wave aided him in getting back into the shallows, where he quickly swam away with his meal.

Everyone was shocked and speechless, except the guide, who beamed with satisfaction. "See? I told you it was coming! Did anyone film that magnificent sight? Anyone? Come now! Someone must have caught it on film!"

Travis was standing there with his camera still aimed at the surf, but he had to admit that he didn't get it. "I was so shocked at what I was seeing, that I didn't think to press the button! All I could do was watch in horror!"

It was the same with everyone else. Though the guide told them what to expect, it was so sudden and horrific that no one even got a photo. The blood splashed beach, was already being washed clean by the rising waves. Soon, it would be white again, and all evidence of the brutal attack would be forgotten. The seal herd re-congregated farther up on the beach, though the move was too late. The shark's hunger was satisfied, and would not attack again that day. The seals yawned and went back to sleep, as though the attack was an every day thing.

"As you can see," the guide said, "in the natural world, death can come very quickly, and unexpectedly. That is the very *essence* of evolution. It is the survival of the fittest, the fastest, and the smartest,… and sometimes just the luckiest."

"The rest of the herd doesn't even seem to be up-set by the attack." the other man said. "I would think they would be so traumatized that they would not be able to sleep, but look at them! If these were humans, they would be needing psychological counseling, to get past the trauma!"

"I think *I'm* going to need counseling!" the man's wife said. "That was horrible!"

Janice was up-set by it too, but not from seeing the seal killed. Her terror was caused from seeing that shark *come up on the shore* to get the seal. Travis knew that Janice's *other* phobia, even greater than her phobia of being around large crowds of people, was her fear of *sharks*.

More than once, Janice had told him about her fear of sharks, which stemmed from her childhood, after watching the movie, 'Jaws' for the first time. And her older sister, Marla certainly did nothing to help matters, when she told her little sister that sharks were *everywhere*, not just in the ocean. Sharks were in every body of water, no matter how small. Rivers, creeks, ponds, and yes, even swimming pools were capable of being visited by sharks. Marla told her young and impressionable sister that a swimming pool has a drain, and that drain was connected to a sewer, and eventually, that sewer was connected to the ocean! Therefore, she reasoned, why couldn't a shark suddenly show up in a swimming pool? At the time, Janice was so young and naïve, that she looked up to her older sister, and believed everything she told her, so why couldn't that be true?

As a result, no matter how far-fetched this sounded, Janice no longer went near the water. She even objected when she was ordered to take a bath, because, as she reasoned, the bathtub had a *drain*, and the drain was somehow connected to the *ocean*, where 'Jaws' lived! Well, her parents soon got her over her fear of bathing, with the more immediate threats of a whipping if she *didn't* bathe, but she still maintained her fear of the ocean, rivers, ponds, and yes, even swimming pools, even after she got old enough to know better, and realize that Marla had been lying to her.

And in recent years, she found out that Marla had lied to her about a *great many* things.

Even after she married Travis, and they had children, Janice would not go swimming with them, because of her deep-seated fear that, just possibly, a shark could be out there somewhere lurking. So was it any wonder that Janice was terrified out of her mind, when she saw with her *own eyes*, a 27 foot shark burst from the ocean, *slide up on the beach* and snap up a seal as big as a human? In her mind, it only justified all those years of irrational fears of sharks! And furthermore, just what the hell was she thinking, when she agreed to a vacation that involved bobbing around on the ocean, like shark bait? Really? Couldn't her husband have taken her somewhere that had fewer sharks? Like maybe the mountains? But to come *here*, to the Galapagos, where the main attraction was standing on the beach and watching the sharks surf onto the shore and kill something? Could he have brought her to a worse place?

After the shark returned to the sea with it's meal, and after the initial shock of witnessing such an event, Travis thought about Janice's fear of 'Jaws', and he thought to himself, *Wow, this can't be a good thing for her. She will not want to get back into that rubber boat. Shit, she ain't going to want to wade out to the rubber boat! I might as well build her a lean-to, and leave her on the island!*

"Janice, are you okay?"

"What do *you* think, Travis?" she snapped back.

Oh-oh. He knew it, she was going to take this badly. He knew it was going to be futile, but he tried to sooth her fears with some kind of rationale.

"I'm sure that seal probably filled up that shark. He won't be hungry again for days!"

The guide heard him, and injected, "Oh no! A shark will constantly eat! They are eating machines! I have seen them maim a seal, and play with it for hours out in the water, before it finally kills and eats it."

"Thanks a lot, fella'! You are not helping!" He grabbed Janice by the arm, and led her up on the beach, where they sat down on a large driftwood log. When they did, the log shifted, and a foot-long colorful lizard darted out from under it, and Janice screamed.

"It's okay! It's just a lizard! He's gone now. Come and sit back down."

"I don't want to sit down! I don't want to explore! I don't want to go back to the ship, because a shark like that could jump up and snap me right off the ship!"

"No it can't!"

"You saw it come up on dry land and get that seal! It could have been one of us! It could have gotten us as we were wading ashore! It could get us as we go back to our boat! It might smash our ship, just like the shark in 'Jaws' did! And don't you even try to tell me it can't, because I know better! I am not going back out on that water! You might as well call a helicopter to come get me, and take me back home!"

"Janice, calm down. Come here and sit down. Here, get a drink of water."

"No, I want to go home!"

The guide was concerned, but stayed at a distance. He had dealt with irrational tour members before, and he knew the best thing was to let her blow off steam, and then she would settle down. He turned to the others and said, "Let us go up the beach to the west. There are many things I would like to point out to you!"

As the group moved away, Janice sat down beside Travis on the log, and took the water bottle from him. She took a drink, then they sat in silence, listening to the waves roll in, and the occasional grunt from one of the sleeping seals. Travis intended to give her all the time she needed. Finally she spoke.

"I'm sorry, Travis! What was I thinking when I said I wanted to come here? To islands, surrounded by hungry sharks!"

"It's okay. No big deal. You'll get past this, just sit here and rest awhile." After a time, he added, "You know, that was the first shark we have seen, and we have been here for three days. I bet we won't see another one the rest of the trip."

"Ha! Yeah, right! I bet the sharks have been watching *us* though!"

"Listen, I know where your fear of sharks comes from, and I get it. But you are going to have to look your fear it in the eyes, and get over it, because you can't stay here, and a helicopter is out of the question."

She didn't say anything, but she knew he was right.

"Look at me. You know how scared I was to get on a boat, because I get sea-sick, but I did anyway. And now I am glad I did, because I learned that with the right help, I can go out on the water and not get sick. The patches help, but part of it is that I really wanted to see the Galapagos, and I knew I had to get over it. Just like you are going to have to do."

"Travis, getting sea-sick won't rip you to shreds, like a shark will do!"

"Hey, I have been so sea-sick in the past, that I *wished* a shark would eat me, to get me out of my misery! I am serious!"

"I don't care what you say, I can't go back out on that water. I just can't do it! I'm sorry."

"Well, the Ecuadorian government won't let you stay here, unless you are an endangered species, so you might as well get used to the fact that you will have to get back on the boat. So, we might as well go join the rest of the group, and enjoy the strange sights here at least."

"Yes, we might as well."

He started to use the rationale that Marla had lied to her about everything else, so she had obviously lied to her about sharks as well. But witnessing the shark attack personally would trump any rationale he tried to use in that regard. Best to let it rest. They got up and walked up the beach to re-join the rest of the group.

When they caught up, the group had broken up, and everyone was gone in different directions, looking at many different things. The guide approached them.

"Mrs. Lee, Are you okay?"

"Yes, I'm better now."

"Well, if it will help any, I already radioed the ship, and told the boat to pick us up down here, in more shallow water, away from where the shark attack occurred. Down here, we can see a shark coming from a greater distance, and they are not as likely to be here, because there are fewer seals. Does that make you feel better?"

"Yes." Janice said, but Travis could tell that it really didn't. But he suspected that she was over it enough that they could get her back on the boat. They walked around, looking at things, turning over seashells and finding flowering plants among the rocks, but he could tell her heart really wasn't in it.

"I'm sorry, Travis. I know I haven't been much fun on this trip. Not just here on these islands, but even back at the Lodge." she said. "You should have brought Rose down here with you. She probably would be tickled to death to visit this place."

"That's okay, Janice. This didn't exactly start out to be a vacation anyway. Remember, we basically *fled* down here because things were going on at home? I think you have done really well under the circumstances, and I'm proud of you. But speaking of Rose, I haven't heard anything from her since I've been back from Egypt. I thought she would be asking to get copies of my photos from there."

"Well, about Rose," Janice started, "I don't think she understood why you sent her home, and you stayed there. She saw right through that 'coin collecting' line you gave her, and she didn't like having to come back home alone."

"She didn't have to travel alone. Pete went to the airport with her, and flew part of the way back with her. You remember me telling you about Pete? The guy from Kansas?"

"Yeah, but she didn't go over there with Pete, she went with *you*. And she suspected that you were involved with something under-handed there, and that didn't make her happy."

"Well, if you will remember, I didn't exactly invite her to go! She heard I was going, and ran to sign up. I think she got the last available spot with the group."

"Yeah, I remember. But I kind of encouraged her to go, because I wanted someone there to look out for you."

"You really shouldn't have done that, Janice. All you did was put her in danger. You did know the real reason I went there, didn't you?"

"No! Do you *ever* tell me *why* you are going on those kind of trips? They are always 'classified' or some such B.S.! And no, I did not tell Rose that your trip to Egypt was anything other than a vacation. That was why she wanted to go. She had so much adventure in Peru, that she wanted to travel with you again. But I don't think she was prepared for what happened to you guys in Egypt, and then the way you sent her home with your stuff, well, she thought that you wouldn't be coming back. Remember, you sent your Passport, wallet and camera home? Even I was puzzled by that!"

"So Rose opened the package I sent home with her?"

"She said the tape you sealed it with came loose, and it spilled out in her bag, so she couldn't help noticing what was in it."

Travis doubted that. The tape he used wouldn't just 'come loose', as she put it. "So did she also read my sealed letter to you?"

"No, the letter was still sealed when I got it. I think the thing that up-set her most, was that she knew there was something going on that you weren't telling her."

"That shouldn't have up-set her, because it was none of her business."

"I know. And the massacre in the Valley of the Kings up-set her too. She said she didn't think she would ever travel outside the U.S. again, because of that."

"Hey, I warned her that traveling with me might be hazardous to her health, but she laughed it off."

"Well, she's not laughing now."

"Whatever. What is that saying? If you can't stand the heat, don't get in the oven?"

"No, it's stay out of the kitchen."

"Yeah, that's it."

"Well, to tell you the truth, I think this is going to be *my* last time to leave the U.S. too! I mean, you can travel all you want to, but leave me at home! Take a lot of pictures, that way I can see the world without having to leave Alabama. All I want, is to just get back home and feel secure. I have done all the traveling I want to do."

"You'll change your mind later. I know you." They held hands as they strolled up the beach, the warm Pacific breeze in their face.

⇥ 43 ⇤

When the time came to leave, the guide had the boat driver come in as close to shore as he could, so Janice would not have to wade too deeply into the surf. She was ever watching out to sea, to see if another 'shark torpedo' was headed their way. The rain clouds had blown away, and the sea had calmed. It was a perfect sunny day. But for Janice, the sea would never be the same, after witnessing the shark attack. To her, the deep blue sea was only a cover for the great white sharks. They patrolled the depths, and when they saw the opportunity, would burst forth and rip apart its prey. And being on the relatively small rubber landing boat was a great concern as well. A shark the size of the one that attacked the seals could easily destroy this little boat, and then would have eight helpless humans treading water to choose from. She wasn't even sure she would feel safe on their ship again. In the movie 'Jaws', didn't a great white shark destroy boats that big, to get at the humans?

"Are you okay, Janice?" Travis asked.

"I'll survive."

They got back on the ship, and went to their cabin to shower and freshen up before lunch. Janice stretched out on her bunk to take a nap.

"Don't wake me for lunch. I'm not hungry anyway."

While Travis was at lunch, the ship got under way, moving around to the other side of the island, where their afternoon tour would be. In talking to the other passengers at lunch, he found that Janice was not the only one shaken by the shark attack. One of the other couples informed their guide that they would not be getting off the ship the rest of the trip.

"What? That is crazy! You paid a lot of money for this tour, and if you do not go ashore the last two days, you will miss the best parts!"

"I know, but it is not worth getting eaten alive over."

"We have never had sharks attack any of our guests, because we take very good care of you! We would not knowingly put you in danger. The attack this morning, I saw that coming, and got you out of the way in plenty of time."

"Did you know that was going to happen before we went ashore?"

"No, that was a rare event, but I have seen it before. That was why I knew what was about to happen. Remember, I had everyone move farther up the beach, to be well out of the way."

"Regardless, we have decided to stay on the ship for the rest of the trip. It is our vacation, and is our decision."

"Okay, that is your right. Does anyone else feel the same way?" the guide asked.

Travis knew that Janice would probably elect to do that, if she was here to make the decision. He didn't plan to tell her about it, because he wanted her to see everything the tour had to offer. After lunch he went up to their cabin, but found her deep in sleep, so he went up on the top deck to watch the sea. While there, his phone rang. The ID said it was his son, Chris.

"Hey Chris! Good to hear from you."

"It's good to hear you too, Dad. I'm calling to let you know that I have just been given my orders to deploy to Iraq."

"How soon?"

"Well, our armored vehicles have been sent to Fort Erwin, California, to be fitted with high tech systems. They said that could take as long as three weeks. Anyway, that's where I am calling you from, Fort Erwin. At the same time the systems are being installed, we are being trained in how to use them. It's pretty neat! Like playing video games, except that we will be destroying enemy armor so far away, that we can't even see it!"

"The technology has come a long way."

"I talked to Joey this morning, and he said that you, Mom, and Calvin are in Ecuador. Is that right?"

"Yes, we came down to help Steve get out eco-lodge up and running. Calvin is there right now, while your mom and I are on a tour of the Galapagos Islands."

"Cool! How does mom like it?"

"Some parts she does not care for."

"So what's the deal with our house burning down?"

"You heard about that?"

"Yeah, from Joey. When I couldn't get your home phone, I called him, and he gave me your cell phone number. He said he went home from school this past weekend, and found the house gone! He stayed with Papa and Mama Lee while he was home. He said there is a crew building a new house near-by."

"Yeah, I hired a contractor to do the work. How is it coming?"

"He said they had the roof on it."

"I need to call Joey, and fill him in on what's happening. Your mother doesn't know the house burned yet. I was wanting to get the new one built before I told her about it."

"Wow, is she going to be surprised!"

"Yeah, and not in a good way. She lost a lot of memories with that fire, and she doesn't even know it yet. Are you going to get any leave time before you ship out in three weeks?"

"No, I'll be busy right up until we leave."

"Oh well."

"Listen, I have to be going. They limit us on our phone calls, and my time is up. I will call you again before I leave."

"Okay Chris. Be safe!"

Janice was going to hate that she missed Chris's call. That was the first time they had heard anything from him since his graduation from boot camp. He decided to go ahead and call Joey.

"Hello, Dad?"

"Yes, how are you, Joey?"

"I'm through with classes for today, but I'm about to go to work in the greenhouse. We're growing tobacco plants for experimentation. So what's going on with you and Mom?"

"Chris called, and told us that we missed you last weekend."

"Yeah. I caught a ride home with another guy that lives in Montgomery. I just stayed with Mama and Papa Lee Saturday night, and went back the next day. A couple of questions: How did the house burn down, and why are you guys in Ecuador?"

"It's a long story, and I will explain it all later. But for now, the important thing is that your mother not know that the house has burned. It is important that I keep her down here in Ecuador until the new house is built. The reason for that too, I will explain later."

"And why are there soldiers guarding your property?"

"Again, I will explain all that later. Are you coming home for Thanksgiving?"

"I sure am. I can't wait to hear the explanations for all this! So Calvin is down there with you?"

"Yes, he is with Steve, at the eco-lodge."

"So that's the property you bought down there?"

"Yeah."

"So is Calvin going to school down there?"

"No, he will have to finish his senior year when he gets back home. He might have to go to Summer School to graduate."

"And he was okay with that?"

"He didn't have much choice. We had to get out of Alabama ASAP."

"I can't wait to hear the explanation for all this. It's bound to be a doozie! I wish you had done this during *my* senior year. I would have liked to go to Ecuador myself!"

"If you hear from Drew, tell him what I told you, about not telling your Mom about the house."

"Okay. I might go see Drew next weekend, if I can find his new apartment in Huntsville. That is, if my buddy with the car goes back home to Montgomery next weekend. I have to hitch-hike any time I go somewhere."

"Don't get your hopes up, but if I can, I'll try to get you a good used car for Christmas. Just something for basic transportation."

"That will be great, if I can scratch up the gas money!"

"I know how you make your spending money!"

"You mean with the sausage?"

"Yeah, I don't think you'll have a problem raising gas money! Listen, I'm going to let you go for now. I'll call you when we get back home."

"Okay Dad. Later!"

After he hung up, he chuckled about the way he found out Joey was making his spending money. Last Christmas, he drove up to Berea College to pick Joey up and bring him home for the holidays. When he got there, he walked up to the third story of his son's dorm, and found a line of guys backed up all down the hall, waiting to for something. The hall was filled with the wonderful aroma of sausage cooking. He passed the line, and found that it ended at his son's room! Inside, he found that Joey was using an electric skillet, (which was against dorm rules) to fry sausage patties, and was selling them for a dollar each, as fast as he could cook them.

He waited about thirty minutes, for Joey to run out of sausage, then the line disappeared, many disappointed that he ran out of sausage before they got theirs. As Joey was cleaning the skillet to put it away, he explained.

"Dad, the food in our cafeteria is so bad that a lot of these guys get desperate for *real* food. I found that out after I got the electric skillet, and began cooking. I tried to close the room off, so the smell wouldn't alert everybody that I was cooking, but you know how smells travel! The guys were just like rats, following their noses! They were beating on my door, wanting food!"

"So you shared with them?"

"Yeah, but I told them I couldn't afford to feed everybody! And man, you should have seen how fast the money came out! I took a few 'donations', then walked down to Wal-Mart, and bought a few 30-packs of Jimmy Dean sausage patties, and the guys practically *begged* me to sell them for a dollar each, so I gave them what they wanted."

"So how much do you pay for a 30-pack of sausages?"

"$2.49, plus tax."

"So you spend $3 and make $30?"

"Yes sir. A net profit of $27 per pack. I cooked ten packages before you got here, and still didn't have enough to satisfy the demand. But I can't cook just anytime I want. I cooked today, because I was told that our dorm monitor is out of town. Everyone knew what *that* meant! It was sausage day!"

"Have you tried selling anything besides sausage?"

"Yeah, sometimes I cook bacon, two strips for a dollar. I tried a lot of things, but sausage gets the best results. I tried something called Chicken 'O' Rings one time, but they didn't sell at all. Everyone wanted to know what part of the chicken the 'O' ring came from. I ended up eating them myself."

"Yeah, that product sounds a little suspect."

"Before I start cooking, I open the window, and turn on the window fan, in reverse, to suck the smoke out, but then I realized it was better advertisement to have the fan blowing in, and with my door open, the smell of sausage hits all four floors of the dorm! Guys come running from everywhere, with dollars in their hands! Sometimes they even come from other dorms!"

"It sounds like you've learned how Free Enterprise works!" Travis said. Even with the scholarship, Joey was having to work his way through school, but that was a good thing. He was learning a lot of useful things.

Janice would have liked to have talked to Joey as well, but he had to talk to him first, so he wouldn't say anything about the house. She appeared to be sleeping well, after her morning adventure on the shore, so he let her sleep.

He went down to the main deck, where he talked to the guide. Their afternoon exploration was not going to be on shore, but would be a tour on board the rubber landing craft. They were going to circle a few small rocky islands, to get photos of the colonies of Galapagos penguins that lived there, and whatever else they saw. The guide said that there were always a few surprises.

He hoped the surprises didn't involve Great White sharks.

Later, when he told Janice what was planned for the afternoon, she told him to get plenty of pictures, because she had no intention of going. She would go, if they were going ashore, but to just bob around on the vast ocean, like shark bait, was just a bit too risky for her. But he couldn't blame her, not after what she had witnessed that morning.

Travis went on the afternoon tour, and found that several of their group had elected not to go. There were only four of them, plus the guide, and the driver, which meant that there was plenty of room in the boat to move around.

The tour was great. The penguins seemed to put on a show for them, as the motored past the rocks that they called home. A small colony of huge walrus also took up residence on the rocks, to the displeasure of the penguins, but there wasn't much they could do about it. There were literally hundreds of these small islands, most of which were nothing more than a cluster of rocks protruding above the ocean. But there was something on every rock, calling it home. It turned out to be a very interesting two hour tour.

Finally, when they had seen enough, they turned the boat out to open water, and headed back to their ship at high speed. They had gone only a short ways, when a wave suddenly broke over the top of their boat. Not a wave of water, but a wave of *fish*! Hundreds of them had burst from the ocean at one time, leaping several feet, and then back into the water. But it just happened that their boat had been under them when they leaped, and dozens of them came down inside the boat with them! One guy on the opposite side of the boat was literally knocked into the floor of the boat, when a two-foot fish hit him in the side of the head.

The boat driver immediately stopped the boat, because they had several large fish in the boat to contend with. The only woman who was on board with them, was screaming hysterically.

"Stay calm, everyone!" The guide was saying. "They are just fish, and they got into the boat accidentally! We will throw them back out! No problem! Please stay calm!"

The fish were thrashing about dangerously, and Travis saw blood in the bottom of the boat, from the guy who was hit in the head. A bony fin had cut him pretty good, judging by the amount of blood everywhere.

"Phil, are you okay?" the guide asked.

"Gonna' need stitches." Phil replied dryly, as he grabbed a fish by the tail and flung it out of the boat.

"What kind of fish are these?' someone asked, while everyone was grabbing them and 'helping' them out of the boat.

"I think they are young Blue-fin Tuna. But I have never seen them jump out of the water like this before, in such numbers!"

The driver said something that Travis didn't understand, and the guide agreed with him.

"Our driver thinks that these tuna all jumped at the same time, because something under the water scared them! Most likely, a large shark. It was just a coincidence that we were in the way when they jumped. If we were fishermen, this would have been a very good omen! Any time a fish jumps into the boat with you, it is a good day!"

"Remind me of that while I'm getting my head sewn up!" Phil said, tongue in cheek.

"Can we take one of these back to the ship and cook it?" Travis asked.

"No, it would be illegal to keep them." the guide said, as he continued to throw them overboard. "Tuna is a commercial fish, and these are not even the legal size to keep. Sorry!"

After they had thrown their catch back overboard, the guide got out the first aid kit and put a temporary bandage on Phil's head, until they could get on the ship. The driver was busy trying to wash the blood off the boat, before it dried. Finally they got back under way, and made it back to the ship.

Travis climbed aboard, more dizzy than he had been the whole trip. He felt behind his ear and found out why. His patch was gone again, so he went to the cabin to get another one. He went ahead and showered, dried, put on his other set of clothes on, then put on a fresh patch. He wondered what the active ingredient was in those patches, that entered his skin, and kept him from getting sick. Whatever it was, it worked well.

Janice wasn't in the cabin, so he assumed she was downstairs in the lounge. He was right. She had been there all afternoon with three other women, and had apparently had several margaritas each. All four of them were so drunk, that they hardly noticed that the tour was back. They were beyond just drunk, they had reached the level of rowdy, vulgar and obnoxious. It was a good thing there were no other passengers on the ship besides them. One by one, their husbands claimed them, and waddled them off to their cabins to sleep it off. When Janice saw the bandage on the side of Phil's head, she asked, "What happened to him?"

Phil replied, tongue in cheek, "Shark bite."

Janice shook her head and said, "See! That's why I didn't want to go!" Travis led her toward the stairway, to get her to their cabin. He thought he would never get her up the stairs, but once he got her there, and onto her bunk, she was out like a light. He took her shoes off her, and covered her with the blanket. She was going to hate the world tomorrow.

After dinner, (which the drunk women missed) the ship got under way, to get them to the next island, for the next days adventure.

⊰ 44 ⊱

The next day their ship was anchored off the coast of yet another island. This one was supposed to have a great diversity of life on shore. For one, there were several large colonies of marine iguanas here. The marine iguana was like the iconic symbol of the Galapagos Islands. Every photo he had ever seen advertising the islands, included a marine iguana.

Before breakfast, Travis took the time to wash out all their previous days clothes in the sink, so they could be drying while they were gone ashore. Janice usually did that chore, but she was in no shape to do anything other than groan about how bad her head hurt.

"I've got no sympathy for you, Dear. Your pain is self inflicted. Are you about ready for breakfast?"

The mere mention of breakfast made her lurch, and run for the bathroom. Afterward, she felt better, but still didn't think she could eat anything. They went down to the dining area together. It was easy to spot the other three women who had gotten drunk the previous evening. They all had the same expression as Janice. None of them ate much more than dry toast.

"You are going to enjoy our shore explorations today and tomorrow," the guide said. "The islands we will visit the next two days are two of the oldest islands, geologically, and therefore, since they have been around longer, they have had more time to accumulate more wayward plants and animals, and those plants and animals have had much longer to evolve and adapt to their environment. All the plant and animal life found in the Galapagos, were brought here either on the wind, or the waves, from the mainland, or even as far away as the shores of the Far East. So everything here has similar origins as other species found elsewhere. But once they got here, the wind and ocean currents prevented them from having contact with species on the mainland. So the longer they are here, the more they evolve to adapt to the unique conditions here. After many centuries, or even thousands of years, they gradually start to look nothing like the species they evolved from. That was what excited Charles Darwin, when he studied the life here. It was similar, but different, because it evolved and adapted to the islands unique conditions."

"So, do you think that we evolved from monkeys?" Phil asked.

"No I do not." the guide said. "The Bible said that we were created in the image of God, so no, I do not believe that we evolved from monkeys. I think Darwin was wrong about that part. But even though we were created by God, I think that Mankind *has* evolved over the centuries. Even we humans must evolve and adapt to our environment. If we do not, then we could perish any time the climate changes, or catastrophic events force us to change our way of living. Life has survived on this planet, because it knows how to adapt and evolve. Life forms that cannot change, are doomed to become extinct,...like the dinosaurs. Their downfall was that they were *too* successful. They thrived in their era, because conditions for life was perfect, causing them to grow to gigantic size. But when events happened that quickly cooled the planet, they could not adapt quickly enough, and they died out.

"Even here in the Galapagos, there have been massive die-offs of some species, in response to changing climate. Just four years ago, because of the El Nino weather systems, that develop in the Pacific Ocean, and move this way, there was a massive die-off of marine iguanas on this very island. I am told that because of El Nino, cooler waters were forced to the Galapagos, and displaced the usually warm waters around the island. The cooler water stunted the growth of algae on the rocks underwater, which happens to be the primary food of the marine iguanas. With suddenly less food, the large colonies of marine iguanas began to die off in alarming numbers. At first we thought the iguanas were the victims of pollution, or toxic chemicals in the water, but after taking water samples, and doing autopsies on over a hundred dead iguanas, they were found to have simply starved to death. In some colonies, there was as much as a 60% mortality rate.

"At that same time, it was observed that the iguanas that did not die, had survived by going ashore, and eating certain varieties of cactus. That was something that they had never been observed doing before. They survived, by adapting. Fortunately, the cool waters eventually moved out, and warm water returned, and the iguana populations quickly recovered. But that is a good example of how life adapts. Because of the abundant algae, the iguana population exploded, but when the food source suddenly disappeared, the ones that depended entirely on the algae perished, and the ones that adapted to a different food, survived. That is a very good example of 'survival of the fittest'. Or perhaps it would be more accurate to say, 'survival of the smartest', or 'more resourceful'. I fear that is going to be the same story of Mankind one day. One day, when our economy, and thus, our civilization collapse, the only people who will survive will be those who know how to adapt. Instead of going to the grocery store for food, they will have to resort to hunting and gathering, like their ancestors. Those who do not know how to hunt, or grow food, will be doomed to starvation. So survival of the most resourceful people will guarantee the survival of the species."

"Then I guess I will be one of the people who go extinct," Phil said. "I've never hunted, and I wouldn't know how to start growing food. I'd have to steal food from those who have it."

"If you try to steal it from me, I'll *help* you go extinct!" Travis said.

"Don't be rude, Travis." Janice said, through her hangover.

"I'm not being rude," Travis said, "I'm just stating a fact. If civilization goes south, there will be a lot of panic and violence. Those who have, will be forced to fight off those who don't have."

"I assure you, I will go extinct very easily." Phil said. "I'm not much of a fighter."

"None of us really knows how we will respond, until it happens." the guide said. "But to get back on the subject, we were talking about the diversity of life on the Galapagos. The Galapagos Islands were all formed by volcanic action, and are very young in geological terms. While no one knows their exact age, the oldest island is almost surely younger than Mankind. And Mankind is generally believed to be, at the very oldest, 200,000 years old. So the life that has evolved here, has done so in a relatively short period of time, and without the intervention of man. I am sure the Polynesians may have discovered the Galapagos, but they did not settle here, as they did on other islands of the Pacific. Perhaps because the conditions here were too extreme, they moved on. So, if everyone will go and get your provisions for the day, we will go ashore in thirty minutes."

"Janice, do you feel well enough to go ashore?" Travis asked.

"Yes, I think so. I don't want to miss seeing the animals. I hate to miss anything, because this is a place I have always wanted to travel to. But the sight of that shark yesterday just…"

"Yeah, I know, it freaked me out too. But you can't let that stop you from going ashore."

There was a stiff wind blowing, as they went ashore, which caused rough water, and even whitecaps, but it was a short ride. When they stepped out of the boat into the waist deep water, no one wasted time in getting ashore. The thought of the Great White shark sliding up on shore to get that seal was fresh in everyone's mind. Janice, normally the straggler of the group, was the first one ashore.

But what they saw was worth the risk, as they saw colonies of marine iguanas that numbered into the thousands. Sunny outcroppings were literally covered with the reptiles. The first thing Travis noticed was that they were a lot smaller than he thought they were. Most were not much bigger than a squirrel, but with a longer tail, of course. On all the nature shows he had ever seen from the Galapagos, the photographer had zoomed in, and since there were no humans in the scenes for comparison, it made the iguanas seem much bigger than they actually were. But still, the sheer numbers were impressive.

There were also more seals here, sprawled out on the beach, enjoying the sun. And there were birds as well. The Blue-footed Boobies were here in large numbers, and all in pairs. Everywhere they looked, they saw boobies engaged in their courtship dance.

"If you think there are a lot of birds here," the guide said, "Wait until tomorrow's tour! The island we see tomorrow is known as 'Bird Island' because of the numerous birds, of all kinds."

They spent almost three hours ashore, seeing all kinds of things that interested them. Birds, lizards, seals, and all kinds of botanical wonders. A beached whale skeleton attracted a lot of interest. Among the surf in a shallow inlet, Travis was looking for seashells, but found dozens of shark teeth. They looked like fresh teeth, not the fossilized kind he used to find in the sand quarry in Byrum County. But the guide told him they were not from sharks that had died.

"When sharks feed, they always lose several teeth. But it is no big deal, because sharks are always growing rows of new teeth, to replace damaged or worn teeth. That is why shark's teeth are always sharp. The fact that you are finding so many teeth here, means that the shallow water in this inlet is a regular feeding ground for sharks. If you come here at night, or at low tide, you might find large schools of fish that have gotten trapped here by the receding water. And the sharks will intentionally allow themselves to get trapped here with them, because they know the fish cannot escape."

"So we don't want to come here to swim at low tide?" Travis asked.

"Absolutely not! But if you want to see a shark catching fish, this will be the place to come."

"Yeah, I think Janice would like to do that."

"I don't think so!" Janice replied.

Travis, Janice and the guide continued to gather shark teeth. He didn't tell Janice what he was going to use them for. He needed a good selection, so he could later take them to a jeweler and have a nice necklace made for her. He might even have small emeralds set in each tooth, since they seemed to have plenty back at the Lodge.

One of the women approached them with a question for the guide.

"Hypothetically speaking, if a lizard were to swallow a camera battery, would it hurt it?" she asked.

"Hypothetically speaking, huh?" the guide asked.

"Yes."

"What kind of *hypothetical* lizard, and how big a *hypothetical* battery are we talking about?"

"Those big colorful lizards, about a foot long. And say, a small round camera battery, about the size of a dime."

"Was this *hypothetical* battery a new battery, or a dead one?"

"A dead one."

"Then *hypothetically*, it probably won't hurt it. The lizard would probably just regurgitate it." the guide said. "But if it was a new battery, it would probably just shock the lizard, *hypothetically*."

"Oh, okay. That's good to know." she said. Later after the guide had left, she admitted to the Lees what she had done.

"I was filming this lizard, when my camera died. While I was changing the batteries, I dropped a dead one, and it rolled down the hill. The lizard ran it down and swallowed it! I guess it thought it was a bug! I was afraid the battery might kill it, so I was reluctant to say anything about it."

"It's probably no big deal." Travis said. "He's probably eaten worse things."

"Are those shells you are gathering?" she asked.

"No, they are shark teeth," he replied, as he showed them off. She hunted in the surf and found a few, then went to show them to the others. Soon the whole group was there, gathering teeth for souvenirs.

When they had been there almost three hours, two other tour ships arrived, and they decided it was time to go. Janice eyed the water critically, looking for sharks, as they sped back to their ship. It had been a good visit.

⊰ 45 ⊱

The fifth day of the tour promised to be a good one, with a four hour stay on 'Bird Island'. Of course, there were other kinds of animals on the island as well, but the landscape was dominated by sea birds. Commorants, Blue-footed Boobies, Red-Footed Boobies, Albatross, all kinds of strange looking ducks, and the usual sea gulls and sand-pipers.

They waded ashore and went inland, to the trail head, where the guide explained a few things.

"As we walk across this island, be aware that there are bird nesting sites everywhere, and not all birds build nests. Some just wallow out a spot in the gravel and lay their eggs. And many times, the eggs are speckled and blend in so well that you could accidentally step on them. Therefore, I must ask that everyone please stay on the designated walking trails. The trails are easily identified because they are marked with a border of rocks. The trails literally criss-cross the island, and you do not have to stay on the main trail. You can branch off and go anywhere you wish, and you may stop and look as long as you wish, but please just stay on the designated walking trails.

"We will be walking through 'nurseries', where the nests will be very close together, and the birds are so accustomed to humans, that they will remain on the nests. You will get great photographs from close up, and you might be tempted to reach out and touch the birds, but please resist the temptation to do so. Some of the birds have been known to bite so hard that they rip the skin. You do not want to be bitten by an irate mother bird! I will lead you across the middle of the nursery, and answer your questions, then you may break up and go where you wish."

The birds were amazing. The first colony they passed through was Blue-Footed Boobies. They were divided up into pairs, and were all doing their little dance. They would face one another, and raise their left foot really high, then their right foot, then left, and then right, then they would lean over and shake their wings, then clack their beaks together, then repeat the ritual. Everyone got videos of the ritual, then they moved on.

On top the flat plateau, it was covered with grass, and was the nesting area of the Albatross. Unlike the other birds, that built their nests in close-knit colonies, the Albatross nests were scattered widely throughout the tall grass. As they made their way to the top of the plateau to get a better view, their guide told them about the Albatross.

"The Albatross has an enormous wing-span, as you can see from those we see flying. They have been known to fly out over the ocean and glide for days, on those enormous wings. They can go up or down, and find a wind current going their way, and travel hundreds of miles. They feed by skimming just over the surface of the water, and grabbing fish as they pass. They must be careful not to go into the water, because it is very difficult for they to take off again, once they are in the water. For all their gracefulness in the air, the albatross is very clumsy in the water, or even on land. Look over there, to the edge of the cliff. See that Albatross waddling over to the edge? Watch what he does."

"He jumped off!" Travis said.

"Yes, that is how they get air-bourn. Instead of flapping their wings, and trying to take off from the ground, they have found it easier to waddle over to the edge of the cliff, jump off and glide! That is why they have chosen this area as their nesting ground, because it is next to a good launching point, to get air-bourn. Now, has anyone ever seen an Albatross land?"

Everyone shook their head.

"Well, you are about to see one land now. Look over there. See that one circling? He is a male, who has been out fishing, and is returning with food for his mate. He circles to locate his nest, and then he will come in for a landing. Here he comes now. Watch closely."

They watched, as the broad-winged Albatross glided in for his landing, his feet out-stretched in an awkward manner, to slow his impact. But it was like he had no way of slowing down, and when he came in, he came in hard, hitting the ground, and tumbling head over feet in the grass, until he came to a stop. He stood up, shook off the humiliation of his crash landing, and waddled over toward his nest.

"It is like that every time!" the guide said. "They know how to launch themselves off the cliff, and they are one of the most graceful fliers in the animal kingdom, but they do not know how to land! Every landing is a crash landing! And sometimes they actually get badly hurt!"

"Bless their hearts!" a woman said. "You would have thought that they would evolve a better way of landing than that, after all these years!" They stood and watched a few more of them land, and it was always the same. The Albatross came in full speed, hoping to stop with his feet, but always crashing and tumbling to a stop. And after the crash, he would get up and re-shuffle his out-of-place feathers, and pretend he had just executed a perfect landing, as he strutted toward his mate.

They moved on up the trail, and came up on a female Albatross who had chosen to build her nest in the middle of the walking trail. When the guide saw this, he stopped.

"We have a bit of a problem here. To get a good view, we must pass by that nesting female, without leaving the walking trail."

"It looks to me like she's the one in violation." Phil said. "She's not supposed to build her nest in the middle of our trail!"

"No, the birds have the right to build their nests anywhere they want." the guide said. "It is unfortunate for us that she has chosen to build her nest here. But we can probably slip past her, if we are very quiet."

"She already knows we are here." Travis said. "And she is watching us pretty closely. Look at that sharp hook on the end of her beak! She doesn't look happy."

"I think she will let us pass." the guide said. "I will show you." He eased up close to the nesting Albatross, and tried to slip past her on the trail, but she was having none of that. She hissed loudly, and struck out at his leg, like a snake. She got a good bite on his calf and twisted, ripping away a piece of his denim pants leg.

"Ow! She got me good!" He raised his pants leg, to reveal a nasty gash on his calf that was streaming blood.

"Okay, I think we can bend the rules just this once." the guide said. "You may leave the trail just enough to stay out of her reach! She is in no mood to tolerate visitors today!" He hobbled over to a rock, where he cleaned and bandaged his wound, then they continued their tour. They stayed on the island well past noon, then finally returned.

They ate a late lunch as the ship got under way, headed toward the port where their tour would end. Afterward they went to the top deck to take in the sun and talk. That was when the guide came to inform them that they would be making one more stop, at Post Office Bay, on Floreana Island. Some of the travelers had heard about it, and expressed a desire to go there, so they would make the stop.

"And if you are going ashore there, bring a post card with you, to mail home to yourself." he said.

Janice shook her head. "I've had enough wading ashore, but you can go, Travis. Get pictures."

Janice was the only one who stayed on the ship, as everyone else went ashore. Like most of the islands of the Galapagos, this one was also void of any signs of human activity. They landed on a lonely beach inhabited by a few boobies, who watched with curiosity as the humans filed past them, and up a trail into the bushes. *An odd place to put a post office,* Travis thought, as they emerged from the bushes into a clearing, with a large make-shift mail box. It seemed to be made out of parts of a wrecked ship that had been gathered and arranged into a whimsical collection of junk. Driftwood, and other floating debris that had washed up here, also found its way into the site. It looked like a collection of junk that could have been assembled by the castaways from Gilligan's Island. The guide opened a door and took out a big plastic bag of post cards.

"Everyone who visits here, leaves a post card addressed to themselves, with no postage. And then you search among the other post cards left by others, and find one that has an address close to your hometown. The rule is, if you take a card from here, you must *hand deliver* it to the address on the card. Later, other groups will visit here, and someone will pick your card, and hand-deliver it to you. Your post card could get home before you do, or it could take *years* to find you again! But that is the fun of doing it, to see how long it takes to get there."

It sounded crazy to Travis, but he left his card anyway, and found a card left by someone from Gadsden, Alabama. He didn't know how long it would be before he would go to Gadsden, but when he did, he would deliver the post card.

Ironically, the makeshift post office appeared to be the only human structure on the island. After visiting the post office, they returned to the ship, and continued on their way. They headed east, reflecting on what all they had seen the past five days.

———◆◆◆———

That evening, they were anchored in the harbor at San Cristobal Island, where they would fly out of for Quito the next morning. (Which meant that there were actually *two* airports in the Galapagos Islands, instead of just the one on Baltra Island) after dinner, while Janice was busy socializing with the other travelers, Travis went up on the upper deck to make a phone call. With this tour coming to a close, he wanted to talk to General Morgan to see if anything had changed. The last word he had, the terrorists who were after him had decided that it wasn't worth the losses to continue going after him. But that was four days ago. Something could have changed, and if it did, he wanted to be aware of it. Instead of Morgan, he got an answering service, which got Morgan on another line, then connected them.

"How is your vacation, Travis?"

"It's great. No one has shot at me the whole time. Does that mean that no one is after me, or do they not know where to find me?"

"According to our eavesdropping, there has been no chatter about you, unless they have substituted a code word for you. The last word we had, was that the Muslim Brotherhood had no resources to go after you, so they contracted it out to Al Qaeda to do it. But after losing six men, they pulled their contract. and told the Brotherhood that if they wanted you, they would have to go after you themselves. Right now, Al Qaeda has got their hands full in Afghanistan. The Northern Alliance, backed by the U.S., is putting the Taliban to route. Al Qaeda is scrambling for their survival. As for the Muslim Brotherhood, they have given no indication that they will continue to go after you. But of course, you know to be ever vigilant."

"Yes."

"We recruited a team of Israeli interrogators to put the screws to those two captured in Ecuador, and we are getting more information than we ever dreamed!"

"But is it reliable information?"

"Yes, much of it checks out. Just yesterday we arrested four members of a sleeper cell in Michigan. Two of them had been in the country for six years, and had already landed jobs that required high level security clearances. One of them had bomb making materials in his garage. Those two are in Gitmo now, about to be interrogated themselves. From what I have already seen, it is scary how vulnerable our country is right now. Most Americans don't realize how serious these terrorists are about bringing us to our knees. Even after 911, most Americans don't realize how determined, and how far-reaching Al Qaeda is. Unless we get serious, and deal ruthlessly with these guys, we are going to see more attacks like 911. And border security! Don't get me started on that! When 9-11 happened, the President should have sealed off our border with Mexico, no later than 9-12. Why? Because most of the sleepers we have interrogated, said that was how they got into this country! And with no one watching, they are *still* coming in! Instead of us trying to start a fight with Saddam Hussein, who by the way, had nothing to do with the attack on us, we should send those troops to the Mexican border, and secure it! But I don't make the decisions, or give the orders, I just do my best to carry them out."

"So there is no chatter about me, huh? Do you think it would be safe for my family to come back home?"

"Probably so. Does that mean you'll be returning soon?"

"It depends on how soon they get my new house built."

"The unit of men I assigned to guard your house say they have not seen anything suspicious since they have been there. But I will leave them in place until you can get back and sort through the remains of your old house."

"Yeah, we might be able to salvage a few things. Janice still doesn't know about it. If she knew, I wouldn't be able to keep her down here. When we leave the Galapagos in the morning, we will go back to the eco-lodge for awhile, then decide how much longer to stay."

"How long will it be before I can expect you to be available again, for the Agency?" Morgan asked, though he knew that was going to be a touchy subject.

"I can be available as a survival instructor, but I just don't know about working for the Agency. Like I told you before, I do not feel comfortable when I'm out of my element. And the Middle East is out of my element. Why? Is there a mission in particular that you are thinking about?"

"No, not in the foreseeable future, but you know how fast that can change. If we go into Iraq, I can almost guarantee that we'll need you for recon missions. If that is okay with you?"

"Recon I can handle, but please, no more hits. I have lost my zeal for that kind of thing. And that last one going so badly…"

"Yeah, that was really unfortunate. But it wasn't your fault. You did the best you could with the information you had."

"Yeah well, I don't want to be put in that position again. You'll call me if anything changes?"

"Yes, I will."

"Then I will talk to you later."

His phone needed to be charged, so he took it to the cabin and plugged it up. Then he went down below to join the party. He found Janice there, but she was conspicuously staying away from the margaritas. Her last hang-over was no fun. To them, the party was a celebration of the fact that neither of them had gotten sea-sick on this entire tour, something that he would not have believed five days ago. Especially after that first night aboard the ship, during the storm.

"So Janice, how are you enjoying your vacation?"

"Oh yes! But I'm a little sad that it is ending. I loved seeing all the animals, but I'll be glad to get off this ship!"

"That makes two of us."

"When will it be safe enough for us to go back home?"

Travis didn't want to tell her that it might already be safe enough, because he knew she was home-sick, and ready to go home. He wanted to delay their return long enough for their new house to be finished.

"According to Morgan, things are improving. They have made some arrests, and are following new leads. I promise you, it won't be much longer. But in the meantime, Steve still needs my help with the eco-lodge, so we might as well help him while we can. You don't mind staying with Felicia a while longer, do you?"

"Actually, yes I do! I put up with it before, but I don't think I can handle that again."

"Then I guess you want to stay at the lodge then? That's the only other option."

"Didn't you say that our bungalow is finished?"

"Yeah, that's what Calvin said, the last time I called Steve. Hey, it's even got electricity and running water!"

"Electricity? How did they do that, way out there?"

"Generators. Actually the electricity will only be on a few hours every day, so you'll have to take advantage of it when it's on. That, and the running water will make staying at the Lodge a lot easier. It'll help, if you just consider the lodge as an extension of your Galapagos vacation. You'll see a lot of animals there that will be different from the Galapagos, but unlike anything you'll see in Alabama."

"So you want me to be a team member, and tough it out?"

"That's right, but it won't be that tough, because the place is starting to shape up. Hey, at least at the lodge, you don't have to worry about shark attacks."

"Okay, I'll give it a try for awhile. Calvin seems to like it there."

"Yeah, he took to it like a duck takes to water! It might be hard to get him to go back home."

"And back to school!" Janice said. "I hate that he's going to have to go to summer school to graduate this year. You know that you're going to have to *make* him go to summer school!"

"Oh yeah, he's going to summer school, whether he likes it or not. Then if he wants to come back down here, that's his decision."

"Will we be home in time for him to go to summer school?"

"Oh yeah, I'm sure we will be back home by then."

"I hope so."

"Janice, one day you are going to look back at this trip to Ecuador, and say, *'that was a real adventure'*, and then you'll be glad you did it. Even though I made you come with me, you'll be glad you did."

"I hope so. Come on, let's see what everyone else is doing. It sounds like a party."

⇥ 46 ⇤

The next morning they flew from San Cristobal Island back to Quito, then transferred to the flight to Coca. They arrived before noon, and Carlos was there to pick them up at the airport.

"Carlos, what's happened while we've been away?" Travis asked.

"Those men who were after you, we caught them, and sent them away on a helicopter."

"What men?" Janice asked.

Travis cringed, because he really didn't want Janice to know about the hit men.

"The men wanted to buy guns," Carlos continued, "So I told them that Steve had guns to sell them. That is what Steve told me to tell them. It worked! I led them right into a trap at the lodge."

"Travis, what men were after you?" Janice asked again.

"It's nothing to worry about, Janice."

"Were they *hit men*? Were they the same people who shot up our living room?"

"No, dear. I killed those two, remember?"

"You know what I mean! Were they sent by the *same people* who tried to kill you at home?"

"Morgan seemed to think they were."

"How did they find us all the way down here? I thought we were supposed to be safe down here! *You* told me that we would be safe down here!"

"We *were* safe, and we still are. Morgan thinks they tapped Jim's phone, because they knew I worked for FBN, and they knew that sooner or later I would call him. When I did call, they heard me tell Jim that I was calling from Coca, Ecuador. So it was *my* fault that they followed us here. Fortunately, Morgan was able to warn me that they were coming."

"So that trip to the Galapagos was just to get away from those hit-men?" Janice asked.

"No, we were planning that before I knew about the hit men. It just happened that the two things coincided."

Janice didn't believe that for a moment, but she let it drop.

"So does that mean that we are going to have to be looking over our shoulders the rest of our lives, or just until they kill you?"

"No, Morgan said that he has evidence that they have already given up looking for me."

"And you believe that? And I'm supposed to believe that?"

"We have to wait and see. That's why we need to stay down here awhile longer, to be sure they have stopped looking for me. It's pretty hard for a Middle-Eastern man to come down here without being noticed. The two they sent down here before, stuck out like black folks at a Klan rally, Steve said."

"So what happened to them? Or do I really want to know?"

"You really don't want to know."

"Okay, enough said."

"Look, Morgan's intelligence source says that the guys who *were* after me, have decided that it was not worth the losses they were taking, to continue after me, so they gave up."

"And how reliable is his 'intelligence source'?"

"Good enough to put my mind at ease. But we still need to stay down here awhile longer, just to be safe. If nothing else comes up in a month or two, we'll head back home."

"A month or two? I was thinking more like in a week or so!"

"No, I need to help Steve get the lodge up and running, and that, in turn, will give us time to make sure it's safe to go home."

"So will it be a month, or two months? I need to know what to expect."

"Let's play it by ear, and see what happens."

"So," Carlos cut in, "Are we going to Steve's house, or to the Lodge?"

"I have had enough of living with Felicia." Janice said. "I want to be wherever you are staying."

"In that case, we'll be going to the lodge." Travis said. "Carlos, take us by Steve's house to get our things, then we'll go to the lodge."

"Si." Carlos replied.

When they arrived at the lodge, they saw that a lot had changed, starting with the landing itself. A large sturdy pier had already been constructed, built on the pilings that had been driven into the mud by the contractors Steve had hired. Workers were busy building a floating pier extension, that would rise and fall with the level of the river. Steve was there to meet them.

"So how did you guys like the Galapagos?" Steve yelled, as they approached.

"It was great!" Janice replied. "It was amazing to see all the animals! But I could have done without seeing the sharks!"

"How do you like the new pier?"

"It looks good." Travis said. "Almost like it was professionally done."

"I think it turned out really well."

"Where is Calvin?" Janice asked.

"He's around here somewhere." Steve said. "He has really been a big help in getting things done. I think he's getting attached to this place too. You might not be able to pull him away, when you leave. He enjoyed the party we had this past weekend. I think he was the only one who didn't get sloppy drunk! I'm sure he'll tell you all about it."

"Wow! Look at that lodge!" Travis said. "It's really looking good!"

"And it's so big too!" Janice added.

"Yeah well, it was designed to be the center-piece of the whole place. It will be the meeting place for our guests, with a restaurant, kitchen, bar, and a large dance floor. I think it's coming along very nicely. Still a lot of work to do there though. We hope to get the cook moved into his new kitchen there in about ten days. I thought about buying the dining furniture, but seeing the skill of our wood-workers, I think I'll let them build the tables and chairs too. They love being able to use such massive slabs of mahogany."

"So, is our bungalow ready for us to move into?" Travis asked.

"Oh yeah! Calvin has been living there for a few days now. We're putting the finishing touches on two more! In a month or so, we could actually begin taking on paying guests. But I would rather keep the public out, until we get everything ready. I want to start with the main lodge, 12 bungalows, and a pool, at least. And of course, all our mining areas need to be secured from prying eyes. I'm thinking that about three months from now, we can announce our grand opening."

"I want to be here to see that, if I can." Travis said.

"Janice, I see that you came here with your bags." Steve said. "Does that mean that you are going to brave the dangers of the jungle, and live here at the lodge?"

"I'm going to try." she said. "It has to be better than bobbing up and down on that boat we were on in the Galapagos!"

"I'll have Calvin spray around your bungalow with pesticide, to thin out the bugs. I know how you hate bugs."

"If it comes down to bugs or sharks, I choose bugs!" she said.

"The sharks seem to have made quite an impression on you. What happened?" Steve asked.

"She saw a shark slide up on the beach to kill a seal. It was a really terrifying sight! Lots of blood. No one wanted to get back in the water after that."

"I can imagine!"

Travis grabbed their bags and headed toward bungalow #1, with Janice and Steve close behind. When they got there, Steve opened the door to show off the new unit.

"As you can see, the construction is simple, but it is really solid," Steve said, pointing out the massive boards. "It is basic shelter, but with the added convenience of running water and occasional electricity. We just brought in a mattress and box springs from Coca, to make the bed more comfortable, because after all, we want our guests to leave here happy. And happiness is a comfortable night's sleep. No matter how many conveniences this place *doesn't* have, if you give your guests a good night's sleep, it will outweigh everything else."

Janice poked her head in the bathroom. It consisted of a new porcelain toilet, and sink. The shower stall was just a tiled in corner of the room, with a drain. "What about hot water?" she asked.

"Not a problem!" Steve said. "All our bungalows will be totally free of hot water, which means that there will be no danger of getting accidentally scalded from out-of-control thermostats. We offer running water that has been cooled by the river itself! Nothing can be more natural, and good for you than that!"

"So you are saying that we have no hot water?" Janice asked.

"That's right, nothing that will blur the aesthetic, raw beauty of living with such basic accommodations."

"I think what Janice is saying is that she would be a much happier camper, if she *did have* hot water." Travis said.

"Sometimes happiness is overrated." Steve said. "The real beauty of a place like this, is not to make you happy, but rather to challenge you to push the boundaries of your own ability to adapt and overcome adversity. And this is also a very beautiful and romantic place, if you take an interest in those kind of things."

"You're wasting your breath, Steve. She's basically a couch potato. She'd rather have the hot water."

"I might surprise you!" Janice said defiantly. "And I am *not* a couch potato! I can put up with this place, if you can."

"You really think so?"

"Yes I can! I have put up with *you* all these years, so I can put up with a whole lot more than you think I can! Put my bags on the bed, and I'll put my things away."

"Okay." He put down her bags, and Steve began to fill him in on what had happened while he was gone.

"I want to show you how well the main lodge is coming along! We have it looking really good. The floor plans didn't do it justice! Seeing it all come together in real wood and stone is awesome!"

"I can't wait to see it."

"Then let's head over there right now. Make yourself comfortable, Janice."

After they were far enough away from the bungalow that Janice couldn't hear, Steve's tone changed, as he got right to the point.

"Travis, we've got big problems! Those smugglers we killed in the jungle? Well, their friends and families think they know what happened, and they are back watching us! For the last two days, they have been watching us, and they are not hiding the fact that they intend to hit us at the first opportunity. I have ordered everyone to stay in groups here close to the lodge. No one goes into the jungle alone."

"Where is my son?"

"He is okay. He's back with Emillio, and they are well armed. Everyone is well armed. I bought forty AK-47's while you were away, and trained everyone in how to use them. If we have to fight, at least we are not going to be out-gunned! Come by my tent, and I'll give you one too."

"Wait a minute." Travis said, stopping in his tracks. "If we are going to open an eco-lodge here, then we have to have a safe, secure area. The picture I'm seeing is *not* a safe and secure area! This is a problem we are going to have to solve."

"Like I don't know that? I thought we had the problem solved, but it looks like we have just stirred up a hornet's nest! That group we ambushed in the jungle apparently represented a much larger group than we thought. And they aren't just going to let this go! They probably want revenge for the guys we killed, and I can't really blame them."

"It sounds like I need to get my family out of here."

"That's probably not a bad idea. I know Janice just got here, but it might be prudent to move her back to Coca for awhile. And Calvin too, if you don't want him in on the fight."

"I hope there won't be a fight. Is there any way we can negotiate with them? At least find out what they want?"

"Like I told you, they probably want revenge for what we did to them!"

"Well, we don't know that until we can talk to them. Is there any way we can send them a message, to tell them we want to talk?"

"They would probably kill the messenger, if we sent one. And leaving a note on a tree probably wouldn't work, because these people are probably not even literate. I don't see any option other than trying out-gun them!"

Travis sighed. "How many people are we going to have to kill, to make this a safe place? And the next question is, how many is *too* many? At some point, we are going to have to decide what cost is too steep a price to pay, to make this project work."

"I say we already have too much invested, to just give this place up!" Steve said. "I mean, even if we never open the lodge to guests, we still need to hold on to this place, in order to mine emeralds. That is our main objective here anyway, remember? The eco-lodge was just a convenient cover story. We are looking at a vast fortune in emeralds here, and yes, to me that is worth fighting for."

"All the emeralds in the world wouldn't be worth the risk of getting my son killed down here." Travis said. "But then, you don't have kids, so you don't know what it would be to lose one."

"That's hitting below the belt!" Steve said. "But you're right. It wouldn't be worth it, if Calvin got killed in the cross-fire. But from what he's told me, he wants to fight too, if necessary."

"He's not old enough to make that decision. I need to talk to him."

"Yeah, I told him to talk to you about that before I let him have a gun, but he insisted that he knew how to use it. He said you wouldn't have a problem with it."

"Yes, I *do* have a problem with it! I don't want him, or Janice to be here if something goes down."

"Then maybe it's time for them to go back to the States."

"No, not until our new house is completed. And are you saying that you gave my son an AK-47?"

"Well, yeah. He knows more about handling guns than I do."

"Where is he?"

"Like I said, he's with Emillio…"

"…And he has an Ak-47!"

"You wouldn't want him defenseless, would you?"

"He and Emillio, where are they?"

"They are on guard duty up beside the water tank on the hill. But get a gun yourself, before you go up there."

They stopped at Steve's tent to get a gun. The place looked like an armory. He couldn't believe what he was seeing.

"Where did you get those RPG's?"

"From the same Russian arms dealer I got the AK's from. He said he could get me a nuclear warhead for 1.5 million in cash. I told him that was probably more fire-power than I needed."

"These AK's are new out of the box!"

"Well yeah! You think I would buy second hand guns? I wanted to make sure they worked. I didn't know that some assembly was required. Calvin and I have been staying up late at night, assembling them, and cleaning off the packing grease. Here, this one is loaded and ready. I need to get back down to the pier. Building that floating pier is more complicated than I thought it would be. You can find Calvin easily. Call out to him before you get there, so he will know it's you."

Travis took the gun, and went up the hill to the new water tank, then called out. Calvin answered from the nearby thicket.

"Over here, Dad!"

He found them with a pair of binoculars, scanning the jungle. Calvin's pet tapir was laying beside him asleep.

"Senor Lee! You have returned!"

"Yes, Emillio. Has Calvin been any trouble?"

"No, not any trouble! He has really good eyes! He is a good look-out! Calvin, I go to kitchen. Be right back."

"Okay."

Travis sat down in Emillio's seat, after he was gone. Loretta snorted, and went back to sleep.

"So, are you having fun yet?" he asked his son.

"I'm having a blast, Dad!"

"It sounds like serious business with these guys. Have you seen anything yet?"

"Oh yeah. There's a guy out there watching us right now! He's been there all morning. I don't think he knows I have binoculars."

"Do you see him now?"

Calvin raised the binoculars. "Yeah, he's right there where he's been all morning. See that really big tree, about 100 yards away? The one with those big fin-like things?"

"Yeah, and that's called a buttress, it helps to stabilize the tree."

"Well, right behind that buttress, you'll see the top of a head. I don't think he realizes that we can see him. Here, take a look."

Travis took the binoculars, and could see the dark haired man raise up and look over the buttress, then scratch the side of his nose.

"Yep, he's there all right, and he's watching us, as we watch him. Is he the only one you've seen?"

"No, there's another guy with big earrings that swaps out with him once in a while. I think they are both behind that tree though."

"They haven't made any effort to get closer?"

"Nope. They're just watching. Emillio says that they are watching, hoping to kidnap somebody. But we're not letting anyone go beyond this point. So how did you and Mom like the Galapagos Islands?"

"It was great! Ask her about the sharks!"

"I didn't think she liked sharks?"

"She *still* doesn't! But now she has a whole new reason not to like them. I'm not going to tell you what happened. You need to hear it from her. I hear you guys had a pretty good party last weekend yourselves."

"Yeah! Did Steve tell you about it?"

"No, he said to ask you."

"Aw, it was great! You're not going to believe what happened! Remember before you left, Steve was saying he was going to have a pig roast for the workers?"

"Yeah."

"Well, he decided to do it the weekend while you were gone. He bought two big pigs, and about twenty cases of beer! It sounded like they were going to stay drunk all weekend, so I decided I would stay here at the lodge, at least until the pigs were done."

"They didn't have it here?"

"No, they went over to that big sand bar on the other side of the lagoon, and set up tables. They built a big bon-fire, and made a big pile of hot coals to cook the pigs with. While the coals were making, they dug a big pit in the sand, and cleaned the pigs. They put the hot coals in the pit, and covered them with green banana leaves. Then they put the pigs in, along with raw vegetables, and covered them with leaves, and then covered the leaves with sand, so it would cook. Then they all got *more* drunk, and had a soccer game on the sand bar, until sunset, then they drank the rest of the night. The next day, they started drinking again, and about 11 A.M. they decided to dig up the pigs, so we could have the feast at noon. They called for me, and the others who didn't drink, to come and join the feast, so we brought fruit and fresh veggies to go with the steamed pork. When we got there, they were digging all over the place! They couldn't find the pigs!"

"You're kidding me!"

"No! They dug all day, trying to find them! They were drunk when they buried them, and then they played soccer over the top of them, and they forgot where they buried them! And they were still drunk when they tried to dig them up! It would have been funny, if we hadn't been so hungry! We ended up eating just vegetables and fruit."

"You mean they never did find them?"

"No! That's the tragic part, Dad! Somewhere out there on that big sand bar, are two roasted pigs, waiting to be discovered! Some of the guys went over there the next day, pushing rods into the sand, trying to find them, but then this security crisis came up, and they had to abandon their search. We've been on high alert, and watching the lodge for the past two days."

Travis shook his head. "I can't believe it! Steve is a geologist, and can find anything underground, but he can't find two pigs!"

"Yeah, and he was with the ones who buried them!"

Travis just shook his head. "How do you like shooting that AK-47?"

"Dad, I need to get me one of these! It sounds like it's falling apart when you shoot it, but it's really dependable!"

"What do you think about moving back to Coca, until this trouble blows over?"

"No! If there's trouble, I want to be here to help out?"

"Listen Calvin, you are still in high school, and things could get ugly as this stand-off continues. I would feel a lot better if you would take your mother back to Coca where it's safe, until this is resolved."

"You mean Mom is *here*?"

"Yeah, she's organizing her things in Bungalow #1 right now."

"That's where all my stuff is."

"There's room for three of us there, until they get another bungalow finished."

"Did you see this water tank we put up? I helped assemble it! I have been doing a lot of pipe work since you've been gone. I'm really starting to get the feel for this place."

"Well, don't get too attached, because you still have to go back home and finish high school."

"What for? I don't need a high school diploma to live down here and help run this place!"

"That may be true, but this place may not survive. And even if it does, you will want to move on to something else one day, and when you do, you'll need to have your diploma. Life is a long journey, and you've barely started. One day, you will be glad you graduated."

"Is that the best reason you can come up with, Dad?"

"Okay, here is a better reason. I'm your dad, and *I say* you will graduate, because that's what your mom wants! How about that? I can still whip your ass, if I have to, but I don't think you want that!"

"I'm just pulling your chain, Dad! I intend to graduate! No need to go postal on me!"

Loretta raised up and looked at them with concern, then snorted and went back to sleep.

"Speaking of school, how much longer are we staying down here, Dad?"

"Don't worry about the Spring semester. You've already missed that. But we should be home in time for you to enroll in Summer School."

"That sucks! What about if I just go back to school next Fall? Hey yeah, then I can play football another year!"

"No, I think you'll be too old to play high school football another year. There is a cut-off date on eligibility."

"Oh well."

Emillio returned from the kitchen with two skewer sticks loaded with roasted meat and vegetables, and gave one to Calvin. He offered the other one to Travis, but he told him thank you, but no, he was just leaving. "Both of you be careful, and don't let anyone sneak up on you here."

"We're on high alert, Dad!"

He walked back down the hill to his bungalow, and found Janice still arranging things inside.

"I saw Calvin. He's staying busy."

"I have killed six bugs, since I have been here!"

"That must be why Steve said he was going to have Calvin spray the place."

"What are you doing with that?" she said, pointing to the AK-47 he was carrying.

"Steve just bought a few for the lodge. I was going to try it out, but I haven't had time yet."

"Why does the lodge need assault rifles?"

"They are a deterrent to trouble, more than anything. So how do you like the bungalow?"

"Did I mention that I killed six bugs?" She stomped the floor beside the bed post. "Make that seven!"

"Well, you have to expect some critters in the rain forest."

"They can expect to be stomped, if they come in here with me!"

"I think they have lunch ready over at the kitchen, if you want to go eat."

"What do they have?"

"I think it's meat and vegetables on skewer sticks. It looks good."

"Okay, let me get my bug repellant."

They left the bungalow together, and passed a cluster of vines, where something was causing a disturbance. Something in there was hissing.

"It's got to be a snake! Be careful!" Janice said. Travis stopped and stepped aside to see what it was, then reported to her, as they continued to the kitchen.

"It was an eight inch lizard trying to eat a four inch cockroach. I think the cockroach was winning."

"So the lizard was hissing?"

"No, it was the cockroach." Travis replied. At the kitchen, they got a plate and went to the long grill, where most of the skewers were still smoking over low heat. They chose one they wanted, and examined the ears of roasted corn.

"I wonder what kind of meat this is?" Janice asked.

"Probably chicken or pork. Calvin said they cooked two pigs while we were gone."

"Oh, so this is probably pork. It's smoked so dark, you can't tell what it is."

Better to let her think it's pork, Travis thought, as he forked an ear of corn, *because those two pigs are probably still missing.* They found a seat at one of the wooden tables. Travis went to get them something to drink. As he was pouring two glasses of pineapple juice, Ortega, the security man, came up beside him.

"I guess Steve has told you about our situation?"

"About the jungle people watching us? Yes, he told me."

"I do not agree with Steve's solution to this thing. I thought I would get your opinion."

"I haven't heard his solution."

"No? Then I will tell you. He wants us to find out where their camp is, and wipe them out again, like we did before."

"But you don't agree with that?"

"No, I think we should communicate with them, and see exactly what they want. We made our point the first time, by wiping out their camp. So they know we are capable of doing that, and there is no need to do it again, unless they force us to do so. But because they know what we are capable of, now they will listen when we talk."

"How do we communicate that to them? Steve said they are probably not literate, so we can't send them a note."

"I will personally take the message to them."

"That might be dangerous. They probably want revenge for those we killed."

"No, I do not think so. I think if I go to them with a chicken, they will listen."

"With a chicken?"

"Yes, as a peace offering. A gift. One does not kill a man bearing a gift. I would like to try this, but Steve is against it. Do you think you can speak to him? You and he are old friends. I think he will listen to you. I think that by talking, we can negotiate a settlement, without further bloodshed. If not, we will at least know the reason why."

"That sounds reasonable to me. Yes, I will talk to him."

"Thank you."

When he got back to the table with Janice, she was carefully nibbling on her meat skewer.

"Is it good?" He asked.

"Yes, it is, but it's not pork. And it's not chicken either."

"So as long as it's good, does it matter what it is?"

"I guess not."

Travis was surprised. That was a departure from her usual response. Maybe she was starting to adapt? Or did she have something else on her mind?

"Why did you bring that gun to lunch with you?" she asked.

"I just didn't think to put it down at our bungalow."

"Really? So why is *everybody* carrying a weapon?"

"Well, Garcia is the security man. He always has a gun."

"Okay, so why does that guy have a gun? And those guys? And those over there? Something is going on, and I want to know what it is.'

"It's just a precaution."

"A precaution against what?"

"Okay, I'll tell you. There is a group of strangers out in the jungle, and we're not sure who they are. Until we find out, it is prudent to take this precaution. If they are up to no good, then just the sight of us carrying weapons should be enough of a deterrent."

"A deterrent against what?"

"Whatever they may have had in mind."

"Couldn't we just call the police?"

"Out here, *we are* the police."

"I never thought I would say this, but boy, do I miss Alabama!"

Steve arrived from his tent, also carrying a weapon. He fixed himself a plate, and sat across from the Lee's.

"How is lunch today?" he asked.

"Not bad, as long as we don't know what it is." Travis replied. "Listen, I talked to Ortega, and he thinks that the best thing to do, is to try to have a dialogue with those guys. He said he thinks he can go talk to them, and get them to meet with us."

"Absolutely not! What if they kill him, like they did Atan? I don't want to lose Ortega. He's too valuable to us."

"He thinks he can do this."

"So what do you think?"

"Hey, Ortega knows more about this than both of us. If he is willing to do it, then I say let him try. He wants to avoid what happened the first time."

"What happened the first time?" Janice asked. She knew nothing about their first encounter with the strangers.

"The first time, we had a 'failure to communicate'," Steve said, glancing at Travis.

"That's why Ortega wants to open a line of communication with them. To avoid mistakes and misunderstandings. I don't think it's such a bad idea, myself. He said as long as he takes a chicken with him, they will at least hear what he has to say."

"What does the chicken have to do with it?" Steve asked.

"A gift for them. He said they will not kill him, as long as he is bearing a gift."

"Hmm, That could be good to know. He might be right. I'll talk to Ortega after lunch. So, Janice, what do you think about the smoked meat?"

"It's good."

"You're not even going to ask what it is?"

"No, I don't think I want to know."

"See? You are making progress! You'll make it here just fine." He turned back to Travis.

"I hope we can resolve this quickly and permanently. We don't need this cloud of uncertainty hanging over us after we open our doors to the public. And by the way, as soon as we can, we need to make another run to Panama. I have 60 pounds of rocks to take Victor. Some of them are very good quality."

"And those came from the foundation of the main lodge?"

"No, actually most of them came to light while digging ditches to bury water lines. And that has me excited, because it means the range of the emeralds are more wide-spread than I previously thought. It means that the amount of emeralds to be found here is staggering! In fact, we might not want to put too many stones on the market at one time, because we would flood the market, and you know what that would do."

"It would cause the prices to drop?"

"Exactly! We should just sell the finer stones, and only a limited number of those. The rest, we can stockpile, and sell them as needed. That way, we can get top dollar for them for years! No one needs to know how big our stock-pile is. The diamond industry has done that for years, and the big diamond producers like DeBeers has made an incredible fortune, by regulating the market. I see no reason we can't do the same thing with emeralds. I'm sure Victor has been doing that with his emeralds."

They talked emeralds all during lunch, and when they finished, they sought out Ortega. They gave him the go-ahead to try to set up a meeting to discuss things. Ortega seemed pleased. He immediately went to the kitchen to get a live chicken.

"While we're waiting on him to get back, come, I need to show you some things in the basement of the lodge."

"In the basement?"

"Yeah, in the space underneath the lodge floor. The entrance to it is around back. You being a retired miner, you've got to like this!"

The massive solid wood floor of the lodge was one of its most impressive features, but the stone work that was going up underneath it was impressive as well. The front of the lodge was level with the ground, but the back and two sides dropped steeply. These three sides were in the process of being enclosed by the stone masons, with massive, solid stone walls.

"This underpinning with stone walls," Steve explained, "will create a 'basement' underneath the lodge, that visitors will presume to be just a storage space. The only access to the space will be this one door in the back side. However, little will anyone know, that this secret space is actually the most important place on the whole lodge! This will be the entrance to our emerald mine!"

"Such a small door?" Travis noted. "That's barely wide enough to get a wheelbarrow through!"

"And once we get the wooden frame set into the stone, it won't be *that* big." Steve said.

"So all the timbers and mining supplies will go in there?"

"Yes."

"And what about all the tailings? The material we dig out that has to be discarded? Will it all come out here too?"

"No it won't. Steve said smugly. "I have another plan for that. Let's go inside and I'll show you."

Inside this basement, Steve turned on a battery lantern to show off his plan. Travis recognized the stone support pillars that he and Calvin had helped build, but it looked a lot different with the massive wooden floor over it, and the sides being enclosed. Overhead, he noted that thin wooden strips had been nailed over the close fitting cracks between the massive floor-boards. "What are those slats for?" he asked.

"So we can turn on lights down here, and they won't be seen by our guests in the Lodge looking down."

"Oh."

"Look over here. This is where the mine entrance will be. I calculate that we'll have to slope downward at 20 degrees, for at least the first twenty feet, before we level off and expand. That way we will be deep enough below the surface, that we can use roof supports to hold the top up. We don't want one of our bungalows to disappear down a sink-hole!"

"No, that would be bad. But what do you plan to do with ground seepage? With the mine opening higher than the mine itself, water is going to accumulate in the tunnels."

Steve had obviously not thought about that. "What do you recommend?" he asked.

"Well, I was of the impression that the mine opening was going to be far enough down the hill that the mine itself would gradually grade *up-hill*, into the emerald bearing rock. That way, any seepage would take itself out of the mine, by means of gravity."

"Yes, that would have been better, I suppose, but I already have it set up here. So that means we will have to have a pump, to get the seepage out?"

"Yeah, a small, 110 volt electric pump will probably do the job. And it runs quietly too, which is what you want, I think."

"Yes, running quietly is a *must*. I probably need to get your advice on how to set the roof supports too. What kind, and how far apart, and that kind of thing. What do you think?"

"I'll have to examine the roof of the mine itself, after you start mining. That's about the only way to be sure. Although, I can tell you one thing already, even before you start. The fact that this mine is going to be so shallow to the surface, and there is a lot of rain here, that means you will have to take special precautions. This is not solid rock you are mining through. It is like a matrix of hard-packed soil, intermixed with the emerald-bearing rock, which is like a hard gravel. It might seem pretty solid, but once you mine under it, I can see the roof and sides deteriorating badly, especially if it is permeated by ground seepage. Therefore, your system of roof support will probably have to be some kind of solid wooden frame, that will hold the roof and sides in place. And it needs to be some kind of water-resistant wood, so it will not rot. Probably the same kind of wood you cut to construct the pier. I suggest 4x4 square wooden timbers, set no more than four feet apart down both sides of the tunnel. These timbers will be holding up cross-timbers, also 4x4, with 1x6 wooden slats across the top, to hold up everything that might fall, even the small stuff. If necessary, you can add 1x6 slats on the sides as well, to keep the sides from crumbling in."

"Wow. It sounds like we need you here, when we start the mining. Your expertise will be a valuable asset."

"Hey, I couldn't have been a coal miner for 25 years, and not learned something about mining! As long as my contribution is only advice. Remember, I had back surgery?"

"Oh yeah, of course! Your contribution will be what you *know*, not what you *do*! We have plenty of strong young men willing to do the manual labor. Someone with a practical knowledge of mining, like you, is exactly what we need! You will be our mining consultant!"

"I like the sound of that. Now, what is your plan to remove the tailings?"

"Oh yeah! You are going to like this! Come over here, to the lower end. See this 8 inch PVC pipe cemented in the wall? This pipe slants downward, at a 35 degree incline, all the way to the river. Step out the door, and I will show you. See the pipe going down the hill?"

"Yes. I saw that earlier, and I was going to ask you what it was."

"This is how we will remove the rock and debris, and deliver it directly to the river! The pipe is so slick, that anything you throw in, slides all the way to the bottom. Of course, before we have guests, that pipe will be covered, so it won't be seen from the outside."

"So we will be shoveling the tailings into this pipe, and it slides down and dumps into the river? That spot won't take long to fill up!"

"The pipe will not be dumping directly into the river. I bought a small barge in Coca that was about to be scrapped. I took it to a fabrication shop, and gave them a drawing of what I want. They are going to modify the barge, with a specially made 'dump door' in the bottom, so it can carry two or three tons of tailings at one time. We'll moor the barge down there under the end of this pipe, and load it, by sliding the material through this pipe. Every time we get a load, we haul it out into the middle of the main river at night and dump it. Out there, the river is so big, and the current is so strong, that the tailings will never be noticed."

"It sounds like a great plan, if the dump door works like it's supposed to. So it's supposed to dump without sinking the barge?"

"Oh yeah! It'll work! I'm pretty good at designing things like that. I might want to get a patent on it, if it does well."

"In that case, when you get the time, you might want to work on a 'roasted pig detector', so we can find those two missing pigs. I bet they are well done by now!" Travis said.

"I guess Calvin told you about that?"

"Yeah, he couldn't wait to tell me about it. I assumed that large amounts of alcohol was involved. But how ironic that someone like you, who can find unseen mineral deposits deep underground, can't find two pigs that *you* buried the day before!"

"Yeah, I know that's pretty funny. Go ahead and laugh, and get it out of your system. But, Mr. Famous Writer, when you get around to writing the story of my life, as a *rich geologist turned emerald producer and philanthropist*, how about doing me a favor, and leaving out that drunken roast pig incident?"

"No way! That's the kind of things that readers want to hear! No matter how rich and famous you become, it's stories like that that will knock you off your pedestal and humanize you! Truth be known, George Washington was probably drunk as a bicycle when he tried to throw that silver dollar across the Potomac River! And though history doesn't say it, I'm pretty sure that dollar didn't make it across."

"Well, that certainly makes *me* feel better!"

"Okay, so if you are going to have to use electric pumps and a ventilation fan, to maintain this mine, it means you will probably be looking at running your generators more than just a couple of hours per day, like you said before. Which could be a good thing, because it will provide our guests with more electricity, for more hours of the day. Janice will be glad to hear that."

"What did you say about running a ventilation fan?" Steve asked.

"Well yeah, I assumed you will be ventilating the mine with fresh air. You *are* going to ventilate it, aren't you?"

"No, I hadn't planned to. I mean, we are probably not going to encounter any methane gas, since this isn't a coal mine, therefore why should we ventilate it?"

"Because your workers will run out of oxygen if you don't. If you don't have some system to pull out the bad air, then your workers will die from what miners call 'black damp', which is nothing more than a lack of oxygen in the mine."

"So we'll need a ventilation fan?"

"Yes, but probably not a big one. As the mine gets deeper, you can extend a 4 inch PVC pipe to the deepest part of the mine. On the out-by end of the pipe, you have the fan mounted, and have it sucking air out of the deepest part of the mine. It will suck out any dust or gas, including radon and carbon dioxide, and will cause fresh air to be pulled in through the shaft."

"Okay, so a ventilation fan is definitely a must have. You know, there is a lot more to operating a mine than I thought."

"Yeah, and if this was a *legal* mine, you would have to abide by all kinds of government safety regulations."

"Then it's a good thing it's illegal! Well, this is where we will mine after the lodge is operational. Until then, we're finding just boo-koos of emeralds everywhere we dig! I can't wait to see what we find when we dig the hole for the swimming pool!"

"If we can't reach an agreement with those smugglers, we might not have a lodge here at all."

"Oh yeah, there will be a lodge!" Steve said. "If it means that we have to deal ruthlessly with them, then we'll do what we have to do. I have put in too much work and sweat here, to be run off by a band of people that have no legal claim to the land!"

"I hope Ortega can set up a meeting with them. Talking will be a lot better than fighting."

≍ 47 ≍

It was almost sun-set, and Ortega had still not returned from the jungle. Steve was up-set, because he was sure that they had killed him. At the kitchen, after the evening meal, he was organizing a search party, to leave out at sunrise the next morning, to recover Ortega's body, when someone said, "We will not have to search far! Here he comes!"

Everyone stood to see if it was really him, and it was. He was returning to them as safe as when he left. He no longer had the chicken.

"So, how did it go?" Steve asked.

"It went well. Now I know for sure who those people are, and what we are dealing with."

"They accepted your chicken?" someone asked.

"Yes, that was a very good idea, to take them a gift, otherwise, they would not have met me."

"Come, sit at the table and eat, and tell us about them." Steve said.

"First of all," Ortega said, "they are Waorani Indians, from across the Colombian border. They have several scattered villages there across the border. For years they have been isolated in that remote area, because they do not like the ways of modern man. They have had run-ins with the Colombian authorities, and even the military. They want nothing to do with them. That is why they have been trading through the backside of Ecuador. Almost 50 years ago, they found that they could bring their trade items through the jungle, and set up on this side of the river, right here in this lagoon. Trade ships would stop and bargain with them, so that became their way of trading with the outside world. When they came here, and had things to trade, they said they would climb that big tree up there on the point, and tie a red blanket. That was their signal to the trade ships, that they had things to trade."

"What kinds of things did they trade?" Steve asked.

"I didn't get into that," Ortega said, "But I got the impression that they would trade anything that they could make a profit on. Not necessarily drugs, though they possibly dabbled in it, as well as other things. They said that trade was good for them. When Exxon came, they built roads, and cleared drilling pads, but they didn't care if Exxon used the land, as long as they allowed them to continue to trade on the river. And for the most part, Exxon hardly noticed them.

"But when you bought this land from Exxon, things changed. We occupied the very spot here, that they used as their trading camp, and they said that was fine with them, as long as we used it and moved on. But we stayed, and then began to build, and dig, and that was when they got up-set. They felt like this was *their* camp, because they had never seen anyone else here before. So they feel that they have a claim to the land here, because they were here first. They said it is their 'homestead'."

"That's nonsense! I bought this land free and clear from Exxon, who in turn, had bought it from the Ecuadorian government. Even if they had homestead rights, they would have to have lived here *continuously* for at least ten years! That's the operative word here, *continuously*! I don't think a temporary trading camp qualifies as a *homestead*!"

"Well Steve, that was what they told me. Obviously, there is room for discussion, and negotiation. And so, they welcome the prospect of meeting with you, so they can make their case that this is their land."

"When do they want to meet?"

"They said they would have to summon their elders from their villages in Colombia, to come here, if you want the meeting to be here. That will take about two weeks, because they are old, and must travel slowly. Or, if you wish to meet sooner, you can make the three day walk to their village, to have the meeting. I think they preferred the latter."

"I prefer meeting right here, but I don't want to wait two weeks for those doddering old geezers to get here! What about going to their village? Do you think it's safe to do that? Could it be a trap?"

"It very well could be." Ortega said. "It would be prudent to send only one person, and an interpreter, to do the negotiations."

"I don't need an interpreter. I speak fluent Spanish." Steve said.

"They told me that the elders speak very little Spanish, and no English. They speak only their native Indian tongue."

"Who can speak that?"

"I can." Ortega said. "My wife is originally from a Waorani village. I can speak it fluently."

"Then you'll be my interpreter. Travis, do you want to go with us?"

"Actually, I thought I would stay here, so when they kill you, then I'll inherit all this!"

All the workers laughed, because they thought he was joking.

"Nothing doing, Dude! If I bite the dust, you'll be right there beside me!"

"Then I guess Calvin will inherit our shares. Sure, I'll go with you. When do we leave?"

"They'll be waiting for an answer tomorrow morning." Ortega said.

"So I guess we pack a bag, and head out in the morning." Steve said. "I want to get this issue solved as soon as possible."

"You *did* hear Ortega say that it *could* be a trap?"

"That's a chance I'm willing to take."

"Okay, I'll have your back." Travis said, not at all sure that they were making the right decision. If he had been asked, he would have voted to wait on the geezers to waddle all the way to *their* camp. The exhausting trip might have softened them up for the negotiations. This was also known as the home field advantage. He wondered how many ambush sites they would walk through to get there.

———◆◆◆———

That night, sleeping in the small bungalow was an adventure, to put it mildly. Travis and Janice slept in the bed, while Calvin rolled out his sleeping bag on the floor. They had a new mosquito net, and spent almost an hour trying to figure out how to install it, so it would work properly. Once it was installed, Janice worried that Calvin would be eaten alive, because he would not be under the net.

"I'll just do like I've been doing." Calvin said. "I'll zip myself up in the sleeping bag, like a worm in a cocoon!"

"Won't that get hot and uncomfortable?"

"Wait and see, Mom. About one in the morning, you'll be freezing!"

"Here in the rain forest? That doesn't make sense."

"You'll see." he said.

Janice imagined all kinds of dangers out there in the darkness. And there was certainly no lack of reasons to think that, because there was constant noise from jungle, as monkeys howled, a jaguar growled, and all kinds of nocturnal birds, animals and insects kept up a racket all night long. She did sleep, but only for short, fitful periods, before something screamed and caused her to bolt upright in bed. Travis just snored on.

But then, about 4A.M., something was on the porch, trying to get the front door open! It was grunting and rooting at the bottom of the door, and she was insane with fear. Something was on the porch, *trying to get the door open*! She couldn't stand it any longer. She shook Travis until he woke.

"What is it?"

"There is *something* trying to get in through the door!"

"What is it?"

"I don't know, but it's something big!"

"So let it in."

"What? Are you crazy? It might kill us all!"

"Well, if it gets *you first*, then maybe I can get some sleep!"

"Get your gun, and see what it is!"

"I don't care what it is! It can't get the door open anyway!"

"Hear it? It's scratching at the bottom of the door!"

"I hear it." Travis said, unimpressed.

"Shoot through the door and kill it!"

"That's a new door, Janice."

"If it gets in, it'll kill us! Get up and do something!"

With a deep sigh, Travis got up and shuffled over to the door. He unlatched the lock, and peeked out. By the moon light, he saw what it was, and opened the door wider, to let it in, then shut the door behind it.

Janice screamed and jumped up on the bed, as Travis turned on the battery lantern, and illuminated the room. The large animal that came into the room had plopped down on the floor beside Calvin's sleeping bag. It was Loretta, Calvin's pet tapir. Calvin unzipped his sleeping bag just enough to get his hand out to scratch behind her ears. She grunted with satisfaction.

"Are you happy now?" Travis said. "I know Loretta is!" He went to the bathroom, then came back to bed. In two minutes, he was snoring again.

———◆◆◆———

They were up at dawn, and went to the kitchen, to see if the coffee was ready. Not only was the coffee made, but a buffet breakfast was laid out as well. A large group of workers were gathered around the hearth, sipping coffee, telling tales, and laughing heartily. Sunrise was when everyone gathered here to socialize, before starting another long day of work. They greeted the Lees, and made room for them at a table. Steve and Ortega were already there, talking quietly among themselves. Travis sat across from them with his breakfast. Janice joined them a minute later.

"So, how do you like the new bungalow?" Steve asked.

"I had no problems with it." Travis said. "It's small, but sufficient and well organized for what it is. For an eco-lodge, it's perfect. Just enough comfort to get a good nights rest, but still 'out there' and close to the jungle, and the jungle critters. That is exactly what people come to an eco-lodge for. I like it."

"What about you, Janice?" Steve asked.

"It was like trying to sleep through a bad 'B' horror movie!"

"Ah, so you liked it!" Steve beamed.

"Let's just say that it is *far* from being a five star hotel!" she added.

"Well then, we have succeeded! That was exactly what we were aiming for! Detached from the civilized world, and connected with the rain forest, and the creatures of the night! Our guests are going to love it!" Steve said, as Janice rubbed the sleep out of her eyes. There was no point in trying to tell him how bad she hated it. He would only take it as a compliment. This early in the morning, she hated to be around an optimist.

"I'm going to get coffee." she said.

After she was gone, Travis asked, "So what time will we leave?"

"As soon as you are ready." Steve replied.

"The Waorani said we would meet a guide on the trail this morning." Ortega said. "He will accompany us all the way to their village. Most of them left last night, heading home, so they can be there ahead of us, to be in on the discussions."

"It sounds like they are really taking this seriously." Travis said.

"Yes, and I'm glad they are." Steve said. "That means our trip won't be for nothing."

"This is just a thought," Travis said, "And maybe I am way off base, but what if we get there, and find out that their tribe has decided not to negotiate. But instead, put us on trial for murder?"

Steve and Ortega looked at one another, then looked back at Travis. That was all the answer he needed. The thought had crossed their minds as well.

"So we could be walking into a really bad situation." Travis said.

"Potentially." Steve replied, and added, "You don't have to go, if you don't want to, Travis. I'm sure we can handle it. And if it *is* a trap, at least you won't be caught in it. After all, you were not a part of the massacre, were you?"

"Neither of us were. Remember, we were gone to Panama, selling stones to Victor? That happened while we were gone."

"But I was there." Ortega said. "In fact, I was the one who ordered the attack. I intended for the attack to be a surprise, and to defend ourselves, if they tried to fight back, but it turned out to be quite different than we anticipated. They initially fought back, but quickly gave up. However our men were prepared for a hard fight, and went in very determined. I did not intend for it to be a massacre. None of us did. We went there as a show of force, to intimidate them into not coming back. But when someone opened fire, and I don't even know if it was our guys or theirs who fired first, it didn't really matter, because we had them out-gunned. I was in charge of the whole thing. So if they want to try someone for the murders, then I'm the guy."

"No one is going to be tried for murder." Steve said. "It sounds like it was as much their fault as it was ours, so we just wipe the slate clean, and start over,...that is, if the subject even comes up. If it doesn't, we don't need to be the ones to bring it up."

"Of course, they may not even suspect us as being the ones who did that." Travis said. "Didn't we leave evidence there that indicated that it was a cartel attack?"

"Yes." Ortega said, "But I do not know how convincing it was. They probably know it was us."

"How would they know, unless someone survived to tell what happened?" Travis said. "Didn't you say that no one got away?"

"Yes." Ortega said. "And the fact that nothing was changed when you went there with us later, tells me that no one had been there since the massacre. They might have a strong suspicion that we did it, but they have no proof. And it was *days* before any of their people found out what happened, so much of the evidence to implicate us had already been scattered by jungle scavengers."

That painted a gruesome picture in their minds, as Janice returned with her coffee cup, praising whoever had brewed it.

"This is the best coffee I have ever tasted!" Janice said. "What does your cook do, to make it so good?"

"It just reflects the atmosphere of this place!" Steve replied. He didn't want to tell her about the 'special' additive that the cook used to enhance the taste. "Hey, do you want to see something, Janice? One of our guys is about to take a bucket of green bananas to the monkey tower. The monkeys are all in the jungle watching him. As soon as he puts the bananas down and leaves, you'll see a mad dash toward the bananas."

They could see the monkey tower from where they sat, so they ate breakfast, as they watched the bananas being placed on the tower. A few of the small, greenish-grey monkeys bravely climbed out the ropes, almost to the tower, as the bananas were being dumped, and as soon as the worker started back down the ladder, the feeding frenzy was on! At least forty monkeys dashed across the ropes, and made quick work of the 25 pounds of bananas. Of course, a few fights broke out, and tails and ears were bitten, but nothing serious. A few young monkeys visited the tower after the frenzy was over, and found a few tid-bits that had been overlooked. But in less than three minutes, it was all over, and the stragglers had returned to the jungle, via the ropes.

"Wow, that was a little scary!" Janice said. "Those little guys don't play around, when it comes to bananas!"

"If they cornered me with a banana in my hand," Calvin added, "I'd give it to them! No need to lose an ear over a banana!"

"Well," Steve said, "I guess we need to be going, if it's a two day walk to their village."

"So you'll be gone four days?" Janice asked.

"Well, let's see," Steve said. "Two plus two equals four, unless we dally along the way, then it turns into five. Travis, do you have your satellite phone?"

"Yes."

"Okay, then we need to leave one of our phones here at the lodge. If we run into trouble along the way, we will call and request back-up.

Ortega, make sure there is an armed rescue team on alert, in case we call for them."

"I have already done that. They will be waiting, if we call."

"Okay, good. Then we're ready to go."

"Which phone will we leave here?" Travis asked.

"Is yours fully charged?"

"No, not quite."

"Then you need to leave yours here on charge, because mine is fully charged."

"Calvin, get the charger out of our bungalow, and plug it up." Travis said. "And take care of your mother. Don't let the critters, or her imagination, carry her away!"

They checked the clips in their AK-47's, and headed out.

⊰ 48 ⊱

Janice wanted to help in the kitchen while Travis was gone, because cooking was something she knew something about, but it didn't take her long to find out that the cook was very particular about who came into his kitchen. He had gone to cooking school in Paris, and apparently the French taught their chefs to be territorial, and defend their kitchen against questionable, untrained cooks. Even though his kitchen was only a make-shift kitchen, it was *his* make-shift kitchen.

"Don't take it personal, Mom." Calvin said. "He yells at everyone who comes into his kitchen. Unless he invites you in, you stay out. Even Loretta knows that by now."

"Well, he's not going to talk to me like he does a dumb animal!"

"Mom, I'm telling you, just let it go. Look at the bright side. At least you don't have to do the cooking, or wash the dishes."

"Well, I was just looking for something productive to do while your father is gone. I don't like him going into the jungle like that, because it seems dangerous."

"They have guns, Mom."

"That's what I mean! Why do they need assault rifles, unless it's dangerous?"

"Don't worry, Mom. He knows what he's doing."

"Yeah, right! Remember, young man, I have known him a lot longer than you have!"

"Yes ma'am."

"I wonder if I can call him on his cell phone?"

"You probably can, Mom, but Steve doesn't have a way of charging his phone, so we'd best not call him unless it's an emergency."

"You're right. If he gets in trouble, he will call us, right?"

"That's right."

"I wonder if I can call home on his phone? We have a charger here, so we can recharge the phone if I run it down."

"Yeah, I guess."

"I'm going to call your grandparents, and see if everything is okay at home." She went and got the phone off the table, where it was on charge. She unplugged it, and punched in the number for Mama Lee.

"It is going to be so good to hear a voice from back home! But don't worry, I know better than to tell them where I'm calling from."

"Hello, Mama Lee?"

"Yes."

"This is Janice! How are you?"

"Oh, I'm doing okay. Are you and Travis back home now?"

"No, we are still out of the country. So, what is happening back there in Alabama?"

"Well, your new house is coming right along! They have got it up, and are bricking it now. I guess the inside is still needing a lot of work, but from the outside, it looks good!"

"My new house? Travis has said nothing about a new house!"

"Oh my! He may have wanted it to be a surprise! I'm sorry I spoiled it for you!"

"Mama Lee, are you saying that Travis is building me a new house?"

"Yes, on top the hill, where you have always said you wished your house was, instead of over the hill. This new house is in plain sight from our house! I like being able to look across the hollow and see your house."

"Why did he build a new house?" Janice asked. "And when did he do this?"

"Well, he said your old one was unlivable, so he wanted to get this new one built before you got back. I reckon he was going to surprise you with it."

"I reckon he was!"

"He was here about two weeks ago, and showed them where to build it."

"Travis was *there* two weeks ago?"

"Yes, he came here after he did that investigation job in Mexico City. He didn't tell you that?"

"No, nothing about that!"

"Yep, I reckon he wants it to be a surprise then. Don't tell him I told you! And when he tells you about it, you need to act like you're surprised, and hearing it for the first time!"

"Yes, I will!" Janice said.

"I want you to know that I've got a whole lot of old photos that you are welcome to make copies of, in case…Hold on, Janice! He needs me to help him get out of the tub! I'll be right back."

Mama Lee was about to tell her how sorry she was that their old house had burned to the ground, and she lost all her things, and was going to tell her that in regards to photographs, she could copy hers to replace some of the photos she had lost. But at that moment, Chester began calling for her. While she was gone, Janice thought about how expensive this call probably was, so when she got back, she was going to go. Mama Lee came back to the phone.

"I'm sorry about that! Chester said he's taking me to town for lunch today, and I told him I wasn't going nowhere with him, until he takes a bath! He didn't like it, but he got in the tub! OKAY, CHESTER! I'LL BRING YOU A DIFFERENT SHIRT IN A MINUTE! Gracious! That old man can't do nothing without me!"

"Then I'd better let you go, Mama Lee. I'll talk to you again later."

"Okay. Good-bye Janice."

She turned off the phone, and plugged it back to the charger, and sat there a moment, thinking about what she just learned. Mama Lee said that Travis was building her a new house because the old one was 'unlivable'. What did that mean? Was he finally acknowledging the fact that she did not feel comfortable in her home, since that murdered man was found in it last year? And prior to coming down here, Travis had personally killed two more men in that same house. He probably knew that she would never feel safe again in that house, with those 'ghosts' of dead men floating around inside it. So, out of his love for her, he was building her a *whole new* house, so she would feel safe again! Wasn't that nice of him? She never knew that he cared so much for her! It was so out of character for him, but she liked it! Calvin came back to the kitchen, from the pier, and she called him over.

"Calvin, how long have you known that your Dad is building us a new home?"

"You mean down here?"

"No, I mean a new house back in Alabama!"

"That's news to me, Mom."

"You mean your dad didn't tell you about it?"

"No, this is the first I've heard about it."

"Mama Lee said he's having it built on top the hill, where the fruit orchard was."

"Sounds great to me! But what was wrong with our old house?"

"I think he wants me to feel safe there. You know, from the ghosts of those men who were killed there."

"Ain't no such things as ghosts, Mom."

"I think it's a nice gesture though. It means he loves me!"

"Maybe y'all can give the old house to me then?"

"That's a possibility. We'll talk to your Dad about it when he gets back." She thought about it a few moments, then said, "I'm going to call Paw-Paw too, to see what's going on with them."

"You do know that Dad left the phone here to be used in case of emergency, don't you, Mom?" Calvin reminded her.

"I know. I don't intend to call everyone I know, just your grandparents. And we have a charger here to keep the phone charged up, so what's the harm in it? I'll keep it brief."

Calvin shrugged his shoulders and went out to help Emillio.

The phone rang four times before Janice's father answered the phone. He sounded agitated.

"Who's calling my number now! You'd better not be selling something!" Herston said.

"It's me, Janice! What's going on, Paw-paw?"

"Hey girl! I ain't heard from you in awhile!" His voice softened when he heard it was her. "Where have you been?"

"Travis and I are gone on a vacation for awhile. How is Maw-maw?"

"How is she? She's as cantankerous as she's ever been! And she's been getting worse every day, it seems. I've been thinking a lot about what your sister Marla has been saying, about putting her in a nursing home, but I can't make myself believe that it would be for the better. Folks that go into nursing homes don't never come out! I ain't ready to get shut of her just yet."

"Well, I didn't call to try and convince you, one way or the other. I just called to see how you are doing."

"We're doing okay. But your sister is getting insistent that I put your mother away, and I had to get ugly with her a few days ago, because

I'm tired of her harpin' on it! And then Marla told us about how two strangers had *kidnapped* her from the Bruno's parking lot."

"What? Kidnapped her? Why would someone do that?"

"She don't know. Said they blindfolded her, and took her out a dirt road, then asked her a lot of questions, then let her go."

"What kind of questions?" Janice asked.

"Questions about your husband, Travis!"

"Why would they be asking about Travis?"

"Well, Marla thinks that Travis is mixed up in some kind of drug deal, and those bad guys were looking for him. Said she thinks they mistook *her* for *you*, and let her go when they found out that she wasn't you."

"That is so absurd! Travis wouldn't be involved with drug dealers!"

"I know, but that's what Marla said. I know she ain't never liked Travis, so I got to think that she's just up to her old tricks. I seriously doubt that she was really kidnapped either. She just wanted to create a little drama, and it ain't like she's never done *that* before either!"

"Oh yeah, that sounds like classic Marla!"

"But she did file a police report about it, so something must have happened. She said they accidentally cut her, when they cut the tape binding her hands together. But the cut wasn't so bad."

"She could have cut herself washing dishes. It sounds like I need to call Marla, and see what this is all about though, since she involved me in her little tale."

"Just remember to take what she says with a grain of salt. It's a shame to have to say that about one of my own daughters, but it's so."

"Paw-paw, have you been out to our house lately?" Janice asked.

"Naw, not since we come back from Alaska. Why do you ask?"

"No reason. I've got to go, Paw-paw."

"Well, okay. Call again when you can talk longer, or come by the house."

When she hung up, Calvin came back into the kitchen, so she didn't immediately call Marla. She knew Calvin would say something about not tying up the phone, in case of an emergency, and she understood that. So she went back to her bungalow to find something to do.

⇥ 49 ⇤

Meanwhile, down the jungle trail, Travis and Steve followed Ortega until they came to the old Waorani camp, and there they found a young fellow waiting on them with a rusty single shot shotgun. He looked more frightened of them, than they were of him. Without a word, he motioned for them to follow him. He was to be their guide to the Waorani village. The headed northeast, toward the Colombian border.

As they walked, Travis intentionally dropped back from the rest, and followed from a distance. He did this in case there was an ambush on the trail. It would be more difficult to ambush them all, if they were not all bunched together. Steve noticed that he had fallen back, but said nothing. He knew that Travis would not do such a thing for no reason, but didn't care to know the reason why.

They made good time along the trail, until Steve could not keep up the pace, and called for a break. Their young guide looked annoyed at the delay. Travis asked the youth how much farther to his village, to which he replied only, 'mas', which didn't tell them much, which was probably the point. When they continued walking, they did so at a slower pace, and continued until the jungle began to grow dark with the closing of the day.

The young man told Ortega it was not safe to continue traveling after dark. He gathered wood, and started a small camp fire, leaving it for them, then he moved away and spread his blanket separate from them. Ortega tried to get the youth to say how much farther, but always got the same reply. 'Mas.'

"There may not be any marker at the Colombian border." Ortega said. "Borders mean little, here in the jungle. The government from neither country would patrol such a border in such an out of the way, and uncontested area like this. That is why there jungle people move back and forth so easily."

"If they like to trade along the river, why don't they move their village there, and become citizens of Ecuador?" Travis asked.

"Because their ancestrial lands, and their dead ancestors are there in Colombia. It would be distressing to leave them there." Ortega replied. When their fire was blazing high, Steve posed a question to his companions.

"Either one of you think to bring food? I'm starving!"

"Then you should have brought food." Travis replied.

"You're not hungry?" Steve asked.

"Yeah, but I've got fat reserves to survive on." he said, patting his belly. "What about you?"

"Well, I don't have any fat reserves." Steve said. "Ortega, ask the kid if he can find us something to eat."

Ortega rolled his eyes. "We are already pushing our luck. They assigned him to be our guide, not out procurer of food. But I will ask him anyway.

"Steve, I can find you some food, if you aren't real particular about what you eat." Travis said.

"How particular?"

"Grub worms, scorpions and centipedes." Travis replied.

Steve sighed. "I think I'll survive, but thanks anyway."

"At least we thought to bring water." Travis said. He looked around and didn't see the young man, and immediately got suspicious.

"Where did the kid go?"

"Maybe to find food." Ortega replied. "I asked if he could find food, and that was when he left."

Travis was suspicious of him leaving, but there was no reason to be. Minutes passed. He kept his gun nearby. He heard someone coming through the darkness, stumbling over deadfall and vines, until he broke into the fire light. It was the youth, and he had an arm-load of strange jungle fruit, which he offered to Steve.

"It looks like dinner is served!" Steve said. "I don't know what some of this stuff is, but it looks better than grub worms!"

As they cut up and devoured the fruit, Ortega carried on a conversation with the Indian youth. He began to open up and talk more freely. Soon the two were laughing and telling tales to one another.

Travis and Steve had no idea what was being said, but that wasn't important. It was good that at least Ortega was becoming more accepted by the youth. A friendship of any kind might be useful later.

———◆———

When they resumed travel at sunrise, they realized that they were leaving the flat jungle, and began climbing into the gently rolling hills of a tropical highland. It was still rain forest, but without the standing water and swamps. And the plants were changing too, in subtle ways. This land appeared to be more livable. At one point on the trail, they saw an animal skull wedged into the forks of a tree, and the tree was in the process of growing over it. The youth pointed to it, and said something to Ortega as they passed. Ortega relayed it to the others.

"He said that skull marks the boundary of their ancestrial land."

"Is this Colombia, or still Ecuador?" Travis asked.

"He probably doesn't even know. Like I said, borders are almost non-existent here. If we're not in Colombia yet, we should be very close."

"And close to their village as well?" Steve asked.

"We have to be getting close."

They walked for another fifteen minutes, and suddenly, they were surrounded by Waorani men, all armed, but not menacing. Some had antiquated guns, some had machetes or hoes, and some just had clubs and sticks. Were it not for their soccer shirts and cut-off denim jeans, they might have been mistaken for primitive, stone age people. Travis noted with amusement that one man was wearing *spark plug* around his neck as a decorative ornament. The Waorani appeared to be a tribe that was caught between the old and the new, and were confused about what to take from each. Ortega explained what they were saying.

"Their village is at the top of this hill, but before they will let us go there, we must leave our weapons here."

"Is that a good idea?" Travis asked.

"I don't think we have much choice."

"Let's do it, guys." Steve said. "We want them to trust us, and that's hard to do, draped with simi-automatic weapons." Travis left the gun, like the others, hanging from a broken tree limb, but he still had his Kabar concealed, in case he needed it.

"This appears to be our escort to the village." Ortega said, as they moved out up the hill. "There is a clearing up ahead. That must be the village."

The closer they got to the clearing, the more evidence they saw that surprised them, and hinted that the Waorani might not be living as traditionally as they might have thought. Scattered among the foliage at the edge of the clearing, were the remainants of many modern day appliances. Travis recognized the tank out of an electric hot water heater, that had been modified into a meat smoker. An eviscerated Volkswagen Beetle frame was being used as a portable storage building, for a wealth of junk and re-usable items. Plastic bottles were used and re-used as drinking vessels, and liquid storage, anything from drinking water, to burnt motor oil. Obviously from the relice they saw, the Waorani had road access to civilization from the Colombian side. With access to civilization by way of a road, Travis wondered why they chose to trek two days through the jungle, to the Napo River. Couldn't they trade much easier by using the road?

There was ample evidence that the Waorani were holding on to old traditions too, in spite the modern day relics. Mixed in with the cannibalized remains of modern man, were relics of a more remote past. The most eye-popping was a row of human skulls that ringed a vegetable garden. It was only natural to wonder whose skulls they were, enemies, or family. When Steve saw the skulls, he said to Ortega, "Don't even ask about them! We don't even want to know!"

"Speak for yourself." Travis replied. "There has to be a story behind them."

"We're not here as anthropologists," Steve said. "We just want to negotiate a land deal, so let's stick to the business at hand."

He said this as they passed something that looked like a scarecrow with a horse skull as a head, and bones and feathers making up the body. The large string of beads around its neck were of suspicious origins. It was most likely the depiction of some dark deity which they looked to for protection, or good luck. Perhaps it cast spells on strangers entering their village.

"Ignore the scarecrow." Steve said. "It's just bones and sticks."

As more tribe members joined the throng of spectators who accompanied them up the hill, they noted that many of the men had pierced, and elongated ear lobes. Some of the women were bare breasted.

These were traits that were once common among many of the Amazon's indigenous tribes, but in recent years, they had all but died out. The Waorani had apparently not gotten the memo.

They were led to the front of what could only be described as a shack, with a rusted corrugated tin roof, and sides that were made of thatched leaves and bamboo. In front of the shack, sitting in an aluminum lawn chair, was a large man wearing dark sun glasses. As they drew closer to him, they could see that he was actually a very old man, with wrinkles, and graying hair. He sat there, unresponsive, and unsmiling, and the visitors wondered if he was even alive, or just the corpse of an elder. The rest of the village quickly assembled around them, as though this was going to be a town meeting.

Steve was unsure of how to begin this meeting, so he fell back on his Alabama instincts.

"Howdy folks! How are you today?"

The 'corpse' suddenly came alive, and barked out something that didn't sound so inviting, and instantly, there was serious mumbling from the entire village, which did not sound good. Ortega leaned over to Steve and whispered,

"Please, let me do the talking! You have already insulted the chief, by speaking before he asked you to speak."

"Oh." Steve said. They stood in silence for an uncomfortable minute and a half, before one of the elders said something to the chief, and he nodded, and directed the question to Ortega.

"The chief asks, what is our business in coming here?" Ortega relayed to Steve.

"Tell the chief that we want to discuss a deal about the location of our lodge." Steve said.

Ortega relayed the message, and got an instant reply.

"He says there is nothing to discuss. His tribe has been using our site as a trading post for more years than he can remember."

"Tell him that I purchased the land legally from Exxon Corporation, a company that had legally bought the land from the Ecuadorian government, and I have a valid bill of sale to prove it."

Ortega relayed the message, and got a short answer.

"He says paper is worthless. And who told the government it was *theirs* to sell?"

Steve was at a loss for words. How do you negotiate with someone who did not recognize the existing laws?

"Tell the chief that since his people do not *live* on the property, they cannot claim it! We are building a permanent structure, and we will be there from now on, and if his people go there, they will be trespassing on *our* land!"

Ortega hesitated, then whispered to Steve. "Boss, I don't think you should word it quite that way. I remind you, that we are in a compromising position just by being here. Remember that our guns are down there in that tree. And someone's heads are out there lining these guys vegetable garden."

"So what do you suggest?" Steve asked.

"I'm going to ask the chief to offer *his* solution to this problem. That way, we will at least know where he stands, before we start negotiating."

"Okay, go ahead." Steve said.

The chief responded with a lecture that lasted almost ten minutes, in his native tongue. Toward the end, he got dramatic, and stood up from his lawn chair, speaking directly to his fellow tribesmen, who responded to his rousing speech, by beginning a chant, which finally died out, and Ortega was able to interpret for Steve.

"So what did he say?"

"He said a lot of things. One thing in particular stood out though, when he said something about the FARC. He thinks that the FARC was responsible for massacring his people last month. And they are still fearful that FARC will come back. So we dodged a bullet there. They don't even suspect us! They are very much afraid that the FARC attack them even here at their village."

"But that's not our problem. What did he say about our land dispute?"

"I'll give you the abbreviated version, Boss." Ortega said. "He said for us to get the hell off his land."

"Did he mean the lodge, or here?"

"I think he meant *both*. So, we'd better thank him for his time, and get out of here, while we still can."

"Wait a minute! We didn't resolve anything! I came here to settle this thing once and for all!" Steve said. "Tell him I want to negotiate!"

"Are you sure you want to push this thing?" Ortega asked.

"If we don't, we're going to lose everything we've worked for so far! We have to work out a deal, that's all there is to it!"

"Okay, so what is our bargaining chip? What do we have to offer him, that he doesn't already have?"

Both of them were drawing a blank, trying to come up with something. Finally Travis entered the conversation for the first time.

"Since they think FARC killed their people, and they are scared shitless of them, let's use that to our advantage. Tell them that we have close ties to some of the inside people associated with FARC. Convince them that we can protect them from the FARC, as long as they establish friendly ties with us."

"But that's a lie!" Steve said. "We don't know anyone associated with them. And as far as we know, the FARC doesn't operate this far to the west."

"But *they* don't have to know that! All they need to know, is that we can shield them from future attacks from FARC. If they believe that, then we will have a bargaining chip."

"I like it." Ortega said.

"But it's not true!' Steve insisted. "There are so many ways that can backfire."

"So you have a better idea?" Ortega asked.

"No, I've got nothing! But at least I'm honest about it!"

"Oh, well if we are suddenly going the honesty route, we should call up Exxon and let them know they have emeralds on some of their mineral rights land!" Travis said sarcastically. "We're going to have to improvise something, or you might as well give that land back to Exxon!"

"I'm good with it. I think we should give it a try." Ortega said. "If they don't believe it, we can try something else."

"So we are going to bluff them into dealing with us? I don't think it will work, but go ahead." Steve said.

Surprisingly, it did work. When the chief found out that they could 'call off' the FARC, he was almost *eager* to deal with them.

Steve then proposed a few compromise measures, and the chief was more receptive to the compromises. He even made a counter offer, and then the negotiating was on.

They stayed there at the village most of the day, negotiating a deal that both sides could live with. The village even put on a short notice feast that afternoon for their guests. By sundown, both sides had hammered out a deal that they could live with. They spent the night in the village, and headed back to the lodge early the next morning.

⫷ 50 ⫸

On the morning of their fourth day gone, they arrived back at the lodge, with the good news that the tentative war with their neighbors was now over. From now on, they were going to be business partners with the Waorani tribe, as long as they followed the guidelines laid down in their negotiations.

The Waorani Tribe would be allowed to establish a permanent trading post on the lodge property, but separate from the lodge itself, by a quarter mile of jungle. The Waorani would construct a traditional village at the trading post, and those tribe members who staffed it, were to dress in traditional Waorani attire. The items they were allowed to sell at the trading post would be traditionally made Waorani crafts. Nothing illegal, like drugs, or banned items, like animal hides, bones or feathers. And most importantly, the Waorani village/trading post was to be open to tourists who were guests at the lodge, once the lodge opened. This would be yet another important dimension added to the eco-lodge.

Visitors could come to the eco-lodge to be close to nature, with nature walks into the virgin rainforest, to photo plants, animals, insects and flowers. They could bird-watch, animal-watch and fish in the lagoon. They could swim and sun-bathe at the swimming pool that was yet to be installed. They could canoe and kayak in the river and lagoon. They could have beach parties on the sand bars (where the roast pig had still not been found). They could enjoy dining on authentic jungle cuisine, prepared fresh daily by their resident Paris-trained chef. At night, they could hang out at the bar, and enjoy occasional live bands, and dances in the big lodge. And now, thanks to the compromise reached with the Waorani tribe, visitors could visit a real authentic indigenous village, and photo the villagers in their authentic dress, and even buy souvenirs direct from the Indians themselves.

And of course, while all this was going on, behind the scenes, Steve would be secretly running an emerald mine, and making a small fortune.

Janice could hardly wait for Travis to get back from the jungle, so she could tell him that she had found out about his 'big surprise'. The new house he was building for her back in Alabama, just because he loved her!

"How did you find out about the house?" he asked.

"I talked to Mama Lee! She told me how good it looks in it's new location! I am so excited! Can we go home now?"

"No, we still have a lot to do here before this place is ready to run. And besides, the new house is not finished yet. We need to stay out of the carpenters way until all of the interior is completed. That could be another two or three weeks."

"That's okay. I can wait! And I will try to be more of a help around here. Thank you for building me a new house!"

Travis thought it was amazing that she had found out about the new house, but apparently knew nothing about the fate of the *old* house, so he saw no need to tell her about it just yet. Why spoil her temporary happiness, with the news that they had lost all their worldly possessions. Well, not all of them, just the ones that were in their old house. That could wait until later.

And he knew something else. With her finding out about the new house, it was going to be hard to keep her down here much longer. She would naturally want to go home and see it. And with the danger appearing to be past, it was going to be hard to justify them not going home. Janice was practically packing to leave when he got there, but now she seemed content to stay, at least for awhile. He sat down with Calvin to have a talk.

"Dad, that new house is all Mom has talked about, since she found out about it. She is really excited."

"Yeah, and that means we will probably be going home sooner than I thought, I'm afraid. And *you* will be going back to school!"

"Aw man! There ain't no need for me to go back now! I've already missed too many Spring classes. Can't I just stay down here, until time to start Summer school? I can leave here the last week of May, and get home in time to start classes on June 4th."

"Have you discussed that with your mother?"

"No, but Steve said he can really use me here until I have to go."

"We'll have to discuss it with her first. I'm going to let you in on a little secret, but don't tell your mother. The reason I had the new house built, was because our old house burned to the ground, about a week after we got down here."

Calvin was clearly shocked. "How did that happen? The terrorists?"

"No, it was an accident. The soldiers that were watching our house were cooking something on the stove, and a grease fire got out of control. The house was a total loss. Your mother is going to be pretty devastated when I tell her."

"Well, so am I! I had a lot of stuff in my room! So that's all gone?"

"Yeah, everything that was in the house is gone. Since it burned, it has been covered with a waterproof tarp, so if anything survived, it should still be there."

"What would happen to gold and silver?"

"Gold and silver? Why do you ask that?"

"Because over a year ago, me and Chris found an old box in the woods. It was full of gold and silver coins."

"Wow, that's the first I heard about that. Exactly where did you find it in the woods?"

"Actually we found it in the floor of Weaver's barn. We were digging a hole to bury something else, and we found that stash of coins. Rebecca knows about it already. I showed it to her, and she said it was probably somebody's coin collection, because all the coins had different dates. And then she got the idea to try to find out who they belonged to. She put a notice in the paper, and she had a lot of people call in, saying that the coins were theirs, but couldn't nobody identify them. At least not until this one old woman from the nursing home called, and was able to identify them."

"So the coins belonged to her?" Travis asked.

"Yeah, they was stolen from her and her husband years ago. They suspected Mr. Weaver, who was a teenager at the time, but they couldn't prove it. But because we found the coins in Weaver's barn, it made sense that he was the thief. The old woman said he was probably so strung out on drugs, that he probably buried them in the barn, then forgot where he put them."

"So why didn't you give the coins back to the old woman?" his dad asked.

"Hey, Rebecca *tried* to give them to her, but she said she didn't want them! She said if she had them, her good-for-nothing grandkids would just fight over them, so she insisted that me and Chris keep them. Rebecca and I went to the nursing home to see the old woman, but she died before we could get there. She must'a known she wasn't going to live very long."

"So you have had them all this time?"

"Yeah. When Chris went into the Army, he told me to hide them and not tell anybody about it, until he got back. But I had about decided to tell you about it when we got back home. But I guess it's gone now."

"Where did you hide it?"

"Inside a wall stud in my closet. Do you think it might still be there?"

"The wall is gone, I know that. It was apparently a really hot fire. The only thing left still standing was the toilet in the bathroom. But I'm sure those coins are still there, even if the house is burnt down. They will be on the ground below where you had them hidden. Even if the fire was hot enough to melt them, the precious metal is still there somewhere."

"Oh. Well, I hope it didn't melt! Some of those coins were really old!"

"Even if they did, the gold price is really high right now, so the gold will still sell."

"That's not the point. Rebecca said some of those coins were valuable because of what date they were. If they melted, they're just worth the gold and silver price."

"That's true. We'll find out when we get back home. I'll help you look for them. So you would be okay with staying down here until May?"

"Sure!"

"Okay then. I'll talk to your mother about it."

"And after I finish high school, can I come back down here?"

"It's your future. That will be your call." Travis replied. He didn't say anything at the time, but he much preferred that he come back down here, and immerse himself in running this place. That would be better than going into the Marines, and going off to fight in Afghanistan, or God knows where this 'war on terrorism' would take them. He already had Chris in the Army, and he wished he wasn't. He had a bad feeling about the way the U.S. was going into Iraq. That country had not been a part of the 911 attacks, yet Bush seemed determined to stir up things there as well.

⊰ 51 ⊱

A boat arrived from Coca that afternoon, with a young couple, and their suitcases, as though they planned to stay awhile. Travis was at the kitchen when they arrived, so he went down to meet them. They appeared to be in their late to mid-twenties. He was a handsome young man, and she was a blond beauty. He wondered if they were movie stars or something. If so, they were either lost or thought the lodge was the set of a 'Survivors' reality show.

"Hello!" he greeted them.

"Hello! You must be Mr. Steve Merideth!" the young man said, as he extended a handshake.

"No, I am Travis Lee, one of the owners of this place. But Steve is here somewhere."

"I am Dr. Danny White, and this is my wife, Ann."

"Pleased to meet you, but this place isn't exactly open to visitors yet. It is still under construction."

"Oh, we're not visitors! We are coming here to work!"

"Come again?"

"Let me explain. I was recruited by Mr. Homer Jones, CEO of Jones Electronics. I was told that you had an opening for a jungle physician, and a school teacher. I am a doctor, and Ann is a teacher, so here we are!"

"So Homer hired you?"

"Yes, he said the place was still under construction, but he encouraged us to come on down and check the place out."

"In that case, welcome to the lodge! Did Steve know you were coming?"

"We tried to call from Quito, and again from Coca, but we got no answer, so we came on out. It was easy to find this place! I love the location! This place is so lush and green!"

"Yes," his wife said, "The jungle is green like emerald gemstones! Translucent and full of life!"

"Yeah, it really is." Travis said. "I'm glad you like it. Then I guess the first thing we need to do, is take your things up to the big lodge, and introduce you to Steve. Right this way."

"I was told that I would be teaching Indian children here. Is that true?" Ann asked.

"Yes." Travis said. "In our original planning, we decided to have a medical clinic, and a school here at the lodge, to provide medical care for the indigenous people who help run this place. They will be living here, and so it made sense to build a medical clinic, and a school, to educate their kids. The nearest village is five miles away by river, so Steve envisioned us being a self sufficient community."

"It sounds like a wonderful plan." the young doctor said.

"Yeah, but we have not had time to build the school or the clinic yet. Right now we are still building up the infrastructure, and the basic lay-out. I have not even asked where the school or clinic will be located."

"Oh. Well, we had the impression that those things were already in place. That's why we came on down here."

"It might be good that you are here. You can help us decide where to put the clinic, and how to lay-out the building itself should be."

The young doctor and his wife looked forlornly at one another and sighed.

"Do either of you speak Spanish?" Travis asked.

"Yes, we both have taken Spanish in college."

"Have you ever used it in a real life?"

"Well, no, only at Mexican restaurants. But how hard can it be?"

"A lot of the Indians you will be treating, and teaching, speak Spanish as their primary language, and know enough English to get by. But they also speak a native dialect as well. So the people you will be dealing with are already tri-lingual."

"That sounds challenging." Ann said.

"Yes, challenging and rewarding, if that is your calling in life. Wait here at the lodge, and I will try to find Steve. Make yourself at home."

Someone told Travis that Steve was over in the jungle, where the Waorani were planning to set up their camp, and that's where he found him and Ortega.

"Steve, have you heard from Homer lately?"

"As a matter of fact, yes, just this morning. He said he's found us a doctor, and a school teacher. Why?"

"They just arrived. The doctor, and the teacher. A husband and wife team."

"What? They are already here?"

"Yes, I told them to wait at the lodge for you."

"I had no idea that Homer was sending them on down here. We don't have the set-up for them yet."

"That's what I told them, but they showed up with all their things, ready to move in and start to work."

"Then I need to go meet them. Ortega, show these guys where their boundaries are on this side, and reiterate some of the ground rules. Especially the part about them not taking a shit just wherever the urge strikes them! I'll be back soon."

When they got back to the lodge, Travis introduced everyone, and Steve wasted no time in explaining the stage of development they were in, and about how long it would take to get things ready for them. Until they got to that point, they were welcome to stay and help with other things, such as the physical construction of the eco-lodge. The young doctor and his wife took a few minutes to talk things over, then got back to them.

"Ann and I have already settled up all our affairs in the States, and made arrangements to be gone for years, if necessary. According to Homer, we were going to love this place. And the fact is, we are already here, so it wouldn't make much sense for us to go back home and come back in six months. So we might as well stay here and help get the place up and running. It would be an investment in our future."

"I'm glad you look at it that way," Steve said, "because we can use the extra hands around here. And once we get the clinic and school built, we can really use you both. If you and your wife can adapt to the primitive conditions here, then you'll do fine."

"So we will be paid for the hours we put in here?" the doctor asked.

"Sure, why not. I assume you and Homer already talked salary?"

"Well, we didn't settle on a salary. He said I would have to discuss it with you. Neither one of us knew what was fair for down here. He just said that if we came down here and committed to this project, he would make it worth our while."

"Then it sounds like Homer is willing to pay you whatever it takes to make you happy. Let me give you and Ann a tour of the place, and tell you about our plans, and then we'll reach an agreement on salary."

Travis stayed behind, and let Steve give them the tour. He had plenty else to do, and not knowing how much longer he was going to be there, he needed to do as much as possible before he left for home. Janice found him as he was leaving the lodge.

"I heard that we have visitors?" she said.

"No, not really visitors. The future doctor, and school teacher for our community. Steve is giving them a tour of the place now. It's a husband and wife team. Ann is the teacher. I'm sure you will want to talk to her, since she is new to the rain forest. You might have some advice to give her about the critters."

"Oh yeah! I've got advice for her all right!"

⇥ 52 ⇤

It was most likely the arrival of Ann to the lodge, that encouraged Janice to try a little harder to adapt. That was why Travis and Janice stayed in Ecuador for three more weeks, before finally heading back home to Alabama. In that three weeks, construction of the bungalows was suspended, and instead, construction was begun on, first the health clinic, and then the school house. With these two things in place, the Indian workers were allowed to bring their whole families, and construct private dwellings in an area behind the lodge, in a location that was out of sight from the future lodge visitors. The lodge had begun to jell into a real village, by the time the Lees left.

And when they left, Calvin stayed behind, to help Steve at the lodge until the start of Summer School in Laurel Grove. Loretta wanted to come home with him, but of course, he had to leave her behind, with the understanding that she *was not* to be eaten.

As Janice and Travis flew home, Janice snuggled up to her husband. It was going to be hard to go back to their old routine. With her kids grown, and Travis going back to work for FBN Investigations, it was going to leave her at home alone almost all the time. She almost wished she could stay at the Lodge in Ecuador, where at least she could have the interaction of other people. Oh well, she could join the YMCA and work out, and meet new friends.

She noticed that Travis was awake, but he had a far-away look on his face.

"What are you thinking?" she asked.

"Who said I was thinking about anything?" he replied.

"I can tell. So what are you thinking about?"

"About how short life is. It seems like only yesterday that we were young, and looking forward to the whole spectrum of life. And now here we are, headed down the back-side, and wondering where all those years went."

"I know where the years went. I lived every day of them, and I loved it! But you're talking like we have reached the end of our life!"

"Well, I'm starting to feel my age. I think everything is going to catch up with me at one time, and I'll officially be an Old Fart!"

"You're not quite there yet, mister! We still have a lot of years to go, and I'm going to look forward to every one of them with you!"

"Do you promise?"

"Yes, I promise!"

He wondered if she would still feel that way, when she gets home and finds her house and all her stuff burned to the ground? The fact that it happened over a month ago, and he still had not told her about it? What would she think about him then? That might be what made their marriage work. Never being able to predict what was around the next bend. Always some new calamity to deal with. With Travis, how could she expect anything else?

———◆———

Begun: July 30, 2012
Finished: December 23, 2013